Runaway Love Story

Sadira Stone

Runaway Love Story

♥

Wrong time, wrong place, perfect guy.

Laurel

Fired again, and now darling Maxie needs my help. That San Francisco art gallery job will have to wait. I'm stuck in Eugene, Oregon, rescuing the auntie who rescued me.

Running into Dalton ignites a sweet flirtation that quickly turns spicy. He's almost perfect: a beloved teacher and coach, wise and funny, and so compassionate with Maxie.

But he wants lasting love, and I'm only passing through. No matter how much I crave him, I can't let him derail my dreams.

Dalton

Between my scheming ex and Mom's dementia, this is the worst summer break ever—until Laurel.

Though she stubbornly denies her artistic gift, she's brilliant, stunning, forthright, and the spark between us grows hotter each time we meet. But she's clinging to big-city dreams, and I can't leave my hometown.

When a social media post about our budding love goes viral, Laurel's insecurities flare. To keep her from running away, I'll have to convince her how brightly she can shine right here.

Come to Book Nirvana for a spicy, funny, heart-wrenching tale of true love and second chances.

Runaway Love Story was previously published and has been revised and updated with new chapters.

To Duncan, my HEA

A note to readers:
I do not use generative artificial intelligence in any part of my writing process. All my books were written by me, with feedback from my human editor and human beta readers. Different "authors" may make different choices, but I believe the best art comes from human minds, spirits, and hearts. Take that, robot overlords!

Contents

Chapter One

♥

Laurel

I told you so.

That's exactly what my dad's going to say, with that smug sneer that makes my jaws clench.

And you know what makes it worse? He did tell me—at length—when I took this latest art gallery job. In fact, his relentless negativity campaign started the day I announced my college major.

"Quit kidding yourself, Laurel. An art major who can't draw? Or paint or sculpt or whatever the hell they're doing on computers these days? Might as well study underwater basket weaving."

Dad always conveniently forgets all the business classes I took—and barely passed. But still.

Besides, my dream is to open my own art gallery, not to be the artist who fills its walls. I love everything about the art world, the way art makes feelings visible, durable, powerful—even if my own artwork resembles a kindergartener's. And what else am I gonna do with all this frustrated creativity? Become Dad's receptionist at Jepsen Heating and Cooling? I'd rather starve.

Stomach churning, I take the turnoff for Cotter's Grove, Oregon. Boomeranging back home at thirty-one is humiliating. And it never fails—after a few days under Mom and Dad's roof, I regress to a whiny, sulky adolescent. Funny—no, painful, the way family roles stick.

It's broiling hot out, and Main Street looks the same: boarded-up storefronts, a second-hand shop with a faded awning, the VFW hall, the diner, the bank, and...damn, that new kebab place already went under. So much for getting a decent meal here.

If not for the lush linden trees lining the sidewalks, this bland, dusty street would be utterly unbearable.

Stalling, I pull over and snap photos of their heart-shaped leaves and the dappled shadows they cast. Memories waft up of childhood summers spent biking down this road, glorying in the endless possibilities of summer.

Whatever happened to that happy, hopeful kid?

With a weary sigh, I climb back into my car. Time to get this part over with. They love me as well as they know how, I guess.

I pull up in front of my parents' house—faded and beige, just like my future. Pushing to my feet, I roll my stiff neck and sweep my hair behind my ears.

"Just a temporary setback," I remind myself as I square my shoulders and stride up the walkway. Just a few weeks at home to lick my wounds, retool my résumé, and focus on my plan. Great-aunt Maxie says a woman with a plan is unstoppable.

I stop halfway to the door. Huh, Mom's playing again, fluid piano jazz drifting from the house. I hardly recognized her in the photo my sister sent, so elegant in her sequined sheath dress, bent with feverish intensity over a baby grand. Sparkly, glowing, passionate.

It's about damn time.

But the front door opens to reveal the same old Mom—tall and rangy like the rest of us Jepsens, wearing pastel capris and a faded floral blouse.

"Laurel." Her cheeks plump like shiny pink apples. "Good to see you, my baby. Lunch is ready. Let's catch up before you hit the road."

I blink in surprise. "Hit the road? I just got here."

Mom waves absently. "Well, you know how afternoon traffic can be on I-5."

Behind her, Willow waddles through the kitchen door carrying a steaming casserole. She sets it down and shuffles forth to welcome the black sheep.

"Laur-bear!" She hugs me tight, her massive pregnant belly prodding me. Pulling back, she gives me a head-to-toe inspection. "You're too thin. Come eat."

"Here." I pull a wrapped package from my bag. "I made something for the baby."

Willow unwraps the unbreakable mirror, its wooden frame painted with colorful dots, zigzags, and spirals. She turns it over and reads aloud, "Welcome to the world, beautiful baby, from your Aunt Laurel."

"The patterns are supposed to be stimulating or something." I tried to mimic the expensive toys in Portland baby boutiques. Now, in my sister's hands, the gift looks clumsy and sad.

Willow flashes a plastic smile. "It's lovely."

No mention of my bad news. Very odd. Last time I lost a job, they laid the recrimination on thick.

You're not a kid anymore. It's time to give up that art nonsense and get a real job. Why can't you be realistic, like your sister?

It's not easy, being the underachieving younger sister of the perfect, blue-ribbon eldest child. But maybe, focused on the arrival of their first grandchild, my parents will cut me some slack this time?

My father's voice booms, "There she is, our little washout."
No such luck.

Dad looms in the doorway, wiry arms crossed, pale eyes narrowed. "What's with the blue hair? Who's going to hire you looking like that?"

Willow lifts my turquoise-tipped ponytail. "I like it. It's—artistic."

Dad harrumphs. "It's juvenile."

I straighten my spine. "I didn't wash out, Dad. My boss and I had different visions for the gallery, that's all."

I'm lying. I totally got fired.

Mom shoots him a tight glare as she pats my arm. "Well, you'll find something in Eugene."

"What are you talking about? Why would I go to Eugene?"

"Didn't you tell her?" Dad asks on his way to the table.

Mom shrugs. "I thought you told her."

"For goodness' sake, let's eat." Willow snags my elbow and tows me to my customary seat. "Lunch is getting cold."

"Not until you explain—"

"Sit, Laurel," Dad orders. "Your mother made your favorite. Show some appreciation."

With a weary sigh, I take my seat, and the past ten years slide away like a coat dropping to the floor. Two days ago, I was an assistant in a trendy Portland art gallery, making big strides toward my dream career. Today, thanks to one stupid decision, I'm a gawky, sullen kid, slumped in my chair.

And gluey chicken casserole topped with potato chips is *not* my favorite.

Willow passes the salad, iceberg lettuce with a sprinkling of shredded carrots and—eew, raisins?

"Something wrong with the food?" Dad asks, his pale eyes sharp.

"It's fine." I force a grin. "Thanks, Mom."

Dad pours iced tea from the plastic pitcher. "So, running away again, eh?"

I flush hotly, but before I can snap out a retort, Mom interjects, her tone smooth as Jell-O, "Let it be, Dave. If that job wasn't a good fit, she'll find another."

He stabs his food as if it were trying to scurry off his plate. "What did she expect, wasting her college education on artsy-fartsy baloney?"

"Dad," Willow hisses, "chill out."

Easy for her to say. My sister's office job at the wastewater treatment plant meets Dad's definition of useful and practical. Another point in her favor: she's married to a nice, boring guy who grew up in our nice, boring town.

"Mom majored in music," I remind him.

"Your mother's music is practical. She plays at church. Why can't you—"

Mom cuts him off again. "Laurel, you need to go help Aunt Maxie."

I drop my fork with a clatter. "Help her how? Is she okay?"

"No, not really," Mom says with a tinge of weariness. "She's been having—she calls them 'spells.' She forgets where she is and how she got there."

I swallow hard around the jagged lump in my throat. At ninety, my great-aunt still lives in a cottage stuffed to the rafters with her oddball art projects. Maxie's the only member of my family who appreciates my artistic ambitions and bohemian style. As feisty as a mongoose, she's always struck me as invincible. Until now.

Willow lays her hand over mine. "Maxy's moving to an assisted living facility. She wants help to sort through her stuff." She pats her belly. "But I can't go in my condition."

"I have my piano students," Mom adds, "and a gig this Saturday."

"Don't look at me," Dad says through a mouthful of casserole. "You know I work long hours." He points with his fork. "You're the only one with time to spare. Considering all Maxie did for you, I'd say you owe her."

I can't argue with that. When I gave up my track scholarship at Oregon State to transfer to the University of Oregon, Aunt Maxie made up the difference in tuition, and she'd always slip me "a little something extra" when my paycheck didn't quite stretch to the end of the month. Aunt Maxie found me an internship at an art gallery, inspiring my dream of owning one. If she needs my help, I have to go.

But the timing sucks. My college bestie lives in San Francisco, where he has contacts in the art scene and a vacant guestroom. And until a moment ago, that bright, shiny hope kept me afloat.

I heave a guilt-laden sigh. "Okay. Of course. I'll go help Aunt Maxie. How long do you think it'll take?"

Dad snorts. "You've seen that rat's maze she calls home."

"I'd give it a good month, baby." Mom pats my hand. "Maybe two."

"Get yourself a job down there." Dad's grin has a sharp edge. "Go work in a coffee shop with the other art majors."

I bite back the snark itching to escape my tightly pinched lips.

Willow's voice drips honey. "Lay off, Dad. Laurel will find her niche eventually."

I shovel gloopy chicken down my tight throat. I can't let this change of plans derail me. In fact, spending time with Aunt Maxie sounds downright delightful, compared to fending off my dad's barbed comments, my mom's cluelessness, and my sister's pity.

I push back my chair and pop to my feet. "Lunch was delicious, Mom, but you're right about traffic. I'd better hit the road."

"Laurel, hang on." Willow follows me out. Gripping my elbow, she guides me to the shade of the big sycamore. "Look, I know it's hard, but can't you just—"

"Pretend everything's peachy?" Bitterness gives my voice a jagged edge. "'Cause guess what? It's not. I'm broke. Maxie's sick." I flap my hand toward the front door. "And they're too busy playing the perfect postcard family to help her."

"They don't get Maxie like you do. Even if they went down there, Mom would throw away all her art stuff, and Dad would boss her around till she cries."

"Or whacks him with her cane."

We both chuckle as Willow pulls me in for a hug. "You know, we've moved past it. Why can't you? Things are better now."

And poof! My feeling of sisterly warmth evaporates. After what we endured as kids, how can she just gloss over that mess? I cross my arms and glare. "It's way past time for someone to apologize"

I climb back into my VW and drive off without looking back.

My car begins to hiccup at the first traffic light off the freeway, and by the time I reach Eugene's Whiteaker district, it's developed a raspy cough.

"Come on, sweetheart, you can make it." I pat the dashboard. "I'll get you fixed as soon as I get my first paycheck."

My bank account is as anemic as my car. Even with Davonte's offer of free couch surfing, I'll have to build up my funds before moving on to San Francisco. I hope Aunt Maxie can help me find a temporary job.

I roll down the window and inhale the fresh, green scent of summer. Maxie's hipster neighborhood hasn't changed, still lush with flowering shrubs and mature trees. But yikes! Did Maxie's house look this rough the last time I was here? Turquoise paint flakes off the wooden siding. Above the porch, sun-bleached Tibetan prayer flags flutter their tattered edges. The once-bright rainbow porch railing has faded to pastels, like dribbles of melting ice cream.

I sit in the driveway, stewing in my guilt. I haven't seen Maxie since Christmastime, and already it's late summer. I could easily have made the trip down from Portland, but instead, I spent my weekends on pointless dates with uninspiring guys. Not one of them ever got me the way Maxie does.

A wisp of scarlet fluff appears in the window, then the front door opens, revealing a beaming Maxie in all her Technicolor glory. Her baby-fine hair glows henna red, and rhinestones twinkle from her cat's-eye glasses. Chunky rings bedeck her gnarled, ropy hands, and her tunic bears a tie-dyed rainbow swirl.

"Laurel," she bellows. Her foghorn voice hasn't lost its power. "Get up here, my precious girl."

Beaming, I trot up the stairs and wrap my arms around my tiny mentor.

"Easy now." Maxie's smile folds her cheeks and forehead into papery pleats. "I'm not so steady on my feet these days." She thumps her cane. Typical Maxie, it's covered with rhinestones, metallic trim, and swirls of bright paint.

"New art project?"

"Oh, this?" She chuckles, her laughter raspy and deep. "One of many." Moving slowly, she settles onto the creaking porch swing. "Tell me, dear heart."

"Tell you what?"

One penciled-on eyebrow rises. "What happened at the gallery?"

I slump down beside her. "Mom told you?"

"She loves you, you know. And she wants you to succeed."

"As long as I do something practical. And boring."

"Now, now." Maxie pats my hand. "It's a mother's nature to worry. So, spill."

My sigh ruffles her baby-fine hair. "The owner put me in charge of a new display while she was on vacation. The artist loved my idea."

Maxie chuckles softly. "What did you do?"

"Arranged the display panels in a maze."

"Sounds fun."

"Right?" My eyebrows shoot up. "I thought, let's invite the customers into a secret world, like Alice Through the Looking Glass. But a customer drank too much free bubbly and knocked into a panel. They all toppled like expensive dominoes." I pick at a fuzzball on my T-shirt. "A couple of paintings got damaged, so Vana fired me."

Maxie snorts. "Her loss. Come inside, my dear."

"Let me get my things." I haul my duffle bag through the living room, over hand-loomed rugs, past mountains of embroidered pillows, through the hallway hung with photos—Maxie on the beach, riding a camel, lounging on the hood of a classic convertible, cradled in the arms of a shirtless young man...

At the guest room door, I brace myself for a flood of memories: cramming for my art history final, weeping into my pillow over Carlo's betrayal, twirling before the mirror in my graduation robe and mortarboard while I dreamt of a dazzling future. And here I am again, but the familiar daybed and vintage day-glo posters are hidden behind a wall of moving boxes.

"What's in all these?"

Maxie sighs, a raspy, weary sound. "Fleeting wisps of joy and love. When you get to be my age, you need something tangible to hang those memories on. Otherwise, they get slippery."

A shiver runs down my back. Soon, too soon, my mentor will be gone. But for Maxie's sake, I paste on a cheerful smile. "You're taking all this to your new place?"

"Oh, no. Only a few dozen boxes. Whatever's left will go..." She trails off, her blue-gray eyes misty and unfocused. "Well, you'll help me figure it out."

My heart squeezes. Leaving the house she's lived in for forty-plus years must be devastating for Maxie. I'll do whatever I can to help my aunt pack up the remains of her long, sparkly life.

Three hours later, I massage my aching lower back. While Maxie directed from the sofa, I've filled a dozen cartons, separating them into a keeper pile, a giveaway pile, and a pile marked *December*. Maxie refuses to explain that one.

"I'll call a few of my young friends tomorrow." With a pained grunt, Maxie pushes up from the sofa. "Stanley will want those Balinese shadow puppets. And Margot would love those black lace doilies."

I finger the lace atop the giveaway pile. "You could make all kinds of cool things with these. Goth flower pins to wear on your lapel or your hat, funky fascinators, maybe Modge Podge them onto picture frames."

"You keep them, kiddo. Have fun."

"Oh, I didn't mean me." I drop the lace. "I mean someone with talent."

Maxie clucks her tongue. "There you go again. You got plenty of talent, kiddo. You just lack stick-to-it-iveness."

I duck my head to hide my grimace. A long line of art teachers hasn't shared Maxie's faith in my potential. Finally, I reached the point where persisting felt futile. And exhausting. And stupid.

But so what? As a gallerist, I can immerse myself in the art world I love and surround myself with fascinating artists without having to put my pathetic dabblings on display.

I push to my feet. "We both could use a break, and I really need a run."

Maxie beams. "Of course, my gazelle. Go stretch those long legs."

From my duffle bag, I dig out my electric-blue running shorts and a sunny yellow tank. I'll need new running shoes soon, but those can wait until I find a job.

"I'll be back in an hour or two." I steer my steps toward the cool, soothing green of Alton Baker Park. I've missed my runs along the Willamette River, the rhythm of my feet slapping the pavement, my breath sliding in and out, steady as the tides. When I run, worries about the future unhook their claws.

Just breathe. Just run. Just be.

Chapter Two

♥

Dalton

On autopilot, my feet carry me through Alton Baker Park. Enough daylight remains for another hour of running, but my sluggish legs protest every step. It's not the workout dragging me down, though; it's the fat envelope that landed in my mailbox today. I knew it would come any day now, but instead of relief, I feel kind of...deflated, I guess.

"Shake it off," I grumble. "Man up. Move on."

This pep talk bullshit seems to help my student athletes, but it damn sure isn't helping me.

And to make matters worse, my water bottle's empty. I duck off the riverside path to gulp from a drinking fountain by the playground.

A pair of little arms clamps around my knees from behind. "Unka Dah-un!"

"Hey there, Princess." I grin down at my goddaughter. "What are you doing here?"

"Swings. Push me." Poufy ponytails bobbing, she skips to the swing set where her parents watch, laughing.

"Hey, Dalton." Destiny reaches up for a hug.

Palms up, I back away. "Been running for an hour. I'm pretty ripe."

She squeezes me anyway. "I'm used to it. Besides, no one out-stinks Marcus after a run."

"Thanks, baby." Marcus lifts their daughter toward the swings.

She wriggles away. "No. Dah-un do it."

Destiny laughs. "Guess she told you." Her phone buzzes. "Sorry guys, gotta take this one." Phone to her ear, she moves to a bench, leaving us guys on swing-pushing duty.

"Wheee! Again." Aliyah kicks her feet, her sparkly tennies flashing.

While I push, Marcus quizzes me. "How's your mom?"

Another sore subject. "Sometimes she's almost her old self. Other times, she thinks I'm one of the nurses."

He grimaces. "Man, that's rough. How about you? Big day today. How you holding up?"

Crappy. I'm thoroughly crappy.

"I've gotta admit, getting those papers was hard. I mean, I wanted the divorce, after what she did, but seeing it on paper's so—"

"Final?" He flashes a wry grin. "Yeah. I can't even imagine. If Destiny ever—"

"She won't."

"Naw. She wouldn't. She's steady. Strong. And she calls me on my shi—" His gaze cuts to his daughter. "On my stuff."

"Again," Aliyah demands.

I grasp the chains. "Okay, squirt. Here comes a super-mega-big push. Ready?" Trilling my tongue in a drumroll sound, I pull the swing backward until Aliyah dangles high above our heads, kicking and squealing. "Three, two, one, launch."

I let go, and she sails skyward, hooting with joy. Her father's cushioning arms bring her back to earth. "Okay, pumpkin. Go play on the climbing castle. I need to talk to Uncle Dalton."

"Work stuff?"

"Yup."

"Okay." She trots off while we settle on a nearby bench.

Marcus drapes his long arms along the back. "So, now that mess is all behind you."

"Almost. Still dickering over the house." I bend to tighten my shoelaces. "Guess her new boyfriend's not as generous as she thought."

"Grasping bitch. Good riddance."

"I thought—" I run my hand over my shaved scalp. Putting my thoughts into words is like wrestling eels. "I thought it would feel good to finally get the divorce, but it just..."

"Dude, it's a big deal. Give yourself time to digest it." Marcus claps my shoulder. "So, what's next, my friend?"

"Nothing much. Just getting ready for the new school year and the race next weekend."

"Don't give me that crap." He nudges me. "See, that's why you need a good woman—to make you answer the important questions in life."

I snort. "A new woman? No thanks. I need time alone to get my head on straight."

"Dude, you've had a year alone—unless there's someone you haven't told me about?"

"There isn't." I slump, elbows on my knees.

Marcus levels me with that one-eyebrow-up stare that pulls confessions from bullies, class clowns, and other disturbers of the peace. "So, when your head is straight again, what do you want?"

I shrug.

His grip on my shoulder tightens. "Don't make me hurt you."

"Ow. Okay, okay." I shake off his grasp. "I want a good woman."

My gangly guru gives a sage nod. "Tell me what she's like, this good woman."

That's a damn good question. I rise and pace on the gravel path. "Someone real, I guess. A partner, like you and Destiny."

"Good. What else?"

"She should be outdoorsy. Maybe a runner. Tiff hates running."

He waves away my ex's name like a bad smell. "Forget Tiffany. Tiffany is over. Tell me about this new woman."

"She's—interesting. And kind. She cares about something beyond herself." Might as well shoot for the moon. "And she loves sex."

Laughing, he pokes my shoulder with his bony finger. "That part's no problem for you, Mr. Anaconda-in-Your-Pants."

I lift one shoulder. "It's a blessing and a curse."

"Hell, wish I was cursed like that."

"No, you don't." I stretch my legs out and adjust the tight running briefs that keep my blessing in place. "Ironic, isn't it? We teachers don't earn half of what we're worth, yet I know how a rich guy must feel. You're never sure if a woman likes you for yourself, or just for what you bring to the table."

"You put it on the table? Damn." Marcus splutters with laughter.

"Shut up." I push to my feet. "I better get back. It's almost dark."

"Don't worry, Cue Ball. Your shiny white head will light the way."

"Look who's talking."

Both of us deal with our creeping hairlines in the same way—shave it clean off.

Destiny steps up behind us and clears her throat. "If you two are done comparing penises, we should get going."

I groan and hide my heated face in my hands.

"See?" Marcus says. "That's the trouble with women. They act all cute and delicate, but they got sneaky ninja skills." He calls Aliyah. "Time to go, baby girl."

"I'm not a baby." She stomps over to her parents, pausing to hug my knees again. "G'night, Unka Dah-un. Sleep tight. Don't let the bedbugs bite."

I wave as the happy family drives off toward home. My best friend is a lucky man. With a wistful sigh, I hit the trail again. Alone.

Laurel

I slow my steps to adjust my ponytail. The river breeze caresses my cheeks and cools my sweaty skin. Deep-blue summer twilight hangs like velvet curtains over the slowly sliding Willamette. I should head back to Maxie's soon, but the air is so delicious, the tree-lined path so inviting, and the fresh, green scent of water and trees beckons me further into the park.

Just a few more minutes, then I'll turn around. There are still lots of people on the trail, so I tune out the inner voice reminding me that a woman alone after dark is asking for trouble. Instead, I focus on birdsong, tweets and chirps and trills and caws and—

"Yo, sweet thang. Don't run away." A guffaw splutters from the bushes.

A higher voice chimes in. "Mmm. Look at that ass. Mama, you make me so hard."

Shitshitshit. In my hurry to catch a run before sunset, I neglected to unpack my pepper spray. My thudding heartbeat picks up speed, and so do my feet. Asshole kids hiding in the shrubbery, harassing women. I almost clap back with a few choice words, but that usually escalates things. Better to ignore them and keep on running.

"Come back, Blondie. I just want a little taste."

Footsteps sound behind me—only one set but closing fast.

I gulp air and lengthen my stride. My quads burn and my sides ache, my reserves nearly spent.

I'll never run without pepper spray again.

The guy is right on my tail, puffing like a bellows.

"Babe, there you are. Hold up." This voice is deeper and lacks the mocking tone of the others.

Without slowing, I risk a backward glance. Tall bald guy. Serious runner, judging by his gear. His face drips from exertion, but his broad smile holds no threat. He tilts his shaved head toward the bushes and rolls his eyes.

I slow, and he pulls up alongside me, exclaiming with unnecessary volume, "I stopped to tie my shoelaces, and you disappeared."

Hard of hearing? Near-sighted?

He throws a glance over his shoulder and lowers his voice. "You okay?"

Understanding dawns. He's rescuing me!

"I'm good, thanks." I jog to a stop and bend over, hands on my knees, gulping air. He waits beside me and scans the bushes, his breathing hard but steady. Expensive running shoes. Above his enormous feet rise long, well-muscled legs encased in snug shorts and the finest ass I've seen in a long, long time—high and firm and muscular. My fingertips itch to trace its contours.

Holy heck, what's wrong with me?

His back to me, he surveys the trail. And what a back it is, outlined by his sweat-soaked T-shirt, narrow at the waist and broad at the shoulders. He runs his long fingers over his shiny shaved head and turns to face me.

Late thirties, I'm guessing. Aquiline nose, straight, pale brows, and deep-set eyes, blue as the summer twilight. A short golden beard covers his jaw. His lips spread in a slow smile, transforming his bony face into something dazzling.

Our eyes meet, and a spark jolts through me, strong and sharp and aimed straight at my core.

Uh-oh.

I've felt this spark before with the college boyfriend who loved me hard and fierce for two years and then dumped me a few days before graduation, shattering my already fragile self-esteem. I'm still picking up the pieces.

Instant attraction spells trouble.

I give my head a shake. This isn't Carlo, just a nice, friendly guy. No need to panic.

I wipe sweat out of my eyes. "Thanks for stopping. Those guys—"

A voice rings out from the bushes. "Blondie, where are you?"

Then another. "Come back and show me some love."

And a third. "You know you want to."

My companion's easy grin slides into a scowl as he sprints toward the voices.

The shrubs explode in a flurry of rustling.

"Shit, it's Mr. Garvey."

"Run!"

Scuffling sounds follow, along with cursing. A moment later, the tall guy emerges, his arms cross-hatched with welts and scratches, clutching a plump, pimply teenager by the back of his shirt. The catcaller, who can't be more than fourteen, squirms in a vain effort to escape.

The man leans in, his expression thunderous, and snarls in the kid's ear. "What do you say to the lady?"

The boy lowers his gaze. "I'm sorry, ma'am."

Mr. Garvey gives the kid a shake. "And?"

"It won't happen again."

Not so brave now, are you, little macho? I swallow a snort of laughter and glare at the boy.

His eyes brim with tears. "Please don't tell my dad, Coach. He'll kill me."

Coach glares like an eagle clutching a rat in its talons. Finally, he relaxes his grip. "Get out of here."

The kid scrambles back into the bushes.

A tickly, nervous giggle escapes my throat. "Coach?"

"Cross country. North Eugene High, home of the Highlanders." He chuckles. "And a few lowlifes like Justin and his buddies." He shuffles his big feet on the pavement, then fixes his blue, blue eyes on mine. "I'm Dalton, by the way."

I extend my hand. "Laurel."

His palm is warm, his grip gentle, and he holds my gaze so long I'm compelled to fill the awkward silence with embarrassed blathering. "Great name for a tall girl, right? Like a tree."

I calculate his height. Six foot six? Or seven? Six feet tall in my bare feet, I seldom meet a guy who towers over me like this. He makes me feel delicate, for once.

I clear my throat. "Are you going to tell his dad?"

He taps his lips with his forefinger, then grins. "Nope. His mom. She works in the school cafeteria."

"Ooo, a lunch lady. They're tough."

When he laughs, his craggy face lights up with a playful energy that makes me want to—what, exactly? I'm definitely not looking for a new boyfriend, or even a hookup. After my last break-up from a Porsche salesman who never took down his dating app profile, I promised myself to go three whole months before dating again, time to reset my priorities, center myself—stuff like that.

I clear my throat. "Well, thanks for being my pretend boyfriend. Best ten-minute relationship ever."

"Let's make it a bit longer." The corners of his wide mouth lift, and a by-God dimple winks in the hollow of his cheek.

"Oh, um..." In my belly, a swarm of fireflies begin their jittery, glowing dance.

"It's nearly dark. Let me run you back to your car."

The fireflies wink out, leaving an odd emptiness.

"Actually, I came on foot."

"Okay, I'll run you home. Which way?"

"It's not necessary, really." But his open, earnest smile tugs me toward surrender. Maybe just a little flirtation to pass the time until I move to San Francisco?

I give myself a mental kick. Nope, nope, nope. Gotta be ready for a fast exit.

Still, it'll be fully dark soon. "Okay, thanks. I'm a few miles back that way, over the bridge."

"Shall we?" He breaks into a slow, loping pace, graceful as a giraffe. I fall into step beside him. We cross the DeFazio Bridge and turn toward Maxie's neighborhood.

"Here's my place." He nods toward a big apartment complex.

"Oh." A lump of disappointment settles in my middle. "Thanks for running with me. Maybe I'll see you later."

He doesn't break stride. "Who said I was stopping?"

"You don't have to—"

"Hey." He slows and glances at his watch. "I'm training for a 10K. I need at least another half hour. And I worry about you running alone in the dark."

Stupid to let a strange man know where I live, but something about him inspires my trust. He is a teacher, after all. And a coach.

"Okay, sure. Thanks."

A few neighbors still linger outside, chatting over fences, and a pair of kids dribble a basketball in their driveway, its hollow plunk, plunk, plunk a counterpoint to our footfalls. But most Whiteaker residents have retreated indoors, their air conditioners humming. TVs glow and flash through plate-glass windows. Maple leaves rustle overhead, still green in the late-August warmth. Soon, this street will blaze with autumn glory.

"Peaceful out here," he says. "Have you lived here long? I haven't seen you in the park."

"I just arrived today. I'm staying with my great-aunt."

"Ah." He points with his bearded chin. "I used to live out here. Over on Adams."

"Why'd you move?"

His voice flattens. "I got divorced."

I wince. Way to put a nice guy on the spot.

"I'm sorry. That sucks."

He lifts one broad shoulder. "Yeah, it does."

"Well, here we are." I trot to a stop in Maxie's driveway. Living room lights blaze through the sheer curtains. "Guess she's still a night owl. Hope I have her energy at ninety."

His eyebrows rise. "Ninety? Wow." He crosses the walkway in a few long strides. "Interesting house. Good bones." The porch rail wobbles beneath his hand. "Better get this fixed. Don't want your aunt toppling into the rose bushes."

"Yeah, the place needs some TLC, for sure."

The screen door bangs open, making me jump.

"Get off my porch," Maxie bellows, brandishing her bejeweled cane overhead. Her flaming hair stands on end, and her thin lips curl into a snarl, reminding me of a mangy Pomeranian.

Dalton steps back, palms out. "Sorry, ma'am. I was just seeing Laurel home."

"Who?" Maxie stabs her cane toward us. "You two get out of here, or I'll call the cops."

My heart gives a wobbly thump. "Maxie, it's me." I step toward the porch light. "Sorry I'm late. I lost track of time."

Her fierce scowl sags. "Susan?"

Suddenly, the expression *Her blood ran cold* hits home hard. I clench my hands to still their shivering.

"I'm Susan's youngest, Laurel. I came to help you move, remember?"

Maxie stares, her jaw hanging slack.

Dalton gently grips my shoulder. I want to lean into him and let his warmth drive away icy dread. Instead, I extend my hand to Maxie.

A lone tear trickles down her furrowed cheek. "Who's this?"

"This is Dalton. He's—my friend. We went for a run. Okay?"

Maxie nods and backs into the house. Her gravelly voice quavers. "Of course. Excuse me." She shuffles into the living room and sinks onto the sofa.

Tears prickling my eyes, I stare after her, then up at Dalton.

He raps on the door frame. "Ma'am, could I borrow a pen?"

Maxie points to the little table beside the door. "In the drawer."

Taking my hand, he scribbles a number on my palm and lowers his voice. "I've seen this before. My mom has dementia. Call me if you need anything. Or just to talk. Maybe I can help." His thumb strokes the inside of my wrist. "I want to help, Laurel." He eyes Maxie, who stares into the distance. "What's her last name?"

"Schmidt."

He leans through the doorway. "Good night, Ms. Schmidt. It was a pleasure to meet you."

"You too, young man," she mutters. "Come visit us again."

Dalton squeezes my arm before trotting down the stairs and into the night.

The cloud over Maxie's eyes evanesces. Her voice strengthens. "Well, come inside, dear. Don't stand there letting the bugs in."

A violent chill rattles my spine.

Oh God, what am I going to do?

Chapter Three

♥

Laurel

Maxie points to a row of parking spaces bordering the broad lawn. "Park right here, kiddo."

I pull her blocky old Volvo into a visitor space. Surrounded by neat boxwood hedges, a wooden sign welcomes us to Willamette Grove Active Senior Community. While Maxie gathers her paperwork and tape measure, I dig in my purse for my phone. Damn, must've left it on the bed. So much for sneaking off to call Dalton.

Less than a month into my self-imposed dating hiatus, I'm definitely not looking for a boyfriend. And if I were looking, it'd be for a passionate artist, not a cross-country coach. Hell, Dalton probably spends his evenings watching football and drinking beer.

But he did save me from those asshole kids in the park. And he handled Maxie's "spell" so skillfully, so gently. The kindness in those intensely blue eyes tugs hard on a part of me that doesn't give a damn about his resume.

I run my fingertip over his phone number, still faintly visible on my palm. Last night, I carefully copied it into my phone and my journal, checking twice for accuracy. How weird, on my first day in Eugene, to meet a sweet, friendly runner who knows how to deal with dementia. That kind of luck never happens to me.

He's too old for me, my annoying practical side wheedles. Though actually, with his shaved head, it's hard to tell. He could be...

"Earth to Laurel." Maxie's cane raps my knee.

"Sorry, I was just..."

"And they say I have memory troubles. Let's go." No question, Maxie is completely herself again, energetic and focused. And bossy.

I follow her to the office building. Really quite lovely for an old folks' home, Willamette Grove resembles a college campus. Tudor-style buildings with dark wood trim surround a neat lawn. Pansies nod from cement urns at every doorway. Beneath a huge sycamore tree, a dozen white-haired residents in workout gear glide through a slow-motion Tai Chi routine.

"Looks boring," Maxie grumbles. "I'm gonna sign up for Zumba class." She toddler-steps up the shallow stairs. "And painting, of course. The art building's over there. The café next door is open all day. Good place to meet fellas." Maxie hands me a spiral-bound notebook. "You take notes, in case I forget anything later."

Inside, a plump woman with freckled cheeks and a short pouf of white hair greets us. "Welcome to Willamette Glen. I'm Pearl. What can I do for you ladies today?"

"Mr. Mendez said I could take measurements for my new apartment. Maxine Schmidt." She pokes the desk calendar with one glittery fingernail. "That's me. Ten o'clock."

"Right. Let me fetch a pass key."

While the receptionist steps away, I whisper, "Ritzy place, Maxie."

She nods. "Been saving for a rainy day. I'm going out in style, my dear."

Maxie's dark humor fills me with a heavy sense of dread. No matter how many bright flowers and fun classes this facility offers, it's still the last stop for its residents.

"This is the nice side, of course," Maxie continues. "Over there, behind the dining hall, there's the wing for the folks with CRS."

"CRS?"

"Can't remember shit." She cackles and smacks the countertop. "But hey, if they gotta lock me up to keep me from wandering off, at least I'll be in a pretty place with cute nurses." She nods toward a buff young man in scrubs. "Hubba Hubba."

The receptionist returns jingling a ring of keys. "Right this way, Ms. Schmidt." She leads us through a side door to a parking pad where a golf cart waits. "Climb in. I'll take you there."

Pearl deposits us in front of a two-story building on the far side of the quad, near the art building and the cafe. "Here we go. Apartment 121. They're not quite done with the renovations. But don't you worry, it'll be finished by your move-in date. Just give me a buzz when you're ready to leave. Number's marked on the phone."

Maxie stands facing the closed door but makes no move to open it. For a moment, I tense, bracing myself for another "spell." Maxie's skinny shoulders lift. "Here goes, kiddo." With a trembling hand, she opens the door.

The sharp chemical odor of fresh paint and new carpet wafts out of the tiny apartment with beige walls and nondescript taupe carpeting. A low breakfast bar separates the living area from the dinky kitchenette. In the rear, a sliding glass door opens onto a little patio flanked by cement planters full of pansies.

Someone must've got a great bargain on pansies.

"Well, shit," Maxie mutters and leans on the door frame.

I rush to her side, but there's no furniture to sit her on.

She swats me away like a pesky fly. "I'm fine. It's just the paint fumes."

Leaning on my arm, she inspects the whole apartment. It doesn't take long. In addition to the main room, a short hallway leads to a small bedroom and a beige-tiled bathroom with a walk-in tub.

"Maxie, are you sure this is what you want? This place is tiny, and it has no, no..."

"Personality?" Maxie's habitual smile droops, settling her face into deep lines. "Honestly, no, it's not what I want. But it's what I need. I'm old, kiddo. And sometimes, I forget things. Pretty soon, I won't be able to take care of myself. I've seen too many friends put their families through hell, pretending everything's fine."

She pats my hand. "Here, I can bring my own things, have company if I want, be left alone when I want. And help is right across the lawn."

My heart squeezes like a fist. How can Maxie squash her bright, bohemian spirit into this beige box? "You could move up to Cotter's Grove instead. Mom and Dad have a spare room."

"Are you kiddin'? Me in that dinky town? I'd go nuts. And I'd drive your parents nuts too." She pats my hand. "You and I aren't made for that kind of life, kiddo. That's why I picked this place out ten years ago. There's a long waiting list, you know. My friends can visit me here. I can catch a cab into town. This'll be okay." Her forced grin doesn't reach her eyes. "I'll cram so much personality into this little box, the neighbors won't know what hit 'em."

Maxie pulls a tape measure from her jacket pocket. "Let's measure the place and get back home." Her voice wavers on that last word, then her face crumples, and she leans against my side, her bony shoulders shaking.

"Oh, Maxie." I hug her tight, our sobs echoing in the empty space.

Dalton

"Mom, tea or coffee?" I grasp her flaccid hand. Sometimes physical contact brings her back, but today is not one of her good days. She stares into the distance, a faint smile on her thin, pink-painted lips. The summer breeze ruffles her hair.

It's so damn hard seeing her like this, knowing how sharp and insightful she once was. Maybe she's dehydrated. If no one reminds her, she'll sometimes go all day without drinking.

"Why don't I get us both an iced tea?"

"That's nice, John."

She thinks I'm Dad again. Shaking my head, I go into the café to place our order. Mom will be okay on the terrace, watching the Tai Chi group do their slow-motion dance.

Dad's across town today, building a potting shed in some-one's yard. Good thing he loves the work, since Mom's room in the memory care center doesn't come cheap.

While I wait, my thoughts drift back to another old lady and the beautiful young woman devastated by her decline. I check my phone again. Still no call from Laurel, no text, nada. Damn.

Like the afterimage of fireworks, she's burned into my retinas—tall, graceful, lovely, and seemingly all alone as she watches dementia destroy someone she loves. A primitive part of me clamors to reassure her, to keep her safe.

I've gotta laugh at my own foolishness. A few smiles from a pretty girl have catapulted me into full-on caveman mode.

"I'm just reaching out to someone who needs help, that's all," I mutter as I collect straws, sweetener, and napkins. "Not looking for a relationship. Definitely not."

What a pretty name, Laurel. What a pretty woman.

Too pretty for me. Too young. She's, what, twenty-three? With her pale, blue-tipped ponytail and her clean-scrubbed face, she radiates youth and innocence. Must be a student at the U of O. Of course, I also noticed her long, smooth legs, her firm, round ass, her striking gray eyes—how could I not? I may be old and divorced, but I'm not dead.

The barista slides me a tray. "Here you go, hon. Give my best to Hannah."

When I return to the patio, my seat is taken by a tiny, birdlike woman, well past eighty, with thin wisps of flaming-red hair. Must be a trend among the seniors. She looks like Laurel's great aunt.

Mom looks up and blinks, then flashes a wide grin. "How nice to see you, dear. I didn't know you were coming by today. Maxie, this is my son, Dalton."

I nearly spill our drinks. Holy crap, it is Laurel's great aunt, the one who was ready to clobber me with her cane last night.

Maxie tilts her fuzzy baby-bird head. "You look familiar, young man. Did we meet at the last art walk?"

"No, ma'am. I—"

"At the microbrew festival?"

"No—"

She fixes me with a squinty stare. "Say, aren't you the artist who sculpts with beer cans?"

Mom's laughter tinkles. "Goodness, no. Dalton doesn't have an artistic bone in his body. He's a history teacher. Now, his sister is a real artist." She launches into a long story about Cassie's latest art show in Denver.

Grinning, I move off in search of another chair. Mom hasn't been this animated in a long time. A good sign?

"Maxie," a clear, high, feminine voice calls. Jolted by a flash of long legs and pale hair, I nearly collide with a tottering old fellow making his slow way to a table.

"Sorry, sir." I help the startled man into a seat, then drink in the glorious sight of Laurel bounding across the lawn. Her silky hair floats loose, its turquoise tips brushing the center of her back, and her colorful skirt clings to her hips and legs as she moves. Hypnotized, I watch her trot to a stop and set a tape measure and notebook on Mom's table. The way she flips her hair out of her eyes, long, wheat-colored strands flashing like a flag in the sunlight...I'm dumfounded. Thunderstruck. Totally, stupidly smitten.

I suck in a deep, steadying breath. Focused on her great aunt, Laurel hasn't noticed me yet—but she will, any second now. A bald, gawky giant is hard to miss.

"Okay. I've got all the measurements and returned the key," she tells Maxie. "Pearl says you can move in any time after the tenth."

I open my mouth, then snap it shut and finally remember to breathe. Maxie's moving in. She'll be Mom's neighbor. I'll see Laurel again.

I bite back a big, cheesy grin.

"I'll get us something to drink." Laurel turns toward the café and bonks right into me.

"Oh, jeez, sorry." Her plump lips curve in a smile. "Dalton!"

"Hi." I give her a lame wave.

Her storm-cloud gray gaze pins me where I stand. "What are you..."

I nod toward the ladies' table. "That's my mom your aunt is talking to."

"How, um, nice?" Her lips quirk to one side.

"It is, actually. These days, Mom doesn't usually take to strangers."

I follow Laurel inside, where she places her order, then lays her hand on my arm. "Hey, could I ask you a few questions?"

Her long pale lashes gleam like moonlight.

Mesmerizing.

We move to a table near the window where I can keep an eye on my mother. "Your aunt's moving in?"

"Yeah." Her gaze drops. "I hate to see her do it. She loves her place. How can she be happy here, in a little beige box identical to the one next door? Maxie's an artist, an adventurer."

I lay my hand over hers and marvel at the softness of her skin. "Does she need the extra help?"

"She says she does."

"And she doesn't want to move in with family?"

She shakes her head. "Doesn't want to be a burden, I guess."

"Well, this is a decent place. They take good care of Mom here."

Her gaze slides away, growing misty.

I grip the table's edge, stifling the urge to enfold her in my arms, which would be totally creepy, coming from a near-stranger.

She sniffles. "I should stay with her, after all she's done for me."

That cute little sniff yanks on my heartstrings.

"I thought the same thing when Mom was diagnosed. But caring for her would be a full-time job. Are you up for that?"

"Not really. I just—" She snarls her fingers in her hair. "I feel like such a shit for letting her move in here."

A wry grin twists my lips. When I told Tiffany the wrenching news of Mom's Alzheimer's diagnosis, she recoiled as if I'd served her a plate of slugs. She visited Willamette Grove with me exactly once, then refused to return, saying it was too depressing. But here's Laurel, turning herself inside out over her great-aunt's decline.

"Hey." I give her hand a squeeze, and she nestles her satiny palm into mine. "She has a say in how this plays out, you know. Has she asked you to move in?"

She shakes her head. "My parents sent me. I was on my way to San Francisco. My friend offered me his spare room. But Maxie needs my help, and I owe her big time."

So much for my stupid hopes. Any day now, she'll leave Eugene to move in with some guy. Figures. Might as well be a good sport about it. I release her hand. "Well, if I had a girlfriend as pretty as you, I'd offer her more than my spare room."

"Girlfriend?" Her eyebrows shoot up, and she splutters a laugh. "Davonte is totally gay. He's like, the crown prince of gaydom."

Thank you, Jesus.

"Besides," she continues, "I have to earn some money first. San Francisco is damned expensive." Her windy sigh lifts a strand of hair from her forehead. "I guess I'll stay for a while, look for a job here."

I straighten in my seat. "Hey, I know someone who's looking for help. My friend Clara runs a bookstore."

"Really?" Her hopeful grin rekindles my pilot light.

"I'll text her to expect you. Book Nirvana, on Willamette Street."

While I tap out a message to Clara, I do my best to calm my over-eager tone. "Our running club meets Saturdays at nine, at the coffee shop next to Clara's place. Maybe you'd like to join us? There are lots of—"

"That sounds great."

"Really?" My voice squeaks like a sophomore's. "I mean, cool."

She grins down at the table. Is she blushing?

The barista calls, "Two superfruit smoothies for Laura."

Laurel rolls her eyes. "I get that all the time." She collects her tray and heads for the door. Outside, Mom and Maxie are still deep in merry conversation.

"Here we go." Laurel sets the bright purple drinks on their table. Maxie takes a tentative sip and screws up her face. "Too sweet."

I step up behind Laurel. "Mom, you've made a new friend?"

Mom's smile slides off like a snowpack from a sun-warmed roof. She glares at me and Laurel, her plump, rosy face contracted in fury. Rising from her seat, she stabs a finger at my chest and shrieks, "You think you can bring your floozy here? Flaunt her in my face? In my home?"

Ice runs through my veins as I back away, sliding Laurel behind me.

"So help me, John, you get that whore out of here." Mom's voice grates like a rusty saw.

I speak slowly and gently, like the doctor recommended, hoping to ease her back to reality. "Mom, it's me, Dalton."

She continues, her fury unabated. "I know about her. The whole town knows about her. You keep her away, you hear?" Knocking her chair over, she stomps across the patio toward the memory care building.

I turn to Laurel. "God, I'm so sorry. She thinks I'm my dad."

"It's okay. Go. I'll see you later." But her stricken expression belies her kind words.

With my belly in knots, I run to intercept my fuming mother before she hurts herself or someone else.

Chapter Four

♥

Laurel

"Don't you worry, doll. We'll find you a fun job." Taking two steps for every one of mine, Maxie tugs me toward a low brick building. A colorful wooden sign above the first entrance reads *Coffee Dreams.*

Great. Just like Dad predicted, I'm going to be a barista.

But Maxie leads me to the second entrance. *Book Nirvana* proclaims the gold-leaf script on the door. Holy cannoli, this is the place Dalton mentioned, where his friend is looking for extra help!

The bell over the door tinkles merrily as we step inside.

"Maxie," a petite, spiky-haired girl squeals and skips over to enfold my aunt in a tight hug. In her slashed jeans and clunky Doc Martens, she reminds me of a punk-flavored Tinker Bell.

"I'm sooo glad to see you." The sprite talks a mile a minute. "Hey, I've used the black lace you gave me as a webpage background. It came out really cool."

"Margot, this is my grandniece, Laurel."

"Pleased to meetcha." Her handshake is surprisingly powerful.

"Laurel is looking for a job," Maxie tells her.

"Cool! Let me get Clara."

While Margot trots down the tightly packed aisles in search of her boss, I check out my surroundings. How did I miss this amazing bookshop during my college years? The sweet scent of old books mingles with the tempting aroma of coffee from the café next door, connected to Book Nirvana by a wide archway. Big plate-glass windows and skylights flooded the space with sunlight, making the colorful book spines really pop. More color shines from scattered armchairs upholstered in bright chintz. On a big round table near the entrance, a vase of yellow mums crowns an architectural stack of books.

And the posters! High above the bookshelves, Peter Max's psychedelic sunset points toward the art books, the Beatles' Yellow Submarine signals the music section, and a lush still life of fruit, bread, and wine hangs over the cooking section. What fun! There are comic book superheroes, a dreamy spacescape, an armored knight charging into battle, and, above a lacquered red door at the rear, Ingres's Grande Odalisque threw a languid glance over her bare shoulder. I recognize her naughty smirk from art history class.

Maxie elbows me. "That's the erotica room."

Why am I not surprised she knows about that?

"Be right with you," someone calls from behind a carved wooden screen near the front counter.

"Prrrrup." A fluffy ginger tabby cat head-butts my ankle, then twines around my legs in a tango of feline affection.

"I see you've met Lulu." A pretty woman of about forty with long auburn hair scoops up the cat and smiles warmly. "Good to see you again, Maxie. Come for more art books? Or did you want the red door key?"

"Not today, dear." She grabs my arm and beams. "This is my grandniece Laurel. Very smart girl. Artistic. Good with people."

"Pleased to meet you, Laurel." Clara clasps my hand. "Wait a minute." She pulls her phone from her jeans pocket. "Are you the one Dalton texted me about?"

"That's me." I hope my smile looks confident.

Clara sets down the cat, grabs a stack of papers from behind the counter, and beckons toward the café. "Let's go next door. Join us, Maxie?"

Maxie waves us off. "I'll visit with Margot."

The handsome barista greets Clara with a syrupy Southern drawl. "'Bout time, dear heart. I was getting worried when you skipped your morning coffee break."

She leans over the counter to peck his cheek. "Inventory hiccup. This is Laurel. She's interested in the job. You remember Maxie? Older red-headed lady?"

He beams. "I do indeed. She's a hoot."

"Laurel is her grandniece."

He scans me from top to toe, then chuckles. "Not much family resemblance."

We collect our coffees and sit beside a bookshelf stuffed with paperbacks.

"Arnie and I combined our shops a few months ago. Now more of my customers come in here to buy coffee, and more of his come to my place to buy books. That's why I need extra help." She sips her latte and grins. "God, it feels good to say that. We nearly folded, you know. The huge chain store up the street almost did us in."

I wrinkle my nose. "Corporate conformity. The worst. Hey, is this the coffee shop where the running club meets?"

"That's right. You're a runner?"

"Yeah. Dalton told me to check it out."

Clara narrows her eyes like an expert appraising a painting. Pretty eyes, deep sea green, and very sharp.

I squirm under her scrutiny, and my gaze falls to the hand holding her mug. "What a beautiful ring."

Clara's expression relaxes as she wiggles the fingers of her left hand. "I can't believe I'm engaged again. Anyway—" She quickly outlines the job duties: stocking shelves, paperwork, ringing up sales, light cleaning during shop hours. "I could use help with decorating, too. I have zero artistic talent, and Margot's busy with her classes at the U of O. Harry, my other helper, is on vacation until October."

"Ah. Well, I have some experience working in art galleries, so—"

"Great." Clara beams and slides an application form across the table. "Just bring this over when you're done. I'm glad to have you on board, Laurel. It's not often I get a candidate endorsed by a good friend."

After filling out the forms, I sit in a chintz armchair by the bookshop entrance and wait for Maxie. And wait. While Clara and Margot help customers, I send a message to my best friend Davonte about my new job, then scroll through photos of my old neighborhood in Portland. God, I'm going to miss that place—the Saturday market, my work friends, my book club, the café where we shared giant sandwiches, the bar where we played darts and danced to local bands. With a wistful sigh, I stand, stretch, and tuck my phone back into my pocket.

"Excuse me," I ask Margot, "have you seen Maxie?"

The red door in the rear of the shop swings open, and Maxie totters out, a large hardback under her arm. "Found a good one." Her saucy grin lights up her wrinkled face.

On the cover, a beautiful, sculpted male nude, deep bronze, is posed to conceal his genitals, barely. Peering closer, I giggle in surprise. This is a living man, not a statue. His gleaming shaved head and oiled skin, along with careful lighting, transform his muscular body into a work of art.

"Quite a hottie, eh?" Maxie winks up at me. "Gonna try some charcoal drawings. Live models are too expensive these days, and they always expect snacks."

I bite back a grin as I imagine my artistic aunt peering over her easel at a gorgeous naked man.

"Looks like your new friend," Maxie adds. "What's his name, Darren?"

"It's Dalton," I whisper—but not quietly enough.

Clara glances up from the register, her eyebrows sky-high. "You've seen Dalton naked, Maxie?"

Maxie cackles. "Course not." She waggles her eyebrows. "Think he's got the hots for my grandniece, though."

Clara draws her head back and blinks rapidly. Uh-oh. Is there history between her and Dalton?

Great, the perfect temp job comes with relationship drama.

Oh well, here's my adulting lesson for the day: keep my personal feelings out of the workplace. If I'd mastered that skill, I might still be working in Portland.

I extend my hand. "Thanks for the opportunity, Clara. Your shop is gorgeous. I'm looking forward to working here." And padding my patchy résumé.

Clara's parting smile is guarded. I make a mental note to tread carefully where Dalton is concerned. Too bad. I don't often meet such a sweet guy, so helpful and thoughtful and tall and cute and...

I give myself a mental smack. Cute as he may be, I know better than to trust a sudden attraction. Look what I got for trusting Carlo, what Mom got for trusting Dad. Better to stick to my plan—help Maxie, make a few bucks, then move on. A big, sparkly future awaits me in San Francisco.

Eyes on the prize, not on Dalton's tempting ass.

Chapter Five

♥

Dalton

I check my phone again. Nada. Why would Laurel even want to hear from me after that ugly scene with Mom?

My little living room sucks all the satisfaction out of pacing—four big strides from the front door to the sofa, four strides back. This must be how a caged tiger feels.

A run, that's what I need. Three more miles to meet my daily training goals. Maybe Laurel would like to join me?

A hungry groan escapes my throat at the memory of her long, lithe body running across the lawn, her hair streaming in the summer breeze, like a slow- motion movie scene. God, she's beautiful. Though I hardly know her, already I can tell she's the polar opposite of my pointy, calculating ex. Laurel is honest, vulnerable, real.

Don't get carried away. You just met her, for God's sake. And you felt just as hyped-up about Tiffany when you met her.

That's a good point, annoying inner voice. But I've learned a lot about relationships since then, and about myself. Still, I'd be wise to take my time and get to know Laurel before letting my goofy heart grab the wheel.

I shuck my jeans and pull on my running gear. As I lace up my Sauconys, my phone pings with an incoming text.

> **Thanks so much, Dalton. Clara hired me. I start tomorrow.**

No mention of Mom's tirade. Something in my gut dances a happy jig. I text back:

> **I'm glad. Up for a run?**

I hit send, then add:

> **Really sorry about my mom. She's not usually so...**

Laurel's reply comes before I can finish the thought.

> **A run sounds great. Half an hour? Meet you at your place.**

Here? Oh yeah, I pointed out my apartment complex the other day as we ran past. And she remembered. Interesting. But also unnerving.

After separating from Tiffany, I fled to this convenient, cheapish spot where lots of my single teacher friends live. Four walls, decent internet, a pool, and a party room. What more could I ask for at this point? But for the first time, I worry about making a bad impression. Will she think this dumpy apartment reflects my personality?

Well, shit. She'll think what she thinks. Can't control that. Better clean up a little, though, just in case.

Fifteen minutes later, all the scattered papers and running magazines are neatly tucked away, the furniture's dusted, and the floor's vacuumed. That's as good as it gets.

Next, I brush my teeth and run my electric razor over my head to smooth the back and sides, then trim my beard. I stroke my chin and grin at my reflection, hoping to see one of those bald action heroes grinning back at me. No such luck.

Once again, this is as good as it gets.

I head out to wait by the front gate. Tingles spread through my chest when I spot her trotting up the street, her ponytail swinging like a banner. Sweat plasters her tank top and shorts to her body. Thank God for the baggy shorts over my compression tights, or she'd see just how much I appreciate the view.

"God. I'm gross." She pulls a bandana from her pocket and wipes her face and her sweat-soaked cleavage. "Hot today."

Yes, you are. "Want a cold drink before we hit the park? I've got some Gatorade in the fridge."

She grins. "That'd be great."

I lead her across the patio and up the stairs.

"Nice pool," she observes, peering over the railing. "Must be fun after a run."

Damn. Now I'm picturing her in a bikini, swimming on her back, her body glistening in the sun.

"Yeah, it's refreshing, if you don't mind the screaming kids."

"Well, you're a teacher, right? You must like kids."

"I do, but not when they land on my head." I hold the door, but she hesitates on the threshold. Smart of her. I'm a relative stranger, after all. Leaving the door open, I trot to the kitchen and peer into the fridge. "Let's see, I've got blue, lime, raspberry, or orange."

"Orange, please. You're well stocked. I'm impressed."

My face heats, which is stupid because she's obviously talking about the fridge.

"Yo, Dalster," Becca hollers as she passes the open door. "Coming to the barbeque tonight?" She grins up at Laurel. "You can bring your friend."

Great. Now everyone from work will hear about my new running friend.

"Laurel, this is Rebecca Knight. She teaches at my school, biology and chemistry."

She seizes Laurel's hand. "You a teacher?"

Laurel blinks like a forest creature facing an oncoming semi. "No, I—uh—I work in art. You know, galleries."

"Laurel and I are heading out for a run." I wink. "Want to come along? Think you can keep up?"

"Are you kiddin'?" Becca guffaws. "On these stumpy legs? Nice to meet you, Laurel."

I hand Laurel her drink and take a big gulp of my own. "Sorry. Becca's good people, but nosy."

She waves it off with a toss of her ponytail. "No problem. Let's go."

"Wait." Taking her elbow, I draw her inside but leave the door open. Her gaze holds mine—beautiful gray eyes, fringed with long, pale lashes, open and trusting and...

"Dalton?"

"Oh, right. Listen, I'm really sorry about my mother's outburst this morning. Lately, she's in and out of reality. Got this crazy notion my dad's cheating on her."

She raises one eyebrow but says nothing.

"Alzheimer's sometimes comes with a side of paranoia."

Her expression softens, and her gaze drops. "Don't worry about what your mom said. I'm learning that dementia makes people unpredictable. I guess you get used to it?"

I grasp her delicate hand. "Not really. But after a while, it doesn't hurt as much." I gulp from my bottle to clear the ragged lump in my throat. "Shall we hit the trail?"

Side by side, we run down the sidewalk, across the traffic-clogged street, and over the graceful DeFazio Bridge into Alton Baker Park. Skaters, skateboarders, and bikers crowd the riverside path, so I peel off toward Pre's trail, the wood-chip path where we'll have less competition for space. The steady thud of our footfalls calms my jittery brain. I keep my eyes on the pathway in front of me and off the stunning, sweaty woman beside me—not an easy task, especially when her ponytail swishes like cool silk against my arm.

Why isn't she saying anything? Is she waiting for me to make the first move?

I clear my throat. "So, you worked in an art gallery?"

"Yeah. Up in Portland. But now, with Aunt Maxie..."

Not very talkative, this one. "You like the bookshop?"

"Yeah, thanks." She flashes a dazzling smile, and I nearly crash into a tree.

Her fingers fly to her mouth. "Whoa there, you okay?"

Way to look like an idiot, you dork. "Yeah, fine." I rub the sore spot on my shoulder.

Laurel shoots me a suspicious sideways glance. "Clara seems really nice. She's a friend of yours?"

"Uh, sort of." I hope my casual grin is convincing. "She's in my running club." Best to leave it at that for now.

Laurel trots to a stop beneath a stand of towering pines. "Hang on, gotta fix my shoe."

She props her foot on a tree trunk. The motion snugs her shorts against her firm, round behind. Transfixed, I enjoy the view until a tightness in my groin prompts me to turn and admire the trees instead.

"All set." Her shoulder grazes mine as she shades her eyes and gazes upward. "I'd forgotten how beautiful it is out here."

I can't help it—my focus slides from the treetops to her graceful, upstretched neck, her delicate jawline, her plump lips open in wonder.

She digs in her running belt for her phone. "See how the sunlight makes a slash of gold on the water?" She moves closer to the riverbank, angling her screen this way and that. Finally satisfied, she shows me her photos.

"Wow." I cup my hands over hers to tilt the screen. "You have an artist's eye for sure."

The corners of her mouth turn down. "I wish. I've tried just about everything—drawing, painting, ceramics, sculpture. Nothing ever comes out the way I imagine it."

"But photography's an art. And this is spectacular. I couldn't have captured that scene the way you did." I'm not just blowing smoke up her running shorts. These images rival shots I've seen in art galleries. "My sister's a sculptor. She says half the battle is knowing where to look, and how. You've got the instinct."

She clucks her tongue. "Snapping photos with your phone isn't art, Dalton."

I gently grip her elbow. "It is when you do it."

When she holds my gaze like this, her eyes soft and welcoming, I have the oddest sense that she sees much deeper than my surface—and is offering me the chance to do the same. And man, do I want to dive in and lose myself in those storm-cloud eyes.

We stand for a long moment, toe to toe. No sound but birdsong and the rush of the river sliding by, until a loud ping slices through my rosy haze.

"Crap. Sorry." She pokes her phone screen. "Hi, Maxie. What's up?"

While she moves a few steps down the trail, I take advantage of the distraction to readjust myself. Better start wearing a double layer of compression shorts for runs with Laurel.

She returns, her smile drooping. "Maxie needs me to take her grocery shopping."

Well, damn. But in our situation, you can't count on long, uninterrupted stretches of private time. Mom's needs have to come first, and I'm sure Laurel feels the same way about Maxie.

We break into an easy trot back toward the bridge. At its apex, Laurel pauses to gaze at the swiftly sliding Willamette below. Her grip on the railing tightens. "You know, it really scared me the other night, when she didn't recognize me."

I prop my forearms on the railing. "It's hard. Wish I could say you'll get used to it, but I haven't yet."

She grips my arm, her eyes glittering with threatening tears. "How do you do it, Dalton? How do you watch someone you love just—disappear?"

I search my brain for a comforting answer, but nothing comes. My gut nudges me to enfold her in my arms, but it's too soon for such an intimate gesture. Besides, our run in the late-summer heat has left me sticky and no doubt pungent.

I lay my hand over hers. "I guess you just show up. Remember, she loves you, even if she forgets."

"Yeah." She blows out a long, windy sigh, and her gaze slides away, toward the glassy green below. "Could I call you sometime? You know, to talk about this stuff?"

I close my eyes. *Yessss.* My inner victory dance complete, I answer, "Of course. Let's have a coffee after running club on Saturday."

"That'd be great." Her bright smile lights up something deep in my chest.

Ten minutes later, we trot to a stop outside my place. As I wipe my sopping head with a bandana, another opening springs to mind. "Hey, there's a 10K race in Springfield a week from Sunday. Wanna join us?"

"I'll think about it." She flashes a grin. "I haven't been training regularly."

"Could've fooled me. You're in great shape."

She bats her long, pale lashes. "I'll bet you say that to all the girls."

Buoyed by her flirtation, I finally work up the nerve to ask her the question that's been nagging me since we met. "Can I ask a personal question, Laurel?"

She waits, eyebrows raised.

"How old are you?"

Something about her narrowed gaze suggests she's been wondering too. "Thirty-one." She digs the toe of her running shoe into the dust. "Where does the time go, right? And you?"

"Thirty-nine."

"For the first time?" She winks.

I raise three fingers. "Scout's honor."

Her gaze slides down my body and back up, leaving a sudden tingly chill, as if she somehow peeled away my damp running clothes to peer beneath.

She nods. "You've held up well, Gramps."

I can't decide whether to wince or laugh. Before I can formulate a snappy comeback, she steps in close—alarmingly, deliciously close—and kisses my cheek, her lips a sweet whisper of pleasure on my skin. She smells like sweaty sunshine.

"I'd better book it. Maxie's waiting. Thank you, Dalton. For the run, and the advice, and the job, and—just, thanks." She lopes away, calling over her shoulder, "See you Saturday."

I stroke the lingering warmth on my skin. When she disappears around the corner, I turn toward home, grinning like a happy idiot.

Chapter Six

♥

Dalton

My post-run shower is filled with steamy thoughts of beautiful Laurel, so I stand there spinning daydreams until the water turns cold. When I turn off the spray, I hear someone pounding on my front door. *Fire?* Is my first thought, followed by *bad news about Mom?* I quickly towel off, trot to the door, and peer through the peephole.

My gut clenches at the sight of my ex-wife fluffing her hair. I ought to keep her waiting while I get dressed. No, fuck it. She's not worth the effort. I tighten the damp towel around my waist and throw the door open with a bang.

"What do you want, Tiffany?"

She looks me up and down like a shopper inspecting a cellophane-wrapped chuck roast, then quirks her glittery lips to one side. "Nice look."

"I'm busy. Why are you here?"

"Come on, Dalton. You're a teacher on summer break." She sniffs derisively. "You've got nothing but time."

"Not for you, I don't." I glare, willing her to disappear.

She rolls her dark eyes and pulls a folder from her huge shiny purse. "Need your signature on the last papers for the house sale. I sent you a dozen texts."

"Got a new phone. Changed my number."

"And didn't tell me. Figures."

"Why would I—" I spin away, giving her my back while I collect myself. No way I'll let her draw me into another argument. That's what she wants, to poke me until I fume and yell and give her the attention she craves.

"Fine. Have a seat. I'll get dressed."

She sinks onto the couch and crosses her shapely, spray-tanned legs. "Don't bother on my account, Dalton. I want you to be comfortable."

I snort. "Having you here is never comfortable, no matter what I'm wearing."

She pulls a tube of lip gloss from her purse and slowly slicks on another layer. Looks like she's had those injections to make her lips puffy.

She wasn't like this when we first met, but people change. Priorities change. Over the seven years we were together, she became more and more obsessed with status and appearances, and it was only a matter of time before the life we built fell apart. Deep down, I was bracing for our breakup even before she cheated on me with Larry the Lawyer.

In the year plus since our split, I've filled three journals trying to figure out my part in all of this. It's a work in progress, and I've learned painful lessons about the danger of assuming everything's okay. If I'd listened more carefully, if I'd read between the lines, I'd have noticed the battalion of red flags my wife was waving. Next time, I'll be smarter.

Tiffany flicks her hair over her shoulders and flashes a slow, calculating smile. "There was a time when we were very comfortable together, Dalton." Her gaze slides down my bare torso, then a little lower.

I clutch my towel tighter. "What's the matter, Tiff? Not getting enough action from Larry?"

A flicker of reaction passes over her painted face, quickly smoothed again as she spreads the documents over the coffee table and uncaps an expensive-looking gold pen. Her voice flattens. "Just sign the papers, Dalton."

"In a minute." I retreat to my bedroom and pull on a pair of jeans and a polo shirt, then blow out a few deep breaths and force my jaws to unclench.

Back in the living room, I drop onto the sofa, as far from her as possible. "Are these the last signatures?"

"Yes." She slides closer and hands me the pen. Her bare arm sparkles like the metallic paint on a Corvette.

While I hunch over to sign at each little yellow sticker, she scoots closer still until her thigh grazes mine.

"Don't." I flip the page.

She lays her hand on my knee. "Dalton—"

I remove it. "I. Said. Don't."

She slinks to the other end of the couch and slips off her high-heeled sandals. With a long, shuddering sigh, she pulls her knees to her chest.

My heart pinches a little at this glimpse of vulnerability. But it's calculated, just an act to get what she wants. I've learned that the hard way.

"Won't work." I sign the last paper. "This is my copy?"

She nods, sniffling.

I stand, roll the papers into a tight cylinder, and stuff them into my rear pocket. "All done."

She doesn't budge. "You can go now."

She squints at me through watery eyes. "After ten years together, how can you be so cold?"

This isn't the first time since our separation she's tried to manipulate me into a meaningless booty call. A sneer curls my lip. "You've made your bed, Tiff. Now go lie in it. I sure won't."

"But I—"

"Go." I stab a finger toward the door.

Her mouth slides into a glum pout as she gathers her things and steps into her shoes. Rising to her feet, she straightens her snug top. "I cared for you, Dalton, but I deserve a better life. Being a teacher's wife in the suburbs isn't enough for me." Her voice rises to a childish, wheedling tone. "You could have been so much more."

"You mean I could have made more money."

She squares her shoulders. "Money is important to me. I'm not ashamed of that. But I miss what we had." Her proud posture relaxes. "We were good together, weren't we?"

I nod. "In bed. Everywhere else, not so much."

"Oh, come on. We had fun. Remember when—"

I cut her off. "Turns out, fun's not enough. See you, Tiff."

She stiffens, stalks to the door, and bangs it shut behind her.

I massage my aching forehead. Damn her for coming back. She could have mailed me the papers. Hell, we probably could've done all this with electronic signatures. Just when I'm riding the high of meeting someone new, she comes around to kick my feet out from under me. Again.

Laurel

"Why the hell did I kiss him?" I mutter as I unpack Maxie's shopping bags.

Kissing Dalton's cheek was just a natural impulse to express my gratitude, but I should know by now how acting on impulse opens the door to big trouble. He's such a sweet guy, and it isn't fair to lead him on. I'm leaving Eugene soon, and no man, no matter how tempting, can stop me.

Still, I smile at the memory: the sexy tickle of his whiskered cheek against my lips, the heat of his body, his soft whoosh of breath as I pressed against him.

Leaning on her sparkly cane, Maxie clumps into the kitchen and pulls a sack of grapes from a canvas tote. "Kissing who?"

I flush hot. "Who said anything about kissing?"

"You did, just now." Maxie nudges me. "I may be old, but I'm not deaf. Was it that beanpole fella?"

When I don't answer, she pokes me again. "I saw the way he looked at you. He's smitten. You're a fast worker, kiddo."

I fling up my hands in exasperation. "I'm not working on Dalton. At least, I'm not trying to."

"Why not? Seems like a sweet young man. Funny lookin', but nice and tall."

"He's not funny looking, he's—"

Maxie cackles. "Aha, you like him."

It's pointless to deny it. I do like him. He's kind and cute. Hunky, too, in his beanpole way. He's got an honest, natural grace about him, and he's so easy to talk to, a welcome change after a long string of self-centered guys more interested in impressing me than listening to me.

Damn you, universe, for your lousy timing.

Maxie hefts a sack of potatoes, despite my protest. "Next week, I'll introduce you to some of my artist friends. You'll fit right in." She dumps the potatoes into a bin beneath the sink.

I fold the empty shopping bags. "Come on, Maxie. We both know I'm no artist. Strictly speaking, I'm a bookstore clerk."

"Pish-tosh. You have the soul of an artist. You just haven't found your niche yet."

I lean on the counter and rake my fingers through my hair. "Once I get to San Francisco, maybe..."

Maxie shoots me a sharp glance. "Rushing off again, eh?"

"Not right away. I'll stay here until you're moved in, of course, but—"

"But what?"

"Once you move out, where will I stay? I'm sort of..." I flap my hands aimlessly, "homeless."

Maxie huffs through her nose. "Nonsense. You'll stay in my house."

"Aren't you selling it?"

She pours herself a glass of water. "I'm working with my lawyer on that. But there's no hurry, and I'm not taking all my furniture. You can use the Volvo, too, when your sad little car dies. So, you just stay put, Miss Scaredy-Pants."

"But I—"

Maxie crosses her arms and scowls. "It was very nice of Clara to hire you on my say-so. Don't repay her by running off after just a few weeks."

"But Maxie—"

"But Maxie, nothing. I know you better than you think." Her scowl softens. "In fact, you remind me a lot of myself at your age." With a grunt, she settles onto a chair and toes off her sequined sneakers. "I wanted a big, sparkly life in the big, sparkly city. So I ran off to New York, to Atlanta, to Chicago. Even spent a summer in Paris, waiting tables in a café that always smelled like piss, no matter how many times I mopped the floor."

I sit beside her. "That's what makes you special, Maxie, all your adventures."

"Baloney." She slaps her palm onto the table. "You know when I came into my own?"

I shrug.

"When I ran out of money and came home to Eugene. Took a job in a bar, the only job I could find, even with my college degree. Gradually, I met people. They introduced me to other people. I started taking art classes. Now I know most of the artists in town." She taps her bony chest and grins. "I'm a big fish in a small pond. And the water's fine."

Gloom descends like a heavy fog. "I don't want to swim in a small pond, Maxie. I want—"

"Those bright city lights, eh?"

Is she ever going to let me finish a sentence?

"Honey." She lays her cool hand over mine. "You don't get your sparkle from those big-city lights. It has to come from inside."

I want to believe her, but my lower lip slides into a childish pout. Maxie may have evolved to the point where she doesn't need outside validation—though she gets tons of it here in Eugene—but I'm not there yet. If chasing renown makes me immature, so be it. I need to feel like I'm more than just a small-town nothingburger. Not that Maxie is, but she's got talent, and I don't. Besides, what's more mature than facing reality?

All this ruminating is giving me a headache. I have a plan, damn it, and I'm sticking to it.

Maxie pats my hand. "Look, this could be a good opportunity. Make some money. Make connections. Build your résumé. After I move, I'll still need your help tying up loose ends. We'll work around your shifts at the bookshop, and your dates with Mr. Beanpole." She elbows me. "He's cute, by the way."

Despite my glum mood, the corners of my mouth quirk upward.

"See, there's one good point about staying in Eugene."

"One."

Maxie grins. "Here's another. Lots of chances to do art here, and—"

I huff. "Maxie, I've told you again and again. I have no talent. Zip. Zero."

She folds her arms. "Says who?"

"Every art teacher ever." I plant my elbows on the table and rest my chin on my palms. "I want to run a gallery and surround myself with amazing art. I want to show the world how much art can express, how it can connect people. That's a goal I can realistically reach."

"You're selling yourself short, kiddo." Maxie squeezes my hand. "Tell you what. You stay here through the holidays, and I'll make it worth your while."

My eyebrows shoot up. "The holidays?"

"I have Christmas plans, and I need your help. Afterward, if you still want to go, you'll leave with my blessing, and a nice Christmas bonus."

I twist my ponytail. "Do I have to decide right now?"

"'Course not. Sleep on it." Maxie pats my shoulder. "I bet you'll dream of that tall fella."

Damn it, I probably will.

Chapter Seven

♥

Laurel

"Shoo, Lulu." I nudge the ginger cat away from my ankles as I tie on my shop apron with *Book Nirvana* embroidered atop fluffy clouds. After a half-hour of dithering over what to wear to work, I finally settled on my Oscar Wilde T-shirt and a wrap skirt made from recycled sari cloth. I left Maxie's house feeling bohemian, even a little artistic. Now, beside Clara's easy elegance, I feel dorky and juvenile.

"Great shirt," Clara says without a hint of the condescension I'd expect from my last boss. Make that my last two bosses, maybe three. "So, you know how to work a cash register?"

"Absolutely." Of course, at swanky art galleries, I didn't ring up many sales. Mostly, I arranged displays and greeted customers.

The brass bell over the doorway tinkles, and a little girl bounces into the shop, followed by her parents.

"Story lady," the little one shouts, throwing her plump arms around Clara's knees.

Clara beams. "Hi, sweetie. You go pick a book. I'll be right there."

She reaches over the counter and lowers her voice. "This opens the red room, where we keep our erotica collection. Adults only, of course. Ask me before letting customers in there." She hands me an old-fashioned key on a silk cord, then points to the rolling rack of books. "These all need to be shelved. Photography books on the left, other art books on the right, erotic stories on the back wall."

The red door swings open into darkness. I grasp the fat silk tassel dangling at chest level and tug, flooding the little room with pink light.

"Oh. My. Goodness," I gasp and gawk at the gorgeous, snug jewel-box of a room lined floor to ceiling with books! A faded, rosy-hued Persian carpet covers the floor. In the center sits an antique red velvet settee whose S-curved seatback would place a couple shoulder to shoulder facing opposite directions. I imagine lounging there, leaning over the divide to gaze at a book in a handsome man's lap. Perhaps a tall man with a shaved head...

Trailing my fingers over the book spines, I circle the room, stopping at the wooden stepladder. Even a tall stork like me would need it to reach those highest shelves. Talk about a fairy-tale library! I half-expect a secret door to creak open, revealing some brocade-clad hero from a romance novel, with mischief in his eye and a most ungentlemanlike bulge in his tight buff breaches.

With a wistful sigh, I shake off my silly fantasy and heft the first volume—pseudo-Victorian photos, dreamy, soft-focus nudes lounging in fields of flowers. I wonder if Alton Baker Park holds a secluded glen like this where a couple might...

Leaning on the bookshelf, I slide into a hazy daydream. Sprawled in the tall grass among gently nodding wildflowers, I reach for the man reclining beside me. His deep blue eyes sparkle in the sunlight. His lips murmur my name, brush my throat...

Voices outside snap me back to reality. Damn, maybe a three-month dating hiatus is too ambitious. I've got sex on the brain, which is not the best state for making decisions. And God knows, I'm facing a big one: Maxie's proposition.

I shelve the volume and pick up the next: *Erotic Art of Ancient Greece*, filled with page after page of graceful figures captured in moments of passion. Men with men, with women, with youths, with dildos, with—Good Lord, is that a goat?

I lift the next book, *Mihály Zichy: Nineteenth Century Erotic Art*. In all my art history classes, I've never seen illustrations like these Baroque courtiers captured in erotic embraces, their clothing half-torn away in sensual abandon. I turn the page. A bewigged gentleman pins his lover with his passionate gaze while he clutches her bare flanks and drives himself deeper into her flesh.

Lucky girl. Is it getting warm in here?

By the time I shelve the last book, my pulse is fluttering, my face flushed, my panties damp. Biting my lip, I open the red door and push the squeaky cart back toward the counter, forcing a smile I hope looks unflustered.

The bell over the doorway tinkles. "Unka Dah-un," a child squeals.

Shit! It can't be. I duck behind a shelf and peer through a gap above the cookbooks. There he is, the man of my spicy dreams, his wide grin aimed at the children's section.

The little girl who called Clara 'Story Lady' skips to him and lifts her arms. "Up."

In one graceful movement, he scoops her onto his shoulders. She pats his shiny bald head and giggles.

Unlike my wannabe artistic self, Dalton is Mr. Suburbia in his boring polo shirt and nondescript khaki pants. He looks so happy, though.

"Hey, Dalton." Clara stands on tiptoe to peck his cheek.

A twinge of jealousy nibbles my gut as I watch their easy affection. They're friends, I remind myself. If they weren't, I wouldn't have this job.

I paste on a nonchalant expression and step out of my hiding place. "All done, Clara. Hi, Dalton."

"Blue hair." The little girl opens and closes her hands like starfish.

Dalton flashes a wide grin. "Laurel, meet Aliyah."

"Your niece?" I flip my ponytail forward for the little one to explore.

"My friends' kid. They're in the back somewhere."

"Baby, quit pestering Dalton." A pretty, petite woman sets a book on the counter, then lifts the little one out of Dalton's arms. "Go find Daddy."

Aliyah trots toward the back of the shop.

"Destiny Sanders, meet Laurel—sorry, I don't know your last name."

"It's Jepsen. Hi."

"I got him." Aliyah returns, tugging a tall, dark-skinned man toward the counter.

"Wow." My fingers fly to my mouth.

Destiny grins. "I know, right? They could be brothers."

"What are you talking about? We are brothers." The guy slings his arm around Dalton's shoulders. Except for the difference in skin tone, the resemblance is remarkable: same impressive height, same slim, athletic build and shiny shaved head. Same wide, welcoming smile. He extends his hand. "This her, D?"

Dalton rolls his eyes and clears his throat loudly.

His friend grins. "I'm Marcus. Pleased to meet you, Laurel." He deposits a stack of sci-fi paperbacks on the counter. "Gotta read some fun stuff while I still have time."

I ring up the first book. "You're a teacher, like Dalton?"

"History and English. Right next door to this guy."

Dalton snorts. "Yeah, if something's missing from my desk, I know where to look."

"Dude, you gotta find better hiding spots for your snacks. I'm just sayin'."

From behind the screen, Clara calls out, "Ten percent educator discount."

"Crap. How do I do that?" I mutter.

Dalton steps around the counter, drops his heavy, distracting hand onto my shoulder, and punches buttons on the cash register. "There you go." He flashes a crooked grin. "I helped Clara with the shop once or twice."

"He helped a lot." She steps from behind the screen. "Hi, Marcus. Ready for school to start?"

He clutches his stomach and grimaces. "Don't remind me."

The doorway bell tinkles again, and in walks the most beautiful man I have ever seen in the flesh. Tall, tan, and elegant, with silver-frosted temples and a tumble of dark curls spilling over his brow, he strides to Clara's side, enfolds her in his muscular arms, and buries his chiseled face in the crook of her neck. They whisper sweet nothings while Dalton's friends take their leave. Then the Greek god looks up, and his smile flattens. "Dalton."

"Nick."

Both men straighten to their full height.

A tingle of warning prickles my nape. What's up with the macho display?

Clara clears her throat. "Nick, this is my new assistant, Laurel."

He turns his high-beam smile on me. "Pleased to meet you, Laurel."

"Nice to meet you, um, Nick." I back away on shaky legs. "I'll just, um, do some books."

I leave the lovers to their whispers and flee to the children's section, which Aliyah has pretty much decimated.

Dalton follows and squats beside me. "Here, let me. Aliyah's kind of a hurricane."

"That she is. Cute, though." His nearness makes concentration difficult, but I have to know before things got weird. Glancing at the counter, where Nick and Clara nuzzle like horny high-schoolers, I lower my voice. "Dalton, honesty is important to me."

He nods, his deep blue eyes sharply focused on mine.

"I need you to be straight with me. Were you and Clara together before Nick?"

He makes a choking sound and topples backward onto his ass. His knee collides with the bookcase, tumbling picture books to the floor.

"Everything okay over there?" Clara calls.

"We're fine. Just—re-shelving books." I raise my eyebrows and wait.

Dalton's face flushes bright red and his gaze skitters away. Finally, he meets my probing stare with a glance of—apology? embarrassment? Either way, it's not a good sign.

"Yeah, we dated for a little while. Nothing came of it. She's with Nick now."

"I see." That makes him my boss's ex. Yikes!

He clears his throat. "I was thinking, maybe after your shift, we could—"

"I'm busy with Maxie tonight." My tone rings sharper than I intended. He doesn't deserve that after his kindness to me and Maxie. I lay my hand on his arm. Blond hairs tickle my fingers. "But I'll see you tomorrow morning, right? At the running club?"

"Right. That'll be—okay then." He stands, hesitating. "See you, Laurel."

I watch him stroll out the door, his long limbs swinging in graceful arcs. His parting glance through the plate-glass window beams worry and hope and longing. I feel an answering tug in my core.

Damn. What have I got myself into?

Chapter Eight

♥

Dalton

Ten minutes to go time. Runners pack Coffee Dreams, but there's no sign of Laurel. I take my place in line at the counter. I'd hoped to get a few minutes with her before we start, but after her pointed questions in Clara's shop, she might not show.

"Hey there, handsome. Coffee before the run?" Arnie, the barista, flutters his lashes.

Helping Clara connect Book Nirvana to Arnie's café this summer, I came to realize his flirtation is toothless, but it still makes me squirm. "Just a single espresso, thanks."

I don't actually need any caffeine this morning. Anticipation over seeing Laurel again has me jittery enough. After replaying our last exchange over and over all night, I'm a freakin' mess. Should I have lied about my brief not-quite-a-relationship with Clara? No, that's no way to treat a friend, and I'm hoping for much more than friendship with Laurel. I can't put my finger on why I'm so drawn to her, beyond her obvious gorgeousness, compassion, humor, unpretentiousness...

Yeah, I've got it bad.

I'm sure there was a spark between us, but her demeanor switched from warm to icy the minute she found out about my history with Clara. To be fair, it's a sticky situation, and—

"Clara-bell," Arnie calls from behind the counter. Clara steps up beside me, blows Arnie a kiss, then pecks my cheek.

"How's it going with the wedding plans?" I ask her.

She peels an elastic band off her wrist and gathers her hair into a ponytail. "Crazy. Flowers, decoration, food, and a gazillion Greek relatives. You're still coming, right?"

"Wouldn't miss it. Maybe once you guys tie the knot, Nick will stop looking at me like I stepped in dog shit."

She chuckles. "Oh, he's not that bad, is he?"

I answer with a raised eyebrow. Clara's completely committed to her fiancé, and I'm at peace with her choice. She knows it, I know it, but it seems I still make the GQ-slick professor nervous.

"Okay, so he's still a little jealous," Clara admits. "Anyway, I told him you came to the shop yesterday to see Laurel."

I glance down at my coffee cup. "Actually..."

Clara hoots. "I knew it. You like her."

My cheeks heat. "I do. She's—"

"Here." She pokes my arm and inclines her head toward the door, where Laurel stands frozen, her wide-eyed gaze darting from me to Clara.

Clara pokes me again. "Go on, talk to her."

I take a deep breath before striding to the door. Hug? Cheek kiss? Something in her stiff posture warns me to tread lightly, so I extend my hand.

She scowls at it as if I'm offering her a dead fish.

Stinging with disappointment, I withdraw my hand and run it over my scalp. "Um, hi there. Come in. I'll introduce you around."

But she remains rooted where she stands. "Dalton, I've got a weird feeling about you and Clara. Have I landed in the middle of some unfinished business? Because I really need this job, and if you two—"

Caution be damned. I seize her hands. "Laurel, there is nothing but friendship between Clara and me." I trace a cross over my heart.

It feels good to say that. Though we only shared a handful of dates, I built a cloud castle of hope around Clara, the first woman to arouse even a tickle of interest since my split with Tiffany. But it didn't take long to see how ill-suited we were. True, she's a beauty and a sweet, kind person, but the attraction I felt for her is just a weak fizzle compared to the spine-tingling jolt I feel with Laurel.

Gaze averted, Laurel purses her lips.

I raise both hands in a gesture of surrender. "You don't believe me? Ask her."

Without another word, she strides past me, right toward Clara.

Laurel

Dalton's height and neon-orange T-shirt stand out among the runners streaming down the riverside path. He keeps glancing backward at me. If he's not careful, he'll run into a tree.

At this pace, I could easily catch up with him. Instead, I'm hanging back with the newbies and the kids—and with Clara. Eventually, he lengthens his stride and disappears around a curve.

"Thought you'd be up front with Dalton," Clara huffs, her long auburn ponytail flopping with each step.

"Yeah, about that." There really was no graceful way to ask, so I jump in with both size eleven feet. "You and Dalton. You have history, right?"

"Me and Dalton?" Her cheeks, already flushed from exercise, glow like neon strawberries.

"There's an energy between you two. I mean—" *Gah, this is so awkward!* "Look, I thought he was flirting with me. But then I saw you together, and it seems like—"

"Damn it, side stitch." Grimacing, Clara chugs to a stop.

Years of track and field training kick in. "Easy now, breathe from your belly. Stretch away from the cramp." I lift her arm over her head. "Better?"

She nods. "You don't beat around the bush, do you, Laurel?"

"I mean, what's the point?"

Clara laughs and links her arm through mine. "Okay. Here's how it happened."

While we walk off her cramp, Clara tells me how, a year after her husband's death, Nick strolled into her shop. On the same day, her assistant Harry set her up with his younger cousin, Dalton. Each guy knew about the other, and both stuck around. She fell hard for Nick, who quit his teaching job in Berkeley to be near her. Finally, she had to tell Dalton that, though she was very fond of him, they simply didn't have the chemistry she felt with Nick. "So now, we're friends. That's all. Just friends."

"But yesterday, in the shop, your fiancé glared daggers at Dalton."

"Yeah, well—he'll get over it in time. Dalton's a regular customer, and with his connection to Harry, he's almost a family member." She squeezes my arm. "And he's awfully cute. Don't you think so?"

I sigh. "I do."

"He likes you. I can tell." Clara gazes out at the green, glassy river. "Listen, Dalton and I didn't get all the way to falling in love, but he's a special guy. He's sweet, and smart, and funny, and loyal, and good with tools, and—" She grins slyly. "—can I share a secret?"

I wait, my eyebrows raised.

Clara's voice lowers to a whisper. "He's very well-endowed. Like, enormous." She elbows my ribs. "Please don't tell him I said so."

An awkward giggle escapes my lips. "But you said you didn't—"

"I said we didn't fall in love. But we did make out a little."

My mouth falls open, but my words stick in my throat.

"Anyway," Clara continues as if she hadn't just dropped a bomb, "I need help in the bookstore, and you need a job, right?"

"Yeah..."

"And Dalton needs a good woman in his life." She shrugs. "Maybe that'll be you, maybe not. But why let someone else's past get in the way of your future?"

Damn, I like this woman!

She breaks into a trot again, and I join her, running side by side in companionable silence until we reach the coffee shop.

"Crap." Clara checks her watch. "We open in fifteen minutes. No shower for me, I guess."

I hold out my palm. "Give me the key. I'll open for you."

She glances at Dalton, seated at the counter with Marcus, then tugs me aside. "So, we're okay?"

"Absolutely." I'm still chewing on what she's told me, but at least I can be sure my interest in Dalton won't endanger my job.

"I'm glad." Clara surprises me with a quick, tight hug. She whispers, "Think about it. He's a good guy, Laurel." She hands over her shop keys, waves to Dalton, and scoots out the door.

Dalton's twilight-blue gaze meets mine, and he flashes a crooked, questioning smile. His hopeful expression reminds me of a sweet, gawky puppy, but man, his strong, lean body is very grown up indeed! My gaze flicks down to his crotch.

Don't be a creep, Jepsen.

I jingle the keys and tilt my chin toward the bookshop door.

He follows and waits while I flip on the lights. "So, did Clara convince you?"

Taming my grin proves difficult. "We had a good talk."

He steps close enough to feel the heat rolling off his body. A flush paints his cheekbones and his long, straight nose. Exercise, sunburn, or something more interesting? The air between us vibrates with tingly energy.

I focus on the floor because looking into his face seems too dangerous.

He inches still closer, so we're standing toe to toe, but he doesn't touch me. "We're good now?"

My gaze skims his long, muscular calves, covered with blond fuzz, to his powerful thighs and the impressive bulge between them, then up his slim torso, his muscled chest, his broad shoulders, until I reach his face. His lids lower. His lips part. As if pulled in by his gravity, my fingertips skate up his arm.

Stop! I drop my hand. "We're good. I'm sorry, Dalton. I saw something between you and Clara, and I jumped to the wrong conclusion."

His smile blossoms slowly. "I'm glad that's all cleared up."

My thoughts are not clear at all, but this is a start, anyway. Another thought pops into my muddled head: I could just kiss him, right here, right now. Get it over with and see what happens next.

Once that seed is planted, it's as if a giant electromagnet switches on, tugging us together. Its power hums in my bones. Invisible sparks crackle between us.

A sharp rap on the front window breaks the current and sends me stumbling backward. It's Nick, Clara's fiancé, scowling through the glass. He points to his watch, then to the door.

Dalton huffs out a laugh. "I'll let his majesty in."

Nick steps inside and rumples his beautiful brow. "Where's Clara?"

"The run took longer than we expected," I tell him. "She went home to wash up."

"Oh. Guess I passed her on the road." He glances from Dalton to me. "You two know each other?"

I slide my arm through Dalton's. "We're—friends." That should satisfy him and get Clara off the hook.

Playing his part, Dalton brushes a tendril of damp hair from my cheek. "Good friends."

Grinning widely, Nick raises both hands and backs toward the door. "Well, I'll leave you to it. Please tell Clara I stopped by."

As soon as he passes out of view, I blow out a breath and release Dalton, but he's not letting me get away so easily. He clasps my upper arms. "Laurel, what is going on?"

"Just...helping Clara. She said Nick's still a little jealous, so..."

His pale brows scrunch. "So, this is just an act? You didn't feel what I felt just now?

Hell yeah, I did, but I shrug, hoping he doesn't see how shaken I am.

"Hmm. Guess it was just me." Dalton starts for the door, then turns back. The corners of his mouth twitch upward. "Too bad. Because if it was something, we could discuss it over dinner tonight."

I chew my lip. It's only dinner, for Chrissakes. No big deal. No pressure. But my crackling nerves disagree. If merely standing near Dalton revs my pulse like this, what will a kiss do to my resolve, not to mention my plan? What happens when he puts those big, long-fingered hands on my body? When those twilight-blue eyes darken with passion?

Shut up, I snap at my annoying inner worrywart. *Why shouldn't I have some fun with a nice guy?*

An almost-wicked smile stretches my lips. "Pick me up at seven."

Chapter Nine

❤

Laurel

I'm wrapping up Maxie's collection of wooden masks from around the world when a clump, step, clump, step pulls my attention from my nest of packing paper.

Maxie pokes me with her cane and waves her Wonder Woman watch under my nose. "Shouldn't you be getting ready for your date?"

"Shoot. He'll be here in twenty minutes." I jump up from the floor. After this morning's run, a long day on my feet at the bookshop, and another hour of schlepping moving boxes for Maxie, I should be too tired for a date. But the prospect of one-on-one time with Dalton winds me up like a triple espresso. All day, I've been daydreaming about what would've happened if Nick hadn't knocked on the window when he did, interrupting our almost-kiss.

After a quick shower, I twiddle with my hair. Up or down? Out of hairspray. Okay, down.

I hum as I rifle through the guestroom closet. This is my first real date in—how long? Over a month, at least. After all those applause-hungry hipster guys in Portland, Dalton is refreshingly normal. But do we have enough in common to get through a whole evening together?

At the mirror, I smooth my silvery tunic over my hips. Nice. Not too plain, not too fussy. With black leggings and strappy silver sandals, I'll pass muster wherever he takes me. Except...I dig into my duffle bag, find my tangled knot of necklaces, and wrestle some blue beads free. Noting how well they match the color of Dalton's eyes, I loop them over my head.

The doorbell sends my pulse revving. Deep breath. Big smile. Here goes.

When I open the door, Dalton's crooked grin washes my whole body in warmth. He's so cute in his going-out clothes—a madras shirt with sleeves rolled to his elbows, crisp dark jeans, and suede loafers.

He holds out a bouquet of sunflowers. "For you and Aunt Maxie."

"How pretty. Thank you. Come in." I gesture toward the mess in the living room. "Pardon the boxes. Have a seat—there's a couch back there somewhere. I'll get a vase."

I scoot into the kitchen, hiding my grin behind the flowers. When I shut off the tap, I hear her voice from the living room. I set the flowers on the dining table and hurry to Dalton's side in case Maxie's in the mood for another round of batting practice.

Lucid and jolly this time, my great-aunt cocks her hip like a flirty girl of sixteen. "So, where you takin' my grandniece tonight?"

"The Thai Pearl on Blair Boulevard, if that's okay with her."

"I love Thai food." I take his arm and tug him toward the door. "I have my phone, Maxie. Call me if you need anything, okay?"

She shuffles after us. "What's your rush? Stay and have a drink first. Elmer brought me some homemade blackberry wine." She totters to the kitchen without waiting for a reply.

I shrug my apology. "Just a few minutes? She loves meeting interesting people."

"No problem. She's quite interesting herself." His shy grin is adorable. "So's her grandniece."

Once again, my fingers itch to touch him. I indulge by brushing a bit of imaginary lint from his collar. He smells fresh, piney, like the crushed-bark trail in the park.

A crash from the kitchen jerks both our heads up.

"Oh. Oh my." Maxie's voice shakes.

Dalton dashes toward the sound with me hot on his heels.

Maxie's standing in a Rorschach blot of dark-red wine and shattered glass. Blood drips from her palm.

"Don't move," Dalton orders. Glass shards crunch as he crosses the floor, scoops Maxie up, and sets her on the counter. "Let's wash this cut."

I start toward them, but Dalton waves me away. "Sandals."

"Right. I'll get some shoes."

"For her too." Maxie's veiny feet dangle in mid-air, clad in jeweled flip-flops.

When I return, Dalton is blotting Maxie's hand with paper towels. "There now," he says in a soothing voice, "it's not so bad."

"Well, shit," she grumbles. "Good thing I'm right-handed."

"Where's the broom, Maxie?" I ask.

"What's that, dear?" Her brow rumples.

"Broom? To clean up the glass?"

Maxie opens her mouth, then closes it, her gaze unfocused.

A chill slithers down my spine, but I keep my tone light and reassuring. "Never mind. I'll find it."

Dalton carries Maxie to the bathroom while I clean up the mess, gripping the broom with jittery hands. It was just an accident. This could happen to anyone.

True, but I can't shake the feeling this mishap signals more to come—lots more. How carefully will I have to watch Maxie?

As I finish my final pass with the vacuum cleaner, they return, Maxie's hand wrapped in gauze. Dalton clears his throat and tilts his head toward the hallway. We leave Maxie muttering in the kitchen.

Once we're out of hearing range, he takes my hands in both of his. "I don't think she needs stitches. The cut's not deep. I sprayed it with antiseptic. But we probably shouldn't leave her tonight. I could go get takeout."

"You mean a date for three?"

"Why not? She seems to be in a good mood. We can still eat Thai food, anyway." He moves a little closer. "And I can still spend time with you."

I gape for a moment, then throw my arms around his neck. "Thank you, Dalton." I press a kiss to his cheek. His solid warmth tempts me to try kissing him for real, but Maxie...

"Right. I'll just, um, go get, um..." He backs toward the front door, his grin a little loopy. "Chicken okay?"

"Anything. Surprise me."

He drives away, and I linger on the porch, tapping my pursed lips with my forefinger and trying hard to ignore the buzzing in my chest. The way Dalton jumped in to help Maxie nudges him dangerously close to keeper territory, and I'm not shopping for a keeper, just a loaner. Maintaining the proper perspective is going to be tough when faced with his kindness, not to mention his gravelly laugh, his disarming smile, and his yummy firm ass.

I'm in trouble.

Dalton

"More prawns, Maxie?" I push the carton toward her. Mindful of Maxie's advanced years, I ordered a few not-so-spicy dishes, but she dove right into the tongue-scorching green curry.

"Mmm. My favorite." She smacks her thin lips. "Pass the sriracha."

Half-full cartons litter the table. Like her great aunt, Laurel has an impressive appetite and loves spicy food. How refreshing to share a meal with a woman who doesn't hide her enjoyment.

Okay, this isn't exactly how I'd imagined our date tonight, but I've gotta admit, I'm having fun. The loving way these two women tease each other, the artistic, half-disassembled mess that is Maxie's home, the easy way they weave me into their banter, it's...homey. Welcoming. Cozy.

"I'll take more prawns." Laurel nabs one with her chopsticks, bites into it, and moans. "Sooo good."

My imagination flies to other scenarios where she might moan like that. Hopefully, no sriracha would be involved.

"Just one more, egg roll." Maxie winks. "How nice your new boyfriend is a doctor."

"He's a teacher, Maxie."

She glances at her bandaged hand. "You sure?"

I laugh. "My paycheck proves it."

There's a smear of peanut sauce at the corner of Laurel's mouth. "Here, you've got a—" I lean in and dab the spot with my napkin. Her plump lips part, her breath whispers against my palm, and my impatient dick inches upward. Again.

All throughout dinner, I've battled for self-control. First, it was the sultry way she slurped her Pad Thai noodles, her tongue flicking out to chase the last bit. When she licked creamy curry sauce from her fingers, I nearly lost it. That pink tongue is going to be the death of me.

I distract myself by focusing on Maxie's rambling story about a young artist friend.

"She welds it all together, hoses it down, and lets it rust." Maxie burps into her napkin. "Calls it industrial decay."

Laurel's leg brushes mine under the table. She lifts her heavy swath of hair, exposing baby-fine curls at her delicate nape. "Hot. I shouldn't have put so much pepper sauce on my prawns." She fans herself and grins.

"You're my little firecracker." Maxie pats her hand.

Yes, you are. Her captivating, unconscious gestures make me dizzy with desire—subtle clues revealing a deeply sensual nature.

With a resounding belch, Maxie breaks through my fog of horny yearning. "Delish. Thank you, Dalton."

The meal seems to refocus Maxie's mind. She pushes back from the table and pats her little round belly. "You kids go out on the porch and smooch. I'll clean this up."

"Maxie," Laurel hisses and hides her blushing face behind her napkin. One gray eye peeks out to gauge my reaction.

I toss my napkin onto my plate. "You heard the lady. Let's go smooch." I lower my voice. "Or take a walk around the block? It's nice out."

"As long as we don't go too far." She carries our dishes into the kitchen and returns with a cardigan draped over her shoulders.

Damn. I was looking forward to feeling her satiny skin beneath my palm. At that thought, my dick rears up again. "Excuse me a minute. Bathroom?"

Inside, I splash cold water on my face and think about faculty meetings until my erection subsides. When I emerge, Maxie pops her head through the kitchen doorway and winks. "Knock her socks off, Ichabod."

I wink back. "I'll do my best, ma'am."

Laurel glares bug-eyed at the tiny jokester before sliding her arm through mine. As we make our way down the porch steps, a breeze lifts her hair, brushing cool silk over my cheek.

She huffs. "I'm sorry, Dalton. She's losing her filter, I guess."

"Don't worry about it. I've been called worse." I clutch her arm and glance around in mock alarm. "Haven't seen a headless horseman in the neighborhood, have you?"

"No, just zombies." She inclines her head toward a couple walking their beagle. "They won't notice us if we don't make eye contact." She squeezes my bicep. "Anyway, you're too fit to be Ichabod Crane."

"Aww, shucks, ma'am." I sling my arm over her shoulder, and she nestles into my side. *Sweet.*

Giddy, tickly hope builds in my chest. I don't know Laurel well yet, but I've seen her kindness, her genuine connection with Maxie. She's got a lot going on beneath her very pretty surface. Maybe this chance encounter on the running path could lead to something real and good and true.

She winds her arm around my waist and hooks her finger through my belt loop. Hip to hip, we amble around the block. The slow summer twilight surrounds us like heavy, deep-blue velvet curtains. Beneath the streetlamps, swallows zoom and flutter in acrobatic loops.

Laurel's lips part in an expression of wonder as she follows the birds' evening dance. "So graceful. Don't you wish you could fly like that?"

"Right now, feels like I am."

She turns those beautiful eyes on me. A smile flickers across her luscious mouth, an invitation. I close the distance and brush my lips over hers, soft and gentle. Her sigh mingles with mine. For a long, sweet moment, we stand there, barely touching, relishing that first tentative taste.

My dick springs to attention, throbbing almost painfully. Embarrassed, I angle my hips away from hers. *Don't be a creep. Take it slow.*

But Laurel has other ideas. Her breath hot on my cheek, she slides one hand to the small of my back, the other around my neck, and presses her warm, yielding body to mine.

Losing myself in her heat, I take her mouth like a starving man devouring a succulent fruit. Ripe and sweet, she opens to my probing tongue. Satin softness welcomes me. Her low moan fires primitive need deep in my gut. I grasp a handful of her hair and press my open mouth to her throat. Her pulse flutters beneath my tongue.

"Eew." A childish squeal jars me back to reality. "Kissing. Yuck." Across the street, three little girls drop their jump rope to point and giggle.

Laurel's laughter bubbles like champagne.

I rest my heated forehead against hers. Beautiful, delicious, and a good sport. I've hit the jackpot.

Smiling, she strokes my chest and cocks her head to the side, her eyes sparkling in the low light. "Well then."

I grin so wide my cheeks ache. "Yes indeed."

She glances over my shoulder. "We'd better get back. I don't want to leave Maxie too long."

Once again, I drape my arm over her shoulder, she slides her arm around my waist, and we start back the way we came. It's uncanny how perfectly our bodies fit together, so comfortable and easy. Her stride matches mine as if moved by music only the two of us can hear.

On Maxie's front porch, Laurel peers through the picture window and beckons. "Look."

Maxie sits at the dining table, a big clipboard in her lap, sketching the vase of sunflowers.

Laurel nestles against me with a sigh. "She looks happy."

"She does," I murmur into her hair. "Even if she loses her way now and then, she still has lots of good times ahead."

I mean it as a reassurance, but my comment pierces our rosy haze.

She pulls away, her smile wistful. "I wish I could ask you to stay longer, but it's Maxie's bedtime."

"Yeah, I'd better get going." I raise her fingers to my lips. "See you soon, I hope."

I want nothing more than to press her against the door and claim another deep kiss, but this situation demands patience. And she's worth the wait.

"Thanks for a lovely evening." Rising on tiptoes, she brushes a kiss across my temple. "See you soon."

Through the window, I watch her bend over Maxie, her blue-tipped hair swinging like a silk curtain. With a happy sigh, I turn and start for home.

Once inside my apartment, I lean on the door and grin, reliving the silky brush of her hair against my cheek, her throat pliant beneath my lips, her soft, willing mouth...

When she broke things off with me, Clara spoke of the chemistry she shared with Nick. At the time, I was too hurt to take in her meaning, but I get it now. I've never felt such a strong pull. Not with Clara. Not with Tiffany. Not with anyone.

Chapter Ten

♥

Laurel

"Wow, Laurel. That's just—wow." Clara clasps her hands beneath her chin and gawks at the window display I'm working on.

A happy blush heats my cheeks. For once, my kinda-sorta art project turned out as well as I'd imagined it—maybe even better. "I still need to make a banner. Which do you prefer, *Fall into a Good Book*, or *Rake in Some Good Reads*? Or something about leafing through a book?"

"Let's go with the rake. I'll bring one from home." Clara fingers a ribbon bedecked with autumn leaves. "This is really clever."

"Well, you gave me lots to work with." Clara's supply closet yielded bins of seasonal decorations and craft supplies, and I had so much fun playing with them, hanging ribbons of leaves from the ceiling and building trees from crumpled brown wrapping paper around round wooden dowels and broomsticks. Between the trees, a stepladder covered with burlap holds fall-themed books, with fall leaves peeping out between their pages.

Grinning with satisfaction, I reinforce a strip of duct tape hidden behind fake foliage. "I figure we can tweak it later for Halloween, add some spooky details and change out the books."

The doorway bell tinkles, and Nick's brisk entrance sets the leaves fluttering. His eyes widen as he admires the display. "Very nice."

Clara smooches his cheek. "Laurel did this. Isn't it marvelous?"

He pats my shoulder. "I hope Dalton appreciates your creative spirit."

"Oh, um, I guess he, you know..." I flap my hands awkwardly and gaze at his shoes. How does Clara get any work done with such a gorgeous man around?

She strokes his beautiful bicep. "Before she moved down here to help Maxie, Laurel worked in an art gallery."

Nick raises a perfect eyebrow. "Maxie? The little firecracker who visits the red room?"

Mumbling at the floor seems rude, so I take a deep breath and meet his gaze. "Maxie's my great aunt. I'm helping her move into an assisted living place."

"Ah." He takes my hands and squeezes gently. "We went through that with my dad. Really nice place, but he hated it. Broke my heart to see him there."

"Yeah. This was Maxie's idea, but it's still hard."

Nick gives me a smile of sympathy before he and Clara duck behind the screen, leaving me to clean up my decorating supplies while they whisper sweet nothings and make out. At least, that's what I imagine them doing.

Speaking of kissing...While I ring up anime books for a pair of teens, my thoughts drift back to last night. Dalton's not leading-man handsome like Clara's Nick—good thing, because I'm no classic beauty like Clara—but something about him touches me in a way mere beauty can't. Is it his deep-set blue eyes, or his shy smile? Or his thoughtfulness? I grin like a goofball, replaying the image of Dalton in Maxie's doorway, holding enough Thai takeout to feed an army, and the sure, gentle way he scooped up Maxie and cleaned her injured hand. And how our first, tentative kiss flared into something powerful, something hard to step away from.

Clara's words echo in my head: "He's very well-endowed. It's enormous."

If it weren't for Maxie's accident last night, I'd likely have found out how blessed Dalton is. Not that I usually jump a guy on the first date, but Dalton and I don't have much time to explore this magnetic attraction. I'll be gone by January, so why wait?

A heavy weight settles in my gut.

Maxie, that's why. Unless I sneak off for an after-work quickie in Dalton's apartment, I'm not likely to taste his charms anytime soon. Two weeks to go until Maxie's move-in date.

Two weeks suddenly seems like a very long time.

Back at Maxie's place, I sit on my heels and push my damp hair from my eyes. What is it about the Northwest? Seems like summer always goes out in a blaze of sticky heat. "These boxes go to the storage place, Max?"

"Yep. I'll get my purse. Car keys are in the drawer there." Maxie bustles to her room and returns dressed for an outing with a jaunty purple beret perched atop her wispy red hair.

Guilt pinches me when I realize this is probably Maxie's first trip out of the house today. While I worked at the bookshop, she filled a dozen moving cartons. Now she rummages in her metallic purple purse, pulls out a marker, and scrawls *December* on five of them.

"Are these your Christmas decorations, Max?"

"Nope." She caps the marker with a snap.

"What's with the labels?"

She waggles her painted-on eyebrows. "You'll see. In December."

After loading the cartons into Maxie's Volvo, I offer her my arm. The second porch step shifts beneath our feet and gives way with a loud crunch. Maxie squawks and clutches the banister.

I lift her onto the walkway, then clap my hand over my thundering heart. "Holy cow, you could've broken a bone. Or worse."

Maxie clutches her chunky glass beads. "Son of a motherless goat, that was a close one."

"You okay?" I run my hands over her skinny arms before stooping to check her legs for bruises or blood.

She swats me away. "I'm fine, child. Just get me in the car."

I help her into her seat, slide behind the wheel, and pull out my phone. "Hey, Dalton, I'm sorry to bother you—"

His chuckle tickles my ear and warms me further south. "You? Bother me? Not possible."

Fear still echoes in my wobbly voice. "I was helping Maxie move some boxes, and her front stairs just collapsed. If I hadn't been holding her, she could've broken her leg. Or her hip."

"Baloney," Maxie mutters, but the tremor in her hands says otherwise.

"Damn. I'm at Willamette Grove with my parents for Sunday dinner. I can stop by later." I hear the clanking of silverware in the background.

"No, no, I don't want to disturb your family evening."

"How about tomorrow morning?"

"I work at ten."

"See you at eight, then. You should put up some tape or something to warn people."

"Will do." I cradle the phone to my cheek, remembering the tickle of his whiskers on my skin. "And thank you."

His voice softens. "Glad to help."

In the background, a woman asks, "Is that the pretty blonde girl? You bring her by, Dalton. I want to ask her some questions."

I giggle. "Sounds like I've been summoned. Or do you have another blonde girlfriend?"

"No, just you. See you tomorrow."

As I tuck my phone away, my mouth falls open. I called myself his girlfriend. And he didn't disagree.

Son of a motherless goat.

Chapter Eleven

♥

Laurel

I never get up this early, at least not voluntarily. After brushing the coffee scum from my teeth, I stand hands on hips in front of my tiny closet. The weather report promises a warm, sultry day, so I pull on an airy sundress and sandals. I've always been self-conscious about my big feet, but next to Dalton's aircraft carriers, my size elevens look delicate. Back in the bathroom, I twist my heavy hair up and secure it with a jeweled clip, then survey my work. To mascara, or not to mascara?

Maxie's sharp knock on the bathroom door interrupts my primping. "Are you spending the day in there, child? I have to pee."

"Sorry, Maxie. Just getting ready for work." I open the door.

"Bull hockey. You're getting ready for your boyfriend." She squeezes my arm as she brushes past. "Good for you, kiddo. Now scoot."

I go to the kitchen to check on my cinnamon rolls. Never much of a cook, I swung by Safeway last night and bought low-stress breakfast fixings: sweet rolls in a tube, orange juice, grapes, and hazelnut coffee creamer. I sniff. Where's that yummy cinnamon scent? Damn it, Maxie must've turned the oven off, and Dalton will be here in a few minutes. I crank the dial up to 400 to hurry them along.

A knock on the door sends my pulse into overdrive. I run my hands over my bodice, tug the neckline to cover a bit more cleavage, then nudge it back up. *Deep breath, here we go.* I fling the door open.

My stomach drops. "Dad."

He stands on the porch, tapping the steel toe of his work boot. No sign of Dalton yet, thank goodness. "What are you doing here?"

"What does it look like?" With a tight-lipped smirk, he hoists his toolbox. "Unless you plan to fix those stairs yourself."

"Dave," Maxie calls and clomps double-time to the front door. She extends her arms and plants a smooch on his cheek, clobbering him with her cane. Her embrace leaves a sprinkling of glitter on his jacket, right above *Jepsen Heating and Cooling.*

I tug Maxie aside and stoop to whisper, "I told you Dalton was coming to fix the stairs. He'll be here any minute."

"Did you?" She blinks up at me. "Oh dear, did I forget?"

Maxie had a lot of talents, but acting isn't one of them. What's she up to? No time to find out, because Dalton's rattletrap station wagon pulls into the driveway behind Dad's work van. He unfolds his long frame and waves, tilting his chin toward Dad, a quizzical look on his face.

Shitshitshit. "Excuse me, Dad." I slide past him, hop over the broken stair, and hurry to intercept Dalton.

"Wow. You look—wow." He leans in, aiming for my cheek, but my dad's prickly stare triggers an old, rebellious reflex. I slide my arms around Dalton's neck and kiss him full on the mouth.

"Mmmm. My favorite breakfast." He grips my waist, pulls me closer, and nuzzles my neck. "Who's the guy giving me the stink eye?"

Reluctantly, I step back from his embrace. "My dad. I'm sorry, Dalton. Maxie must've called him."

He squares his shoulders. "Introduce me?"

"It's just..."

He waits, one eyebrow raised.

Ugh. This makes me feel so juvenile. "Dad and I don't get along. Just so you know."

"Hey, I'm a teacher. I'm used to dealing with difficult parents. It's kind of my specialty." He takes my hand and tows me toward the porch, gracefully stepping over the ragged hole in the middle stair.

Dad opens his mouth to comment, but Dalton beats him to it with a wide, disarming smile and an extended hand. "Pleased to meet you, Mr. Jepsen. I'm Dalton Garvey."

Dad glares from me to Maxie, then fixes Dalton with a squinty stare. "My daughter's been down here, what, four days? Fast worker, aren't you?"

"Five days." I fight to keep my voice even, my lips un-snarled.

"Oh, we're just getting acquainted." Dalton rubs his palms together. "So, what are we going to do about this staircase? I brought some lumber and my dad's circular saw."

"Your father's handy?" He gives Dalton an appraising, up and down scan.

"Contractor, carpenter. There isn't much he can't fix."

Judging by Dad's raised eyebrows, Dalton has scored some major points.

I move toward the kitchen. "I'll go check on breakfast."

The cinnamon rolls are only slightly burnt, and the gooey icing covers the damage nicely. I wipe glitter off the dining room table, cover the paint smears with mismatched placemats, and set out plates. Family breakfast it is. Not what I had in mind, not by a long shot, but might as well make the best of it.

Maxie sets a ceramic bowl of grapes on the table, rubs her hands together, and beams. "Now, isn't this nice?"

"Not really, Max." I cross my arms. "Why did you call Dad? And don't give me that 'I forgot' BS."

Maxie lowers herself into a chair. "I did forget, kiddo, and let me tell you, it's a crappy feeling when you realize you've lost a chunk of time." She passes her gnarled hand over her wispy hair. "But here's the thing. When I remembered your young man was coming too, I thought, why not let Dave meet your new admirer? I don't know why your dad has such a hard time seeing your sparkle, but that tall fella, he definitely sees it. I do too. Today, your dad's outnumbered." She pats my hand. "Maybe it'll help."

I blink away sudden tears. "Maxie, that's—thank you. Your love means a lot to me. I'm sorry I fussed at you."

"I love you too, kiddo. If I'd had a daughter, she'd be like you, I think." She chuckles. "You know what they say about good traits skipping a generation. Your mama has a serious shortage of spunk. But you've got enough chutzpah to push through Dave's bullshit." She rubs her hands together. "Now let's eat."

Breakfast is a reasonable success. When Dad grumbles, "Men need protein," Dalton and Maxie adjourn to the kitchen to scramble some eggs, leaving me alone with him.

He nibbles a cinnamon roll, curls his lip, and sets it down. "So, a teacher, eh?"

"Yes. History."

He snorts. "Not your type."

"I don't have a type, Dad."

"Sure you do." He wiggles his fingers in the air. "Artsy-fartsy. Fancy clothes. Big words. Phonies. The only one worth a hill of beans was that Carlo fella."

Leave it to Dad to rip open that scab. I close my eyes, silently count to ten, then add another five for good measure.

"Here we go," Maxie warbles as Dalton carries in a steaming dish of scrambled eggs. "Your boyfriend found some green onions in the fridge. Doesn't this look pretty?"

It did look pretty, the creamy yellow eggs flecked with rings of green. Maxie conveniently forgot her son-in-law hates onions. *Isn't that too damn bad, Dad?*

"Lovely." I help myself to a big scoop. "Thanks, Dalton."

"A man who cooks. Hmm." Dad chomps his cinnamon roll.

"Oh, scrambled eggs are about the extent of it. And spaghetti, with sauce from a jar."

I shoot him a grin. "I love spaghetti."

After breakfast, I help Maxie with the clean- up while the men resume their construction project. I find them tête-à-tête over a wicked-looking power saw.

"I'd better get to the bookstore." I'd hoped for a private moment with Dalton, hard to come by with my dad watching our every move.

"'Scuse me, Dave." He follows me to my car, a playful grin tugging at the corners of his wide mouth. He knows exactly what he's doing, handling Dad like a salesman gentles a disgruntled customer.

"He hasn't scared you away yet?"

"Nope. Trust me, I've dealt with much worse. He's just protective of his daughter." He takes my hand. "Long shift today?"

"Until three."

"Run afterward?"

"Yes, please." I stroke the inside of his wrist with my thumb. His pulse leaps beneath the smooth skin. God, I want to touch him, to explore his lanky limbs, his broad chest. Is it covered with blond hair, like his arms and legs? Is his delectable behind smooth or furry? And what about the huge cock Clara promised me?

I clear my throat. "Maybe I can thank you properly afterward."

His grin widens. "No thanks needed, but I look forward to finding out what you mean by properly."

I drive off, leaving him to fend off Dad's barbed comments. He can handle it. If Dalton is even half as attracted to me as I am to him, he'll stick around. This chemistry is powerful stuff.

When I return to Maxie's house, Dad's still stooped over the staircase, a paintbrush in his hand. Without turning, he barks, "Use the back stairs."

"And good afternoon to you."

He harrumphs and continues painting. "Looks good. Did you replace all three stairs?"

Another snort. "No point waiting for the next one to go. Replaced the railing here and around back. Porch needs fixing too, but that's a bigger job for another day. Gotta get back to work."

"I'll help you load all this into the truck."

He stands, grimacing as he massages his lower back. "Better change out of your airy-fairy outfit first."

Anger heats my cheeks and narrows my eyes. "I'm dressed for work in a bookstore, Dad. A nice, practical job, just like you wanted. Don't give me grief about my clothes."

He blinks in surprise. I seldom take such a direct approach with him, but it's about damned time I did. Maybe this change of scene is doing me good.

"Well, go on," he grumbles.

I return a moment later, wearing running clothes and carrying two glasses of iced tea.

Dad's eyes bug out. "Good Lord, Laurel. You always work half-naked?"

Can't let anything pass without comment, can you, Dad? "I'm not half-naked. It's a hot day, and I'm going for a run with Dalton."

"Oh." He gulps his tea and wipes his sopping brow. "Nice kid, Dalton. Respectful."

"Hardly a kid. He's thirty-nine."

Up fly Dad's wiry gray eyebrows. "Pretty old for you, don'tcha think?"

"Nope." I sip my tea and refuse to take the bait. "The brushes go in this box?"

He grunts and stoops to string yellow plastic Caution tape across the freshly painted staircase. "'Bout time you found a steady fella to date."

I bite my lip hard.

"You're not getting any younger, you know. Wait too long to get married, and you might end up an old maid, like Maxie."

That. Is. It. Rage narrows my eyes to slits and tightens my jaws. "Of all the people I'd take marriage advice from," I hiss, "you come in dead last."

He stumbles back and raises both hands. "Now wait a minute—"

"After what you put Mom through, how dare you talk to me about marriage?"

"I just meant—"

I stab my finger into his chest. "I don't give two cold dog turds what you meant. Pack up your stuff and get home to Mom. God knows why she stuck with you. I sure don't understand it."

Silence stretches between us. Fists clenched, he glares at the ground. Finally, in a raspy voice, he mutters, "Your mother forgave me long ago. Why can't you?"

I fight rising nausea. "You betrayed her, Dad. You betrayed *us*."

He clasps my shoulders, his callused hand rough on my skin. It's been so long, I've forgotten what his touch feels like.

Too wobbly to resist, I let him walk me to the wooden bench beneath Maxie's sycamore tree and pull me down beside him.

He rests his elbows on his knees and stares at the patchy lawn. Finally, he reaches down between his worn work boots and plucks a tiny daisy. He twirls it in his fingers for a moment, then tucks it behind my ear.

I blink hard against traitorous tears.

When I was little, the two of us would lie on the lawn and tell stories. I'd bedeck his bristly crewcut with daisy chains. This fleeting glimpse of that long-ago dad, the man who could fix anything from skinned knees to broken bicycles, the man I idolized, the greatest of all super-heroes—it pierces my heart.

In a voice as scratchy as his stubble-dusted jaw, he croaks, "I loved Mary. And she loved me. But I gave her up to hold on to your mom and you girls." He swipes his eyes with the back of his paint-spotted hand. "She was a good woman."

"Good women don't have affairs with married men."

"Now wait a minute." He stiffens. "Mary and I, we never..."

"It doesn't matter, Dad. You gave her your heart, and you broke Mom's. And mine." My voice trembles. "I found her, Dad. I was only twelve, and I found my mother half-dead beside an empty bottle of pills."

The year that followed is sharply etched in my memory. A hired nanny kept Willow and me fed and clothed but offered no comfort. Dad was distracted, distant, often gone. His business suffered as news spread of his affair and his wife's suicide attempt. Willow spent every afternoon with her best friend next door, giggling over Barbies. They never invited me. During that dark time, the art supplies Maxie brought on her monthly visits provided the only color in my life.

When Mom finally returned from the psychiatric hospital, she glided ghost-like through the house, strung out on anti-depressants, her eyes vacant. For the rest of my years in Cotter's Grove, the Jepsen family kept the local therapy clinic busy: group sessions where we all sat, stiff and awkward, and private sessions to help me sleep again and forget the terror of finding my mother sprawled and pale and still.

Side by side, Dad and I stare into the distance, silent but for our sniffles. Finally, he speaks, his voice thick with emotion. "She's happy now."

"Mary?"

"Your mom. She had every right to leave me, but she stayed. Things are better between us. A lot better. We talk. We go dancing. She's performing again, too." Pride glows in his smile. "I forgot how good she is. And she wants to buy an RV, take a cross-country trip."

"Will you go?"

"Yeah." He pushes himself up. "I don't know why she forgave me, but I'm gonna do my best to make her glad she did." He turns toward his truck. "Anyway, paint'll need eight hours to dry. Try to keep Maxie off the steps."

Our long-delayed heart to heart is done. Just as well. I wasn't prepared for this emotional bomb, and I need time to process. So does he, evidently. He climbs into his van without saying goodbye.

"Dad, wait," I yell, rushing to the van. Through the open window, I lay my hand over his, white-knuckled on the wheel. In time, I'll figure out what to say, what to feel. For now, a truce. "Thanks for helping Maxie."

He grips my hand. "Of course, Laur-Bear. She's family. And family's the most important thing."

I stare at his white panel van until it disappears. Finally, my phone pings, signaling a text.

Still up for a run?

Dad's burst of honesty left me wrung out and limp, but a hard run will clear my head and calm my buzzing gut. I send a thumbs-up emoji and

See you in 20 min.

I go back inside to check on Maxie, napping peacefully. I splash cold water on my face, then tape a note inside the front door: *Wet paint. Use the back stairs. Gone for a run. Back in two hours. Call if you need me.* Before leaving, I add one more line. *Love you, Maxie.*

Chapter Twelve

♥

Dalton

While waiting for Laurel, I prop my foot on a graffiti-covered bench and lean into a hamstring stretch. My pulse kicks up a notch when she lopes into view, but something's off. Her face is tense and stormy, brows contracted, lips pressed together. She trots to a stop and squats to adjust her shoe. No greeting, nothing.

"You okay, Laurel?"

She blows out a long breath. "I've been better. Glad to see you, though." Compared to our steamy kiss this morning, her peck on my cheek is cool and far too brief. "Thanks for being patient. I had to talk to my dad first."

She doesn't elaborate, but her downcast gaze tells me enough. A few hours working beside Dave Jepson revealed the man's character: taciturn, critical, bossy. Hard to imagine a free spirit like Laurel flourishing under his roof.

"So, the park again?" I ask.

"Yeah. Let's do Pre's Trail." A wry grin twitches her lips. "It's been a hard day. I could use something soft."

I keep my pace slow at first, hoping for more conversation, but once we reach the bark-chip path, she shoots ahead.

Okay, I get it. Many a time, during my last few years with Tiffany, I'd run until my feet bled, pounding my frustration into the pavement.

I lengthen my stride to match hers, and we run in silence for a good ten minutes. Laurel's blue-tipped ponytail bobs and sways while her hips jiggle deliciously beneath her shorts.

Finally, I clear my throat. "You're quiet today."

She shoots me a sheepish glance over her shoulder. "Yeah. Sorry."

"I enjoyed meeting your dad."

"Liar." She slows her pace and gives me a crooked smile. "I'm being a jerk, aren't I?"

"No, just mysterious."

She touches my arm—progress, at least. "Thanks for helping with Maxie's stairs. You must have more interesting things to do with your summer vacation."

"Not really."

Her eyebrows rise.

"I mean, yeah, I'd rather travel, do some rafting maybe. Last year, a bunch of us went down to Baja the last week of summer break."

"Not this year?"

"My mom..." I shrug because what's the point of getting upset over things I can't change? "I'm needed here." I run my palm down her slender arm and take her hand. "Though I'd love to show you my favorite camping spot near Cannon Beach."

She grunts and closes her eyes. "Dalton, I really like you, but I've gotta be honest."

My gut frosts over. Damn, I should be used to this by now. Women as lovely as Laurel don't fall for gawky guys like me.

"Hey, don't look at me like that." Her sweaty brow rumples. "It's just, I'm not planning to stay in Eugene."

"So you said."

Still clasping my hand, she starts to walk. "Do you mind? I think better when I'm moving."

"Okay..." If she keeps holding my hand like this, I'll follow her all over town just to enjoy her delicious warmth.

She sucks in a breath. "My friend Davonte has lots of artsy friends in San Francisco. I hope he can help me find a job in a gallery." She squeezes my hand. "That's my dream—and to tell you the truth, it's the only thing that's kept me from giving up hope I'll ever be more than mediocre." She stops and tugs hard on my arm, spinning me to face her and piercing me with a look so full of yearning I can feel the burn behind my own eyes.

"I love art, Dalton, and I suck at it. Can you imagine what that feels like? But running a gallery—*that* I can do. I know it deep in here." She thumps her breastbone with her free hand. "And I can't let anything sideline me."

It kills me that someone so bright and compassionate and freakin' extraordinary is so filled with self-doubt. But having met her father. I'm not surprised. Over and over again, I've seen kids internalize the kind of shit he shovels. Makes me want to smack him upside his thick skull.

I grip her upper arms. "Laurel, you are the least mediocre person I know. And we have art galleries in Eugene."

"Yeah, but not as many as San Francisco."

"All the more reason for you to stay. Help build up the arts scene here." An idea zings into focus, an opening, maybe. "Our running club sponsors a charity race every September. This year, it's Run for the Arts. Proceeds go to an art program for disadvantaged kids. You could—"

She cuts me off with a huff. "Dalton, I admire people who dedicate their lives to helping kids. Really, I do. But that's not—Arrgh." She presses her fists to her eyes and growls like a feral cat. It's pretty damn hot.

I pull her to the side of the trail, out of the path of a noisy pack of teens jogging toward us.

"Hey, Coach." My cross-country team captain waves. "Enjoying your summer break?" She glances at Laurel and flashes a knowing grin.

"What's left of it. See you on Sunday? It's your chance to outrun me."

She grins and tosses her long braids. "Challenge accepted. See you there." The girls trot off, their giggles like tinkling bells.

Laurel leans on the trunk of a tall pine. "You really like teaching, huh?"

"I do. It makes me feel good to contribute, you know? I don't have artistic talent like you, but I can help kids achieve their potential. Maybe teach them a little history along the way, give them a sense of where they came from, so they're better prepared for where they're going."

She doesn't comment, just gazes at her shoes.

"Maybe you could use your art talents to help that youth program?"

Her voice tightens and her eyes flash. "Look, teaching is a noble profession and all, but..." She pushes off the tree and paces, glaring at the ground. "All my life, I watched my mom sacrifice her sparkle and channel her musical talent into giving music lessons because that's *sensible*." She hooks her fingers into snarky air quotes. "My parents' favorite word."

I tense from scalp to soles. Have I picked another woman who scorns my career? Is teaching not 'sparkly' enough for Laurel?

She talks faster and faster, waving her hands like her fingernails are on fire. "I don't want to spend my life helping others develop their talents. I want to develop my own. I want a big, colorful life, like Maxie's."

I choose my words carefully because if I let my own baggage bleed through, I'll snap at her and douse this budding attraction before it ever fully lights.

"Let me understand you, Laurel. You're saying you don't want to settle for a supporting role?"

Eyes blazing, she throws up her hands. "Exactly!"

I cross my arms and try to relax my expression. "So, becoming a teacher means I've settled for less than I could be?"

Laurel's jaw drops. "No! That's not what I meant at all. Dalton I—" She tilts her head to the sky and squinches her eyes shut, growling, "Shit, I'm not saying it right."

I wait for her to untangle her thoughts.

After a moment of heavy breathing through flared nostrils—unbearably sexy despite the tension between us—she tries again. "What I mean is, my mom's a gifted pianist. Really, really good." She cracks a wry smile. "She's finally performing again. My sister showed me pictures. She was glowing, Dalton. Under those lights, she seemed really happy for the first time in years. And for a long, long time, she wasn't. Happy, I mean." She sighs and digs her fingers into her hair, clutching her head as if it might otherwise explode. "I can't let that happen to me. I just can't."

I wish I could understand the turmoil hurting her right now. Clearly, there's a lot she's not telling me, and I have no right to demand painful details.

Stymied, I pull a bandana from my pocket and mop my sweat-drenched face. "Look, I'm not questioning your dream. I have no doubt you'll make an amazing gallery owner. And if I sound defensive, it's because I get pretty sick of people putting down teaching. It's important work. If it's not for you, that's okay, but it means a lot to me."

The fire banks in her gray eyes. "I didn't mean to put down your work, Dalton." Eyes downcast, she inches closer. "Your students are lucky to have a teacher as dedicated as you."

"And maybe, instead of making assumptions about your mom's happiness, you should talk to her." I cram the damp bandana back in my pocket. "I doubt she'd teach music all those years if she didn't enjoy it."

She stares, open-mouthed, then cracks a sheepish smile. "Maybe."

"And isn't it a gallery owner's job to make artists' work shine? To help them achieve their potential?"

"I mean…" She winces. "Yeah, I guess. That's not all they do, but…touché."

"Not unlike coaching. And another thing." Toe to toe, I cup her jaw. "I'm not trying to squash your sparkle, okay?"

"Okay." She's smiling fully now, her eyes glimmering with warmth and humor again. And then she darts forward and kisses me—sweet, sweat-sticky, breathless, dissolving all the tension between us.

I grin against her lips. "Sure you want to risk kissing me, since you're leaving and all?"

"Not until after Christmas. If this turns into something interesting, well…" She winds her arms around my neck. "San Francisco's not the dark side of the moon."

I slide my hands to her hips. "So, I have until Christmas to change your mind?"

She pulls back and narrows her eyes. "I'm not changing my mind, Dalton. I really like you, but I will leave after Maxie's big Christmas surprise."

"Fair enough." I duck my head to hide my grin.

Challenge accepted.

Laurel

Our turbulent conversation leaves me buzzy and lightheaded, but the steady rhythm of Dalton's footfalls beside me, the soft whoosh of his breath, the surrounding birdsong all combine to lull me into a more peaceful state. I feel like I've expelled something toxic and can finally breathe freely.

As we run back toward his place, I fall back a few steps and watch him. The late afternoon sunlight gilds his muscular calves, his powerful thighs, the broad expanse of his shoulders beneath his yellow T-shirt. The golden hair covering his limbs reflects the sunlight too, like glints on the river.

"Dalton, hang on."

He shoots me a quizzical glance.

I hold up my phone. "The light's really beautiful right now. I'd like to get some still shots."

"Of the river?"

"Of you."

He swipes his hand over his smooth scalp. "I'm not exactly looking my best."

"Oh, but you are. All golden and glowing and…"

"Sparkly?" He bats his eyelashes.

"Come on, humor me for a minute. Just run back as far as those trees, then run this way again."

He shrugs. "As you wish." He takes off, flashing a goofy grin over his shoulder.

"No, don't look at me," I call. "Pretend I'm not here."

He runs back and forth a few times, a self-conscious smile on his lips, but keeps his gaze averted. I shoot a burst of photos each time he passes.

He chugs to a stop beside me. "Enough?"

"Yeah, perfect." I show him a few shots. "See how beautiful you are?"

He cups his hand over mine, angling the screen, then shakes his head. "I see why Maxie calls me Ichabod Crane."

"Oh, stop it." I elbow him. "You look like some figure from Ancient Greece, carrying an important message to the battlefield. What was his name, that Marathon guy?"

"Pheidippides. According to the legend, he dropped dead as soon as he delivered his message."

"Oh. Well, let's say you look like some other ancient hero who didn't drop dead."

"If you say so." He flashes a crooked grin. "You're weird, you know that?"

"Why? Because I think you're pretty?" I pocket my phone and resume running.

He falls into step beside me. "What'll you do with all those photos?"

"Dunno. Just practicing." I simply felt moved to capture this moment, to remember his long, graceful body, the strength and wisdom in his deep-set eyes. To remember how good he makes me feel, even after I nearly bit his head off.

Putting down teaching as not interesting enough—what the flaming hell was I thinking? "Not interesting enough" could never describe Dalton. He's a good man—like deep-down, all the way to the marrow of his bones good. The world needs more people like him.

At his front gate, I pull out my bandana and wipe my sweat-stung eyes while he punches in his pass code.

He inclines his head toward the courtyard. "I don't know what the Ancient Greeks drank after a race, probably wine. I just have Gatorade and beer. Come up?"

I hesitate, calculating how long I've been gone. "I hate to leave Maxie alone for too long."

"Just a few minutes. I promise not to molest you." He cocks an eyebrow. "Unless you ask me to."

I wrinkle my nose. "No molesting. I'm sticky and I smell like a goat."

He leans in and nuzzles my neck. "Mmm. Sweaty woman. My favorite flavor."

"Eew." Giggling, I push him away. "But I will take a beer."

"Right this way, beauty."

Blushing, I follow him upstairs. While he rummages in his fridge, I check out his lair. Bland but comfortable. Running magazines strewn across the coffee table, squashy couch, huge TV, typical guy stuff. Books on history and outdoorsy themes stuff a wobbly-looking bookshelf. I peer at the family photos over the sofa, then jump when he presses a cold bottle to my nape.

"Yikes." I snatch it away, and we clink. After chugging half the bottle, I wipe my mouth. "Thanks. I really needed that."

He watches my lips as if hypnotized.

"What? Did I do something sexy?" I waggle my eyebrows.

His voice lowers half an octave. "Laurel, everything you do is sexy."

"Oh yeah?" Clutching his shirt, I pull him closer, brush my lips against his ear, and release a resounding belch.

Laughing, he slides his hand to the small of my back. "Even that was sexy. So, come run the 10K in Springfield?"

"This Sunday?"

He nods, his gaze still on my mouth. His big, broad hand rubs my back in a lazy circle, warming and soothing my muscles. I want to relax into his caress like a purring cat. If it weren't for my sticky, smelly state, I'd do just that—and more. Instead, I rest my chin on his shoulder. "I don't know, Dalton. I haven't trained much lately."

"You could do it with your eyes closed."

I snort. "Bad idea. I'd probably land in the river."

"Mmm." He kisses me behind my ear. "Now I'm picturing you all wet."

I *am* all wet, and tingly, and completely ready to melt into his embrace. Except...

"Dalton, I'm gross." I squirm against him.

"You're earthy." His lips brush my throat. "Animal." They caress my temple. "So beautiful." He claims my mouth, coaxing my lips apart with his cool, beer-flavored tongue.

Indulging my curiosity, I stroke his smooth scalp, softer than I imagined. He shifts, and a hard ridge of flesh presses into my belly. Clara's words flash in my memory: *It's enormous.* The friction ignites an almost painful tingle between my thighs. God, I want him! Want to feel the slide of his hot, sweaty skin on mine, feel those strong muscles beneath my fingers, feel the glorious hard length of him parting my folds, pushing...

His phone buzzes. He releases me. "God, sorry."

He digs in his pocket, pushing aside the pole that tents his shorts. I stare, mesmerized, but his wide-eyed, stricken expression breaks the spell.

"It's Mom." He dashes to the door. "Can I drop you home?"

I wave him on. "I'll walk. You go."

He thunders down the cement stairs, his footfalls echoing in the courtyard. I grasp the metal railing and close my eyes in a silent prayer.

Please, let her be okay.

Chapter Thirteen

Dalton

"Fractured tailbone, multiple contusions, but nothing that won't heal." Doctor Wong slides a packet of papers across her desk. "As for her mental condition, well..." She slumps back in her chair and tents her fingers. "Wish I had better news for you."

Seated beside me, Dad pales. I take the papers and squeeze his hand. "Doctor, was this fall related to her Alzheimer's?"

"It's hard to say. She could've been disoriented, or it could be just one of those careless moments we all have. She insists it's the latter."

"Good." Dad nods, his lips compressed in a tight line. "Not her fall, but..."

The doctor leans onto her elbows. "Mr. Garvey, it's been four years since your wife's diagnosis. She could remain fairly stable for a few more years, or she might spiral into late-stage Alzheimer's at any time. Once she transitions, she'll need round-the-clock care."

Dad sniffs hard, tears sparkling in his eyes. I feel it too, the weight of impending loss.

"Mom seems happy at Willamette Grove," I tell the doctor.

"It's a good facility." She lays her hand over mine. "Spend as much time with her as you can. And don't fret if she has a bad day. These ups and downs are a normal part of the disease's progression. It's no reflection on her love for you."

Dad draws a shuddering breath. A lone tear spills down his weathered cheek.

I slide the box of tissues closer and take one for myself. "Can we go see her now?"

"Sure. Just a few more tests and paperwork, and she should be ready to go home later this afternoon."

We find Mom propped up in her hospital bed, chatting with a nurse. Dressed in floral pajamas from home, her hair neatly combed, you'd never know she'd spent the last three days being tested from top to toe.

She clasps her hands and beams. "There they are, my boys."

The nurse briefs us on her aftercare. "Now, remember Hannah, ice and the donut cushion for the next four weeks."

"You heard the man." She aims a teasing grin at Dad. "Iced donuts. Doctor's orders."

"And try to sleep on your stomach," the nurse adds.

She grimaces. "Ouch. Squishes my boobies."

I scrub a hand down my face. You're never too old to be embarrassed by your mom. Set to silent, his phone buzzes in my pocket. I take a discreet glance.

Mom notices. "Your new girlfriend again? What's her name, Tiffany?"

"It's Laurel."

"Bring her by to visit."

Not likely, after you called her a whore.

"Go on, son, talk to your friend." Dad sits on the bed and takes her hands. "So, flirting with the nurses, are you?"

She titters like a schoolgirl.

Out in the hallway, I press the Call Back button.

"Hey there." Laurel's breathy voice slides over my skin like honey. "Guess where I am."

"At work?"

"In Clara's red room. Have you seen it yet?" Her laughter holds a spicy edge.

"I haven't worked up the nerve." Leaving that room with a hard-on under Clara's watchful eye is not a good idea. With Laurel, on the other hand...

"I miss you. How's your mother?"

"In good spirits, but she'll be sore for a while. They're releasing her later today."

"Broken tailbone, eh? What a pain in the...Sorry." She giggles. "That was truly bad."

"At least I'm still on summer break. Dad's taking it pretty hard. Guess he feels guilty he wasn't there to protect her."

"She could just as easily have tripped at home."

I massage my aching forehead. "We sat up late last night looking at photos of Mom before she got sick. A real sob fest."

"I wish there were something I could do to help."

What the hell, it's worth a try. "As a matter of fact, she wants to meet you."

"Oh. Um..."

I chuckle. "Hey, don't worry about it. She'll probably forget she asked."

"No, I'd like to meet her."

"Even though you're leaving?"

Her sigh vibrates the phone's speaker. "Not until after Christmas. I promised Maxie."

"Good. I'm not ready to let you go yet."

I hear her sharp intake of breath, then nothing else for a long moment. Finally, she chirps, "Well, give me a call when she's settled in. Gotta go. Clara's calling."

Phone in hand, I stand staring into space. All around me, nurses bustle, patients shuffle, and gurney wheels squeak on the polished gray linoleum.

God, I miss her. That last kiss—such a powerful, hot connection. Fiery and funny and refreshingly honest, Laurel has jolted something inside me back to life.

She doesn't need to move away to find her inner sparkle. She's dazzling already. But I'm just an ordinary guy. How can I tempt her away from those big-city lights?

Laurel

With a wistful smile, I tuck my phone into my pocket. Talking with Dalton unknots the worry I've been nursing since his mother's fall on Monday. Texts can't match the comfort of his deep, raspy voice.

I get back to work on a cartful of new books for the pet section. Right on cue, Lulu pads over, tail high, demanding my attention.

"Yes, yes," I mutter, stroking the cat's silky fur. "You're the boss. All hail Queen Lulu." The kitty rolls onto her back, paws in the air, before bolting toward the back of the shop.

"Cute little weirdo." I shelve the final book and wheel the cart behind the counter, where Clara's pricing used books. In the children's section, Margot entertains a pair of toddlers. "The big green dragon swooped down on the little village. All the people screamed, Look out!"

"Look out!" the kids echo, giggling.

"So, how's Dalton?" Clara asks.

I nibble my lower lip. Tell her or don't tell her? They're friends, after all. "You haven't heard about his mom?"

Clara clutches the locket between her annoyingly perfect breasts. "Oh no. What happened?"

"She had a fall. She's in the hospital."

She dashes back to her desk and returns clutching her phone.

Damn. Not that I want to deny Dalton the comfort of a close friend, but does comfort have to come in such a pretty package? Clara's green eyes flash as she waits for him to pick up. He does. Right away. Double damn.

"Laurel told me about your mom." Worrying a thick hunk of auburn hair with her free hand, she paces behind the counter. "Uh-huh...That's good...Uh-huh."

The doorbell jingles. Margot's still reading to her kiddie fan club, leaving me to handle the trio of older women in colorful tunics and chunky silver jewelry.

"Red door key, please," the shortest one holds out her be-jeweled hand.

Clara nods and points to the key. I hand it over.

"Thank you, dear." As the women make their way toward the back, one says, "She's striking. Beautiful lines."

Finished with her storybook, Margot nods toward the red door. "Artists, all three of 'em. The short one sells a ton of paintings."

"Oh really?" Meeting artists could lead to meeting gallery owners. A calculating grin stretches my lips.

"Speaking of art, what are you working on?" Margot asks.

"Pardon?"

"Clara says you're quite the artist."

I snort-laugh. "That's a stretch. I love art, but I have zero talent." I fish my phone from my skirt pocket. "I did try something the other day." I flip through my photos of Dalton running in the park. I've culled them down to the dozen most promising shots and played a little with filters, bringing out the golden glow of the late-afternoon sun on his skin.

"Really nice." Margot swipes the screen with her fingertip. "I especially like this one. Interesting angle."

I'd squatted to take this shot of Dalton running up the path with the sun at his back, highlighting his legs' muscular contours and impossible length. His eyes are in shadow, his jaw set in heroic determination.

Clara joins us. "Dalton says hi. So does his mom. Apparently, painkillers make her talkative." She reaches between us to angle the phone screen. "Wow."

Margot's nod wiggles her spiky hair. "Excellent composition."

Clara clasps my shoulder. "You've really captured his essence here."

I bite my lip hard. *Just how much of his essence have you captured, Clara?*

"Hang on a minute." One finger aloft, Clara trots back to the counter and rummages underneath. "Here it is." She hands me a flier from the Willamette Road Runners. "They need a poster for this year's charity run. See? Run for the Arts."

I squint at the small print. "Too bad. Deadline's Saturday."

"So?" Margot's blue eyes widen. "That's enough time. Just edit this up a bit. You got a Mac?"

"Are you kidding? Not even an iPad."

Margot chews her knuckle for a moment, then brightens. "Tomorrow's your day off, right?"

"Yeah, so?"

"I can sneak you into the graphic arts lab at the U. We can make an awesome poster of this pic. Add some text above his head, contact information here. Piece of cake."

I hug my tiny coworker. "It's a date."

The artists emerge from behind the red door. "There she is," the tallest calls as they round the corner. "Catch her, quick."

"Oh dear." Clara pulls me close and whispers, "You don't have to say yes."

"Huh?"

The shortest woman marches up, her brisk gait jingling her beaded earrings.

"Let's have a look at you." She crosses her arms over her considerable bosom and circles me. "Yes indeed, interesting lines. Lovely bone structure."

What am I, a horse? "Ummm, thank you?"

The artist fumbles in her pockets and pulls out a business card. *Agatha Andrews, Rising Wind Studios*. "What's your name, dear heart?"

"Laurel Jepsen, ma'am." I haven't ma'amed anyone in years, but the artist's queenly bearing pulls it out of me.

Agatha claps her hands. "How perfect. Laurel, like a tree. Graceful, savory."

"Like bay laurel?" the middle-sized woman asks. "Doesn't that grow on a bush?"

The taller woman flaps her ring-bedecked hand. "Who cares? The point is, we'd like you to pose for our life drawing class."

Ah, so that's what Clara meant.

"Tomorrow at four." Agatha's nod makes her double chin jiggle. "Here's the address. Nice warm studio, women only. Ninety minutes of posing. Homemade muffins. Good ones, not that gluten-free crap."

I finger the card. "Oh, I don't know."

"Pish-tosh, my girl. Give it a try. It's an experience everyone should have." She pats my hand. "A hundred dollars sitting fee."

I've always prided myself on being adventurous, but it's the sitting fee that tips me over the edge. I shake Agatha's hand. "You're on."

"Splendid." The women pay for their purchases, one book each from the red room. I scoot around the counter to peek at their choices. Agatha's buying a book of erotic photography. The tall woman has a book of Asian temple carvings, couples and groups making love in acrobatic poses. The middle one chose a Japanese pillow book. On its cover, a stylized, elegant couple sit face to face, his voluminous kimono parted to reveal an impossibly large, purple, veiny penis. The geisha gapes as if bracing herself for a painful assault.

Would sex with Dalton be like that? I make a mental note to buy some lube, just in case.

Chapter Fourteen

♥

Laurel

Stuck at a traffic light, I roll down my window to ease the late-afternoon heat. That beer garden up the street looks inviting and conjures a vivid sensory memory of Dalton's delicious, beer-flavored kiss three mornings ago. Between his ailing mother and Maxie's failing memory, when will we finally carve out some alone time?

I turn onto Maxie's street, where a green canopy of oaks and maples dapples the sunlight and cools the breeze. I pass a barefoot dad chasing his squealing kids with a garden hose, the scent of water on hot pavement as sweet as any perfume. A bearded hippie grandpa raises his hand in greeting as I cruise past.

Damn, I love it here. Maybe I could...

Nope! I slam the lid on that stupid impulse. No matter how welcoming, how relaxing, how funky and free-spirited, I can't allow this town to seduce me away from my dream, even if it does offer a few art galleries, some fun nightlife, pretty parks, miles of running paths...and Dalton.

"Keep your eyes on where you're going," I grumble, gripping the wheel tightly. This latest defeat has sucked the wind out of my sails, but I'm not giving up.

Sucking in a deep breath of lawn-clipping scented air, I visualize my gallery's grand opening. I picture myself in a chic, sleek, sparkly dress, a flute of champagne in hand, welcoming a crowd of art lovers to my first vernissage. There I am, wearing a serene smile and fabulous statement jewelry as I sashay through displays of abstract paintings, striking photos, surprising sculptures, and intricate jewelry pieces in gleaming, lighted cases. Here I am, posing for publicity photos beside grateful artists. I see the headlines: *Serendipity Gallery*, Triumphant Newcomer to the SF Art Scene—or San Jose, or LA, or San Diego. Because I *will* make my dream gallery reality, and I'll prove them all wrong, every boss and teacher and family member who ever doubted me.

I owe it to myself to—how did Maxie put it? To live loud. Or big. Or sparkly. Something like that.

I pull into Maxie's driveway and heave a sigh. I'll miss this place, but the longer I stay, the harder it'll be to pack up my meager belongings and drive south toward new opportunities. If only I could wiggle out of my promise to Maxie...

"No." I slam my fist down on the steering wheel, eliciting a feeble beep from the horn. "After all she's done for me, I won't let Maxie down."

"Of course you won't," a gruff male voice agrees.

That's when I notice the dented old pickup at the curb, and the young, ginger-bearded guy walking toward it, his muscular, tattooed arms wrapped around a moving carton.

"Afternoon, miss." As I climb out of my VW, he gives me an unabashed up-and-down glance. "You must be Laurel."

Maxie steps onto the porch. "There you are, kiddo. You almost missed Elmer."

Ginger-muscles sets down his load and extends his hand—broad, callused, and tattooed with a foaming beer mug.

Gripping the newly reinforced railing, Maxie wobbles down the stairs. "Elmer works at—what's the name of that brewery, dear?"

"Raven's Gulch." He gives her a fond smile. "Maxie's one of our favorite customers. Sorry to see you move away, Max. Maybe your grandniece can bring you over for a beer sometime?"

"You betcha." She pats his tattooed bicep. "Elmer's one of my art friends. He makes dishes."

I tilt my head. "Artistic dishes?"

"Beer mugs are my best sellers, but I do ceramic sculpture too."

Maxie dangles her car keys. "Let's go, kiddo."

"Now?" I pluck at my T-shirt, damp from the sweaty ride home.

"Why not? You look fine." Maxie heads to her Volvo, which I notice is stuffed with more boxes.

"Very fine." Elmer wiggles his eyebrows, then hefts the carton onto his shoulder.

Show off. He's cute, but I have enough to worry about with Dalton and Maxie and nude paintings.

I help Maxie into the Volvo and follow Elmer to Willamette Grove, where we tote boxes into the empty apartment. The painting crew has finished with the living room, but the kitchen is still draped with plastic tarps. Electrical wires dangle where the ceiling lamps should be.

"You sure it's okay to leave your things here, Maxie?" I ask.

"Mrs. What's-her-face said it's fine." She turns to Elmer. "Now, don't forget. The Saturday before Christmas."

"Wouldn't miss one of your epic parties, Max." He plants a smooch on her weathered cheek, then ambushes me with a bear hug. "Great to meet you, Laurel. See you around, I hope."

I watch bug-eyed as he lopes out the door. Just friendly, or a flirtatious creep?

"Isn't he the nicest boy?" Maxie pokes my ribs. "Sure you wouldn't prefer him to Ichabod Crane?"

"Yeah, I'm sure." Guilt pinches me hard. Dalton's such a sweet guy, so helpful to Maxie, and here I am looking forward to leaving them both behind.

"So..." I drum my fingers on a moving carton. "That's your big Christmas secret, an epic party?"

She flashes a sly grin. "You'll see. I'm counting on your help."

"Of course, but what—"

"Never mind. Let's get back. I don't want to miss *Jeopardy*."

We're about to head home when another pickup pulls up beside us. The driver taps his horn. I glance up to find Dalton waving from the passenger seat. After three days of forced separation, his sweet, hopeful smile tickles my heart like kitten fur.

I roll down my window. "Hey there."

"We're just bringing Mom back. Got a minute?"

"Actually, Maxie wants to get home."

"Don't be ridiculous," Maxie chirps. "We're in no hurry."

Leaning past him, his mother peers at me. "Is this your girlfriend, Dalton?"

He quirks an apologetic grin as we all climb out of our vehicles and made introductions. I'm tensed for another outburst, but Dalton's mother just smiles and envelopes my hand in both of hers. "Nice to finally meet you, Tiffany."

Dalton takes her elbow. "It's Laurel, Mom."

Unease flickers across her face. "Oh, right." She pats my hand. "Sorry, dear. Alzheimer's is a bitch."

Dalton's jaw drops. His father passes a hand over his face, covering his grin.

"I like you better, anyway." She tucks my hand into the crook of her elbow. "I'm Hannah, by the way. Let's go have a coffee."

Dalton's father, tall and rangy like his son but with a full head of wiry gray hair, offers Maxie his arm. "John Garvey. And you are?"

"Maxine Schmidt, Laurel's great-aunt. Call me Maxie."

As we make our way to the little café, John catches my eye and grins, then turns to Maxie. "So, Dalton tells me you're quite the artist."

Dalton falls into step beside me and leans close. "Sorry," he whispers.

"It's fine." I smooth my rumpled skirt.

"Look at those long legs, Dalton," his mom says. "I'll bet she can keep up with you."

He bumps my arm with his. "Oh, she's already caught me."

Oblivious, Hannah nods. "Good quality in a mother. Gotta outrun those kids."

"Hannah." John chuckles. "The kids just met. Give them some space."

"Space, schmace," Maxie chimes in. "Anyone can see they're a good match."

Oh, for cripe's sake! Not twenty minutes ago, Maxie was pushing me toward Elmer. Now, she's playing matchmaker with Dalton's parents?

We find a free table on the café's patio.

"Why don't Laurel and I go fetch coffee?" Dalton suggests.

Hannah shoos him with a wave of her hand. "You go. I want to talk to her."

"I'll help you, son. But first—" John pulls his wife up and slides a ring-shaped cushion onto her seat.

"Ah yes, my donut." She pats his arm. "Much better. Thank you, Dalton."

John chuckles, and Dalton throws a sheepish glance over his shoulder. I wave him off. With Maxie's help, I can handle his mom.

"So, Miss, er..."

"Laurel."

"Right. You're a teacher, like our Dalton?"

"No, ma'am. I work in a bookstore for his friend Clara."

Hannah purses her lips. "Never liked that woman. Greedy. Conniving. Mean."

"Clara?" I can't imagine applying those words to my kind, patient boss.

Hannah shakes her head. "No, no, the other one. The wife. What's her name?"

"Tiffany," I volunteer.

"Nasty girl. You met her?"

"I, uh, haven't had the pleasure."

Hannah snorts. "Count yourself lucky. She's a piece of work. Only after my boy's body." She lowers her voice and brackets both hands around her mouth. "He has a nice big dingle, just like his daddy."

Maxie hoots with laughter and pounds on the table. My cheeks aflame, I close my eyes and pray for the ground to open up and swallow me whole.

The men return with paper cups and two insulated pitchers, plus cream and sugar. Dalton eyes my flushed face. "Oh Lord, what did she say?"

Maxie wipes her eyes. "We were just discussing your love life."

"Mom," he moans.

"Don't make such a fuss," Maxie says. "Let us old ladies have our fun. Decaf for me, please."

Dalton sits beside me and squeezes my knee.

Hannah doses her coffee with a stream of sugar. "Look how well you two fit together. What pretty babies you'd make. I'm glad to see Dalton settling down with a sensible girl who's devoted to her family."

I wince. *Sensible.* Dad's favorite word.

Dalton shoots his father a pleading look.

John clears his throat. "So, Maxie, Dalton tells me your porch needs work."

Dalton pushes his chair back, the iron legs scraping the rough cement. "Will you excuse us for a moment?"

"Go on, son." John chuckles. "Get out while you can."

I take Dalton's hand, grateful for the reprieve. Fingers interlaced, we stroll across the freshly mown quad to a wooden bench beneath a spreading oak tree. Dalton sinks onto it and tugs me down beside him, then closes his eyes and pinches the bridge of his nose. "Words cannot express how sorry I am. Mom is just..."

"I get it. No filter, like Maxie. I'm sure they'll be best friends."

He traces my jawline with a feather-light touch. "I've missed you, Laurel." His twilight-blue gaze makes my heart dance—a steamy tango with swirls and dangerous dips. He lowers his head and kisses me, and for a moment, I forget all about keeping my guard up, about San Francisco and anything beyond his lips on mine, his nearness heating my whole body, opening me like a blossom, soft and willing, ripe for the plucking.

Deep in his throat, Dalton makes a rumbling sound halfway between a purr and a growl. He scoops my legs across his lap, cradles my nape with one hand and grips my thigh with the other, and kisses me senseless. His velvet tongue teases my lips apart, and he tastes of sugary coffee. The world around us fades into soft focus, leaving just our two bodies, calling and answering, breathing in sync, our pulses beating the same rhythm.

"Get a room, why dontcha."

He jerks away. I press my hand to my kiss-swollen lips and blink, discombobulated by the sudden interruption.

Two old ladies, one tall, one tiny, stand glaring at us. The tall one clucks her tongue. "Decent people live here, ya know. We don't wanna witness your smut."

Dalton clears his throat and releases his grip on my leg. "Sorry, ma'am."

I hide my heated face against his chest and giggle until my eyes stream.

"Go on, off with ya." The shorter woman jabs toward us with her cane.

He shifts on the bench. "I, uh, just give us a sec, please."

The tall one cups her hand to her friend's ear, but her stage-whisper carries. "Will ya look at the schlong on him."

Oh God, Dalton's khaki shorts are tented like the big top.

He crosses his legs, which must be painful. Tittering like raspy sparrows, the two old ladies totter back toward the café.

Dalton doubles over. "It is not possible to be more embarrassed than I am right now."

"Don't be. It's kind of flattering." I lean my cheek on his shoulder. "For what it's worth, if they could see the effect you have on me, they'd probably call the fire department."

His eyes crinkle at the corners. "Really?"

"Really really." I kiss his temple and push myself upright. "But it's been a long day, and your family's waiting for you."

"Yeah. Turkey dinner tonight. I promised Mom I'd stay."

"Too bad. I have some things to do tomorrow afternoon."

"Morning run?"

"I'd love it." Grinning like a loon, I back away. "Nine?"

"Perfect." He stays hunched over. "I'll just stay here until..."

"Gotcha. See you tomorrow." I trot back toward the café. When we pull out of the parking lot, he's still there, legs crossed, looking adorably miserable.

A sharp thought slices me between the ribs. How miserable will he look when I drive away from Eugene for good?

Chapter Fifteen

♥

Laurel

Shit, shit, shit. I strip off my grubby work clothes and glare at my reflection in the bathroom mirror. What happened to focusing on the plan? A few hot kisses with Ichabod, and my determination melts like ice cream on the fourth of July. I can't let myself fall for a guy who'll never fit into my future.

He's not Ichabod to me, though. More like what's-his-name, the one who ran the first Marathon—a hard-working, earnest, honest hero who sacrifices for his family. Temporarily, anyway. Sad as it is to admit, his mom won't be around forever.

An icy finger strums my ribs. Maxie won't be around much longer either. Suddenly, the so-called determination I'm clinging to feels like a selfish betrayal. Even Dad did better in the end. Sacrificing a few months for my family isn't a big ask.

Yeah, but a few months can turn into a few years, then forever.

I crank the shower spray full blast, squirt on shampoo, and scrub hard to release the tension gripping my scalp. But the kind of release I crave doesn't come in a shampoo bottle. As

I soap my skin, an image teases my imagination: Dalton's tall, rangy body behind mine, his strong hands stroking suds over my skin, circling my breasts, gliding over my hips, his monster cock probing between my thighs...

The water turns cold. My daydream has exhausted the tank. Shivering, I towel off and wipe steam from the mirror. "Traitor," I snarl at my naked reflection. "You could get sex anywhere. Why fixate on Dalton? Why not that Elmer guy? He's cute. He's interested. A penis is a penis." I prop my foot on the toilet lid and dry my leg in long, rough strokes.

Dalton's long fingers slide over my tense muscles, softening my flesh...

"Arrgh." I ball up the towel, pitch it into the hamper, and stomp to my room.

"What's got into you, Lady Godiva?" Maxie calls from the dining room, where she's sketching a bowl of mangos.

"Sorry, forgot my robe." I shut the guest room door, slide into yoga pants and a loose T-shirt, and pull my phone from my bag. My thumbs fly.

Hey, D. Got a minute? Need perspective.

I stretch my legs on the narrow bed and wiggle my toes. All this running has worn the blue polish at the edges. I rummage in the dresser drawer for the polish bottle and dab at my toenails while I wait for Davonte's call.

When it comes, my best friend's voice rumbles slow, sweet, and spicy, with a hint of peachy Southern drawl—funny from a guy who grew up in the suburbs of Portland. "Hey, doll-face. Long time no hear. How you hanging there in Eugene? God, I miss that place."

"Really? Eugene?"

"Yeah. Fun town. Small enough to make friends, big enough to hold surprises." Papers rustle in the background. "Sorry, working late tonight. Hey, is that crazy club still open? The one with the glitter moose head?"

"Don't know. Haven't been out there yet."

He clucks his tongue. "Girl, why not? You were always good at finding fun. Go paint the town fuchsia."

"I'm a little low on fuchsia paint right now." I give him a quick run-down of Maxie's condition, my new job, my nude modeling gig, and Dalton.

"I really like him, D, and that worries me."

"How come?" He slurps into the phone. Probably mainlining coffee like he did in college.

"I usually have more control than this. Every time I'm with him, I want to rub my hands all over that lanky body of his. I want to lick his bald head, nibble his furry chest."

"Sounds tasty. Did I tell you I met a cute bald guy? Maybe I can talk him into a road trip. We could double date."

"You'd come up here?"

"Soon as I get some time off. I want to see if this bean pole is good enough for you."

"That's the trouble—he's probably too good for me."

He snorts.

"No, really. He's selfless. Kind. A really good guy. Makes me feel like a total shit, knowing I'm leaving right after Christmas." When he doesn't answer, I blather on. "You'd think a high school teacher living in a cookie-cutter apartment would be boring, but he's not."

Silence.

"D, you still there?"

"Listen, Laurel, you know I love you, right?"

I sniffle and swipe at my teary eyes. "You're the brother of my heart, D. I miss you so much."

"I miss you too. Don't get me wrong, the back room's got your name on it. But listen..."

My belly muscles tense. Et tu, Davonte?

"Three months isn't very long. Maybe you should stick around for a while. You're always flitting from place to place, job to job. Eugene's a great town for figuring out your shit. I mean, you've got family there, a free place to stay, and a cute fella."

I groan and curl into a ball on the lumpy bed.

"Besides, art galleries are always opening and closing. We'll find you a job when you get here. Gorgeous and artsy-fartsy as you are, they'll be competing to snap you up."

I grunt. Davonte's painfully right, damn it—not about my desirability as an employee, but about giving myself time to catch my breath.

"You have lots of fine qualities, baby girl, but patience ain't one of 'em. You're like a big ol' leggy racehorse, straining at the bit." More rustling papers. "You like that bookstore?"

"Yeah. It's nice." And I haven't told Clara I'm planning to leave after Christmas, which means I'll be leaving her in a bind. And I really like her. Margot too. Crap. Yet another difficult convo in my future.

"So, stay put a while. Get a good letter of recommendation. After the fiasco in Portland, your résumé needs some cush-ion."

As always, Davonte strikes the perfect note between no-bullshit and compassionate. He knows me to the marrow of my bones, and he likes me anyway. I'm lucky to have such a wise friend.

I blow out a windy sigh. "I'll think about it."

He giggles. "Think about it while you're posing naked."

Muffled voices behind him. "Gotta go. Love you, Laurel Tree."

"Love you, D, the most handsomest, cleverest actor-to-be in San Francisco."

I stretch, yawn, and wiggle my freshly retouched toes. Big day tomorrow. Poster making with Margot, nude modeling, and a morning run with Dalton. The way we're sparking, I'll probably spend the morning in his bed rather than on the trail.

I clutch the pillow to my chest. Is that really such a bad idea? My lady parts vote in favor, but my brain still holds reservations. Can I enjoy being his post-divorce rebound fling without catching feelings? Even if I hop into his bed tomorrow morning, it'll be a four-month romance, at best.

So what? None of my romances since college ever lasted that long. Time after hurtful time, the universe has shown me that love doesn't last. After I gave him my whole heart and he promised his undying love, my college boyfriend left me for his high school sweetheart. And none of the guys I've dated since really gave a shit about me as a person; they only cared about having a leggy blonde on their arm. So why not give into this chemistry brewing between Dalton and me? It's starting to feel inevitable. And whether I indulge or not, this attraction will reach its expiration date.

The ones I want most never stick around. That's just how it is.

Chapter Sixteen

♥

Dalton

Standing at the bathroom sink, I hum as I run my electric head shaver over my skull. Without this daily ritual, I'd resemble a circus clown—springy blond fuzz surrounding a glassy crown, my plight since I started losing my hair in my mid-twenties. At least the chrome dome look is stylish these days. I finish with a layer of sunblock in preparation for my run with Laurel.

Lovely, luscious Laurel. Feisty and funny and so dazzling she nearly scorches my retinas. My dick stirs at the memory of our last kiss, so I pull on very loose running shorts over very tight compression shorts. That oughta keep any surprise public boners contained.

My doorbell dings at five till nine. I grip the doorknob.

Deep breath. Be cool. Don't drool on her.

Like an exceptionally pretty flamingo, Laurel grins while grasping one foot behind her, stretching her quads. Her silky shorts and skimpy singlet leave most of her smooth skin on display. Already sheened with sweat along her brow and collarbone, she smells like a day at the beach.

"Your neighbor let me in, the science teacher." She tugs a bandana from her pocket and swipes it across her face. "Ready?"

"Almost." I clip on my hydration belt. "Want to try something different today?"

Her gaze skims down my body and back up. She tilts her sleek blond head and flashes a saucy grin. "What did you have in mind?"

Beads of sweat form along my brow. "Skinner Butte Park? A little hill work?" *Or you could just come inside, drop those shorts, and make me the happiest man in Oregon...*

Her lids lower, and her long, pale lashes cast shadows on her cheeks. "I don't know. I'm not in great shape, like you are."

"We can turn back anytime."

She scrunches her lips to the side as if pondering layers of meaning. Finally, she nods. "Okay. I'm game."

The promise of a scorcher shimmers in the morning air as, side by side, we jog through several residential blocks toward the towering Basalt Columns fronting the Butte. Laurel stops to watch the climbers crawling up and down like ants on a tree. "You ever try that?" she asks.

"Just once. How about you?"

She swipes her bandana across her brow, down her throat, and between her sweet, perky breasts. She said something too, but all my available brain cells are tied up following that square of cloth.

"Up this way." I point. "Nice view of the river."

She trots ahead of me up the wooded path. Filtered by the trees, sunlight dapples her smooth, strong thighs like a fawn's hide.

"Really pretty up here," she puffs.

"Really pretty back here."

She grins over her shoulder. "That's why you let me lead, eh?"

"Well, you never know when a bear might attack."

"What if he attacks from up front?"

I chuckle. "Guess you'll have to protect me."

"Lucky for you, I've got pepper spray." She pats the pocket on her belt.

We turn onto a steep, narrow path.

"Man, you're a tough coach." She chugs uphill, her calf muscles flexing, her long ponytail bobbing like a silk flag. At a switchback, she stops and grips the railing. "Rock in my shoe." She stoops to untie it, then grins up at me. "Watch out for bears, will you?"

I salute. "Will do." But my gaze rivets to her behind as she fiddles with her laces. Holding my arm for balance, she dumps the grit from her shoe. When she bends again to refasten the laces, her foot slides on loose gravel.

"Oops. Sorry." We collide, my thigh between hers, her hand on my chest, our faces inches apart. Her mouth opens on a sigh. Her lashes flutter down. Her breath strokes my cheek. *Kapow.* The energy simmering between us flares into a supernova.

I clutch her waist, pull her in tight, and crush my lips to hers. She welcomes my probing tongue. She tastes like cinnamon, sweet and hot. My pulse gallops, and my dick throbs painfully.

Somewhere in the back of my brain, an alarm blares. A cluster of teens is coming down the trail, their shouts and laughter growing louder.

Laurel angles her hips, pressing her damp heat to my thigh, and whispers the sweetest words I've ever heard, "Dalton, please."

"This way." I tug her through a narrow opening in the bushes, probably a deer trail. Twigs scrape my skin, but at this point, I'd push through rusty blades to get at her. Resting my back on the trunk of a tall pine, I pull her tight against me. She giggles into my shoulder.

"Sshh." I touch my finger to her lips. She licks it, her tongue scorching hot.

God help me.

Ten feet away, the teens guffaw and shout and snap selfies. In here, shielded by undergrowth, a secret garden blooms. The forest loam is soft beneath our feet, and the tang of pine needles mingles with her intoxicating scent—floral shampoo, beachy sunscreen, and hot, juicy woman. My hands slide beneath her tank top and over her damp skin.

She tugs my T-shirt free from my belt. "Take this off," she whispers while she unfastens her waist pack and pulls her top over her head. Pressed against me in just her shorts and sports bra, she fumbles with my belt while I strip off my shirt.

Her fingertips skim over my furry chest. Should I have shaved that too? I feel like a skinny blond gorilla, exposed in the open air.

"I love this." Her fingers weave into my thatch. Her thumbs circle my nipples, igniting shivers of tickly pleasure.

All righty then. No shaving.

While her hands slide over my back, I cup her sweet, soft breasts through her damp bra. Her nipples pebble hard beneath my palms. I search for a bra clasp and, finding none, tug the strap over her shoulder. She slides her arm free, and her right breast plumps into my hand, silky and warm and delicious. I have to taste her.

A mere ten yards away, the kids cackle like manic chickens. God help us if one of them needs to pee in the bushes.

Despite the tree bark scraping my back, I scoot down until my mouth finds her beautiful, rosy nipple, firm and hot beneath my tongue. I suck greedily.

Laurel moans and clutches me closer with one hand while she tugs her bra down to her waist.

There's a shriek of laughter from the path. Straightening, I cup her jaw and incline my head toward the noise. "Shhh."

She nods and flashes the most beautiful, wicked smile. My heart nearly bursts out of my shuddering ribcage when her hand trails down my belly, dips to the front of my shorts, and grasps my aching erection through the cloth.

"God, yes," she whispers, slowly stroking me. "So hard, so big."

My jaw unhinges. My eyes cross. My heart stops. My hand, though, has a mind of its own, burrowing between her smooth thighs. Even through her shorts, I feel her blooming beneath my touch. She buries her face in the crook of my neck and releases a trembling sigh while she rocks her hips.

From the trail, a nasal voice rings out, "Carlos, c'mon. Move your fat ass." More shrill laughter.

Powerless to stop, I join the dance, my hips echoing Laurel's rhythm, thrusting with delicious slowness into her hand. Blinding bright pleasure washes through me. With eager fingers, I pull her shorts and panties out of the way and slide inside to stroke her sweet, hot pussy, as smooth as my head and slick with her excitement. "So wet," I whispered, probing between and inside.

"God, I want you." Her hand tunnels into my compression shorts, tugging the tight fabric away from my skin. When her fingers close around me, I bite my lip to keep from groaning aloud. Her thumb finds the tear of pre-cum at the tip and strokes in lazy circles, readying me to glide into her.

Pulse hammering, I yank my shorts down, clutch her thigh, and lift her toward me. She grasps my shaft and rubs the swollen head at her entrance, sliding, gliding, the sweet ache building my need to thrust...

It costs everything I have to stop. "Wait." I draw back. "I don't have a condom."

She squeezes her eyes shut and leans her forehead into my chest. "Damn, I'm so close." She sinks her teeth into my shoulder, but the sting only intensifies the pleasure sizzling through me.

Maybe I can't have the complete fulfillment I crave, but I'm not going to leave her like this, aching and unsatisfied. Not when she's on the edge, hot and wet and willing. I wind her ponytail around my fist and slant my mouth across hers. With my free hand, I tug her shorts aside again, slide one finger inside of her, then a second, and brush my thumb back and forth until I find the firm little button that makes her quake and moan. Her slick flesh clings to my fingers with each stroke.

With a gasp, she takes me in both her hands and milks my shaft hard and fast, sparking bright electric jolts beneath my skin.

"God, I can't, Dalton..." Eyes shut tight, she hisses through clenched jaws as her inner muscles clutch my fingers, fluttering in waves. So beautiful, her throat arched, her breasts bared to the sun. She curls forward and keens softly into my chest, coming, coming...

My own climax blasts through me like a fiery rocket, spirals of impossible pleasure throbbing, pulsing, my blood roaring as I surrender to primal bliss.

Dizzy with release, I cling to her, letting my breath slow.

"Oh," she finally whispers, "Oh, my." She releases my softening cock and, giggling, presses her damp cheek over my heart. "What a mess."

Wincing, I survey the damage.

Both my chest and hers are smeared with cum.

"Oh, jeez. Let me..." I pull my bandana from my shorts. Is she grossed out? Apparently not, thank God, because she holds onto my shoulders, laughing softly as I wipe the mess from her beautiful pale breasts and belly, then my own furry front. I dig a hole with my toe and bury the crumpled cloth. "A sacrifice to the forest gods."

Grinning, she kisses me softly. "I think they'll be pleased." She picks up both our shirts and gives each a good shake before handing mine over and pulling hers on. "Oops, backwards." Her laughter rings like magical fairy bells. "Feels like I'm drunk."

I pull my shirt on, and she picks pine needles from my chest.

"Let me get your back." She plucks at the cloth, then laces her fingers around my middle and hugs me with a happy sigh, her face between my shoulder blades. "Wow. I've never done that before."

"You've never made love in the forest?"

A sharp intake of breath. She freezes, clutching my shirt, her body stiff.

I hold my breath. What did I say?

Exhaling in a whoosh, she softens and rubs her cheek against my back. "No, I never have. Before now."

I turn, cup her face, and stroke her perfect cheekbones with my thumbs. "Well, I'm honored to be your first. In the woods, I mean."

"Thank you." She pulls me in for a gentle kiss, then glances at her watch. "Hey, it's ten-thirty. I have to be somewhere at noon, and I sure can't go like this." She gestures at her rumpled, pine-flecked clothing. "We'd better hit the trail, Coach."

"As you wish, beauty." We emerge from our hideaway and set off down the trail, jogging downhill at a relaxed pace. When we round a curve, we find the path blocked by a half-dozen chattering, giggling teens.

"Excuse us," I call out.

"Hey, it's Mr. Garvey. How's it goin', man?"

I curse under my breath. The kids who gathered just ten yards away while Laurel and I groped and groaned were all students from my school. I recognize two girls from last year's world history class, and Kyle, a skinny kid who runs hurdles. "When's cross country practice start, Coach?" he asks.

"Um, it's on the school website. See you soon." I catch Laurel's hand and leave the kids whispering and tittering behind us.

Her eyes are huge. "Oh my God. You think they heard us?"

"I hope not. Kids goofing around hardly ever notice adults, even adults trying to get their attention."

Her laughter rings over our thudding footsteps. "I can see the yearbook now—Mr. Garvey: Most likely to fool around in the woods."

When we reach my apartment door, I tug her inside, enfold her in my arms, and kiss her breathless. "Round two?"

Her gray eyes sparkle with promise. "I wish I could, but I have a couple of appointments today, and I need to clean up." She glances down at her rumpled shirt, still flecked with dirt and pine needles.

"Guess not." I kiss the tip of her nose. "Sorry about the mess."

"Are you kidding?" Her fingertip traces lazy swirls on my chest. "That was sooo hot. I can't wait to try again when we have more privacy and can make some noise. But I have these two projects today. They mean a lot to me, Dalton." She pecks my lips. "Can I call you tonight?"

"If you don't, I'll come howl outside your window."

Before trotting away, she flashes a smile that lights up the darkest corners of my bruised heart.

I close the door and lean into it, my mouth slack with wonder. Caught up in my misery, I wasn't looking for this, wasn't expecting it. But it seems a bright angel of hope took a wrong turn and landed right in my path.

I'll do whatever it takes to hang onto her.

Chapter Seventeen

♥

Laurel

"Scooch a bit to the left, my angel."

I flinch as Agatha's icy fingertips nudge my bare hip into position.

"Perfect. Now, focus your gaze on that blue vase." She steps back and surveys my nude form from top to toe. "Lovely. Janice, would you adjust the lamp? I want a little more shadow beneath her jaw here." She points to the spot. "Good. Let's have some music to help you relax." Soothing strains of Enya fill the art studio.

I struggle to keep my gaze on the vase, and not on the dozen women eyeing me over their easels and sketch boards. It was surprisingly easy to drop the terrycloth robe Agatha provided, and it's not too hard to relax under the artists' steady, impersonal gaze. There's no sense of judgment here. I know, from the many art classes I barely passed, the artists are focusing on shape and line, light and shadow. I wish I were on the other side of an easel, sketching a brave model who bares it all for art. But a hundred bucks for ninety minutes of lounging around is too good an offer to pass up, not to mention the chance to meet an influential artist.

The session opens with a series of one-minute standing poses. I shift my position whenever the timer dings, raising my arm, looking over my shoulder, angling my head up or down. Afterward, I settle onto a stool covered with a cheap polyester tablecloth, complete with—*Please, let those be gravy stains.* The artists, a dozen women from twenty-something to well over seventy, scribble rapidly with each pose. Easy peasy.

But holding a pose for twenty minutes at a time? That's a different story.

A wall clock ticks off the minutes. After two sweeps of the second hand, my nose begins to itch. I try hard to ignore it, focusing instead on Enya's lilting harmonies, the soft scratch of pencils on paper, the drip, drip, drip in the stainless-steel sink.

Five minutes. My stomach rumbles. My knee itches. The arch of my left foot cramps.

Ten minutes. The stuffy, paint-scented air weights my eyelids. The music's rise and fall laps like tepid waves against my body, slowing my breath...

My chin jerks up. "Sorry," I whisper.

Agatha peeps around her easel and flashes a bright, apple-cheeked smile. "Take a few deep breaths, darling. I'll crack a window." Her earrings tinkle as she waddles over to the tall windows, admitting a breeze, traffic sounds, the smell of exhaust, the shouts of passing kids...kids like we met on the trail.

Did Dalton's students hear us? In moments of passion, I always have trouble restraining my loud cries. With all the groaning and rustling, it's a wonder those kids didn't burst through the underbrush to investigate what must've sounded like the death throes of some wounded beast.

The delicious memory sends a shiver down my spine and through my limbs. Dalton's strong hands on my body, sliding and caressing and clutching and grasping. His furry chest tickling my breasts. His long fingers inside me, thumb strumming me like a guitar. He has magic in those hands. And his mouth—on my lips, my throat, my nipples. Delicious, ferocious, tender, demanding. And that monster cock of his, thick and long, its plush plum crown slick with pre-cum, ready to thrust into me with such force...

"Are you cold, dear? Shall I shut the window?" Agatha's round pink face pops above her easel.

I blink hard. "Oh, I'm fine."

"You sure? You're shivering, and, erm..." She gestures with her pencil toward her own heavy breast.

Yikes! My nipples have hardened like diamonds. I flush from my crotch to the roots of my hair. A kitchen timer dings, echoing off the cement floor. *Saved by the bell.*

"Ah well, break time." Agatha sets down her pencil and stretches her plump arms overhead. "Have some tea, Laurel. That'll warm you up."

I shrug into my robe, then glance at the stool. Crap, a wet spot. Trying to be discreet, I fold the cloth to hide the stain.

God, how embarrassing. So much for distracting myself with thoughts of Dalton. Better pick a safer subject.

During the next twenty-minute pose, I make a mental list of every job I've ever held: my earliest babysitting gigs, waitressing in a diner, selling cheap designer knock-offs in a strip mall, filing papers in the campus admissions office, slinging espresso in a pretentious coffee bar, three short stints in art galleries, and now the bookstore. Not much of a résumé. Davonte has a point. This job at the bookstore could provide a valuable reference. Should I list "artist's model" on my résumé? Um, no. Dumb idea.

The timer dings again. Thank goodness. I really have to pee. Through the thin plywood door, I hear the artists chatting around the tea urn. "Beautiful lines on her...squirmy, though. Twitchy. ...ask her back?"

I comb my fingers through my hair, then grasp the doorknob.

"There's our girl." Agatha slides her arm through mine and walks me back to the dais, where she's arranged several mismatched cushions. "For our last pose, let's have you lie down. I'll just drape this cloth over the top—"

"I'll get it," I chirp with artificial brightness. I snatch the cloth from the stool, spread it over the pillows, and stretch out on my side. "Like this?"

"Right leg a little forward, relax your elbow." Agatha makes a few gentle adjustments. "Lovely. Twenty minutes." She cranks the little tomato-shaped timer. "Here we go."

This time, I visualize a solo run along the river at sunset. Sun glints on the water. A fresh breeze lifts my hair, drying the sweat on my brow. That does the trick. No jerking, no twitching. Before I know it, the timer dings again.

"That's all for today, dear. You can get dressed now."

Behind the wooden screen, I pull on my jeans, T-shirt, and sandals. When I emerged, the artists are still at work. Fascinated, I stroll around the studio's perimeter. Here I appear as a translucent watercolor nymph with floating hair. There, an almost abstract figure sketched in bold charcoal swaths. Another artist uses pastel crayons to shade the curve of my thigh, as powerful as a cartoon superheroine's. The woman looks up and grins. "You're a runner, right?"

I nod.

"I can tell. Great leg muscles."

But Agatha's is the best of the bunch. She's sketched me seated in three-quarters profile, my hair spilling across my shoulder like a river of silk. Agatha has transformed my lanky, angular frame into graceful, sensuous curves. The image's Mona Lisa smile reflects my steamy daydreams of Dalton.

"Wow," I whisper.

"That's how you look to me, my dear. Like you're dreaming about some delightful secret." Agatha sets her pencil down. "But we've kept you long enough. Come." She pads on bare feet to a cabinet, rummages in her purse, and hands me an envelope. "May I call you for another sitting? I'll want more time to finish this portrait."

"Of course. And thank you."

Agatha pats my hand. "You're an interesting subject, Miss Laurel. Lots going on below the surface."

Should I ask? The worst she can say is no.

"Actually, I'm working on an art project of my own. Would you mind taking a look?"

Her bright, round eyes twinkle. "Show me."

From my backpack, I pull the carefully rolled poster Margot and I had printed at the university's graphics lab. I slide it from its cardboard tube.

"Interesting composition. You've a good eye for lines and motion." She nudges me with her elbow. "Is this the young man you were dreaming about?"

I stammer.

"I'm just teasing." She beckons to a wiry-haired woman working with a charcoal pencil. "Katie, come see."

"Oh, I love what you've done with the psychedelic sunset background."

"Sort of an homage to Eugene's hippie past." I explain.

Soon, a half-dozen women gather around their teacher.

"So, it's a competition for the best poster?" one asks.

"I guess." I shuffle my feet. "I've just joined the group, and—"

"Oh, you'll win, hands down. This one's a real eye-catcher."

"Rainbow Center for Youth Arts." A petite woman with a snowy crown of braids taps the poster with her fingernail. "I've been there. Good program. You should teach them photography, Laurel."

"Well, I'm just an amateur."

"Nonsense. Amateurs don't have your eye for composition. See how well you've captured his motion? I can almost hear his footfalls, his breathing."

Blushing hotly, I re-roll the poster. I'd been nervous about presenting it to the running club at tomorrow's meeting, but the artists' praise bolsters my confidence. I thank them profusely, backing out of the studio into the still-bright sunshine.

While rush-hour traffic zooms by, I take a deep breath of the exhaust-scented air and grin. What a glorious day of firsts. First photography project, first art poster, first modeling gig and, best of all, first sex with Dalton. Even if we didn't technically go "all the way," our passionate moment in the bushes left me energized and giddy. I can't wait to tell Maxie about today's adventures—except our tumble in the bushes, of course.

I check my phone, set to silent before the art class. Two messages from Dalton, and one from Maxie, sent an hour ago:

sidnk

Did she drop her phone? Sit on it?

Maxie picks up on the third ring. "Hello? Who is this?"

"It's Laurel. I just finished with the art class."

"Who?" Traffic sounds nearly cover her scratchy voice.

"Laurel," I enunciate carefully. "Where are you, Maxie?"

"Something's wrong with my car."

Oh God, is she driving?

A loud honk blares, followed by screeching tires.

"I better take a look under the hood," Maxie mutters.

"No! Stay where you are." *Shit, shit, shit.* Heart galloping, I dash for my Beetle. "Where are you?"

Maxie's voice cracks. "I'm not sure."

I start my engine, set my phone on speaker, and pull onto the busy street. "Stay where you are. Just tell me what you see."

"Trees. Buildings. Cars."

"You gotta be more specific, Max."

"Oh look, there's Elmer."

A muffled male voice, then Maxie again, "Here. You tell her."

"Hello? Who's this?"

"It's Maxie's grandniece, Laurel."

"Oh, hey." His flirtatious grin comes through loud and clear. "What's Maxie doing here by herself? Her car's blocking the parking lot entrance."

"Could you please get her somewhere safe? I'll be right there."

He gives me the address. Thank God Maxie landed only a few blocks from home. Friday evening traffic is thick as magma. Despite my skittering pulse and shaky grip on the wheel, I make it across town in twenty minutes, kicking myself all the way for having left her alone for so long.

I spot the Raven's Gulch Taproom, a squat brick building with picnic benches out front and bikes clustered beside half-barrel planters. A long line of customers snakes toward a food truck parked at the curb.

Wrapped in her fuzzy yellow cardigan, Maxie is easy to spot. I park and jog to her table.

"Hey there." Grinning above his ginger beard, Elmer intercepts me, a pizza box in his hand.

I throw my arms around him. "Thank you," I murmur into his muscular shoulder.

"Whoa. Don't wanna drop Maxie's pizza."

"Sorry. I'm just so glad you saw her before she hurt herself."

He grins and shrugs, his long-lashed hazel eyes twinkling. "No bigs. She's a regular. Someone would've recognized her. Wish she wouldn't drive, though. Maybe it's time to, ya know, hide her keys."

"Absolutely." I slide into the seat opposite Maxie while Elmer sits beside her and opens the pizza box. "Olives, mushrooms, pesto, and extra cheese. Bon appétit." He plants a smooch on Maxie's cheek.

She giggles like a teenager. "Your beard tickles. Isn't he cute, Laurel? You should ask him out."

I roll my eyes. Elmer is awfully cute, with his mischievous grin and heavily inked, muscular arms, but after this morning's escapade, it'll take much more than a cute brewer to tempt me away from my new running partner.

"Maxie, I'm with Dalton, remember?"

"Who?"

"Ichabod."

"Oh, him." She takes a huge bite of pizza, smearing her chin with tomato sauce. "Mmm. Good."

Elmer helps himself to a slice. "Have some, Laurel."

Worry still clenches my stomach, but the tempting aroma of wood-fired crust and melted cheese soon revives my appetite. I inhale my slice while Elmer fetches more beer.

I wipe my greasy mouth and fold my hands on the wooden picnic table. "Maxie, you told me you didn't drive anymore."

She stares into her beer mug. "Guess I forgot. I was hungry."

"We have food in the house, for goodness' sake."

"I was bored, too. And lonely." She sighs, her eyes soft and watery. "I'm sorry, kiddo. I thought I could handle it." She pulls the Volvo keys from her pocket and presses them into my hand. "You hang onto these." She slurps her beer, foam settling into the lines around her thin lips. "This is really good. Promise me, once I'm moved into my new place, you'll bring me here on pizza night."

I squeeze her hand. "I promise, Max. And I'm sorry too. I should've checked on you sooner. It won't happen again."

The weight of my statement sinks in. Until Maxie moves into her apartment, I'll have to stay as close to home as possible. That won't leave much time for Dalton.

I check my phone. Another text, and a voice mail.

"Excuse me just a minute, Maxie. I'll be right over there." I point. "Don't leave, okay?"

Maxie nods, intent on her third slice of pizza. For such a skinny little woman, she sure has the appetite of a horse.

"Dalton? Hey, it's me."

"Laurel." His deep voice vibrates in my bones. "I was getting worried you'd changed your mind."

"About you?" I huff a laugh. "No, sir. You've been very much on my mind. The thing is, I got the chance to work on a couple of art projects I've been wanting to try, and then Maxie called. She decided to take a drive."

His voice tightens. "She okay?"

"She's fine, thank God. You know Raven's Gulch Brewery?"

"I'll be there in ten minutes."

Our pizza finished, mostly by Maxie, Elmer follows me to the food truck line. He drapes his beefy arm around me and points to the menu board. "You're too skinny, Laurel. Let's try the Fat Boy pizza, extra meat, extra cheese."

Too damn handsy, this guy. I stiffen and slid out of his grip.

"I think she's just right." Dalton's voice rumbles behind me. My jolt of surprise morphs into a full-body flush when he slides his arm around my waist. His eyes narrow. "Introduce me to your friend?"

Elmer raises both palms and steps away. "Hey, no offense, man."

Uh-oh. I return Dalton's embrace and kiss his tight mouth. "Dalton Garvey, this is Maxie's friend Elmer. He rescued her from the parking lot over there."

The two men exchange curt nods.

"I'll go check on her before I get back to work." Elmer slinks into the crowd.

Dalton raises one eyebrow. "He works here?"

"Yeah. Beer brewer and potter."

"Like Harry?"

"Like ceramics."

He scowls at Elmer's retreating back. "Didn't I see him at Willamette Grove yesterday?"

"He helped us move some boxes into Maxie's new apartment. You hungry?"

We order a large pizza with pepperoni, mushrooms, and Shishito peppers. Stepping aside to wait, he nestles behind me and winds his arms around my waist. "Maxie's trying to fix you up with that guy?"

I lower my voice, twist to face him, and lace my fingers behind his neck. "I'm with you, Dalton. You." I nuzzle the smooth skin below his ear. "This morning was so…"

"Mmm." He rocks his hips against me, just a tiny motion, but enough to speed my pulse and dampen my panties. "Amazing. Delicious. When can we try again, preferably without an audience?"

"That's the problem." I quickly relate Maxie's close call. "She got lonely, and off she went."

He strokes his short, golden beard. "She won't be lonely at Willamette Grove. When's her move-in date?"

"The tenth."

He ticks off on his fingers. "Today's the twenty-fourth. School starts on the fifth. That leaves us less than two weeks to entertain Maxie."

"You mean babysit her."

"Elder sit," he corrects me. "But, yeah. Maybe that Elmer guy will sign up for a turn."

We carry our steaming pizza to the table. "Thanks, man." Elmer helps himself to a slice and takes a big chomp. A thread of mozzarella clings to his flaming beard. "So, you guys coming to the vernissage tomorrow night?"

"Umm…" Dalton's forehead rumples.

I translate. "Opening night at a gallery exhibit. Lots of Maxie's artist friends will be there. Wanna come? There'll be wine. And snacks." I squeeze his leg under the table. "And me."

"I'm in." He lowers his voice. "But I'd rather be alone with you."

"Sorry. I promised Maxie. Maybe after?" I brush a kiss to his earlobe.

Elmer narrows his eyes and grunts, then presses his fuzzy face to Maxie's cheek. "Good to see you, Max." He moves back toward the taproom.

"Elmer, wait." I trot after him, thank him again, and explain my problem with leaving Maxie alone.

He strokes his beard. "I could bring her to the pottery studio for a while. Let me think about who else could help. We'll talk tomorrow." As he glances at Dalton, his lips stretch in a sly grin. "It was really good to see you, Laurel. I'm glad you came to Eugene." He ambles away.

Is he just teasing, or stirring up trouble for the fun of it?

After finishing our pizza, Dalton slides behind the wheel of Maxie's Volvo. "I'll walk back later and pick up my car."

"I'm riding with Ichabod," Maxie announces. "I got some questions for you, mister."

I bite my lip. I haven't told Dalton about my adventure in nude modeling. Will Maxie spill the beans?

Chapter Eighteen

♥

Dalton

"A triple date." Maxie cackles as I pull into her driveway. "Sure you can handle both of us?"

It's impossible not to love this sassy old sprite. No doubt, Laurel gets her spark from this side of her family, not from her tight-lipped, critical father.

"I'll do my best," I assure her as I open the passenger door and offer my arm.

Maxie titters like a middle schooler. "Classy, this guy," she tells Laurel, who's waiting beside the car. "Too bad he's not artistic, like us."

That's true enough. I'm about as far from artistic as Eugene is from Hong Kong.

"My sister got all the artistic talent, I'm afraid."

"And what did you get?" Maxie asks.

A wicked grin tilts Laurel's lips. Her gaze slides down to my crotch.

"I saw that," Maxie crows. "Good for you, Ichabod. Now, let's talk about my porch."

Blushing like a beet, I pace off the length of the porch. "About five yards." I probe a soft spot with my toe. "This needs shoring up. I've got some time this week."

Laurel grips my arm. "Oh Dalton, that's so much work."

I take her hand and weave our fingers together. "Hey, I can't entertain you with my artwork, but I can do this. Let me, okay?"

With a heart-melting smile, she leans her forehead on my shoulder. "Okay. Thank you."

Give me a steady supply of those smiles, and I'll rebuild the whole damn house.

"Bring him inside, Laurel. I want to see what you were working on all afternoon."

Her eyes flash. "Maxie, it's supposed to be a surprise."

Maxie turns in the doorway, the picture of feigned innocence. "Oops. You know how forgetful I am, dear."

"Fine." She huffs. "It's only fair, I guess." From her VW's back seat, she pulls a cardboard tube.

"Is this your art project?" I ask.

"One of them. The other's also a surprise, unless Maxie already told you."

She didn't, but now I'm intrigued.

The cottage has emptied considerably since my last visit. A stack of folded packing boxes leans against the flagstone fireplace. Most of the artwork is gone, leaving pale squares and rectangles on the walls.

"Moving day's getting closer," I murmur as Maxie clumps into the dining room, leaning on her cane.

Laurel sighs. "Yeah. It makes me sad to see her personality draining out of this place."

"You kids want some wine?" Maxie calls.

"No thanks," Laurel says. "Some of us have to run tomorrow morning."

"Wimp." Maxie grins up at me. "Dalton?"

"No thanks. I have to drive."

"You aren't staying here with Laurel?"

"Maxie," Laurel hisses. "Besides, it's just a single bed."

"Where there's a will, there's a way." She prods Laurel with her fancy cane. "Okay, show time."

"Right." She pops the plastic cap off the cardboard tube. "I hope you like it, Dalton." The hopeful tilt of her eyebrows makes me resolve to like it, whether it's any good or not.

It is good. Really good. Her poster for the charity race shows a solitary runner in three-quarter profile, sprinting away from the camera into a rainbow-hued sunset. Glowing rays vibrate around him in the psychedelic style of 1960s pop art. Cartoonish lettering announces *Run for the Arts*, along with the race's date, time, location, sponsors, etc. Artistic, eye-catching, easy to read. The runner looks more like a painting than a photo, with his impossibly long legs, his determined jaw, his shiny shaved head...

Holy shit. "Is this me?"

She nods, her grin sheepish. "Do you mind?"

I hold the poster at arm's length, then up close. "How did you do this?"

"Margot helped me. She studies graphic design, and she—"

"But I don't look like this. This guy's—"

She stops me with a soft touch on my arm. "Dalton, this is exactly how I see you."

Now, I hold no illusions about my looks. Gawky, too tall, with huge feet, and bald to boot, I've never drawn a woman with my appearance. But Laurel has transformed my image into a work of art. A bubble of emotion rises in my throat: gratitude, wonder, admiration, and something else I can't quite name, something that makes my eyes prickle and my chest tingle.

I carefully set the poster down, then stroke my thumbs over her cheekbones, beneath those sparkling gray eyes, and I kiss her, slow and sweet.

She rests her chin on my collar bone. "You're okay if I submit this for the race poster competition?"

My voice comes out raspy. "More than okay. I'm honored."

Maxie raps the table with her cane. "Tell him about the other thing."

She stiffens. "Not now, Max."

"You made something else?"

"No." She takes a deep breath and softens. "It's just a class. If it turns out well, I'll show you when it's done, okay?"

"Okay." I smooch her forehead. There's no reason to push her. We've only spent a short time together, and already I can tell she's not a person who opens up easily. And that's fine. We've got...damn, only until Christmas.

"What a fun day." Maxie rises. "I'm pooped. Gonna have a nice, hot bath before bed."

"G'night, Maxie." Laurel pecks her cheek.

A moment later, the strains of salsa music drift from down the hall. Laurel steers me toward the couch and settles beneath my outstretched arm. A shuddering groan in the wall makes me jump.

She laughs. "The plumbing needs work too."

"You're staying here after Maxie moves?"

"I guess." She stretches her long legs and crosses her ankles. "I love this place, but it won't be the same without her."

Nuzzling her temple, I inhale the fresh, flowery scent of her hair. "It has good bones. Like you. I could help you fix it up."

"Won't you be busy with school and coaching?"

I sigh. "I love my work, but it does gobble most of my time."

She strokes my scalp, her touch light and soothing. "Will you be too tired to run with me in the evenings?"

"Maybe, but I'll do it anyway." I brush my lips across her mouth, her nose, her closed eyelids, her throat. Tingling energy vibrates wherever I touch her. She feels it too, because she purrs and shifts closer. I scoop her legs across my lap, keeping one hand on her thigh while I caress her hair and kiss her deeply, learning her mouth with each stroke and slide. When I cup the delicious softness of her breast, she moans and arches into my touch. My pulse picks up speed, a drummer urging me to go further, faster, *now*.

But the sofa is way too small to accommodate the passionate embrace of two tall people. Laurel squirms beneath me and cants her hips against my erection, arousing a primitive urge to thrust, to claim this woman. All we need is a little time, a little privacy...

"All day," she whispers. "All day, I thought of you. Wanted you. This is crazy, Dalton."

"I know. Crazy fast. Crazy good." I roll my hips, and she shudders like those aged pipes. My aching cock clamors for release.

"Ay ay ay, cómo te quiero..." Maxie's scratchy voice warbles from the bathroom.

We both quiver with hushed laughter.

"Her timing is impeccable," I murmur into Laurel's silky hair.

"Yeah, she loves her salsa music." She tugs my shirt from my waistband and slides her hands beneath.

I rock against her in rhythm with the music. Her breath stutters.

"I feel like I'm in high school," she whispers, and her nails rake my back, a sharp, delicious sensation.

"Two more weeks." I nudge her T-shirt up and nibble her lace bra. "Once she moves into Willamette Grove, we'll have time. And space. And privacy."

"I can't wait two weeks." Grasping my arm, she rolls me on top of her, so we're pressed together from lips to loins. Her long legs around my waist, she grinds her pussy against me, nearly tumbling us off the narrow couch and onto the floor.

"I want you so much, Dalton." Her breath heats my throat. Her hands clutch my hips. My throbbing need demands I push inside her, fast and hard, before Maxie emerges from her bath.

Do I have a condom? I meant to slip one into my wallet, but I left the house in such a hurry—I can't recall, can't think, can only feel, and taste, and want.

"Ow!" A big splash, then another. "Laurel, help!"

I scramble to my feet, and Laurel bolts down the hallway, tugging her shirt down as she runs.

"Maxie?" She rattles the knob. Eyes wide, she beckons. "Maxie, the door's locked."

The squawks continue, interspersed with blubs and splashes. Laurel's panicked expression hits me like a bucket of ice water.

"Stand back." The narrow hallway doesn't leave much room to build momentum. With a whispered prayer, I lurch forward and slam my shoulder into the door.

"Shit," I hiss through clenched teeth. Doors from the 1920s are solid oak, not the flimsy hollow-core stuff used today. And the doorknob has a key slot, too. Why didn't I notice? Oh yeah, the screaming. Plus, all the blood that normally services my brain was tied up further south. "Get me a flat-tip screwdriver. Or a steak knife."

While she rummages noisily through drawers, I press my ear to the door. "We're coming, Maxie."

"Ow," she yelps.

"Here." Laurel presses a screwdriver into my hand. I insert the blade into the slot and jiggle until it finally turns. I'm about to charge into the room when she yanks me back. "Let me."

I almost barged in on a naked ninety-year-old!

Laurel's tight voice echoes on the tiles. "Maxie, what happened?"

Muffled conversation follows, along with a sob. A moment later, Laurel emerges, her arms around a damp, quivering Maxie, wrapped in a too-big terrycloth robe, her thin red hair plastered to her scalp.

"Let's get you an ice pack," Laurel murmurs as she guides her great-aunt into the kitchen. "You too, Dalton."

With calm efficiency, she scoops ice cubes into freezer bags, wraps them in kitchen towels, and applies one to Maxie's pale, mottled shin, another to my aching shoulder.

Maxie wipes her nose on her sleeve and explains how she'd been reaching for her bath salts when she accidentally knocked the handle all the way to hot, scalded herself, slipped, and dunked her head. "Got a big snootful of water. Guess I panicked."

"All the safety bars and non-skid mats in the world won't help if you don't use common sense, Max," Laurel grumbles. "Thank God I was home."

Maxie snuffles. "I just wanted a nice bath. My new place has one of those walk-in tubs. You can't stretch out in those." She seems to shrink under Laurel's scolding glare. "I'll miss my bath. One more thing I have to give up."

"Oh, Maxie." Laurel's voice quavers. She gathers her aunt into her arms, and they rock together, weeping softly.

The tears prickling my eyes have nothing to do with my sore shoulder. I clear my throat. "I should probably take off."

Laurel glances up, her beautiful eyes puffy and red. "See you tomorrow morning, I hope. Would you take the poster, just in case?"

"Of course. Good night, Maxie."

"Good night, Ichabod. Thanks for rescuing me."

"Anytime."

I shut the front door, lean on it, and sigh. Dizzy, frustrated, giddy, sad—how to name this emotion vibrating my bones? Only ten days since we met, but already Laurel has slid beneath my ribs and filled all my aching, empty spaces with tingling heat. Scary fast, scary good. And for some bizarre reason, she wants me as much as I want her. Tonight, if it weren't for Maxie, we'd have tasted paradise.

But Maxie's here—so dear to Laurel, so vulnerable. Maxie has to come first.

"Two more weeks," I whisper.

Chapter Nineteen

♥

Laurel

Arnie elbows his way through the crowd of runners. "Hot coffee, coming through. Shift your skinny butts, people." He sets the tray in front of Maxie, perched on his cushiest armchair. "Here we go, ma'am. This mob will clear out in a minute. Then you and I can shoot the shi—I mean, breeze."

She flashes me a merry grin. "Oh, I like this fella. You should tell Davonte about him."

That's my Maxie—stubbornly single, but a matchmaker at heart.

Back at the counter, someone dings the old-fashioned reception bell.

"No rest for the wicked." Arnie hustles away.

Maxie sips her cappuccino. "Your runner friends are so colorful. Like a tree full of parrots."

She's right about that. We're surrounded by every shade of running gear from hottest pink to acid green to road-cone orange. Clara's violent yellow top gives her face a greenish cast.

Standing next to my boss, Dalton furrows his brow and beckons. I trot over to join them.

"Clara's not feeling well," he tells me.

"May I?" I press my hand to her pale brow. "No fever. In fact, you're a little clammy."

She winces and hugs her middle. "Clams. Ooo, that's probably it. We had pasta with clam sauce last night. Must've got a bad one. I'll call Nick."

Dalton nods. "Just a short run today since we have the 10K tomorrow. We'll be back in plenty of time to open."

Clara claps her hand over her mouth. She fumbles with the lock on the glass door connecting the bookshop and café, tosses me the keys, and bolts toward the restroom.

I wince. "Poor Clara."

"Attention, please. Voting closes in five minutes." Dalton's friend Marcus points to the bulletin board holding the three poster entries for Run for the Arts.

Stage fright speeds my pulse.

Dalton slings his arm around me and presses a kiss to my temple. "Want to check out the others?"

"Sure." We move to the bulletin board where they're displayed. One poster is mostly text, arranged on a hot pink background with a border of artist's palettes. Fine, but not especially eye-catching. The other features a pair of running shoes superimposed beneath a photo of the Rainbow Art Center. I bite my lip to tame my grin. For the first time I can recall, my artwork shines!

The club choses my poster by a landslide. As we gather on the sidewalk, they heap me with praise and thanks until I have hide my flushed face against Dalton's chest before I burst into happy flames.

"Proud of you, babe," he murmurs.

I'm someone's babe. And an artist.

I yank on my inner reins. One little hit of validation doesn't make me an artist—just an amateur photographer who got a lucky shot. And this thing with Dalton can never be more than a short-lived fling.

Still, giddy energy propels me through our Saturday run.

Too winded for conversation, I relax into the effort and enjoy the summer breeze, the fluttering leaves overhead, and the tempting view of Dalton's muscular behind flexing with each step. I finish our three-mile run at the front of the pack, ahead of the other women.

"Careful now," Dalton pants beside me. "Save something for tomorrow."

"Piece of cake." I swat his butt as we trot to a stop. "Six measly miles. I'll be right on your tail the whole time." Coffee Dreams' doorway bell tinkles a welcome. Inside, the place is library-quiet, with only a few college students clicking away on laptops.

A worry-mouse nibbles my gut. "Where's Maxie?"

"Probably in the restroom." Dalton checks his watch. "I'll go home and change, then stop back to check on you."

"Thanks, Dalton. You're the best." I smooch his sweaty cheek.

He purrs into my ear, "Actually, you don't know that yet."

A hot flush washes over me and settles at the apex of my thighs. After making sure no one's watching, I squeeze a big handful of his ass. "I'm looking forward to finding out."

The restroom door opens, and a young mother emerges, pushing a stroller.

That mouse of worry morphs into a large, ravenous rat. "Arnie, where's Maxie?"

He raises one perfectly groomed eyebrow. "Calm down, cupcake. She went to look after Clara. Nick picked them both up."

"Thank God. Is Clara okay?"

He wrinkles his nose. "Puked up her toenails. She sends her apologies about the restroom. Guess it needs a touch-up before you open."

Armed with latex gloves, a bottle of disinfectant, and a jumbo can of air freshener, I clean the bookshop's little WC, breathing through my mouth the whole time. Finished, I venture a sniff. Piney lilacs, with no hint of puke. But only fifteen minutes until opening, not enough time to get home and shower. Crap. That means working in my running shorts until Clara returns.

Ten minutes later, Dalton arrives looking crisp in khakis and a sky-blue polo shirt that brightens the color of his eyes. He ties on a Book Nirvana apron. "I'll man the fort while you go change."

"You, sir, are a peach." I hug him tightly.

"More like a nectarine." He rubs his freshly shaved scalp.

After a speedy shower, I return to find Dalton sprawled on a beanbag chair, reading to dark- haired twin preschoolers. He punctuates his narrative with comical gestures and sound effects, his deep voice booming. "Stanley the steam shovel scoops up a big mouthful of yummy dirt and rocks. Nom, nom, nom."

The twins giggle and roll on the carpet. At the counter, their mother waits with a stack of romance paperbacks. "He's good with kids," she remarks. "I bet he's a great dad."

"He's a teacher," I tell her, "but he doesn't have kids of his own."

She flashes a knowing grin. "Not yet. Mark my words. He's a natural."

Another peal of laughter from the kids' corner. On all fours, Dalton pushes the beanbag chair with his head. "Barny the bulldozer puuushed the big pile of rocks." He grunts comically.

Whooping with glee, both boys tackle him.

Their mother hurries to rescue him. "Now, now, let the poor man get up."

My conscience wipes the grin off my face. The woman is right—Dalton is a natural with kids. He deserves a partner who'll stay in Eugene and build a family with him. I'm distracting him from his true path. If it weren't for the chemistry pulling us together like an industrial-strength electromagnet, I'd never pick a guy like Dalton. Sweet, dependable, generous, outdoorsy...

Shit. Except for not being an artist, he's pretty much perfect. Leaving him in December is going to be damned painful.

But that's my M.O., right? When the going gets rough, I run. This time, it's not Dad's voice nagging me, it's my own.

Still, I've been honest with him. He knows about my plans, and he's not holding back. Why should I? Why deny myself his friendship and a physical connection of volcanic proportions?

Because I'm messing with his heart, that's why. And my own.

When the mom herds her twins out the front door, I squeeze my eyes shut and tense as if I'm about to dive into icy water. I have to tell him, right now, before he kisses me again and I lose this moment of clarity. He steps around the counter and drapes his comfortable arm over my shoulders.

"Cute little monsters, aren't they?"

I turn to face him. "Dalton, I think we're making a mistake here."

His happy grin slides right off. He grasps my arms and runs his big hands up and down, as if warming me from a chill. "What do you mean?"

Already, the physical contact is blurring my best intentions like ink in the rain.

"You. Those kids. You deserve better." Tears prickle my eyes, and my traitorous voice quivers. "You deserve someone steady, someone who'll stay here. With you. And build a family." I swipe a tear and force myself to continue. "Not some flake like me who's just going to leave you, and..."

"Hey." He squeezes my arms. "Look at me, Laurel."

The tenderness in his blue eyes quiets my blubbering.

"You've been honest with me. I'm not complaining. And I'll tell you a secret." He pulls me against his chest and rubs soothing circles on my back. "I'm hoping you'll change your mind. If you don't, well, you know what they say. Better to have loved and lost than never to have loved at all."

Love. He said love. I shiver in his arms, afraid to look at him, afraid to speak.

I loved once, with my whole heart, but it turned out I was only a placeholder until Carlo graduated from college and returned to his high school sweetheart and his cozy hometown that held no room for an artistic weirdo like me.

Mom loved once, and it nearly killed her.

Dalton loved his ex-wife, and he's still recovering from their split. Rebound relationships never last, and...

"Besides," he murmurs into my hair. "I never said I wanted kids. I get my kid fix at work."

I've seen his easy rapport with those twins, with his friend's little girl. But it's not my place to challenge him on this.

"And I'm not dreaming of white picket fences, either." He lifts my chin. "Okay?"

I sniff and nod. "Okay."

I want to believe him so badly, I'm willing to risk it. If I'm strong enough to endure everything I've been through up till now, I'm strong enough to guard my heart.

The doorbell chimes, and Clara walks in with Maxie on her arm. Clara glows pink and healthy, as if she hadn't spewed her guts up a few hours ago. "Hey, Dalton." She gives him a quick hug, then spins him to untie his apron and pull it over her own head. "Thanks for stepping in. I hope you didn't..." She gestures toward the restroom.

"I took care of it." I cringe inwardly at the easy intimacy between my new boyfriend and his old lover.

Clara flashes a sheepish grin. "Thank you, Laurel. I'm really, really sorry about that."

"Feeling better?" Dalton asks.

"Yeah." She shrugs. "It was the strangest thing. Once I threw up, I felt just fine. Energized, even."

Leaning on her cane, Maxie grins. "Better get one of those sticks you pee on."

Clara's eyes bug out. "No. It couldn't be. Not at my age…"

Having blown poor Clara's mind, Maxie turns to Dalton. "Give a girl a ride home?"

"Sure." He fishes his keys from his pocket. "We'll take a look at that porch of yours."

"What a peach, this guy." Reaching as high as she can, Maxie pinches his cheek.

Before leaving, he pulls me into a side-hug and whispers, "Is this a dressy thing tonight?"

"Um, a little. I guess. You never can tell with artists."

Maxie chatters like a sparrow as she and Dalton make their slow way out.

I scoot behind the counter to help the boss unload a box of books. "I'm glad you're feeling better, Clara. Guess it really was just a bad clam."

Her dreamy expression floats somewhere between wonder and confusion. "Yeah, I guess. I'll…" She drifts toward her desk, rubbing the back of her neck.

"I know how you feel," I mutter. Already emotionally wrung out, I have a long day of work ahead of me, then a fancy date with Dalton and Maxie—my first introduction to Eugene's art scene, besides posing for Agatha. Even though I'm not planning to stay, this opportunity feels important, and I really want to make a good impression. You never know which connections might prove to be crucial.

Chapter Twenty

♥

Dalton

I straighten my tie in the rearview mirror. Then loosen it. Then tighten it. Cupping my hand over my nose and mouth, I check my breath for traces of the tuna sandwich I gobbled for dinner, then pop another mint, just to be sure. I haven't been this nervous since my junior prom. This event at the art gallery feels like a test I haven't studied for.

Earlier, while measuring Maxie's front porch, I quiz her on how to dress, what to say, what to do, but as the afternoon wore on, she became more and more vague, jumping from one topic to another like a grasshopper fleeing a lawnmower.

"Just wear something nice," she told me, patting my hand. "Put a little personality into it."

Personality is sorely lacking in my wardrobe. At work, I default to khakis or jeans, with Oxford shirts or polos. Ties come out only for open house and graduation. Fortunately, Marcus and I wear the same size. Decked out in my best friend's deep blue dress shirt, paisley tie, and charcoal slacks, I feel like a kid playing dress-up. But Destiny assured me I look suave.

I hope Laurel agrees.

"Knock 'em dead," I mutter to my reflection before pushing up from my car, stiff and sore after four hours of hauling and cutting lumber. I bet Laurel gives a killer back rub. I'd rather spend the evening stretched out with her on Maxie's couch—better yet, on my bed. How sweet it would be, her hands kneading my muscles, her long hair falling like a curtain around her beautiful face, tickling my bare skin...

Later. If I'm lucky. First, I have to show my appreciation for her art world. That's my best chance at keeping her here in Eugene. Probably my only chance.

A near-stranger answers the door, her blond hair upswept in a complicated knot, her eyes thickly lined in black, her lips glittering with goo. The neckline of her short, slinky dress slides off one shoulder. Her feet are strapped into towering, painful-looking sandals, like a Roman gladiator in drag.

I blink in stupid surprise, then force my mouth into a smile. "Wow, you look—wow."

She tugs her dress over her thighs and shifts on those ridiculous shoes. "You too, Dalton. Great tie."

Maxie calls from the living room, "Come in, sweetheart." What a sight she is tonight, with glittery spray in her sparse hair, a sequined T-shirt dress thingy, and her boney chest piled high with massive necklaces. She takes my hand and spins me around like her dance partner. "Don't you look dapper! See how handsome he is, Laurel?"

"Very handsome." She plants a sticky kiss on my cheek. I wait until she's not looking to wipe it off.

"And what do you think of your girlfriend now?" Maxie's clearly not shy about fishing for compliments.

"Very, uh, fancy." I'm a lousy liar, always have been, and Laurel looks like a villainess from a science fiction movie, all shiny and hard and a bit scary.

Maxie excuses herself to fetch her purse, leaving us alone in the living room. Like a wobbly baby giraffe, Laurel totters to the mirror by the front door and sighs at her reflection. "It's too much, isn't it? I was going for avant-garde chic, but..." She plucks at a strand of hair stuck to her forehead.

Stepping behind her, I place my hands on her shoulders. "You're beautiful no matter what you wear. I've just never seen you this—done up."

"I look ridiculous." With a cluck of her tongue, she tugs at the pins anchoring her hair.

"May I?" I carefully pull out a pin. One silky curl tumbles free, settling against her bare back. One by one, I remove the others until her hair lies in messy waves. I press my face into the wheat-blond silk and inhale her fresh scent. "Simple. Beautiful. You."

Her sparkly face relaxes into a smile. Turning, she winds her arms around my neck and moves in for a kiss.

"One more thing." I brush the corner of her mouth with my fingertip and hold it up for her to see. "Sticky."

"Okay, okay." Laughing, she wipes her lips on the back of her hand, leaving a glittery snail trail. "Better?" When I nod, she kisses me. Thoroughly.

My hands slide over her slippery dress to rest on her hips. Her throaty purr sends a bolt of anticipation right to my groin.

"Thanks for coming, Dalton. This really means a lot to me."

I remember her words in the bookshop: "You deserve someone better...someone who'll stay here with you." Wrapped in her arms, I know deep in my bones there is no one better. Not for me. And if I have to dress up and go to fancy parties to keep her here, well, it's a very small price to pay. I stroke the enticing silk of her bare back and kiss her again, slow and soft and—

"Ay ay ay. You two. First the show. Then the kissing." Maxie prods me with her cane. "Let's go."

·♥·♥·♥·♥·♥·

Broadway is packed, so I drop Maxie and Laurel in front of the gallery and park two blocks away. When I return, I push through the noisy crowd and find them chatting with that smarmy, red-bearded guy from the brewery. At least he's not hanging all over Laurel this time, but he damn sure looks like he wants to. I note with satisfaction how, in her stratospheric high heels, Laurel towers over him. I allow myself a tiny inward gloat when she winds her arm through mine and tells him, "You remember my boyfriend, Dalton."

Elmer's grin lifts on one side as he eyes my tie. In jeans and flannel shirt, sleeves rolled to his elbows to show off his tattoos, he looks far more comfortable than I feel.

"Shall we go up?" Laurel nods toward the entrance.

At the landing, a pink-haired person checks our IDs, even Maxie's, then stamps our hands. "Champagne's over there, by the installation."

"Hoo-boy, bubbly," Maxie cackles.

The echo of conversation nearly drowns out the electronic music. With polished cement floors, bare brick walls, and futuristic neon lights, the space feels more like a nightclub than an art gallery. Art fans crowd around paintings hung on the walls, sculptures mounted on white pedestals, and mobiles dangling from the ceiling. Most guests wear jeans and casual shirts, making me feel like an overdressed bumpkin.

We find a bar set up beside the "installation," a hip-high mini-Stonehenge on a low dais. Instead of stones, the artist glued together packing peanuts, painted to resemble granite. Laurel and Maxie bend to examine the thing while I collect plastic glasses of sparkling wine. Booze in hand, Maxie totters off.

Laurel scrunches her face and paces a slow circle around the sculpture. "Intriguing choice."

More like some kid's history-fair project. "Do people buy things like this?"

"Probably not," she admits, "but it's fun. Draws people in, you know?" She sips her wine and grimaces. "Too sweet."

"You sold stuff like this in Portland?"

"Even weirder." She grins. "Once, we had this sculpture of a hairy naked fat guy, totally made of rusty barbed wire and twinkle lights."

"And...that's what you want to do? For a career?"

I recognize my mistake as soon as the words slip from my mouth.

Laurel's lips tighten. Her eyes narrow. "Yes. Absolutely."

Backpedal. Fast.

"I, uh, I mean, it's all very interesting, but not what I usually imagine when I think of art."

She seizes my arm, her eyes sparkling with evangelical fervor. "That's just it, Dalton. We need to expand the definition of art. Make it more experiential. More exploratory. More inclusive."

"Uh huh. Absolutely." *I have no idea what you're talking about.* But the glow on her face could light the room.

She softens her tone. "Don't worry. Most art galleries earn their bread and butter from more conventional stuff. Like this." She leads me to a canvas covered with wide swaths of bright reds and oranges, dotted with black and white.

I squint at it, back up, and squint again. "Reminds me of a campfire."

She chuckles. "Abstract artists hate it when you say that."

"Campfire?"

"No, silly." She slides her arm around my waist. "It's supposed to communicate a feeling, not a concrete object."

"Ah. Okay." I pull her closer and gaze at the canvas. "It reminds me of how I feel when you kiss me."

"Very good." She smooches my cheek. "And this one?" She indicates a canvas the size of a garage door, painted in streaks of deep blue.

"This is how I feel when you're not around."

"Awww," she purrs into my ear. "Excellent answer."

I nuzzle her nape. Maybe I can learn to enjoy modern art, especially if it makes Laurel horny.

Maxie interrupts, as usual. "Laurel, come see Elmer's sculpture."

Laurel doesn't miss my eye roll. "Come on," she urges with a teasing laugh. "He's Maxie's friend. Just a quick peek."

I paste on a smile and follow her through the crowd.

A dozen heavily inked art fans gather around Elmer's display, mostly ceramic beer mugs decorated with funny faces. In the center sits a large urn glazed in greens, blues, and earth tones. A gleaming river of iridescent paint winds up and around, finally disappearing inside. On its banks, tiny, sculpted bikers, runners, parents with strollers, kids on skateboards, dog-walkers, an artist with an easel—everyone you'd see on a sunny day along the Willamette. On the lip of the vessel, a pair of children hold hands and grin as if daring each other to jump.

Fucking brilliant. Jealousy stabs my gut. I can barely draw a stick figure. With her passion for art, how am I going to hold Laurel's attention while the other guy sniffing her butt can make this?

"What do you think?" Maxie beams up at me. There's nothing for it. I have to say something complimentary or I'll come off as a pouty, jealous asshole—exactly how I feel.

"It's, uh, really good. Lots of detail."

Maxie nods. "Elmer's gonna let me visit his studio and make something outta clay. I'm thinking a mermaid for my new bathroom. She can hold the soap." She lifts her glasses, dangling from a beaded chain, onto her nose. Peering up into my face, she purses her thin lips. "You okay, hon'?"

Are all the women in Laurel's family this sharp-eyed?

I force a nonchalant grin. "Me? Oh, I'm fine."

Leaning on her cane, Maxie taps her foot. "I'm not buyin' it. You look tense. Too much running, not enough smooching. Say, where'd Laurel get off to?"

I spot her beside the mugs, talking to Elmer, hands dancing and swooping in animated discussion that ends with a loud laugh from his red-bearded mouth.

My face heats. "Excuse me, Maxie." I step up beside Laurel and put my hand on her waist.

"Oh, there you are." She gives me a sweet smile, as if she wasn't just heaping praise on my rival. "Elmer was just telling me about an art fair next month."

Elmer's grin edges toward smugness. "Yeah, same day as that Run for the Arts thing. Hope to finish my next project by then."

Yeah, well, Laurel will be running that day. Not admiring your art. Or your beard. I stroke my jaw. Should I let my beard grow longer?

"See you later, Elmer." She flashes a conspiratorial grin. "And thanks for, you know." She tugs me back into the crowd.

"Thanks for what?"

"He's lining up some of his artist friends to visit Maxie while I'm at work. So far, he's got her covered through next week."

Okay, maybe he's not a total asshole.

"So—" She laces her fingers through mine. "What do you think of the gallery?"

My spine stiffens. "It's, uh, very interesting."

"Hey." As sharp-eyed as her great-aunt, Laurel notices my discomfort and gently massages my rigid shoulder. "You're being a really good sport. I know this isn't your thing."

"Not yet." I give her hand a squeeze. "You keep showing me how your art world works. I may be slow, but I'll get it eventually."

She taps her pursed lips. "Okay, art appreciation 101. You ready?"

I nod. Truly, I'm ready to get out of here, but if it makes Laurel happy, I'll do my best to get with the program.

She sweeps her hand in a flourish, taking in the whole crowded space. "Show me your favorite piece."

I wrap my arms around her waist and turn us both in a slow circle, considering all the possibilities. Finally, I point at a pedestal near the entrance. "There."

I guide her to a wire and metal sculpture of a tree. No leaves, just finely textured bark, branches, and twigs. With my forefinger, I trace its shape from root to tip.

"See how it seems to move? This reminds me of those coastal pines at Cannon Beach. The wind bends and sculpts them until they're like twisted old men and women, all gnarled and full of character. This is the one I'd buy."

I check the price tag and whistle. "If I won the lottery."

She hugs my waist, her eyes sparkling with unspoken promise. "You have excellent taste, Dalton."

I cup her jaw with both hands. "I fell for you, didn't I?"

She tilts her head, brushes her lips over mine, and sighs. All around us, laughter and conversation fade into background noise as my focus narrows to her eyes, her voice, her breath.

Until a familiar form catches my eye, making me stiffen in Laurel's arms. And not in a fun way.

"Well, well," Tiffany's nasal voice drawls. "This is the last place I'd expect to find you."

Chapter Twenty-One

♥

Laurel

Dalton's whole face shutters as he turns toward the rude interloper. I curl my hand around his bicep, hoping he feels my support, but I'm not sure he even registers my touch. He stands stiff and tense, planted in front of me like a roadblock.

Clinging to the arm of an Armani-suited guy in his fifties, a petite, curvy brunette regards us, her glossy lips quirked to one side. Very pretty, thick makeup, impressive cleavage framed by a little black dress. Malevolence flashes in her dark eyes.

Dalton slides his arm around my shoulders. "Let's get out of here."

"Yeah, run away, Dalton," the woman sneers.

"Come on, Tiff. No need for that." Mr. Armani attempts to turn her away, but she stands her ground like a feisty little terrier.

"He's a big boy. He can take it." She toys with her necklace, a silvery tassel tipped with sparkly stones. Zircons? Judging from her companion's polish, those rocks are probably the real thing.

Dalton's eyes narrow. His nostrils flare. His jaw muscles bunch. Damn, he's hot when he's angry.

Squashing that unhelpful thought, I slide my arm through his and murmur, "You okay?"

His words come out in a whispered growl. "My ex-wife."

"Ah." This staring contest is getting boring. Might as well take the bitch by the horns. I force a broad smile and step forward, my hand extended. "You must be Tiffany. I'm Laurel."

While Tiffany looks me up and down, I toss my hair. *That's right, he's my man now. You had your turn, and you blew it. Move along.*

But instead of backing down, Tiffany puffs out her chest. "You're wasting your time here, honey." She waves her pointy-nailed fingers. "He can't afford any of this."

"Always shopping, aren't you, Tiff?" Dalton slides his arm down to my waist. "We're here to check out the art scene. Laurel's new in town." He presses a kiss to my hair. "She's an artist."

Mayday! A blush scorches my cheeks. Dalton probably means well, but he has no idea what it takes to earn that label. The artists in this room have trained, paid their dues, and people actually pay money for their creations. A lot of money. Nothing I've made comes close to their level. How can he not see the difference?

"An artist, eh?" Tiffany's companion assumes the same posture as Dalton, claiming his woman. "I'm Larry, Tiffany's fiancé." He emphasizes that last word and tugs Tiffany against his side.

"Pleased to meet you." I manage a tight smile.

"What sort of art do you do?" Larry asks.

"Oh, this and that..."

"Photography," Dalton inserts. "She's very good."

Larry nods as if he's buying this nonsense. "I look forward to seeing your work, Laurel." Still clutching Tiffany's waist, he backs away. "Let's go get some wine, babe."

Dalton glares after them as they move toward the bar.

"Hey." I grasp his arm and spin him to face me. "Why did you say that?"

He blinks as if awakening from a blackout. "Say what?"

"That I'm an artist."

"Because you are."

I huff my hair from my eyes. "Don't put me on the spot, okay?"

"But I just—"

"Your ex is an asshole. I get it. But taking one nice photo doesn't make me an artist."

Dalton's forehead rumples as if he's working a difficult math problem. "I wasn't exaggerating, Laurel. You're very talented."

Before I can explain why his compliment pushed all my buttons, Maxie totters up. "I'm pooped, kids. Let's go."

"Sure, I'll, uh…" Dalton squints at me, worry etched all over his face. "I'll go get the car." He slides away through the crowd.

I release a shaky sigh. "Did you have fun, Maxie?"

"You betcha. I visited with lots of my friends." She pats my arm as we start toward the door. "Remember that when you're old, kiddo. Always have young friends. Keeps you from getting boring."

We've almost reached the entrance when Tiffany slithers across our path, a gleam of challenge in her beady eyes. She ignores Maxie, never a good idea, and rises on tiptoe to hiss at me, "Take it from me, honey. Dalton's boring. No ambition." She quirks a snarky grin. "Or maybe you're just after his big dick."

"How rude." Maxie slams the tip of her sparkly cane on Tiffany's toes.

While Dalton's ex squeals and hops, Maxie tows me toward the door. "Let's get outta here before they sic the bouncer on us."

Covering my astonished giggle with one hand, I elbow my way to the exit, towing Maxie behind me.

"Watch it," Maxie calls, "Old lady, coming through." On the sidewalk, she fixes me with a sharp look. "Dalton's a nice fella. Are you just after his big dick, like she said?"

Mortified, I duck my head. "Maxie, please."

"Nothing wrong with a little fling, but I think he's pretty serious about you. You're not leading him on, are you?"

Dalton's arrival saves me from having to answer. He helps Maxie into the back seat, then spears me with his pained gaze. "Look, I'm really sorry about Tiffany, but I don't understand why you got so upset about being called an artist."

"I'm not mad, Dalton, it's just—" I step closer, trying to wrap words around my flaming insecurity, when my left foot slides off the curb and into the gutter. A split second too late, he reaches for me, but I crash down like a Jenga tower. A hot stab of pain slices up my leg. "Ow. Crap. Stupid shoes."

"Here, let me help you."

Clutching his arm, I gingerly try leaning my weight onto my left foot, but it buckles.

Dalton eases me into the passenger seat and crouches beside me. "That ankle doesn't look good. Let's get you out of these." He unfastens the straps of my mega-high heels and slides them off. "Why did you wear them, anyway?"

Pain and embarrassment tighten my voice. "I was *trying* to look *elegant.*"

Gently cradling my heel, he examines my swollen ankle. "Why not just be yourself? You're stunning, Laurel."

Wincing, I snap, "You don't understand what a woman has to do to be taken seriously as a gallerist. I can't just schlump around like an artist can."

He gently squeezes my calf. "Maybe you're not a gallerist at heart. Maybe you're one of them." He flaps a hand toward the gallery. "Seriously, you lit up like Christmas in there. Those are your people." His smile shimmers with good intentions, but he just doesn't get it.

My voice cracks as tears blur my vision. "I'm not an artist, Dalton! Don't you think I've tried? I love art more than anything, and I suck at it."

He closes his eyes and runs his hand over his scalp. His chest rises and falls in a deep inhalation. "Okay. I'm sorry if I overstepped."

I'm crying in earnest now, tears dribbling down my cheeks. So much for the smoky eye effect I spent half an hour perfecting. I must look like a raccoon.

"Sorry for snapping." As if I weren't embarrassed enough, now I've got the hiccups. "Can you take me home, please?"

"Of course." Dalton lifts my injured leg into the car, then climbs behind the wheel. It's fully dark now, but the streets are buzzing with people streaming downtown to enjoy the bars and restaurants—while I slink home to ice my stupid ankle because I fell off my stupid shoes.

It's not Dalton's fault, damn it. Why did I have to bark at him?

I sneak a sideways glance. He grips the wheel, jaw firm, eyes on the road—and off me.

What a crappy way to end what I hoped would be a special evening. I was so eager to show him my world, but everything's crumpled into bad slapstick comedy.

In the ten minutes it takes to get home, Maxie falls asleep, snoring in the back seat.

"We're home, Maxie," Dalton says in a gentle voice. She blinks up at him. "What? Who?"

I lean over the seat back. "It's us, Maxie. Laurel and Dalton. You remember Dalton? He's fixing your porch?"

Maxie rubs her head, making her hair stand up in wispy spikes. "Of course. The fella with the big willy."

He grimaces but says nothing as he helps Maxie up the steps and into the house. I struggle to my feet and hop toward the porch, hissing with pain each time my left foot touches the ground.

Dalton trots back down the stairs. "For God's sake, let me help you."

His impatient tone makes me bristle. "I've got it." I grasp the railing and try hopping up the steps. Bad idea. "Ow, shit."

With an exasperated eye roll, Dalton scoops me up and carries me into the house as if I weigh—well, far less than I do. He sets me on the couch. "Now stay put while I get you some ice."

"Bossy," I grumble, secretly impressed and a bit turned on by his he-man display of strength.

He returns with a plastic bag of ice cubes and a kitchen towel. Sitting beside me, he pulls my ankle onto his lap and drapes the ice pack over it. "Not too swollen. Probably a two-week sprain. You should see a doctor, though. There's an urgent care clinic on West Eleventh."

"I'll find it tomorrow."

We sit in silence for a long moment, his hand warm on my shin. My apology sticks in my throat, trapped by a bubble of disappointment. Stupid shoes. Stupid me for trying to be fancy in a town that doesn't care about fancy. Stupid ex-wife. And now, the one thing Dalton and I have in common is off the table for two weeks. At least.

Finally, he squeezes my knee. "Again, I'm sorry about Tiffany."

"Not your fault," I mutter.

"She had no right—"

"Don't worry about it." I know I'm being an asshole, but I can't quite force my mouth to un-pout.

"Hey." He slides his hand up my thigh. "You mad at me?"

"No, I..." My shoulders sag. "None of this is your fault, Dalton. I'm just tired and in pain. You've been great, but—can we call it a night?"

He withdraws his hand, and right away I wish he'd put it back. The warmth on my skin fades as he gently removes my ankle from his lap and stands. He opens his mouth as if to say something but only sighs, his shoulders slumped. "Can I call you tomorrow?"

I nod. "G'night, Dalton."

When he closes the door, I swipe a tear from my cheek. He's such a good guy, caring and tender. He deserves so much better than what I can give him.

Why did I have to meet him now? It's not fair.

Chapter Twenty-Two

♥

Laurel

Maxie tightens the ace bandage around my ankle before fastening the clasp. "That'll do 'er. Now, finish your breakfast. We're running late."

"For what? I have today off, remember?" Even though I have zero appetite, under Maxie's eagle eye, I fork up my last bite of scrambled eggs and push the plate away.

"For the race, silly. I'll get my jacket."

I gesture to my useless leg. "You know I can't run on this."

Maxie returns lugging a pair of aluminum crutches. "My neighbor brought these over. Think they're tall enough?"

"They'll give me crutches or a boot at the clinic."

Maxie clucks her tongue. "We'll go after the race. It's important to be there for your friends, right?"

"My friends?" Having grumped at Dalton last night, a blunder for which I've been kicking myself ever since—with my good foot, of course—I'm feeling pretty friendless at the moment.

"Your new running friends. Especially Ichabod." She crosses her skinny arms and raises one penciled-on eyebrow. "Besides, you owe him an apology."

"I was pretty awful, wasn't I?"

"Like a pouty kindergartener. And I need that young man to finish my porch."

"Damn." I heave a sigh. "Okay, I'll get my camera." I haven't yet played around much with the little Nikon Maxie gave me for Christmas.

My mood is as dark as the circles under my eyes as I help Maxie pack folding chairs, a picnic blanket, snacks and water into the Volvo. After the way I treated him, I doubt Dalton will be thrilled to see me at the race. Ending this now would be the smartest thing. Holding onto what can only be a temporary fling will make my departure harder on both of us. But how can I cut him off now, when my whole body tingles every time he's near? And he did reassure me he's up for a short-lived connection, so...round and round my mental wheels spin.

When we reach Sladden Park, I grab our gear and hobble toward the starting line.

"Over here, Maxie," a hugely pregnant woman calls from the shade of a linden tree. "Come sit with us." Three young mothers scoot over to make room. Maxie makes introductions while their toddlers zoom toy cars around our feet.

Spectators pack the sidewalks near the starting banner, and the air is filled with happy chatter, colorful signs to cheer on the runners, and music blasting from the P.A. system.

Maxie's pregnant friend gestures to my wrapped ankle. "Bet you wish you were out there, eh?"

"Yeah. Stupid accident."

"Frustrating to just watch." She pats the dome beneath her blouse. "I'll be back at it once this one drops. I'm bummed that I have to miss Run for the Arts next month."

Maxie interjects with a proud grin, "Laurel made the poster for that race. She's a photographer."

"The rainbow running guy? I saw it at the farmer's market. Really good." She grabs her son, who's making off with one of my crutches. "No, Liam. The lady needs those. She has an owie."

Little Liam, all curly hair, huge eyes, and dimples, switches from race car driver to doctor. "I fix." He squats at my feet and pats my bandage. "You need a shot." He pokes me with a stubby finger, his cupid face solemn.

I can't help grinning at this cuteness overload. "Oh, I feel much better now. Thank you."

He rewards me with a plump-cheeked grin, then picks up his plastic car and zooms away.

I snap a few shots of the runners warming up and pinning on their race numbers. Across the street, a half-dozen teens hold a hot-pink poster board painted with *Go Highlanders*. A familiar figure trots into view.

"Hey, Mr. Garvey." Shouting and laughing, the kids gather around their coach, whose shiny shaved head towers above them. I focus my lens on his smile, so fond and genuine as he greets his students with fist-bumps and back-slaps.

They're lucky to have such a great coach. I'm lucky to have such a great boyfriend—if I haven't driven him away with my stupid, snotty behavior.

Shrill voices carry through the crowd. "Mr. Garvey, I saw your poster."

"Our coach is famous," a girl squeals.

Dalton's reply is too soft to hear as he exchanges elaborate handshakes with two of the boys.

Of course, people will recognize him from the poster. Even facing away from the camera, there's no mistaking his smooth head, his broad shoulders, his firm, round butt...

Heat spreads between my legs as I drink in his form, clearly outlined in his snug shorts and sleeveless tank. This is ridiculous. I can't think straight when he's around. I zoom in on his profile, then jolt backward when he turns and looks right at me. His smile slides off, his brows contract, and he stalks toward me. I lower my camera and notice Maxie beside me, waving like a maniac.

Dalton stoops to peck Maxie's cheek.

"Good morning, dear heart," she coos. "We came to watch you win the race."

"I'll do my best." He frowns at my wrapped foot. "You should have that elevated. Have you been to a doctor yet?"

"Don't worry, Coach, it's our next stop." I flash a sheepish grin. "Help me up?"

Lips compressed in a straight line, he hauls me to my feet.

"I, uh—" My cheeks flush hot. His students are watching, and Maxie is listening. I hop a little closer and lower my voice. "I was a jerk last night. I'm sorry."

Still tight-lipped, he glances at my camera, then raises one eyebrow.

I feel my shoulders creeping toward my ears. "Might as well take some pictures of the race. You can use them for your team, or something..."

He nods, still silent. I wish he'd say something to break the tension crackling between us.

Little Liam's mother steps up. "Hey, aren't you the guy on the race poster?"

Dalton's face relaxes. "Yeah, that's me." He nods toward me. "She does good work, right?"

"Really good," the woman agrees.

Liam totters up to his mom and raises his chubby arms. "Up."

She hefts him onto her hip. "Oof. You're getting heavy."

The tot smooches his mother's cheek, then twists and extends his arms to me. "Up."

"Me?" I gesture to my wrapped foot. "I'm kinda wobbly. Afraid I might drop you, buddy."

Liam's lower lip protrudes.

Dalton winds his arm around my waist. "I've got you. Go ahead."

Trapped with no way to decline graciously, I take the child into my arms. Surprisingly solid and heavy, he smooches my cheek and rubs the blue tip of my ponytail over his face. My heart thumps with a surprise surge of warmth.

Holy crap, now is not the time, ovaries!

"So precious. Let me take a picture." Liam's mom digs in her purse and snaps a few shots. "Liam makes friends wherever he goes."

I can't help giggling as the boy tickles Dalton's nose with my hair.

"See there?" Dalton whispers. "You are good with kids, and you're a good photographer too. Don't sell yourself short, Laurel." He brushes a kiss in front of my ear, sending shivers skittering over my skin. No getting around it. I want him more than I fear wanting him.

The P.A. system shrieks to life and calls the racers to the starting line.

"Down you go, buddy." Dalton pulls the little one from my arms and sets him on the ground. "See you after? We need to talk."

"Yeah, okay. Good luck."

He trots to join the other runners, a look of quiet concentration on his face. At the starting line, he jiggles his powerful thigh muscles and stretches his long arms high overhead. At the starter pistol's bang, the runners surge forward.

I squat to photograph the tangle of legs flashing by, then collapse into my seat. Warmed by the sun and lulled by the women's chatter and kids' giggles, I soon drift into a pleasant doze, until a sharp poke rouses me.

Maxie jabs me again with her cane. "Here they come."

Grasping my camera, I heave myself to my feet. Liam's mother helps with my crutches, and I claim a spot near the finish line.

In the distance, a half-dozen figures approach, closing fast. The first man across the finish line is about twenty, his ebony skin gleaming in the sun. Next comes a skinny kid of about sixteen, his flaming ginger dreads flopping with each step. Across the street, teens and parents wave *Go Highlanders* signs.

My imagination flashes to an image of Dalton in a kilt, his strong, blond-fuzzed legs disappearing beneath the tartan. I slide my hand beneath the pleats and caress the smooth curve of his hip, the sweet indentation on the side of his ass, the swelling of his—what's the name of that big pole they toss at the highland games?

The sound system crackles. "And here comes the leader of the thirty-five to thirty-nine division, Daltonnn Gaaarvey."

Face dripping and flushed, long arms pumping, he gobbles the distance in fierce strides. His students go nuts, stomping and cheering, "Garvey, Garvey, Garvey."

I snap bursts of photos as the Highlanders close around Dalton and empty their plastic cups over his head. The steady stream of finishers prevents me from hobbling across the road to congratulate him, so I content myself with snapping photos of his victory, his mile-wide grin as he wipes his face, his booming laugh, the hugs and high-fives. He's so happy, so alive, so beautiful.

Finally, after the bulk of the runners pass, Dalton lopes toward me, mopping his face and neck with a bandana. He slings his arm around my shoulders and murmurs into my ear, "Get some good pictures, Ms. I'm-not-a-photographer?"

"Got some nice shots of you, Mr. I'm-not-good-looking." I show him the camera's little screen and scroll backward through the images.

The corners of his mouth quirk upward, then drop again. He strokes his palms up my arms, his gaze locked onto mine. "Laurel, we've gotta figure this out. This isn't just flirtation for me. I was up all night trying to understand what I did to make you mad." Pain swims in his deep blue eyes. "Have you changed your mind about us? Because I meant what I said. While you're here, I want you. If you're still determined to leave in December, we'll decide what happens next."

"Dalton, I—" His nearness ties my gut in knots. I flatten my palm on his damp chest. "I wasn't expecting this. I had a plan, you know? Maxie taught me that. A woman with a plan is unstoppable. Meeting you..."

He hugs me tight and chuckles into my hair. "I screwed up your plan?"

"Yeah." He's so near, sweaty and hot and solid and real—how can I concentrate on my future with him around?

"Good." He brushes a kiss across my lips. "Now get your ankle looked at. Call me when you're done?"

Across the street, someone hoots, "Git it, Mr. Garvey."

"Dalster!" His friend Marcus trots up and claps Dalton's back. "Man, you beat me by miles today." Grinning, he nods to me. The two men move off.

"You heard the fella. Let's get your ankle fixed." Maxie wrestles with her camp chair.

"Let me." I collapse both chairs and stuff them into their carrying cases. "You heard all that?"

"I heard enough." Grinning a mile wide, she taps her ear. "I'm old, but I ain't deaf."

Chapter Twenty-Three

♥

Dalton

The ping of Laurel's text wakes me from my post-race nap.

> **Maxie's in Sacred Heart Hospital. Can you come?**

What the hell happened? The old gal looked fine a few hours ago. With my heart slamming my ribs, I reply,

> **On my way.**

I grab my keys and bolt down the stairs. Despite the bad news, a warm, giddy feeling fills my chest because when Laurel needed help, she turned to me.

I find her pacing in the E.R. waiting room. Head down, her left ankle in an elastic brace, she mutters while hobbling back and forth on crutches. I plant myself in her path. Focused on the floor, she nearly knocks me over.

"Whoa, sorry." She flashes a smile weighted with weariness. My first impulse is to wrap my arms around her and comfort her, but after our tense exchange this morning, my better judgment urges caution. "How's she doing?"

"They're waiting on the cardiologist." Her voice wobbles.

Caution be damned. I pull her tight to my chest, crutches and all. She nuzzles my neck and lets me rock her. The flowery scent of her hair fills my nose, and a tingly glow spreads through my belly, as if I've swallowed a whole packet of Pop Rocks candy. This woman arouses feelings I never expected to experience again.

Finally, she snuffles and pulls back. "Thank you for coming."

"What happened?"

"We went to the urgent care clinic for my stupid ankle. When I came out, Maxie's legs and feet were really swollen, and she was groggy."

"Like before, when she didn't recognize you?"

Laurel shakes her head. "This was different. She knew me but couldn't get the words out to describe how she felt, so the doctor sent us here."

"Well, it's a big hospital. They'll figure it out."

She rests in my embrace until a high, reedy voice calls her name and she goes rigid.

The woman hurrying toward us has to be Laurel's mother. Tall, pale, and thin, same high forehead, same gray eyes, same wheat-blond hair. Worry lines etch her brow and bracket her mouth.

Laurel accepts her tight hug but keeps her hands clamped on her crutches. The woman glances at me and raises an eyebrow.

"Mom, this is my friend Dalton Garvey."

"Susan Jepsen. Pleased to meet you, Dalton." Her glance is appraising but not unkind. "I'm glad Laurel has a friend by her side today." She drops her smile, all business now. "Where's Maxie?"

"In there. We're waiting to hear from the doctor."

Susan closes her eyes for a moment, then squares her shoulders. "Let's get you off that hurt foot." She drops into a plastic bucket seat and pats the one beside her. "What happened?"

Laurel fills her in. A few minutes later, a nurse appears in the doorway. "Ms. Jepsen?" Both Laurel and her mom spring to their feet. "Doctor Martinez is ready to see you."

Laurel grasps my hand and squeezes so hard I stifle a yelp.

Eyebrows high, Susan glances at our interlaced fingers. "All righty then, let's go."

The nurse leads us down a long hallway crowded with equipment and bustling with medics, nurses, doctors, patients, relatives, and one grumbling janitor trying to mop the floor around them all. At the doorway of a small office, the nurse tells Laurel, "I'll get an extra chair for your husband."

Laurel's mouth forms a perfect O.

I bite back a grin, secretly pleased at the slip-up.

Susan chuckles. "You two have news you're not sharing?"

Before Laurel can answer, a petite doctor with curly dark hair bustles in. "I'm Doctor Martinez. You're Maxie's family?"

Susan answers. "She's my aunt."

The doc gives a crisp nod. "She's a pistol, that one. A little too stoic, though. Says her feet have been swelling for a while. She just chalked it up to getting old." She sits behind the desk, leans onto her elbows, and ticks off on her fingers. "Here's the plan. First, a low-sodium diet. Second, we'll try some new meds to help her kidney function. Next time her feet swell, I want them up as high as she can manage." She taps her keyboard, then scribbles something on a sheet of paper. "The pharmacy has some good compression socks, but she'll probably comply better if they're colorful. Try this website."

Laurel clears her throat. "Doctor, what's wrong with Maxie?"

"Well, she's ninety. And she's suffering from congestive heart failure."

"Failure?" Laurel's nails dig into my arm. I pry her hand loose and hold it gently.

"Scary diagnosis, I know," the doctor continues, "But if we keep an eye on her symptoms, she may have a few more good years." Her warm smile returns. "If I have her energy at that age, I'll count myself very lucky."

Susan scribbles notes while the doctor outlines Maxie's new restrictions. Then we follow her to a curtained-off cubicle where Maxie's cackling with a nurse over a gossip magazine. She looks a bit pale and rumpled, but otherwise very much herself—full of piss and vinegar, as my dad would say.

"There's my girl." She beams at Laurel and Susan. "Willow, how nice to see you, dear."

"It's Susan, Maxie." Unperturbed, Laurel's mom bends to kiss Maxie's cheek.

Maxie grins up at me. "And Ichabod. Everyone, this is Fred. Isn't he cute?"

The nurse heads for the door. "I'll go check on your discharge papers. Nice to meet you all."

Laurel touches her mother's shoulder. "Could you take her home? I haven't eaten in hours, and..."

Maxie waves as if shooing a fly. "Scoot, you two. Go smooch."

"See you back at Maxie's house," Susan adds.

Pale and silent, Laurel hobbles on her crutches to the hospital entrance, where I leave her staring into space while I hurry to bring my car around. I help her into her seat, stow her crutches in the back, and slide behind the wheel. "So, what's your pleasure? Sandwich? Gyros? Sushi?"

She opens her mouth, but no words emerge, and then her beautiful face crumples into violent sobs.

A heavy chill settles over me. I know this pain all too well, and there's nothing I can do to save her from it. I search for wise, eloquent words, something more helpful than a comforting touch in a beat-up car in a busy parking lot.

"I know, babe. It's hard," is the best I can come up with as I rub slow circles on her back.

She clutches my knee, her hand a white-knuckled claw. "She's gonna die, Dalton. Any day now. Her heart's gonna quit and she'll just—just die."

The same fear scrapes me raw whenever my mom lands in the hospital. So many times, over the last four years, I've sat alone in a hospital parking lot, wondering if this is the day she won't come home.

I stroke Laurel's hair back from her tear-dampened cheek.

"I don't think I can do this." Eyes wide and wild, she grasps the door handle as if to fling it open and sprint away.

"Of course you can. Your mom's here, and Maxie's friends. And me."

In a sandpaper voice, she whispers, "I'm no good at this part."

The ragged emotion in her eyes brings tears of sympathy to mine. "No one's good at this part. You just get through it and let your loved ones prop you up."

Let me help, Laurel. Let me in.

She snuffles. "You're going through the same thing, aren't you?"

"Yeah, pretty much."

She finally meets my gaze. "What's your mom's prognosis?"

"Maybe a few more years."

"God. I'm sorry." Fresh tears dribble down her cheeks. "You've got so much on your own plate. I shouldn't have called you."

"Hey, I'm glad you called. Really." I release her and turn the key in the ignition. "Let's get you something to eat."

She huffs a dry chuckle. "I know I need to, but I don't know if I can."

At the soup and sandwich place, she traces figure eights in her tortilla soup with her spoon, then opens a packet of saltines and crumbles them into microscopic bits, her gaze downcast.

Maybe a change of topic? "Tell me about your mom. Are you close?"

The corners of her mouth twitch. "Not really."

I nudge her knee with mine. "I'm a good listener, you know. Kind of a job requirement."

Another cracker becomes dust in her trembling fingers. Finally, she clears her throat. "Let's just say Dad did a bad thing, then Mom reacted badly, and my sister and I suffered the fallout. For years."

"Ah." I clasp her icy, crumb-dusted hands. "Well, if you ever want to talk about it, I'm here, okay?"

Her gaze flicks up to mine. "Thank you, Dalton." She fiddles with her spoon again. "You know, I can hear Maxie's voice in my head."

"Yeah? What's she telling you?"

"To talk this out with Mom. And eat my soup. And thank my boyfriend for being such a great guy."

At last, a crumb of hope. "I believe her favorite words on that topic are 'Go smooch.'"

"Good advice, right?" She leans across the table and plants a good one on my lips before setting to work on her soup.

Not forthcoming with the family secrets, but at least she called me her boyfriend. That's progress. Excellent progress. Grinning, I bend to my own bowl.

Chapter Twenty-Four

♥

Laurel

Dalton's lingering goodbye kiss isn't enough to erase the pain of the doctor's news, and it isn't enough to steel my nerves for a much-needed heart-to-heart with my mother. But it helps, and the warmth of his embrace clings to my skin as I open Maxie's front door.

Raised voices echo in the nearly empty living room.

"I don't care what the doctor said. I'm not eating this crap."

"For goodness' sake, Aunt Maxie."

I hustle to the kitchen where, fists on hips, Mom looms over Maxie, who's glowering at a plate of beige food.

Great, now I'm the referee. I swing over to the table, lean my crutches in the corner, and drop into a chair. Holding my hair back with one hand, I give Maxie's plate a sniff.

"Smells boring, right?" Maxie grumbles.

I give her bony shoulder a squeeze. "You have to eat, Max."

She screws up her face. "If this is all I can eat, I might as well curl up and die right now."

"Maxie," Mom and I chorus, but she just harrumphs and glowers.

I draw Mom aside and whisper, "What did you make her?"

"Plain boiled chicken breast and mashed potatoes, no salt, no butter."

When I wrinkle my nose, Mom plucks a pamphlet from her purse and slaps it onto the counter. "Think you can do better? Be my guest." She stalks from the room. The guest room door slams.

"Great. Now, where am I going to sleep?"

"Go bunk with Ichabod," Maxie suggests. "But first, order me a pizza."

"Now, now. Let's be reasonable." I page through the leaflet that promises *Flavorful, Heart-Healthy Recipes*. I've never developed my cooking chops beyond the bare-bones basics. Time to remedy that. I take a quick inventory of the fridge's contents. A Styrofoam tray holds three more chicken breasts. Riffing, I douse them with lemon juice, dump on some chopped garlic from a jar, and sprinkle them with salt-free Greek seasoning. "Right. Salt-free Greek chicken. What else can we do?"

"Garlic mashed potatoes?"

A bag of frozen kale gets the lemon and garlic treatment as well.

Mom follows her nose back into the kitchen and chuckles as she watches me dish up our new and improved dinner. "Will wonders never cease?"

Maxie digs in. "Not bad, kiddo. In fact, it's darned tasty. Needs salt, though."

Mom pounces on the saltshaker and tosses it into the trash can.

"For goodness' sake, child, I was kidding," Maxie chides.

"Nevertheless." Mom raises her fork in a salute. "All for one, and one for all."

After dinner, Mom washes up while I sit on the porch swing and call Dalton. Just the sound of his rumbling voice relaxes me.

"Greek chicken, huh? Make it for me sometime?"

"For us, you mean? Yeah. I'd like that. But with a little salt." I laugh, because it's either that or cry again, and I'm all cried out. "Poor Maxie."

Mom opens the screen door, steps onto the porch, and stretches her long arms high overhead. "What a glorious evening."

Dalton's voice gentles. "Time to talk to your mom?"

I groan softly.

"Laurel, you've got this. I know it's hard, but you won't regret clearing the air. You'll breathe easier afterward." He chuckles. "Okay, apologies for the bad pun."

"Thanks for everything, Dalton. I'd never have made it through today without you. Talk to you tomorrow." *I love you.* The words hover on my lips, as easy and natural as saying good night. My heart gives a heavy thump as I bite them back. I can't possibly love Dalton, not this soon. And considering love's track record in my life, diving into that cesspool would end our friendship. And right now, I really need a friend.

"G'night," I whisper.

"G'night, beautiful one. I'll dream of you."

Clutching the phone to my chest, I stare unfocused into the gathering dusk. The breeze ruffles the leaves on Maxie's big sycamore tree. A trio of kids zoom by on their scooters, their laughter ringing in the sultry evening air.

Mom settles onto the porch swing beside me. "Talking to your new boyfriend?"

I nod.

"He's a keeper," she remarks.

I wrinkle my nose. Mom's idea of what constitutes a keeper is miles away from mine, and anyway, keeping Dalton is out of the question.

Ignoring my reaction, she continues. "He's strong, that one. And gentle. And he loves you."

I'm starting to suspect that's true, but I scoff anyway. "Mom, how could you possibly—"

She tilts her head back toward the house. "Maxie says so. But I saw it too."

Pain throbs behind my eyes, an echo of hurt so deep I still haven't healed. "Mom, you're not exactly qualified to give me advice on my love life."

Mom's sharp inhalation drives another aching thud into my skull. What a crappy daughter I am, snarking like a teenager. I should have moved beyond this by now, but the memory still sears.

"All right." Mom leans her elbows onto her knees. "I guess this is long overdue. Willow and I talked this out years ago, but—"

"But what, Mom?" I blink back the tears prickling my eyes.

"Guess I was waiting for you to ask. I figured you would, someday, when you were ready."

My throat constricts, tightening my voice to a raspy whisper. "Why, Mom?"

"Why did I want to die?" She shakes her head slowly. "It seems so far away, you know? I'm a different person now."

"Are you?"

She nods, her eyes glassy with tears. "I was devastated. That town, that marriage, they were my whole world. And everyone knew." A lone tear spills down her pale cheek. "I didn't have the strength to face the shame, to start over somewhere else, taking care of you girls on my own. How could I put you through it? I was just...defeated. And I wanted the pain to end."

"Leaving us to Dad?" Despite my burning resentment, I cover Mom's hand with mine. This is as hard on her as it is on me.

"And to Mary." She turns her palm up and weaves our fingers together. "She wasn't a bad person, you know."

My spine stiffens. "Mom, she was a horrible person."

Mom sighs. "We can't always control our feelings. Sometimes, people just—fall in love. And it changes everything." She squeezes my hand. "Your father didn't want to hurt us. He just fell in love."

There it is again, the big L word that brings chaos and leaves a trail of wreckage.

How can she forgive him? How is that even possible? I wipe my eyes with my forearm and, when I trust my voice not to break, ask the question I've held back for so many years. "Why did you stay with him?"

"He gave her up." Mom's voice is mild, her gaze soft. "It took me a long time to appreciate his sacrifice. Finally, after a lot of work, we found our way back to loving each other." She cups my cheek. "I'm happy now. I have a strong, steady partner, and we'll spend our golden years together, until God parts us."

She pulls me closer until our foreheads touch. "He cherishes me, baby. That's what I wish for you, a man who cherishes you. As for the rest, I can apologize until the day I die, and it'll never be enough. But I am truly deeply sorry for what I put you through. I was weak and stupid. I hope someday you'll find a way to forgive me."

My mouth hands open, but I have no words. My insides feel as hollow as a cavern. Maybe I'll never understand my mother's choices. Maybe my understanding doesn't matter. Finding my way to acceptance will take time, but I won't punish Mom's wrenching honesty by shutting her out. I wrap my arms around her and sob against her soft cheek.

Finally, Mom straightens, pulls her ever-present wad of tissues from her pocket, and wipes her eyes. "Now then, there's the matter of who sleeps where."

My teary laughter croaks. Here's the strong, practical mother I barely remember. "You take the bed. I'll take the couch." I push to my feet and gather my crutches. "How long can you stay?"

"A few days." She flashes a teasing smile. "Why don't you go visit your young man? I'll bet he has a comfortable bed."

"Mother," I yelp, my eyebrows sky-high.

She shrugs. "What? You're a grown woman. Life heaps enough sorrow on us—more than enough. When an opportunity for happiness comes along, you should grab it."

Chapter Twenty-Five

♥

Dalton

With my bare feet propped on the coffee table, I half-watch, half-ignore a mediocre action movie and imagine Laurel beside me on the couch, her head on my shoulder, her pale hair soft against my cheek. The hero creeps through a dripping underground passageway toward unspeakable evil, the only sound his raspy breathing, the drip, drip, drip of slimy water—and the ping of an incoming text. I snatch up my phone.

> **Maxie's asleep, Mom's staying tonight. Can I come over?**

A flush of anticipation heats my skin from toes to top. My thumbs fumble on the screen.

> **Yes, please and thank you.**

> **See you in fifteen.**

Thank God I've already showered. I dash through the apartment, opening windows to air out the echoes of my dinner, then re-brush my teeth for good measure. I rip the sheets from the bed and replace them with a fresh set. While I fluff the pillows, I whisper a prayer that my efforts won't be in vain.

My pulse races at the sound of Laurel's knock.

"Hi." Leaning on her crutches, she gives me a weak smile. Damn, she looks exhausted and tense and so beautiful my heart skids sideways. The evening breeze lifts her thin hippie skirt and her unbound hair. No makeup obscures her red, puffy eyes. Chuckling, she bats away a moth that bops against her forehead, drawn by the glow of her blond silk.

"You're here." No use fighting my goofy grin.

"Yeah." Gazing at her feet, she raises one shoulder and lets it fall. "I need a friend tonight."

Angel, I'll be your friend and so much more, if you'll let me.

Reaching around her crutches, I fold her into my arms and inhale her fresh, springtime scent. Her deep exhalation lands somewhere between a sigh and a moan, and she winds her arms around my neck, pressing her soft breasts into my chest.

"You feel so good," she whispers.

My primitive animal brain roars, urging me to take her now, fast and hard, right here against the wall. *She wants it. You want it. Why wait?* I snap a mental whip and send the beast back to its cage. Laurel is hurting. Now is not the time.

I release her. "Come in. Get off that injured foot."

"I, uh..." She gestures to the overnight bag by her feet. "I wasn't sure, so..."

Thank you, Universe! I scoop up her bag and step aside to let her hobble in. "What did the doctor say about your ankle?"

"One to two weeks. Elevation and ice. Nothing too bad." She eases herself onto the couch and props her foot on the coffee table, giving me a sad-puppy pout. "I'll miss our runs."

"Me too. But you're not leaving yet. We still have lots of time. To run, I mean." I back toward the kitchen. "I'll get you some ice. Something to drink?"

"God, yes." She laughs, deep and throaty. "I mean, yes, please. It's been quite a day."

I return with a gel ice pack, a bottle of wine, and two glasses. "Will this do?"

She checks the label and whistles. "Utopia Chardonnay, Willamette Valley. Very nice."

"Some of us teachers did a winery tour last June. Got a little tipsy and bought a case of this stuff."

She slides the elastic brace off her ankle and adjusts the ice pack. "Wine, ice. You're ready for every contingency."

I sit beside her and bend to uncork the bottle while she strokes lazy circles on my shoulder. Distracted, I nearly stab myself with the corkscrew. When I reach for the wine glasses, she winds her arm around my waist and rests her cheek on my back. Inside me, two desires play tug-of-war—to stay there, relishing her easy trust, or to wrap her hair around my fist and kiss her until our clothing incinerates.

Caution wins, for the moment. I fill our glasses. "What shall we drink to?"

Her long, pale lashes flutter down as she swirls her wine. "How about, to good friends—the kind who push us to do the right thing."

"To good friends." We clink glasses. Does she mean *just* good friends, or...?

She swallows half her glass, leans against my shoulder, and weaves our fingers together. "So, I talked to my mom."

"Did it help?"

"Yeah." She drains her glass.

"That rough, eh?" I pour a refill.

"Pretty much." Her fingertips trail along the sensitive skin of my inner arm, making it hard to concentrate.

"Look, Laurel, it's not my place to pry, but—"

She blurts the words as if spitting out something bitter. "She tried to kill herself. With pills. Because my dad cheated. I found her. I was twelve."

My chest constricts. I force a deep breath, then another. Holy shit, no wonder she's so skittish. I brush away the curtain of hair she's hiding behind and tuck it behind her ear. "I'm so sorry you went through that, Laurel. Thank you for trusting me enough to share your story."

She leans her cheek into my hand, a gesture so sweet I nearly whimper. "It's funny. I do trust you. I've only known you for, what, two weeks? But I feel like I don't need to hide things from you."

A tickly glow fills me as I kiss her palm. "I'm glad."

"I was so angry, you know? And I never understood why she stayed with him."

"Did you talk about it?"

"Yeah. I still don't quite get it, but—it's their thing to work out."

"And they have?"

"So it seems." Chuckling, she nuzzles my neck. "Guess who urged me to come over here?"

"Maxie?"

"Mom. Said something about grabbing an opportunity for happiness." She slides her hand up my arm and gently kneads my shoulder.

Her mouth shimmers like a luscious fruit, and I take it in a ravenous kiss. Her lips part, her wine-scented tongue hot and sweet. Suddenly, she jolts backward and grimaces.

No no no. What's wrong?

"Sorry. Garlic breath. I brushed, but I can still taste it."

Laughing, I rake my fingers into her hair and press my forehead to hers. "Laurel, you could snack on roadkill, and I'd still want to kiss you." So I do, murmuring against her mouth, "You are so delicious."

"Mmmm." She relaxes in my arms, offering me the satiny skin of her throat. I take my time, kissing my way from the soft, secret spot behind her ear to the enchanting hollow at the base of her throat.

My impatient dick urges me to claim the heaven she's offering, but this is a moment to savor, not to rush. Careful of her injured ankle, I lean her onto the sofa pillows and lift her legs across my lap. Through half-closed lids, she watches me with a lazy, knowing Mona Lisa smile while I slide my hands to the indentation of her waist, down the curve of her hips and back up to the buttons of her blouse. "May I?"

"Please." She stretches languid arms above her head and waits, her deep breaths lifting her beautiful breasts.

Reverently, I undo the bottom button, revealing the perfect oval of her navel. I can't resist trailing one fingertip around its contours.

She squirms. "Tickles."

Laughing, I unfasten the rest of the buttons to expose her pale belly. Its steady rise and fall is hypnotic. I sweep my thumbs up toward the front clasp of her bra, where a tiny silver heart dangles. Laurel arches her beautiful neck as I fumble with the fiddly clasp until her breasts spill free. Heaven! I close my mouth over one silky mound and softly knead the other. Her nipples tighten beneath my eager tongue.

"More," she moans deep in her throat while her fingertips trace tingling circles on my head, neck, and shoulders.

I reach for the waistband of her skirt, held together by a cloth belt. Thanking heaven and my Boy Scout training, I undo the knot and unveil this longed-for gift.

Laurel mewls and rolls her hips on the sofa as I trail kisses down to her wispy lace panties. I've already stroked her here, on that morning when we lost our minds on Skinner Butte, but now her most secret place is mine to see, to touch, to taste. Her flesh blooms pink and soft beneath the transparent fabric, so tempting I have to lick her through the lace. With a gasp, she lifts her long legs, then hisses when her injured ankle collides with the wall.

She pushes up on her elbows and huffs her mussed hair from her eyes. "Bed, please."

A slow, wide grin stretches across my face. "Yes, ma'am."

Laurel

When Dalton slides his strong arms beneath my knees and shoulders and lifts me, I flush with self-conscious delight. Never has a guy carried me to bed. How corny, how old-fashioned, how incredibly hot! He kisses me again, deep and delicious, then strides to the hallway, eases me through sideways, and kicks the bedroom door open.

"Oh, my," I giggle into his chest. "You're a wild man."

He growls into the crook of my neck before gently depositing me onto the bed and sits beside me. He strokes his broad, warm hands over my bare skin from shoulder to hip, raising goosebumps of pleasure.

I open my eyes. "Hey, you're still dressed. Why are you still dressed?"

Wordlessly, he rises, pulls his T-shirt over his head, and steps out of his loose gym shorts. Wearing only thin boxer-briefs that barely contain his straining erection, he prowls toward me, his eyes dark and glittering.

I stay him with my raised hand. "I want to see you." Rising on one elbow, I drink in the sight of his nearly nude form, displayed just for me. "Magnificent."

This first chance to appreciate his tall, lean, muscular body from head to toe is a moment to relish, and I mean to take my time. Everything about him is masculine, strong, graceful, like Michelangelo's David. In the low light of his bedroom, shadow heightens the contrast between muscle and bone. My fingers itch to stroke his furry blond chest and follow the golden arrow of hair down the center of those tight abs. Low on his hips, a V of muscle points the way to paradise.

I've never seen such a magnificent cock, long, thick, and pulsing. Impatient, but restraining himself for my sake, Dalton clenches his hands at the ends of those long, golden, lean-muscled arms. In a moment, he'll wrap those arms around me, but for just a moment, he's mine caress with my eyes, my own beautiful work of art. The powerful curve of his thighs—

"Enough," he huffs, his voice husky with desire. Kneeling on the bed, he straddles me and frames my face in his hands. His heavy-lidded gaze lasers onto mine as he lowers his body closer, closer, until only a millimeter of heated air separates us.

I glide my hands over his sides and tug his shorts down. "I want to see you."

He kneels and lets me strip away this last barrier. His erection bops against his stomach, inviting my touch. Clara was right: it's an impressive sight.

"Oh. My. It's so..." I grasp his length, silky and ruddy and surprisingly smooth with a plush purple crown. When I stroke my thumbs up the sensitive underside, a tear of pleasure appears. Curling into a sitting position, I swirl my tongue around the plump head.

Dalton's ragged breath rings out in the silent room. "God, Laurel, so good."

Dizzy with desire, I wonder how I'll fit this monster inside me.

"My turn," he commands. Extricating himself from my caressing hands, he stretches out beside me and kisses me with a fierce hunger. His lips feather down my throat, and when his hot mouth seizes my nipple, a spark jolts straight to my sex and dances there like heat lightning.

As he slides to the foot of the bed, he tugs my panties down and tosses them away. Nudging my thighs open, he nibbles and kisses his way up to my center, then pauses, his breath the barest whisper of sensation on my pulsing clit. "You are so beautiful."

With a sexy grunt, he seals his hot, hungry mouth to my flesh, and everything else falls away. My whole world becomes waves, spirals, lightning bolts of pleasure. While his magic tongue licks and teases, he inserts one long finger and strokes in and out in a rhythm that makes my hips dance. A second finger joins the first, opening me, making me ready.

Eyes shut tight against the overwhelming sensations, I stroke his smooth, warm head and clutch his shoulders. A sweet, honeyed heaviness builds between my thighs, pulsing electricity that sparks around his every touch. "God, Dalton, I'm going to—"

"Yes, baby," he murmurs against my thigh. "Come for me."

"But I want you inside me."

"Soon. Give me this first." His broad tongue slides over my clit, and I tumble into sweet oblivion.

When awareness slowly returns, I find myself collapsed onto the pillows, sated and boneless. Dalton kneels between my thighs, a condom packet in his hand. Fascinated, I watch him roll the thin sheath over his rigid shaft.

I giggle. "I didn't know they made condoms that large."

He flashes an aw-shucks grin and pulls a tube of lube from the nightstand. "I don't want to hurt you, Laurel. I have this."

Feeling every inch the wicked temptress, I roll my hips. "I don't think we'll need any." I stroke a finger between my folds and lift it, glistening.

His furry chest and thighs tickle my skin as he lowers himself over me. Supporting his weight on one hand, he notches his cock at my entrance, then pauses, his twilight-blue gaze drinking in my body, my face.

I hold my breath.

He begins. One slow push, easing in just the fat crown, then withdrawing. His pale lashes lower, and his mouth opens on a sharp inhalation. Another push, a few more inches of delicious fullness. My breath escapes in a rush. I clasp my legs around his hips. He pushes deeper, stretching me completely. A razor-thin edge of pain dances atop the pleasure, but need builds deep inside me.

"Are you okay?" he whispers, his breath hot on my cheek.

I dig my nails into his muscular ass. "More."

Achingly slowly, he withdraws until only the plump head of his cock rests at my entrance. Deliciously slow, he drives into me again. "So good. So sweet," he murmurs, his hypnotic gaze pinning mine. The amazing width and length and heat of him scrapes every nerve ending, electric and sharp and almost too much to bear. With a groan, he settles into a smooth rhythm, stroking deep, pausing at the peak of each thrust. His breath comes in little gasps as his bucking hips pick up speed. Each invading push tugs my clit, igniting bright sparks that dance down my legs and into my center. My body tenses as a second climax rumbles closer, like a train shaking the tracks with its inexorable approach.

"God, Dalton," I gasp. My bare calves clasp his hips, our sweaty bodies slick and sliding.

He clutches my hip, his lids fluttering. "Laurel—I can't—oh God—"

Beyond words, I cry out, keening my pleasure as he drives into me, once, twice, then freezes, and the pulsing of his cock fires off another earthquake orgasm that obliterates everything but this incandescent moment, this breathtaking man.

Slowly, as if awakening from a deep dream, I come back to myself and feel his lips against my temple, the weight of his sweat-slicked body, the rise and fall of his breath.

"Heavy." I gently push his chest.

"Phenomenal," he whispers. "Miraculous." He rolls off me, removes the condom, and showers my face and throat with kisses before trotting toward the bathroom, his muscular ass clenching with each step. I close my eyes and drift, my body humming with contentment. *Don't think. Just rest in this moment, with this sweet, wonderful man.*

When I awake, darkness envelopes me. Dalton's long arm rests across my waist, pinning me to his warm, heavy body, soft with sleep. I snuggle my back to his furry front, and his cock stirs against my butt.

He murmurs, "Laur..." my name sliding into a gentle snore.

My breath catches. A surprise tear slides across my nose and plops onto the pillow. It would be so easy to stay here. Dalton would love me and cushion me from the sorrow of losing Maxie. I could build a life with him. A good life. Not a big, sparkly life, but I'd be comfortable. And for a moment, the promise of ease wafts like a siren's song through the midnight silence.

Let go. Lay down your struggles. Be content.

All I have to do is give up my dream, to live with never knowing if I could have made it.

Shivering, I snuggle closer to Dalton, but his warmth doesn't penetrate where I need it most. He can't help me through this. I have to choose—Dalton or my dream. Either way, I'll lose.

Chapter Twenty-Six

♥

Dalton

I yawn and stretch, as relaxed and refreshed as if I've been sleeping on clouds. A grin stretches my lips as I recall the reason for this cozy contentment: *Laurel. The most amazing woman in the universe and the hottest, sweetest night of my life.* I reach for her, joy fizzing in my veins, but there's only a Laurel-size dent in the mattress, still warm from her delectable body. Cutlery clinks in the kitchen. A cabinet door closes.

She's still here! Clutching her pillow to my chest, I thank all the chubby little angels who usually overlook guys like me—but not last night, when Laurel slept nestled in my arms, her soft ass cradled against my hips. Unused to company in my big, lonely bed, I woke a dozen times to inhale her scent and rub my cheek against the cool silk of her hair.

I'm not really the praying sort, but I whisper a fervent prayer to whatever gods might be listening: "Keep her here with me."

The sound of her poking around in my kitchen fills me with hope. A partner who actually gets me, who's easy and honest and real—maybe that dream is within reach after all.

I need a good-morning kiss before she slips away. Still naked, I pad into the kitchen and find her leaning on her crutches, dressed again in her hippie skirt and thin top, her bed-mussed hair spilling down her back. Her hips sway to some internal music, slow and enticing, as she pokes the buttons on my coffee machine.

I am the luckiest man in Oregon.

Stepping behind her, I wrap my arms around her waist and join in the dance.

She giggles and cranes her neck to kiss my jaw. "Hope you don't mind. I needed coffee." Her hips swirl in a lazy figure eight.

Make that the luckiest man on the West Coast.

"My goodness." She strokes my bare flank. "Rise and shine."

"Yes, ma'am," I mutter into her hair. "I'm rising, and you're shining."

Reaching over her shoulder, I push the button, and the coffee machine splutters to life.

"Ah. Noted." As she leans her crutches on the counter, her gaze flicks down to my erection. Grinning, she wraps her arms around my neck. "Sausage for breakfast?" Her minty-fresh kiss tickles my lips.

I hold a finger to her lips. "Wait right there. Don't move." I jog to the bathroom, brush my fuzzy teeth, and return, clutching a foil packet, my eager dick bobbing with each step.

She laughs again, her head thrown back. "That's adorable."

I lift her onto the counter. "I'm glad you think so." While the coffee machine belches and sputters, I kiss her luscious lips, taste her toothpaste tongue, run my grateful hands up her sides and cup her heaven-soft breasts.

"Dalton?" she purrs against my throat.

"Hmmm?" I bunch her skirt and lift it above her hips.

"I have to be at work by nine."

I check the clock on the coffee machine. "We have plenty of time."

"I have to go home and change."

"You can wear my clothes." I stroke up her smooth thighs, and hallelujah, she's not wearing panties.

Luckiest man on the continent.

"I left in a hurry last night," she confesses. "Forgot to pack underwear."

My fingertips part her silky folds, already slick and ready.

She sighs into the crook of my neck. "Mmm, you're so...ohhh." Her fingers close around my shaft and tug me toward her center.

With a goofy growl, I tear the condom packet with my teeth and sheath my aching dick. She shifts her hips forward on the counter and crosses her ankles around my lower back, pulling me in. Her elastic brace scratches, but the discomfort is quickly obliterated by the heaven of her hot, wet flesh closing around me, her lips against mine, her breath heating my skin, her moans in my ear...

Afraid I'll come too soon, I withdraw and rub my shaft between her swollen inner lips, sliding over her most sensitive spot, making her leg muscles jolt. She bites her lip and whimpers.

"Yes," I murmur against her throat. "Come for me, Laurel. I love to feel you coming."

Her panting breath and the way she tenses in my arms tells me she must be close. Stroking her clit with my thumb, I drive into her hard and fast while she shudders and gasps, her inner muscles fluttering.

"Yes, angel, give it to me. God, I love—"

"Don't." Her nails dig into my back. "Don't speak. Just feel." She shuts me up with a fierce kiss.

Anything you want, Laurel. Anything.

She's quaking, sobbing, and I'm falling with her, or flying, or both at once, spinning in a vortex of impossible pleasure.

Slowly, the kitchen re-materializes around us. Panting, I withdraw and peel off the condom. I reach toward the trash can, but Laurel holds me in place, her face buried in the crook of my neck.

With my free hand, I stroke her hair back from her sweat-dewed face. "So, no talking during sex?"

Into the crook of my neck, she whispers. "It's just that one word."

Shit. What did I say?

"Dalton, I..." She cups my jaw, her brows drawn together, her eyes moist with...sadness? Fear? "Damn. I don't know how to say this right."

Not fear. Regret.

Time stops. My belly tenses for the coming blow. How could I have got it so wrong? She doesn't want me. She just wants sex.

I spit out the words like shards of glass. "Just tell me, Laurel."

Her voice is tight, brittle. "I really like you, Dalton. A lot. And this—" Her gaze softens as she skates her fingertips over my bare chest. "This is amazing. I'm so grateful to you for being there for me and Maxie, but—"

With a violet shudder, I step out of her arms. I must look ridiculous to her, naked and clutching a used condom while she tears my heart out.

She clutches the counter's edge to keep from falling off and draws a deep, ragged breath. "What we have is special, but please don't call it love."

"No problem." Ice drips from my words. I back toward the hallway, unable to tear my eyes from her—clothes half-off, her hair in disarray, her thighs glistening with her arousal. Inside and out, dressed up or in sex-mussed, Laurel is stunning, but her heart holds no room for me.

And that's what I get for being a naïve, love-struck idiot. Put a pretty woman in front of me, let her show a little kindness, a little humor, and BAM, I'm in love. You'd think after Tiffany, after Clara, I'd finally take the hint the universe keeps bashing me over the head with.

For a little while, a few happy days, I thought I'd found the one. But I'm a fool to trust my judgment.

Rooted where I stand, washed in shame, all I can do is stare.

Laurel's chin trembles. "I really care about you, Dalton. Can't we just—" She sniffles and swipes her eyes with the back of her hand. "Can we take this slow?"

What the hell does she want from me? This makes no goddamn sense. "You mean no more sex?"

"That's not what I mean." Awkwardly, she slides off the counter and coaxes the goopy condom from my tightly clenched fingers. She tosses it into the trash can beneath the sink, and the natural intimacy of her gesture stabs me right between the ribs.

She takes my clammy hand and fixes me with a pleading look. "I just want to keep things—easy, casual."

A gray pall falls over my vision. "You've got someone else."

"No!" she squeaks, eyes wide, and then her brows slam together as she scoops up her crutches, anchors them in her armpits, and stabs her fingers through her hair. "Shit, I'm making a mess of this."

I clench my jaws against the roar of frustration trying to escape. "I've got all day."

For a long moment, she stares at the floor and wrings her hands. Finally, she meets my gaze, her expression grim. "I'm scared, Dalton."

"Well, that's just—" I huff at the ridiculousness of this whole fiasco. Of all the timid, wimpy people I've ever met, well—Laurel definitely isn't one of them.

I lean against the counter and inject false calm into my voice, like when I'm defusing a fight between students. "That's not what I see, Laurel. Look at you, taking charge of Maxie's care. That's incredibly hard. Hell, Dad and I struggle to stay on top of Mom's needs, and there are two of us. But you're handling a tough situation with grace and I—" Damn, I almost said the L word again. "With ingenuity. You're stronger than you know."

She throws up her hands. "You don't know that! And you don't really know me." She's pacing now, hobbling back and forth in my cramped kitchen, her long legs swinging, her eyes blazing. "You've found your path. You've got friends, a career, students who adore you, and a family who love you. All I've got is this dream of a future where I can be...*more*. More than ordinary. More than small-town successful. My whole life has conspired to keep me small, Dalton. Insignificant. And no matter how much I want to be with you, I can't surrender."

If that's how she sees herself and her situation, she's right. I don't really know her.

And no matter what her reasons, a kiss-off is still a kiss-off.

Shaking my head, I pivot and stride toward the bedroom. If I can't argue from a position of strength, at least I can pull some clothes on.

Laurel's crutches thud and squeak behind me. "Don't you see, Dalton? If I fall in love with you, I'll have to stay in Eugene."

"A fate worse than death." I don't bother reining in my snarky tone as I pull on a T-shirt, ripping a seam it in my haste, then step into the shorts I discarded last night. I wheel on her. "Look, Laurel, I'm gonna feel what I'm gonna feel. You can't stop it." Frustration roils my gut like a nest of snakes. "And Eugene is my home. If it's too confining for you, I guess this is goodbye."

I want to stomp out and slam the door behind me—but we're in my place, and that would look ridiculous. So I just glare.

Moving slowly, she gathers her things, hefts her overnight bag, and hobbles into the hall. When she turns to face me one last time, her beautiful, stormy eyes glitter with tears. The sight pierces my wounded pride, but I tighten my jaw and stand my ground.

"I'm sorry, Dalton." She swings away, closing the front door softly behind her.

I crumple onto the bed and bury my face in the pillow that still holds her scent.

How stupid to think my luck has changed. Why should Laurel be any different? Time to put my pointless hopes on the shelf and get on with my life.

Chapter Twenty-Seven

♥

Laurel

"Stupid sex." Perched on a wheeled office chair, I shelve books in the red room, the door propped open to ease the stuffy warmth. This assignment is the last thing I need after yesterday's fight with Dalton. Each sexy book I touch is a sharp reminder of how I got myself into this mess.

I should've kept my mouth shut, should've let him deal with his feelings in his own way. I was honest with him. He knew about my plan, about our connection's expiration date.

Bitterness fills my mouth and sours my stomach. Who the hell am I kidding? I'm a complete and utter asshole, using Dalton for comfort in my time of need when he deserves so much better. He's sweet, compassionate, and decent to the marrow of his long bones. Of course he's going to catch feelings.

He thinks I'm strong? Bullshit—I'm pathetically weak if I can let a passing infatuation distract me from my plan. And now I've hurt a good man. Like, truly, deeply, one of the best people I've ever met.

It would be so easy to let myself fall in love with him. And then the cascade of dominoes begins. I talk myself into giving up my dream. I persuade myself that I'm happy in Eugene, and it works for a while, until it doesn't, and I start to resent him, and it poisons our connection, and...

Click, click, click, faster and faster, it all comes crashing down.

A tear plops onto the book in my lap, a collection of erotic artworks from ancient India. I shelve it and pick up the next new arrival, a catalogue of sex toys ancient and modern. Should've stuck with something like this. No distractions, no complications, no messy feelings. A battery-operated boyfriend wouldn't care if I move away tomorrow.

Of course, it also wouldn't keep me warm at night.

My memory flashes to Dalton's body spooned against my back, his hips cradling my butt as he sleeps, his breath soft on my neck. No amount of battery-powered fun could ever replicate that delicious comfort.

Damn it to hell and back. I wasn't supposed to feel so much for him, and these memories are merciless: Dalton's beautiful, hopeful smile as he trots into the kitchen, naked and aroused and so damn happy to see me. His groan as he draws a fierce climax from my sleepy body. The shattered expression on his face when I pull away and shutter my heart.

But I have to pull away.

With a growl, I slam the remaining books willy-nilly onto the shelves, hoping Clara wouldn't notice. As I'm reaching for the red door, a bejeweled hand pushes it open.

"There you are, my dear." Agatha sweeps in. Wearing a gleaming emerald silk tunic and an elaborate breastplate-necklace thingy of hammered copper, she beams like a mother goddess. When she notices my expression, her plump cheeks deflate. She gestures to my ankle brace. "You're wounded. And weeping. What's wrong, my muse?"

"I'm not crying. I'm just…"

Agatha folds her arms over her considerable bosom and lifts one eyebrow.

I'm as transparent as cellophane. "Okay, it's a guy."

"Ah. Lovers' quarrel?" She pats my arm. "Well, give it time. Most problems settle themselves if you do." She rubs her hands together. "Are you free tonight? I'd love to finish that portrait."

"Let me check."

I phone my mom. Good news: she's staying for a few more days, giving me a little wiggle room. Also, Davonte called and talked to Maxie for a long time. Lots of loud laughter—God knows what Maxie told him. That's what I get for not answering my bestie's texts.

I agree to meet Agatha at seven, a good excuse to forestall a painful conversation with Dalton. Will he even want to talk to me after this morning's debacle? I pocket my phone and return to the counter.

Clara glances up from her pile of paperwork and grins. "Margot," she calls.

The little sprite pops up from behind the cookbooks. "What's up?" She bounces on her toes, which can't be easy in those clunky Doc Martens.

"I just got a call from my doctor." Her pinched lips don't quite hold back her wide grin. "I'm pregnant."

"I knew it," Margot squeals and claps her hands. "Didn't you just know it, Laurel?"

I choke out a feeble imitation of happiness. "Great news. Congratulations."

Clara rubs her slim belly. "Under the circumstances, we're moving up the wedding. If we wait much longer, my dress might not fit. So, Sunday, the ninth. We'll close the shop. I hope you can both come."

Margot elbows me in the ribs. "You and Dalton are next, right?"

Don't cry. Please don't cry. I snatch up a rag from beneath the counter and quick step back to the red door. "Noticed a smudge. I'll clean it up."

While Clara and Margot giggle and hug, I polish the brass doorknob as if wringing its neck. A whispered sob escapes, and I smother it in the dustrag.

Ever since my breakup with Carlo years ago, I've guarded my heart like freakin' Fort Knox. Somehow Dalton has pried open the door, and now I'm drowning in a stew of goopy, confusing, frustrating feelings.

"Sit taller, please." Agatha taps her paintbrush on her palette. "Just five more minutes, then I'll make us a nice licorice tea."

Forget tea. I need a shot of whiskey. I'm alone in the studio with the artist, who perches on her stool while Dido croons from the old boom box. The still, heavy air lulls my senses, but my mind whirs.

Dumped. Used. Discarded like a sneezed-in Kleenex. How else could he feel? We made passionate—I stop myself. Even inside my head, I don't dare say it. *We had passionate sex, and then I blurted out half-formed thoughts. When will I learn to think before I speak?*

I sniffle hard and try in vain to still my trembling chin.

"Oh, dear." Agatha sets down her brush and picks up a rag. "Here, this one's clean."

I hold it limply between two fingers.

"Go on, wipe. I can't paint a weepy muse." She clucks her tongue. "Pity. Last time, you were vibrating with sensuality, languid with pleasure. Now look at you. Deflated."

I swab my leaky eyes. "I'm sorry, Agatha. It's been a truly awful day."

She shifts to a second easel and clips on a fresh piece of paper. "What did that boy do to you?"

My voice quivers. "Nothing. He did everything right. I was in the wrong."

"I see." She makes one of her wise old guru nods, perfectly serene. "Even harder, eh? Well, I suppose you'll have to apologize."

"I can't." I hunch over, cradling the pain. "He'll think I'm in love with him."

"Are you?" Agatha chooses a pencil from her case.

I hug my uninjured leg to my chest and rest my cheek on my knee. "I can't be."

"But are you?"

Shit on a flaming stick, I probably am.

"Let your hair fall forward." The pencil scratches rhythmically. Agatha's gaze travels over my bent form, not judging, not probing, just seeing. "Your poster is gathering a lot of interest. I've seen them all over campus." She scrubs the paper with a bit of kneaded eraser. "Coffee shops, too. And the art supply store."

"Really?"

"Don't move, dear. Hold that pose." She waddles closer and shifts a lamp. "My friend Lorenzo was impressed. He's a photographer, you know."

I suck in a breath. "Does he give lessons?"

"He might do." Agatha's grin blooms, slow and calculating. "If a friend asked him to."

My pulse kicks up a notch. Careful to move only my lips, I ask, "Would you? for me?"

"I suppose I might. On two conditions. Don't smile."

"Sorry. What's the other condition?"

Agatha's throaty chuckle echoes in the empty studio. "That's not a condition. I just want your lovely melancholy expression. Think of the boy you wronged."

Dalton's voice echoes in my aching head, my hollow gut. *"I guess this is goodbye."*

"That's it. Good girl. Here are my conditions. First, you'll pose again. I like your lines."

"All right. And?"

"You'll apologize to your boyfriend before our next session." She sets her pencil down. "You're lovely when you're sad, but I much prefer your satisfied smile. La Joconde has nothing on you, dear."

That's going to hurt like hell, but I have to do it. I need Agatha's help—and even if Dalton is done with me for good, I need him to know how sorry I am. None of this is his fault. It's all on me, and I can't bear the thought of him suffering for my stupidity.

I give her a clipped nod. "Agreed."

"Splendid. I'll have Lorenzo call you tomorrow."

Chapter Twenty-Eight

♥

Dalton

The screen door's bang jerks my focus from the board I'm measuring.

"Hoo-boy, still hot out here." Maxie sets two frosty glasses of sludge on the porch table, then wipes her furrowed brow with her sleeve. "Mango, spirulina and beet juice. This'll put hair on your chest."

My dad laughs. "Thanks for the refreshments, Ms. Schmidt, but my son and I are hairy enough."

She pats his arm. "I like a furry man. Very sexy." Even at ninety, Maxie's a charmer.

Dad's phone tootles. "Oops. Gotta hurry. Date night tonight. Hannah loves her bingo. Can I leave you with this, Dalton?"

"Sure. Kiss Mom for me. I'll be by later."

He fixes me with a probing gaze.

I wave him off. "I'm fine. See you later."

I'm not fooling him, but my dad's too kind to poke at a sore spot.

I still haven't told anyone about my argument with Laurel—not Dad, not even Marcus. After a long, steamy shower that washed away Laurel's scent but not the ache of her rejection, I came right to Maxie's house and fulfilled my promise to repair her porch. I need something to focus on other than the hollowness in my center, the place Laurel used to warm. It's uncanny how fast, how easily we came together, how well our humor meshed, how perfectly our bodies fit. In less than two weeks, I fell so damn hard for her.

Getting over her will take a lot longer.

The physical effort of sawing and hammering provides a welcome outlet for my churning emotions. With Dad's help, I've strengthened the porch supports and replaced the last of the soggy floorboards. Painting will have to wait for another day, though, since Laurel's shift ends at seven. No way I can face her tonight. The plea in her beautiful gray eyes, the wobble in her voice—the memory clamps around my heart and twists. One more soft touch on my arm, one more tear sliding down her smooth cheek, and my resolve would crumble.

First Tiffany, then Clara, now Laurel. Three strikes, you're out.

Leaning on her sparkly cane, Maxie watches from the doorway.

"That should do it." I latch my toolbox.

She claps her gnarled hands. "What a fast worker. My grandniece is a lucky girl to have a fella like you, Dave."

I let the name slip-up pass without comment. Ditto the needling remarks about Laurel. Maxie doesn't know yet, does she?

She shuffles over and holds out an envelope. "Here's a check to cover the materials, and a little something extra to say thank you."

"I told you, that's not—"

"Nonsense. You've been busting your cute butt for us instead of enjoying your summer vacation." Her blue eyes twinkle. "I've dated a teacher or two. Actually..." She counts silently on her fingers and smiles at some distant memory. "Anyway, I know how hard you work, and I appreciate your sacrifice." She lowers herself onto the porch swing.

Gingerly, I sit beside her. The wooden seat creaks but holds my weight. "Well, thank you. What are your plans for this place, if I may ask?"

She purses her thin lips and gazes into the distance. "Been talking to my lawyer about it. Could donate it to an arts foundation, but I'd rather keep it in the family."

The Whiteaker District is perfect for a budding artist like Laurel. And she's already made some artsy connections, it seems. With Maxie's help, she could make lots more, if only she'd stick around. But those bright city lights blind her to our town's appeal. And to mine.

"Well, I'd better get going." I stand and stretch my stiff shoulders.

"Don't you want to wait for Laurel?"

"No, I have, um, stuff to do." I heft my toolbox. "It's been a pleasure, Ms. Maxie."

"Take care, Ichabod."

With an aching back and a leaden soul, I drive back to my empty apartment. I crave a punishing run. Maybe if I run far enough, hard enough, the pain outside will blot out the pain inside.

I should've turned back an hour ago, but despite my heavy legs, my aching feet, my burning lungs, I keep pounding along the riverside trail. So much for distraction. Thanks to the balmy August weather, the path is land-mined with couples holding hands, kissing on benches, and sprawled on the river-bank. Love is in the air, as irritating as pollen.

"Hey, it's that running guy from the poster," a woman calls. Shrill giggles follow. "Hey, hashtag running man."

Well, shit. I slow up and paste on a smile. "Evening, ladies."

It's a trio of girls in University of Oregon T-shirts. "I saw you on Insta," one squeals. She fiddles with her phone and shows me the screen. "You and your girlfriend are so cute."

My jaw sags. It's the photo taken by Maxie's friend at the 10K race—my arms around Laurel as she holds that cute kid and beams at me as if she loves me. But she doesn't. She's made that damn clear.

The caption reads: ***The guy from the race poster and the artist who made it. So cute together. My kid, not theirs, but wouldn't they make the sweetest babies? #EugeneRunningMan.***

"Holy shit," I mutter under my breath.

"Can we take a picture?" phone girl chirps.

"Um..." I pluck at my sopping shirt. "I'm kind of gross."

"So what?" They cluster around me and snap selfies, mugging for their own cameras. "What's your name, running man?"

"I'm Dalton." An idea flickers to life. Why not use this unwanted publicity to do some good? "Wanna help me out? Race for the Arts, September fifteenth. Add it to your post." I give them my widest smile. "See you there?"

"For sure. Hey, where's your girlfriend?" Phone girl taps her screen.

"She, uh, hurt her ankle."

"Aww. You two are mega-cute together." With a cheery wave, the girls trot away.

Great. A viral breakup. Next time someone asks, I'll just admit Laurel and I are no longer a thing. Perhaps Ms. Right was waiting for him out there, scrolling through her social media feed.

Except it doesn't feel over with Laurel. If it were over, the pain wouldn't be this sharp, needling me to do something, to explain, to hit the rewind button and try again.

Don't be an asshole. She doesn't want you. Leave her alone.

Weariness dogs my steps as I plod toward home.

Laurel

When I get home from work, a Prius sits in Maxie's driveway. Must be another of her artist friends. As I hobble toward the porch, a young woman with a shiny black bob pops from the car, holding her phone aloft. "Hey there. It's Laurel, right?"

"Um, yeah."

"I'm Jessica Alvarez, from the Eugene *Register-Guard*."

My whole body clenches. "Er—"

"I'm just gonna record this so I don't misquote you, okay?" Before I can answer, she bulldozes ahead. "You guys are totally going viral. How does that feel?"

I glance around for something, anything, to explain this non sequitur. "We're—I'm sorry, what?"

"You haven't seen it?" The reporter taps her phone screen and passes it over.

Oh no. Please no. My stomach plummets like a runaway elevator as I scroll through images and comments: my poster for the running club, photographed in shop windows, on restaurant counters, on streetlamp poles. Here's the photo of me and Dalton at the 10K race, gazing into each other's eyes like lovers. There are photos of Dalton running in the park without me. He's grinning with cute college girls, all handsome and sweaty and not mine anymore.

"Thanks to you, a hometown guy has his own hashtag. It's popping up as far away as Portland. See?" The reporter pokes the screen with her lacquered nail. "Everyone loves a love story." She glances at my wrapped ankle. "Too bad you can't run with him. But hey, this exposure will boost your art career."

I blink, dumbfounded. "My, uh—pardon?"

"You're a photographer, right?"

"Well, I like to take photos, but..."

She charges on, oblivious. "Do you miss running with Dalton?"

The corners of my mouth twitch upward. Here's an opportunity to make things right.

"You know, I really do. Dalton is—" I heave a sigh filled with sincere longing. "He's wonderful."

She claps a hand over her heart. "Aww, how sweet. How'd you guys meet?"

"On the trail." I relate how Dalton saved me from teenage harassers by pretending to be my boyfriend.

"And now he really is your boyfriend. What a great story." The reporter tucks her phone into her bag. "When can I get a picture of the two of you?"

"Oh, um..."

"Here's my card. Text me, okay?" Without waiting for an answer, she slaps the card into my palm, hops into her car, and drives away.

With shaky fingers, I pull my phone out and scroll through my Instagram feed. #EugeneRunningMan really is trending. Frickin' bizarre how strangers seize on a few images and spin their own narrative. Shaking my head, I scan the comment thread.

@RoadRunnerMama posted a photo of Dalton running alone on the riverside trail. ***"Doesn't he look sad without his sweetie?"***

"Laurel, honey?"

I jump at the sound of my mother's voice from the doorway.

"Who was that?"

"A reporter. She's, uh, doing a piece about our running club."

Mom nods. "Ah, those posters you made. Very nice. I didn't know you did photography."

"You saw it?"

"At the bank. And the beauty parlor. Maxie stole one from the Safeway bulletin board." She lowers herself onto the porch steps and pats the space beside her. "You can get away with all sorts of mischief when you're ninety."

I sit. "Thanks for staying today. And last night."

She quirks an eyebrow. "So. That young man."

Avoiding Mom's probing gaze, I adjust my ankle brace.

"No date tonight?"

"Nope," I mutter, my gaze downcast.

"Ah." She gently squeezes my shoulder. "I'm sorry, dear."

"Me too."

We sit side by side, listening to the cricket symphony and the whispering leaves.

Resting my cheek on my knees, I examine Mom's familiar face. There's a new softness in her crinkled gray eyes and the upward tilt of her lips. She looks—peaceful.

"Mom, is love worth it?"

"Worth what?"

"Giving up what you could've been?"

"Still chewing on that, eh?" She stretches out her long legs. "Who's to say what I could've been?"

"Are you kidding? With your talent, you could've played in a symphony, or a jazz band, or—"

"I am playing in a jazz band."

"But you could've—"

"Laurel." Mom waits until I meet her level gaze. "These woulda, coulda, shoulda games are pointless. If I never married your father, if I put my music first, I might've been a star. Or I might've been a mediocre pianist, playing in the Holiday Inn and living alone in a single-wide trailer." She lifts a lock of my hair and rubs it between her fingers. "And look what I would've missed. So, yes. Love is worth it."

Tears blur my vision.

"And look how your art career has taken off since moving to Eugene."

"My art career? Mom, I work in a book shop."

Mom waves off my protest. "Your posters are all over social media, and a reporter tracked you down to cover the story. Pretty impressive, kiddo."

I huff stray hairs from my forehead. "It was just a lucky shot. I don't have enough talent to be a photographer."

"Lots of people disagree. Eugene seems to have inspired your muse."

My lip wants to curl, but I force it back down. "But in San Francisco, I'd have more opportunities."

"There are a lot of photographers in San Francisco."

"Lots of competition, you mean?" My jaw clenches. Give up my plan for one poster? No way, no matter how many likes it gets on social media.

"Don't be so close-minded. There are opportunities all around you." Mom pats my back, stands, and goes inside, leaving me alone on the porch stairs.

"I'm not close-minded, I'm realistic," I mutter, hugging my knees. After a long mope, I haul myself to my feet—and notice the smooth, new, unpainted boards beneath them.

My mouth falls open in wonder. Dalton came back, even after I rejected him. He kept his promise to Maxie. Fresh tears prickle my eyes.

No boyfriend ever stood by me like this. And I sent him away. I am the stupidest woman on the planet.

Chapter Twenty-Nine

♥

Laurel

Lulu trails me as I roll down the cooking aisle on Clara's office chair. Cookbooks are perfect for my raw mood today. No roiling emotion, no sexy pictures, just cakes and pies and vicarious comfort.

The reporter said she wants a photo of us both—a golden opportunity to meet Dalton again, to apologize, to explain. But my text to him remains unanswered. With a defeated sigh, I get back to work...and yelp when a large hand clamps onto my shoulder and spins me around. Startled, I drop the heavy cookbook, barely missing Lulu's tail. The poor cat yowls and streaks away.

Tall as a redwood, Dalton glowers, his wide mouth pinched, his blue eyes icy. He brandishes a rolled-up newspaper. "What the hell is this?"

"I don't—"

"You break up with me because I said the big, bad L word. And now we're the love story of the year?"

A flush of heat shoots through me, and not the sexy kind. "Now just a damn minute. I never broke up with you."

"Sure felt like it." He crosses his arms and sticks out his lower lip, a pose that would be cute if not for the looming and snarling.

"Well, you sent me away before I could explain." I push to my feet. "I wanted to give you time to cool off. And the reporter didn't say she was going to run the story yet. She wanted a picture of us together first."

"That's what reporters do, Laurel. They run stories. Jesus." Clutching his skull with clawed hands, he stalks away, then pivots back and shoves the newspaper into my hands. "And she has plenty of pictures, thanks to your friend at the race."

I open to a column on page two. *Run for the Arts Leads to Runaway Love Story.*

Below the headline, my poster and the photo from social media. *North Eugene High School teacher and coach Dalton Garvey and photographer Laurel Jepsen make friends and warm hearts at the Springfield 10K. Their love story is an overnight viral sensation.*

I scan the article, my breakfast curdling in my stomach. The reporter twisted my story of Dalton's rescue into the ultimate rom-com meet cute.

He resumes his pacing. "It's bad enough you jerk me around like this. But to do it in public, in front of all my friends, my colleagues, my students, my family…" With each addition, his voice tightens like thumbscrews.

Customers are gawking at the crazy man. Eyes wide in alarm, Clara darts out from behind the counter. "Dalton, what the hell?"

He presses his fists to his eyes and drops into a chintz arm-chair. "Tomorrow's our first teacher workshop day. Everyone's going to ask about the story, and I get to tell them how you dumped me. Won't that be fun?"

Clara glares at me. "You dumped him?"

"I didn't, I swear." Embarrassment zaps all the power from my voice.

Dalton's having none of it. "First you tell me love is off the table, then you tell a freakin' reporter we're in love? A stranger?" If his eyes bugged out any farther, they'd fall onto the floor.

"I didn't tell her—"

He snatches the newspaper and stabs it with his long forefinger. "Paragraph two."

"Stop it, both of you." Clara grabs the red room key and thrusts it under my nose. "Here. Go talk this out in private." When neither of us moves, she shoves Dalton's shoulder. "Go on."

"All right, all right. Jeesh." He trudges to the red door and waits, breathing noisily on the back of my neck while my trembling hands fumble with the key.

When I switch on the overhead lamp, Dalton stalks past me and plops onto the antique settee, knees splayed wide, arms crossed, clenched fists making his biceps bulge. He looks—

Fierce. Powerful. Sexy. Damn it.

I set my crutches against the wall and lower myself into the other seat. At least we have the S-curved seatback to separate us. Touching him now would be a bad idea. Confusing. Distracting. Delicious.

I gulp a few breaths before diving into the deep end. "I'm sorry she took liberties with our story, Dalton. When she surprised me in front of Maxie's house last night, I was tired and in pain and really, really sad." My fingers knot the key's satin cord.

"Why should you be sad?" He counters, glowering at the rows of books. "You know what you want. And what you don't."

"Actually, I don't know. Not anymore. But I do know what a great guy you are. And how shitty I feel for hurting you." Despite warning bells clanging in my head, I lay my hand on his shoulder. The tense muscles there are hard as granite, but warmer—much warmer. And he doesn't shake me off.

"What happened to your plan?" His gaze softens, those long golden lashes shading vulnerability. If only I could untangle my tongue and my thoughts and my stupid, stupid heart and make him see how much I want him.

"My plan is in flux." I rest my chin on his shoulder and inhale his scent, clean and fresh and simple.

"Hmmph." When those blue velvet eyes pin me, my resolve drains away and puddles at my feet. The empty space leaves me light-headed. I need a solid anchor before I float away.

I grip his forearm. "Okay, here's a question. What do you want, Dalton?"

For a split second, his eyes widen.

Gotcha. You don't know either.

His mouth quirks to one side. "Funny. A friend asked me the same thing a few weeks ago."

"And what did you tell him?"

"Hard to remember, with you looking at me like that."

"Like what?"

"All pretty and sad and wide-open." With one finger, he lifts a strand of hair from my forehead and tucks it behind my ear. "Did I mention pretty?"

"Thank you. You're pretty too."

He snorts. "I'm a gawky beanpole."

I give his arm a playful smack. "Fishing for compliments?"

His lips twitch. "Wouldn't hurt."

"Okay." I clasp the back of his neck and gently knead the tight ropes of muscle. My thumb circles the ridge at the base of his skull. "I find you very attractive, Dalton. Distractingly so. When you're this close, my plan starts to crumble."

He cocks an eyebrow. "And that scares you?"

"Shitless."

His chuckle warms my icy core.

"You still haven't answered my question." I hold his cobalt gaze until he blinks.

"Okay. What do I want?" He pushes to his feet and slowly circles the little room, running his fingertips over the book spines. He pulls one off the shelf, huffs through his nose, and puts it back. He tries another, flipping through the pages. "Wow." Back onto the shelf. Finally, he stops behind me and rests his hands on my shoulders, tracing circles with his thumbs. "I want—a partner."

"Uh huh?"

"Someone who's real. No pretense. No games."

"Okay."

"And she has to be at least as pretty as you."

"Gotcha." Hope flutters in my chest.

"If she likes to run, that's a plus." Round and round, his thumbs knead my muscles, squeezing, soothing. "And she has to be kind."

I've got some work to do on that front. "Anything else?"

"Yeah." He slides into the seat opposite me, spearing me with his intense stare. "She has to be here, Laurel. Because I can't leave. My sister's in Denver. My brother's in jail. My parents need me. And that's where we're stuck."

A chill descends over me, making it hard to speak. "But you said—"

"I know. But I'm starting to see your point of view. I can't fall in love with someone who comes with a ticking detonator. Count-down to goodbye." He cups my cheek. "It's too hard, Laurel. So, I guess you're right. Until you figure out where you want to be, I'd better keep my distance."

My heart, a moment ago filled with fizzy, sparkly hope, tips over with a thunk. All the joy runs out, drips away...gone.

A knock on the door. Clara leans in. "You two sorted things out?"

"For now." Dalton pushes to his feet and holds out his hand. He pulls me up, then lets me go. In a few swift strides, he slides past Clara and out the door.

After closing the shop at seven, I wrestle my damn crutches into my Beetle and slam the door. The car's interior is stifling. Sweat prickles my forehead and soaks my bra band. At the rate I'm going, it'll be years before I can afford a car with AC. Even with the windows down, the muggy air barely stirs.

Traffic sucks too. Cars and trucks choke Willamette Street on both sides, and the radio traffic lady warns of more blockages. If it weren't for Maxie, I'd keep on driving all the way to San Francisco, just leave my belongings behind and start fresh, forget I ever set foot in Eugene. Forget running. Take up rowing, or biking, or yoga—anything that doesn't remind me of him. Of what I threw away.

I should just end it. Hell, Dalton thought I already had, so he's got a head-start on suffering. It's cruel of me to ask him to keep his feelings on hold until I untangle this knot of conflicting thoughts and desires and emotions. If I bow out now, he'll be healed soon and can move on with his life, and I'll be nothing more than a brief, bad episode, and...

I coast to a stop in the shade of a huge maple, fold over on the steering wheel, and sob.

Where the hell did this come from? I'd nearly convinced myself Dalton wasn't worth a change in plans. So why is my heart jackhammering my ribs? Why is my stomach trying to turn itself inside-out? I wipe my streaming eyes and pull out my phone.

Please answer, Davonte. Please, please, please.

"Hey there, doll-face. What's up?"

My voice catches. "I can't, it's all, it's just, oh God, D." My words dissolve into pathetic blubbering.

"Oh, my dear Lord, did Maxie pass?"

"No." I switch the phone to speaker and honk into a tissue. "I fucked it up, D. It's all gone to shit."

"You got fired again?"

"Worse. I think, maybe—" I sniffle hard and swipe my streaming nose. "Maybe I fell in love."

His voice takes on a sing-song rhythm, as if calming a hysterical kindergartener. "Laurel, that's a good thing. Love is what we all want, right?"

"But I botched it, and now he doesn't want me anymore." I hunch in my seat, shoulders heaving, fists clenched around my soggy Kleenex.

Davonte clucks his tongue. "Listen, we wrapped up a show last night. I've got a few days off. I'm coming up there."

"Up here? To Eugene?"

"No, to Paris. Of course to Eugene."

"But you—"

"But me no buts, young lady. We'll go paint the town, just like in the old days."

"Okay." I sniffle, the waterworks slowing to a trickle. "That'd be nice."

"Hell, yeah. Now, chin up."

"Yes, sir," I mutter, but he's already clicked off.

I check my reflection in the mirror. Red, swollen eyes, pale lips clamped tight, blotchy skin. There's no way I can sneak past Mom and Maxie without comment. With my belly grinding like the gears on my VW, I steer toward home.

Chapter Thirty

♥

Dalton

Marcus flings open the door. "My best friend's a celebrity. What happened, Cue Ball? We go to the beach for a few days, and you go viral."

I palm the back of my neck. "Wasn't my idea, believe me. Some friend of Laurel's snapped our picture with her kid and posted it on Instagram. Now it's everywhere."

"So's her poster. Best we ever had. Your girlfriend's talented."

I slump against the door frame. "She's not my girlfriend. Not anymore."

"Oh shit." Sympathy shines in my friend's dark eyes. "Sorry, man. I thought she really liked you."

Destiny sweeps into the living room, her sundress swishing around her legs. "Shut the door, guys. You'll let in all the bugs." She stands on tiptoe to smooch my cheek. "All ready for an exhilarating day of teacher meetings?"

Marcus and I both groan.

She chuckles and pats her husband's behind. "Poor babies, in shock after summer break. Sandwich, Dalton? We've got ham, roast beef, and turkey."

"No thanks, Miss D. I'm not hungry." Actually, my stomach feels like a bottomless pit of doom, but food won't fix that.

Marcus brightens. "I'll take a sandwich, babe."

She snorts. "Fix it yourself. Aliyah needs a bath." She starts up the stairs, calling over her shoulder, "Unless you want to bathe the baby and let me drink beer with Dalton."

Not a bad idea, actually. I could use a woman's perspective, especially a smart, no-nonsense woman like Destiny.

Marcus waves her off. "We're good."

I trail him into the kitchen and perch on a stool while Marcus assembles a monster roast beef and cheddar sandwich. My stomach rumbles. Guess it didn't get the message that we're in mourning.

"See?" Marcus pokes my shoulder. "Big guy like you needs fuel."

Armed with cold beer, a sandwich, chips, and deli potato salad, I sit beside Marcus on the rear deck, chewing in companionable silence. Beyond the glow from the house, quiet summer darkness thrums with insect song and the faraway hiss of freeway traffic.

I wipe my mouth on a paper napkin. "You have a beautiful place out here."

Marcus empties his bottle and sets it on the low table between us. "You regret giving up your house in the Whiteaker?"

"Sometimes. But you know, lawyers, bills."

"Yeah. Sucks."

I huff a bitter laugh. "Sucks. That word pretty much sums up my summer."

Marcus cocks an eyebrow. "It's not that bad, is it?"

"It's that bad." I slump back in my seat and stare out into the darkness.

He playfully punches my arm. "Come on, bud. Spill it. You'll feel better."

"No I won't."

"Bullshit. Gotta lance the boil. Squeeze the poison out."

I wrinkle my nose. "You're disgusting, you know that?"

"It's what my grandma always said. The bit about boils, I mean."

I swallow, my throat suddenly parched despite the beer. "It just feels like it's never gonna happen for me."

"What's never gonna happen?"

I sweep my hand in an arc, taking in the deck, the yard, the house, the trees. "All this. Home. Family. Love."

"Is this what you want?"

My chin drops to my chest. "What's the point of wanting something you can't have?"

"Who says you can't?"

"Fate, I guess." I slump further in my Adirondack chair. "It's like, every time I think I've found the one, she turns out to be rotten. Or taken. Or both."

"And which is Laurel?"

"She's taken."

Marcus straightens, stiff with indignation. "She has another guy, but she went after you? That's cold."

"Not another guy. Another goal." I raise my bottle, find it empty, and set it down with a sigh. "Wants a big-time art career. Gallery owner, manager, curator. I'm not sure. Neither is she."

"Then what's the problem?"

"Got her heart set on San Francisco. Her friend's gonna get her a job in a fancy art gallery. I can't compete with those bright city lights." I pick at my beer label, and flakes of colored paper flutter onto my lap like dandruff.

With a grunt, Marcus stands, goes into the house, and returns with fresh beers. He hands one to me. "Guess the newspaper story's like salt in the wound."

"More like gravel. And all that social media shit." I gulp my beer. "They say we all get our fifteen minutes of fame, but I hoped mine would be more meaningful, you know?"

We prop our oversize feet on the table and drink in silence.

After a long moment, Marcus sets down his bottle and tents his fingers in front of his face. "Here's the most important question. You still want her?"

I close my eyes and exhale until my lungs are completely empty. Memories wash over me, swirling like autumn leaves caught in a whirlwind—Laurel's silvery laugh, the glow on her face in the art gallery. The way she nuzzled my sweaty neck after a run. The way she upended her life to take care of Maxie. Her soft, warm body relaxed against mine in sleep. Her steady footfalls beside me on the trail. The raw vulnerability in her storm cloud eyes when she confessed she doesn't know what she wants or where she's going. Her feelings for me scare the shit out of her, but at least she's honest about it.

I drew a deep breath, cool, clean air rushing into my lungs. "Yeah. I still want her."

"Okay then. You need a plan."

Chapter Thirty-One

Laurel

Flick, swish, my rag chases dust and cat hair from the front table display. I sneak another glance at my boss. Her thick auburn ponytail swinging, Clara hums merrily as she restocks paper bags behind the counter. It's been two days since Dalton left the Red Room. Did he tell Clara about our breakup? If so, she's a damn good actress. No sharp glances, no reproving scowls, just a dreamy, contented grin. She catches my eye, pats the breast pocket of her satin blouse, and pulls out a slip of paper. "Hey, I almost forgot. You got a call this morning."

My heart breaks into a gallop. Dalton? Why would he call the shop?

"Ernesto Diaz, down the street. Owns that furniture place. Gorgeous hand-carved stuff. Expensive as sin."

"He called me?"

Clara hands me the notepaper. "Wants to talk to you about doing his front window display."

"How—what?"

Clara's smile holds a tinge of mischief. "Don't look so surprised. He likes what you did here, and when I told him you made the running man poster, he wanted to see what you could do with his place."

My face must reveal my abject panic because Clara gentles her tone. "He's a nice guy. He won't bite you. Give him a call."

"Um, okay."

The front doorbell tinkles for a chatty trio of teen girls wearing cat-ear headbands. Clara points behind the wooden screen and raises her hand in a telephone gesture.

Gulping down the huge, prickly lump in my throat, move to Clara's office space, pull out my phone and dial the furniture dude's number.

Five minutes later, I emerge, my teeth clenched in a giddy, manic grin.

"So, everything good?" Clara asks.

"Yeah, he, uh...I'm meeting him at four." The sum he offered me to redesign his window display left me dizzy, even a bit nauseated.

She beams. "Great. Just promise me you won't run off to open your own firm."

"Doing what?"

"What do they call it—" She rotates her wrist.

Margot's spiky head pops up from the children's section. "Visual merchandising. Told ya. You're good at this stuff." She beats out a drum riff on the shelf before squatting down again among the picture books.

On my lunch break, I grab my crutches and hobble up the street to check out the furniture store. Clara's right. Those gorgeous, elaborate chairs look like they grew organically, with their twisting legs, arm rests, and backs of gleaming polished wood, plus velvet and satin seats. They'd be right at home on the set of a fantasy movie set—thrones for elven kings. That's what I'll do, surround them with a magical forest of towering paper trees, Spanish moss, ferns on the floor, maybe a wizard's hat and a magic wand on the table, and a book of spells, as if the wizard had just stepped away...

·♥·♥·♥·♥·♥·

Back at the bookshop, Margot flashes a sly grin. "You're popular today. Someone's waiting for you." She points toward the performing arts aisle. "He's mega-cute."

My breath catches. Dalton? I smooth my batik tunic over my leggings. *Keep cool. Don't freak out and scare him off.* On my crutches, I swing down the aisle.

Davonte hops up from a chintz armchair and flings his arms wide. "Doll-face." His tight hug sends my crutches clattering to the floor.

"D, you came," I squeal and rain kisses all over his gorgeous face.

He releases me and gives me a quick once-over with his bulging dark eyes. "Christ on a cracker, what happened to you?"

"Fell off my stupid heels. God, it's good to see you." I squeeze his shoulders. "Ooo, you've been working out." He's always had gorgeous legs, ever since we met on the U of O track team, but now his upper body has filled out beautifully.

"Of course, doll. In my line of business, appearance matters." He purses his lips to the side. "Is this your artistic look?"

"Oh, er...Guess I'm just trying to blend in. You know, hippie-dippy Eugene."

"Girl, that psychedelic bus left long ago."

I rescue my crutches, and we move toward the front of the shop. "Thank you for coming up here. I need a big shot of your wisdom."

Behind the counter, Clara and Margot whisper. Margot pipes up. "Introduce us to your friend, Laurel?"

"Davonte Thomas, meet my boss, Clara Martelli. And this is Margot DuPont."

Margot leans onto her elbows and sighs. "You are so pretty."

His thick, glossy lashes flutter in a display of false modesty. Davonte knows he's a stunner, with those enormous eyes, satiny bronze skin, and a chiseled physique. And does he ever know how to work it! His voice purrs like a double bass. "Why, thank you, dear lady. I do what I can to make up for my utter lack of talent."

Clara asks, "Are you an artist too?"

"Actor. Failed actor, so far. But I do love theater folk, so I work in theater management."

"Ah." Clara nods. "Like Laurel wants to work in art galleries."

"Exactly," I agree. "If I can't be an artist, I can still surround myself with art and hang out with artsy people."

Davonte arches one perfect eyebrow. "Who says you can't be an artist? The barista next door showed me your poster. That's good stuff, girl." He leans closer and whispers, "You were right. He's mighty cute."

My cheeks flush. "Well, he's—"

"The barista, I mean. Your boyfriend's okay too."

I roll my eyes. "I only took the picture. Margot did the rest."

"Bullshit." Margot plants her fists on her hips. "I just taught you how to work the graphics program." She grasps Davonte's arm. "Laurel's all over Insta. Have you seen it? Hashtag Eugene Running Man."

He nods. "Arnie showed me. So, where's your running man, Laurel?"

He ran away.

But I can't say that in front of Clara, so I change the subject. "My shift ends at four, then I'm meeting with a guy up the street about some design work. Can we meet for dinner?"

"Of course, baby. I'll just check out your shop, then go visit a few friends." He touches his forefinger to his lips. "Now, what did that charming man say? Ah yes, the red door."

"I don't know, Laurel." Clara scowls in mock sternness. "Do you trust this guy?"

"With my life." I lean over the counter and snag the key. "The question is, if we let him in, will we be able to drag him out?"

Grinning, he snatches the key and disappears behind the red door.

I glance back there after twenty minutes. And again after forty. Did he somehow slip out without my notice? I'm arranging new arrivals on the front table when the red door creaks open.

With trembling fingers, Davonte clutches a stack of books to his chest. "Oh my dear Lord. Laurel, why didn't you tell me? I woulda been up here weeks ago."

I bite back a knowing grin. "Find something interesting back there?"

Slack-jawed, he nods. "Ring me up." The books he plunks onto the counter include two volumes of homoerotic photography, an explicit manga book, and a volume entitled *The Phallus: A Treatise*. Clutching his purchases, he trots toward the coffee shop like a kid with a delicious secret to share.

Come quitting time, I peek into the café. Davonte's standing behind the counter as if he's been working there all along. While Arnie pulls espressos, Davonte hands him syrups, milk pitchers, and other coffee accoutrements. As soon as the last customer in line is served, they turn their backs and giggle over a book open on the rear counter. Arnie whispers into Davonte's ear. Davonte laughs and hip-bumps him.

Well, at least somebody's love life is clicking. "Hey Arnie. Hey D."

Both men turn, and Arnie's cheeks flush a becoming shade of pink.

"I'm heading to my meeting. I'll text you when I'm done, okay?"

"Sure thing, doll. Sushi for dinner?"

"Yes, please."

They turn away, Davonte's hand on the small of Arnie's back. A twinge of jealousy pings behind my eyes. I loved it when Dalton touched me that way. Will he ever again?

Chapter Thirty-Two

♥

Dalton

Sweat trickles down the back of my neck as I pace on the griddle-hot sidewalk in front of Clara's shop. I tug my Oregon Ducks cap low over my eyes and make another pass. No sign of Laurel. Clara catches my eye and beckons me inside.

I sidle up to the counter. "I feel like a spy."

She nods at my hat. "If that's meant to be a disguise, you're going to have to up your game."

"Trench coat and fedora?"

"And a pistol hidden behind a folded newspaper." She pulls her phone from her pocket. "Speaking of which, the newspaper story on you and Laurel is keeping your hashtag alive."

"Jeesh. I wish that business would just die down." As I predicted, almost every staff member of North Eugene High School teased me about that story during today's meetings. I even caught the supply clerk snapping my photo for her Instagram—as if greater Eugene gives a rat's ass about their running man making photocopies of his syllabus.

"Everyone loves a love story." She pulls me behind the wooden screen that conceals her office space. "So, Mr. Super-Spy, your plan is working."

"The furniture guy?"

"She's there now. If that goes well, the beauty salon around the corner will probably bite next."

I squeeze her hand. "I really appreciate this. With your connections, we can keep her busy."

She scrunches her lips to one side. "It's creative work, but will she see it as art?"

"Well, I've got something artsy-fartsy for her. Our school's art teacher helps out at the Rainbow Arts Center, the one—"

"Ah, the charity race." She punches my arm playfully. "Good thinking, you."

"Maybe. Laurel doesn't seem too fond of the whole working-with-kids idea. But it would give her the chance to set up an art exhibit."

"I hope this works. Laurel's a real help here. I'd hate to lose her."

"You and me both."

The doorbell jingles. Clara steps toward the counter. "Well, Laurel, how'd it go?"

I suck in a deep, centering breath and pull off my ball cap. *Just say hi. No big deal.* She's only a few steps away, and yet my feet remain glued to the floor—until a baritone voice says Laurel's name and she answers with a delighted squeal. Glue dissolved, I peek around the screen.

A muscular guy stands at Laurel's side, his arm around her waist. His dress shirt and slacks reek of money, and his exaggerated pompadour gleams. Rich and movie-star handsome. No way could I ever compete with him. My stomach sinks like a boulder in a pond. Blub.

And then I remember Marcus' question: Do you still want her?

Damn straight I do. Squaring my shoulders, I stride to the counter and flash my best imitation of a nonchalant grin. "How's it going, Laurel?"

She jolts, eyes wide, voice tight. "Hi, Dalton. It's, um, going great, actually."

The movie star just grins at me with gleaming, perfect teeth. Then at Laurel. Then at me. He elbows her.

"Oh, right. Dalton, this is my friend Davonte. From San Francisco."

The gay BFF? Relief floods me.

Davonte extends his manicured hand. His grip is soft, but his eyes are sharp as he rakes his gaze up and down my body, lingering below my belt. "Delighted to meet you, Dalton. Laurel has told me so much about you."

She glares at her friend and clears her throat.

"Likewise," I tell him.

The guy's sly, bulging eyes slide to Laurel. "We were just going to get some sushi. Why don't you join us?"

I take a step backward. "Oh, I wouldn't want to intrude. I just need a quick word with Laurel before you go."

The guy actually pushes Laurel toward me, then sashays toward the coffee shop. "You know where to find me."

Clara dangles the key to the red door. "You two need some privacy. Here you go."

"Fine," Laurel huffs. She snatches the key and swings away on her crutches.

Once the red door closes behind us, she leans against the bookcase, arms crossed, teeth worrying her lower lip. I know that look. She's got something to say, but she's all knotted up inside. Should I wait her out? *No, knucklehead, she's waiting for you to start.*

I sidle closer and trace the curve of her elbow with my forefinger. "First of all, I want to apologize for being such an ass the other day. The newspaper story, all this social media stuff—I should have handled it better. None of it was your fault." I slide my hand down her arm and wrap my fingers around her clenched fist. "I'm really sorry, Laurel."

She keeps her gaze downcast, and her voice rings flat, with none of the spark I've come to love "None of that was your fault either. I'm sorry you got caught up in it." At last, she looks at me, her gray eyes swimming with pain—hurt I inflicted by being a grumpy, conclusion-jumping jerk.

I pry open her fist and weave my fingers through hers. "Listen, what I said the other day is true. I can't leave Eugene, but I'm not ready to give up hope. I'm still interested in you. In us."

Her brows contract as if she's going to cry, and I hurry to change the subject before the tears come and I start babbling nonsense, desperate to comfort her.

I drop her hand. Gotta get some distance so I can think clearly. "So, I have a favor to ask."

"Oh?" I'm convinced she's faking cool composure as she pulls a book from the shelf and opens it.

I glance at the page, an illustration of Baroque lords and ladies cavorting in a garden, fucking on benches, beneath trees, against a wall, the women's frothy skirts flung high to expose rosy, round rumps.

A memory zaps into focus: Laurel pressed against me in the woods, my fingers inside her, her head thrown back, her gasps and moans...

"What favor, Dalton?" Her clipped tone yanks me back to reality.

"Our art teacher helps out at the Rainbow Arts Center. On race day, they're doing an exhibit of kids' artwork. Some of my students go there."

"Uh huh?" She flips another page. A seated man, naked, bearded, and muscular. Astride him, a lushly curvy woman crouches in reverse cowgirl, sneaking a shy look over her shoulder as if to say, "Am I doing this right?" Laurel wouldn't be so shy. She'd flash a wicked grin as she rides me, her long hair swaying with each roll of her hips...

I clear my throat. "Your poster has brought them lots of media attention. They want your help to organize their exhibit."

She scowls, clearly suspicious. "Why would they want my help?"

"Because you're good, Laurel." I squeeze her shoulders.

Her muscles yield to my touch, softening, but her tone does not. "They don't know that. They've never seen my work besides the poster."

"Babe, why are you so stubborn? You're good at this stuff. Arranging art. Photography. Shop windows."

She whirls on me, her gray eyes squinty and sharp. "What do you know about my shop windows?"

Mayday! Our plan won't work if she knows Clara and I are setting up jobs for her. I step back and gesture toward the front of the shop. "Clara's window never looked better."

She scoffs but doesn't contradict me. "How's your ankle?"

"Not too bad. Splint comes off next week."

"I'm really sorry you're hurting." Let her interpret that as she wishes.

"Yeah. Well." She claws through her blue-tipped hair. Loose today, like a silk curtain. My fingers itch to touch it. "You've got their number?"

"Oh, right." I fish a business card from my pocket and press it into her palm. Tickly warmth slides up my arm when her fingers brush mine.

Her gaze flicks up, her beautiful mouth set in a grim line, tight and guarded. "Anything else, Dalton?"

Desire overrides thought. "Yeah. Just one thing."

I wrap my arms around her tense shoulders and smash my lips to hers. This wasn't part of the plan, but touching her is inevitable, inescapable. She gives a sharp little gasp but doesn't fight me.

"Laurel." I inhale her scent, her heat. A sigh parts her lips, and I stroke my tongue over hers, sweet as sugared velvet. Her body fits mine perfectly, soft breasts pressed over my heart, long, smooth thighs parting to let me in...

And strong arms pushing me back. I stumble into the loveseat, gouging my palms on the sharp wooden curlicues.

"That's not fair," she growls. "You can't keep jerking me around, Dalton."

Caught between passion and frustration, I fling my arms wide. "I'm jerking you around? Who tumbled into my bed and then pushed me away?"

"You wanted it as much as I did."

"More. I still do." I gape at her for a long, silent moment.

She glares back, and then her gaze drifts downward, right to the huge boner pressed against my zipper.

Great. This is why I avoid this room. Too dangerous. No one out there will know it was Laurel, and not the racy books, who triggered this reaction. They'll just point and laugh at the disgusting perv. Another juicy image on Insta.

To my horror, she scoops up her crutches and hobbles out the door, leaving me to calm myself. Fat chance of that.

From outside come raised voices and a blast of light. I peer around the red door. At the counter, a shaggy guy aims a big TV camera right at Laurel's pale, stunned face while a bubbly reporter thrusts a microphone at her.

Trapped by a boner. I have to help her. Driven by panic and protectiveness, I frantically search for a shield. Just outside the doorway, I spot a large hardback volume of cupcake recipes. Perfect. I clutch it over my crotch and stride forth to save my woman, whether she likes it or not.

"There he is, the man of the hour." The reporter swivels to me, and her cameraman follows.

Laurel faces me, so pale and shaky I'm not sure if she's going to pass out or throw up. Her gaze drops to the book I'm holding over my still-insistent erection.

Time to improvise.

"Thanks for helping me find this one. My sister will love it." I plant a kiss on her temple.

"It's Dalton, right?" the reporter chirps. "Sandra Wong from KVAL. How does it feel to become an overnight celebrity?"

I roll my eyes at the absurdity of the whole situation. Cupcakes, public boners, real/pretend romance, all playing out on Instagram and TV. What next?

"It's pretty weird," I tell her. "Right, Laurel?"

She flashes a manic, wide-eyed grin. "Very weird."

"I'll bet you miss running with your girlfriend."

God, yes. I put my arm around her shoulders. "I really do. It's lonely out there on the trails without her."

Laurel catches my eye, and her frozen expression thaws just a little.

"So, what's next for you two? Wedding bells, perhaps?"

She stiffens. "Um, we just—"

"We're just taking it day by day, you know," I chime in. "Laurel's pretty busy, what with her photography and her shop windows. And she's helping out at the Rainbow Arts Center."

The reporter beams. "My niece goes there. What a great program for Eugene's youth. So, you do shop windows too?"

Clara points. "She did this one. I'm so pleased with her work."

The cameraman zooms in on the front window display.

"You're the owner?" the reporter asks.

Clara introduces herself and makes a quick plug for Book Nirvana.

The camera closes in on Laurel again. "So, tell us about your photography. What are your favorite subjects?"

"Oh. Um." She blinks rapidly. "Runners, I guess."

The reporter laughs. "Good choice for Track Town, USA."

Chuckles all around, though Laurel's sounds more like choking.

"Where can we see more of your work?"

She gapes, frozen.

I nudge her. "Aren't you going to show some photos at Run for the Arts?"

"Um, yeah. Maybe." Out of the camera's view, her hand slides around my waist and pinches me so hard I bite my lip to keep from yelping.

"We look forward to it." The reporter motions the cameraman back for a shot of the two of us, pressed together in a false display of loving contentment.

I keep my grip on Laurel as the TV crew packs up and leaves. Outside, a dozen onlookers aim their phones through the shop window. When she squirms in my grasp, I press a kiss to her ear and whisper, "Smile, we're on camera."

She nuzzles my neck and whispers, "What the hell, Dalton? Maxie is dying. My life is a shambles. And now you're giving me homework?" With a sexy growl, she bites my earlobe, and not in a fun way.

"Ow. I'm sorry, all right? I just thought—"

She smiles prettily for the camera, but her eyes shine with cold fire. "You just thought you could manipulate me into staying in Eugene." She drops her grip, backs away, and hisses, too quiet for the others to hear, "Think again."

Chapter Thirty-Three

♥

Laurel

My forehead aches, my eyes sting, and my lady bits tingle. How is it possible to be so pissed off and so turned on at the same time?

Davonte shoots me a worried glance. "You look like you need a minute, doll. I'll go check on our order." He hops out, leaving me in the parking lot of the sushi place, resting my folded arms on the steering wheel.

Dalton wants me back. That should make me happy, right? But his blatant manipulation has me seething. Obviously, the window design job was his doing. And his friend just happened to want my help at the Rainbow Arts Center? How convenient. But ambushing me on camera was a jerk move. He knows damn well I'm not a trained photographer. Thanks to him, the whole town will see my race poster was a fluke—smoke and mirrors and graphics editing software.

Maybe he really has faith in me? Dismissing the thought, I push to my feet and slam the car door.

Waiting at the restaurant entrance, Davonte fiddles with his phone. I peer over his shoulder at a lively, emoji-filled discussion in progress. An eggplant pops onto the screen.

"Who are you talking to?"

He slides the phone into his pocket. "Just a friend."

"I wish my love life was as busy as yours, D."

"It only takes one, darlin'." He bumps my hip with his. "The right one."

"Is Arnie the right one for you?"

He gapes. "How did you know?"

"You've been flirting with him all afternoon." I hobble to the takeout line. "Honestly, I'm a little jealous."

"You have no reason to be jealous." He clucks his tongue. "That tall drink of water is totally besotted with you."

"How do you know?"

"Hello, the way he handled that reporter? Full-on protection mode."

I swipe my hand down my face. "You saw all that?"

"Watched the whole thing from the café doorway. You didn't see me?"

"My attention was focused elsewhere."

He laughs. "The way you stared all bug-eyed, I worried you were gonna puke on camera."

Good point. Without Dalton beside me, fielding the reporter's questions, I probably would have looked like an even bigger ass. Still, his interference sticks in my craw like a fish-bone. "Did you hear what he said about taking photos?"

Davonte shrugs. "So, take some photos. You always take good pictures."

"That's not the point, D." I knuckle my eyes. "My parents. Dalton. Maxie. I'm so sick of everyone trying to manipulate my life from behind the scenes. I feel like a fucking mari-onette."

"Wow. Defensive, much?" He hooks his arm through mine. "Must be low blood sugar. Let's get you fed."

While we wait in line, I check my new phone app for tracking sodium. "Plain rolls are okay. No fried crispies, no tasty sauces."

He elbows me. "Speaking of tasty sauce, tell me about Dalton."

I snarl my fingers into my hair. "He's—shit."

"He is not." Davonte plants his fists on his hips. "He's a lovely man, and he's over the moon for you."

"I don't mean *he's* shit. I mean, I can't figure it out. It's tearing me up, D."

"On the phone, you told me you were in love with him."

The couple ahead of us in line pause their conversation.

Davonte pokes the man's shoulder. "Mind your business."

"Aren't you that artist?" His girlfriend points to the counter where the race poster hangs beside concert fliers and a lost cat notice. "I saw you on Instagram. Such a sweet love story." She raises her phone.

Davonte snarls, "Girl, you snap her picture, and I will snap your phone."

"Jeez, okay." With a snotty huff, she tucks it away.

Great. Now strangers recognize me on the street. No doubt, it'll get even worse after the eleven o'clock news. Damn nosy reporter. When will this stupid story finally die down? And how can I figure out my feelings for Dalton when strangers keep shoving our phony relationship in my face?

Twenty minutes later, we pull into Maxie's driveway. Davonte climbs from the car. "Old place looks the same. Someone fixed the porch?"

"Yeah. Dalton."

"Before you had your big fight?"

I sigh. "After." Because of course he did. On top of all his other fine qualities, he's honorable too.

Davonte whistles. "Integrity and a big dick. That guy's a keeper."

I drop my keys. "How did you—"

"Arnie told me." He winks. "He has a keen eye for such things."

When I open the door, Maxie looks up from setting the table. With her typical flair, she's dressed for the occasion in a silk kimono over patterned leggings.

"Dante," she crows, throwing her arms wide.

I close my eyes on a groan.

Davonte elbows me and whispers, "Oh hush. All old people mix up names. Maxie knows who I am." Squealing with glee, he runs to Maxie, scoops her up, and spins her around.

She pats his cheek, her face pleated with smile lines. "Good to see you, dear heart." She inclines her downy head. "You sure you haven't changed your mind? You and Laurel would make such a cute couple."

"Sorry. It's out of my hands. I'm firmly on team sausage."

Maxie cackles.

We unpack our sushi feast and dig in. Between mouthfuls, Maxie tells us about her day with one of Elmer's friends, a sculptor who works in driftwood and plastic trash she finds on the beach.

After cleaning up, Davonte and I sit on the porch swing and watch the neighbor kids chase a soccer ball, their squeals and laughter ringing in the heavy, deep-blue twilight.

He stretches his legs. "Ahh. This really is like old times. You and me on Maxie's porch, talking about life, love, sex..."

I prop my injured ankle on my knee and dig at an itchy spot beneath the brace. "Life was simpler then. Easier."

"Not really." He pats my knee. "Remember how torn up you were when Carlo told you he was going home to his old girlfriend? Thought we were going to have to sedate you."

I groan. "I was beyond furious. And so heartbroken." I pivot and grab his hand. "See, that's the problem. You open up to someone, relax your defenses, and they stab you right in the gooey parts."

He pats my hand. "So, this new guy stabbed your gooey parts?"

"Yeah." I slump in my seat. "He's looking for love. I'm not. I mean, what's the point? I'm not staying here, and falling for a local guy will just make leaving harder." I sniffle and swipe at my eyes. "I can't go through that mess again, D."

He tucks a loose strand behind my ear. "Sounds like it's too late. You already fell. Otherwise, you wouldn't be torn up like this."

"It's just, I can't, arrrgh!" I scrub both hands down my face.

Davonte is probably the only friend who'll put up with my nonsense long enough to sort out this tangled mess. I gulp a deep breath. "Okay, so we had sex."

He shrugs. "Of course."

"And it was really great." A shiver dances over my skin. "I mean, really, really great. Astonishing."

"Good for you. So?" His kind, dark eyes glitter under the porch light.

"I woke up in his bed and realized I was on the verge of giving up my dream. For a guy. How pathetic is that, D?"

He taps his pursed lips with his forefinger. "Now see, that's where you lost me. Why does loving this guy equal giving up your dream?"

I snarl my fingers into my hair. My position is getting harder and harder to defend. "The thing is, there aren't many gallery jobs in Eugene. In a bigger city like San Francisco—"

"You wouldn't have a social media following. You'd be one tiny guppy in a huge shark tank." He squeezes my hand. "Take it from me. I'm starting to wonder if I wouldn't be better off building my résumé somewhere smaller before tackling the big city theater scene."

My chest hollows. "You might leave SF?"

"I mean, I'm really just a secretary. If it weren't for my uncle's generosity, I could never afford to live there. And my work keeps me too busy to take the acting classes I obviously need."

"But you're so talented, so pretty."

He kisses my cheek. "Thanks, love. But so's everyone else competing for those roles. And I miss Eugene. It's a fun town, all artsy and funky."

This can't be happening. If he leaves, where will I go when I'm done here?

Davonte slumps in his seat and runs his hands through his hair, mussing his suave pompadour. "Dreams are a powerful motivator, love, but there's a time to face reality. I step over used needles and drugged-out addicts on my way to work. San Francisco isn't what I expected." He gulps the rest of his iced tea. "Wow. Maxie hasn't changed her recipe."

He grimaces and wipes his mouth. "All I'm saying is, don't be so quick to write off this place. You could build something here."

I stare out into the night, my head throbbing in time to my heartbeat. "But it *hurts* to give up my dream, D. I really love art, and running a gallery is my only chance at a career in the art world. That vision of my future got me through all the shit times after Carlo, all the hassles with my family. Who am I without my plan?"

"You're a photographer, it seems. And a window display designer." He nudges me. "And a nude model."

"Damn it, Maxie," I grumble.

His warm laughter rings out like a jazzy saxophone. "The point is, you're already involved in the art scene here. And you're falling for a nice local boy. Quit fighting so hard and try just riding the wave. Maybe it'll peter out. Maybe it'll float you to a shiny new beach."

"Maybe it'll drown me."

"You're a strong swimmer." His phone tootles in his pocket. He taps the screen and grins. "I've got a date." With a few more taps, he summons a rideshare, then pushes to his feet and gives his ass a saucy shake. "Some of us aren't afraid to take the plunge."

"Okay, okay. Enough with the water metaphors. I have to pee." I hug him hard. "Will I see you tomorrow?"

"Absolutely. You and I are going out. On. The. Town." He tries to spin me. "Oh. Shit." He frowns down at my ankle brace. "Well, we'll drink, at least."

"Screw it. Let's go dancing. I'll borrow one of Maxie's canes."

"That's my girl." The shine in his eyes is just the medicine I need tonight.

When the driver pulls up, Davonte smooches my cheek and rides off toward adventure and romance—or at least a hot night with a Southern cutie.

I trudge back into Maxie's, my head buzzing with arguments and what-ifs, and the sneaking suspicion Davonte is right, damn it.

Chapter
Thirty-Four

♥

Laurel

"Arrived," my phone navigator chirps. My asthmatic VW chugs to a stop in front of the address Agatha texted me. Is this right? This Craftsman bungalow doesn't look like a famous photographer's studio, but a small brass plaque below the doorbell reads *Lorenzo LaFontaine, Fine Art Photography. By appointment only.*

My imagination lights up: here I am, ten years from now, opening the door of a gorgeous old house to greet a client. What does an artistic photographer wear? Probably something like Maxie's outfits, lots of color and funky accessories.

Slow your roll, Laurel. First, take some pictures that don't suck.

I lean on the adjustable cane Maxie lent me—not quite tall enough, but a huge improvement over those damn crutches—and hobble up the stairs. Despite Agatha's reassurance that Lorenzo is "a pussycat," my finger shakes as I push the doorbell.

"Coming." A round little man throws open the door and beams. "You must be Laurel." Bearded, bald as an egg on top with a scraggly gray fringe, he wipes his fingers on his Bob Marley T-shirt before grasping my hand.

"Sorry, just finishing breakfast. Come in, come in." He welcomes me with a sweeping gesture. "Not every day I entertain a celebrity."

"Excuse me?"

"I've seen the fuss on social media." He squints. "You look taller in person. This way."

I follow him into a sunny kitchen where a TV natters faintly.

"Your story just aired. Have you seen it?"

On the screen, the chirpy KVAL reporter giggles with the weather guy.

I swallow rising bile. "No, I haven't."

"No worries. It'll play again at noon and six." He switches off the set. "Sweet love story. Nice to see some good news for a change." He smacks his palms together and rubs them briskly. "So. That poster. Good work, my dear. Show me more."

From my bag, I extract my basic Nikon and pull up the photos of the 10K race: churning tangles of legs; contorted, sweaty faces, jaws clenched in pain, gritted in determination, slack in surrender; and shot after shot of Dalton, striding across the finish line, surrounded by his cheering students, grinning through a waterfall of acid-green Gatorade.

Surprise tears prickle my eyes at the sight of his beautiful, wide-open smile. I turn away to hide a sniffle.

Lorenzo clicks through the sequence. "Excellent. Lots of life here. Authentic. Emotional." He slaps the little camera back into my palm. "What do you want to accomplish?"

"Well, a friend—" An interfering, manipulative jerk with a great smile and big, warm hands and a big, delicious... "He sort of volunteered me to display some photos at the Run for the Arts."

"That's, what, two weeks away?"

I gulp and nod.

"Then we'd better get started." He leads me to a sunny office. "My studio, such as it is." An expensive-looking computer and printer sit atop a battered wooden desk. Surrealistic photos cover a corkboard on the wall. I examine the whimsical compositions: a crotchety old woman, her rickety shopping cart stuffed with laughing children. A suited businessman reads a newspaper while his bus seat floats into a cloudy sky. A procession of teens hunch over their phones as they walk up the wall of a brick building.

"These are amazing." I peer closer. "Hey, I know this guy." His red beard glowing, Elmer floats shirtless on an air mattress in one of his hand-thrown beer tankards.

Lorenzo chuckles. "Eugene's a small town. Most of the artists know each other." He pulls another photo from the tray of his printer. "Check out this one, for example."

I splutter with laughter. "Marvelous." Clutching a hot-pink feather fan, Maxie grins into the camera from inside a champagne glass, her jeweled flip-flops dangling over the rim. "How did you do this?"

"Not too hard." He pulls an extra chair up in front of his computer station. "I'll show you."

The next hour flies by. Together, we meld a photo of kids climbing on a playground structure with a shot of rainforest trees from the Olympic Peninsula. The finished image shows the kids dangling from the jungly trees like circus acrobats.

"You could do something like this with your runners."

I heave a wistful sigh. "There's no way I can afford a computer like this, much less the editing software."

Lorenzo taps his pursed lips. "Tell you what. Maybe we can work out a trade."

I wait, barely breathing.

"Portland Art Fair's in October. My usual helper moved out of state. Take his place, and I'll let you use my computers. I'll even throw in some photography lessons if you don't mind carrying my camera bags around town."

I pinch my lips together, but a wide grin still breaks through. "Deal."

"Good. In the meantime, go shoot the background scenes you want to use."

I grip his extended hand like a drowning woman clutching a life preserver.

"Easy now." He chuckles, extricating himself. "Mind my arthritic knuckles."

"Sorry. It's just—thank you so much."

"Glad to help a promising young artist."

Despite my ankle brace and cane, I have to restrain myself from skipping back to my car. I check my phone. A voice mail from Maxie. "Better look at InstaBook. Those twits are going nuts."

Just like that, my giddy mood fizzles. I poke the screen.

@sparklegirl95 posts: ***Don't believe the crap on KVAL. Saw Laurel last night, ordering sushi with her REAL boyfriend. Says Dalton is shit. #EugeneRunningMan #phonybitch***

The string of replies is growing by the minute. With a trembling finger, I scroll through dozens of tweets condemning me as a hard-hearted user, a cheater, and other misspelled deprecations. And then, a reply that nearly stops my heart.

@runcoach: ***It's me, #EugeneRunningMan. All is well with me and Laurel. Please respect our privacy. #RunfortheArts September 15.***

I tap his profile. Dalton's face grins from the screen, beads of sweat sparkling on his shiny head as he squints into the sun. Probably a candid photo from a race.

I stroke my fingertip over his image. God, I miss him. So, he wants me to stay. Is that so bad?

Should I post something, or would that just add fuel to the fire? After several minutes of dithering, I tap out my reply.

Thanks, Dalton. You're the best. I scrunch my face, searching for words to express my keen longing. Nope, not in front of all these people. Better wait for a private moment.

Stupid sprained ankle. I miss our runs. #RunfortheArts.

Funny, with the letters smashed together, the word "hearts" stands out.

One last look at the comment thread.

@Nikegirl adds: ***If she doesn't want him, I'll take him. Nice ass, #EugeneRunningMan.***

Well, crap. Dalton's sudden celebrity status will attract lots of attention from single women, especially if they think we're not together anymore. Feeling queasy, I crank the ignition and head toward the park to photograph more runners.

Chapter Thirty-Five

♥

Dalton

"Come on, slowpoke." Destiny tugs Marcus's arm. "You promised me four art galleries before we stop for a beer."

"But, baby, I'm so thirsty," he protests. "Aren't you thirsty, Dalton?"

I raise both palms. "Don't drag me into this." I know better than to argue with Destiny. Besides, if I'm going to persuade Laurel to stay, I'd better educate myself on Eugene's art scene.

I haven't been downtown for the First Friday Art Walk in years. From the Fifth Street Public Market to the far end of Broadway, art galleries and shops ply visitors with flashy displays, live music, even wine. Kesey Square is well stocked with food trucks and a band, which is good because weird art definitely goes down easier with snacks and alcohol.

But a promise is a promise, and Destiny is determined to get her art fix. She snags her husband's arm. "Let's check out this place."

I admire a painting in the gallery window: a watercolor panorama of Mount Hood, its snow-covered peak reflected in the glassy waters of Mirror Lake. Will I ever get the chance to hike up there with Laurel? I picture her blue-tipped blond ponytail bobbing up the trail, hiking shorts gripping her sweet, round ass, those long legs flashing in the sun—

Destiny tugs me inside. "Look, a new Agatha Andrews." She hustles toward the back of the shop, leaving me to gawk at the mob obscuring the artwork. Her hand appears above their heads. "Dalton, you're going to want to see this."

Easier said than done. A dozen excuse-me's later, I finally reach the painting in question.

"Holy sh—" I clap my hand over my mouth.

It's Laurel. Naked.

She gazes over her bare shoulder, her lovely face relaxed into a dreamy Mona Lisa smile, her pale skin glowing as if lit from within. Her satin hair flows down the sinuous curve of her back. Above the cloth-draped stool, her ass blooms plump and tempting. The artist perfectly captured the strong, graceful lines of her legs, her storm cloud gaze that roots me to the spot and strips me bare.

She looked just like that after we made love. Right before she told me not to love her. Caught between arousal and shock, I sway on unsteady legs.

Oblivious to my stunned reaction, Destiny points to another pair of nudes, sketched in rough strokes of charcoal. Here, Laurel folds inward, cradling a painful secret. Her gaze lowered, her hair drooping, half-hiding her face, she seems...

"Heartbroken." Destiny reads from the label beside the image. "Wow. Makes me sad just to look at it." She turns to me. "Say, isn't she—"

Marcus slings his arm around her shoulders. "Baby, they're serving wine back there. Come on."

"Okay, but—"

He lowers his voice. "Let's give him a minute."

I stare at the mournful image. Is this what I did to her? Just when she needed someone by her side, I cut her off because she wasn't moving fast enough for my impatient ass.

How could I have handled my mom's illness without my family, my friends? Laurel's going through the same thing with Maxie, and she's all alone.

I'm a stupid, selfish asshole.

"Hey, isn't that the guy from Instagram? The running dude?" The voice snaps my reverie like a potato chip.

"No photos, sir." A gallery employee pushes past me.

Whispering a prayer to the gods of social media, I hurry to the exit. Outside, I text Marcus:

Heading to Kesey Square. See you there.

The Square rings with voices, laughter, and blaring music from the funk band on stage. Packed onto a makeshift dance floor, dancers sway and gyrate. Tempting odors of BBQ, fried goodies, and spicy Asian food compete for my attention. I skirt the dance floor, aiming for the sushi burrito stand—until something whacks my shin painfully, drawing a yelp.

"Oh, hey, sorry." The woman who clobbered me with her cane whirls to face me.

"Laurel?"

Gray eyes wide, she freezes in place. "Dalton—oh—hi."

We blink at each other, stock-still amidst the churning crowd. Just like one of those slow-motion scenes in a movie, the air between us stills.

When the song ends, the singer purrs into the mic, "We're gonna slow things down, so take hold of the one you love. The night is young, the sky is blue-jean blue, and it's time to move closer."

The thunder of my heartbeat drowns out the music. Her gravity's gaze leaves me no choice. I slide my hand to the small of her back and pull her close. She doesn't resist.

"I'll just take this." Her friend with the bulgy eyes grabs her cane and melts into the crowd.

She shrugs. "It's kismet, I guess."

"Shall we dance?" I take her hand. "I mean, can you?"

"If I lean on you."

"I wish you would, Laurel." It's not like me to find the perfect words at the perfect time, but there it is, my heart's truth, my desperate plea.

As we slowly sway, the crowd around us blurs and flows like a watercolor. I wish I had Laurel's artistic talent so I could capture this moment, her warmth, her sparkling eyes, the tilt of her plush lips.

"Laurel?"

"Hmm?"

"You still mad at me?"

She nestles her cheek to mine. "Sort of. I don't like being manipulated."

"I'm really sorry. I was trying to make you see—" I shake my head. "Doesn't matter. I wasn't honest with you, and I was wrong." My fingers itch to stroke her hair. My impatient dick itches to press against her. Lots of itching. I restrain myself, barely. "How can I make it up to you?"

She chuckles. "Well, you called off the social media hordes before they tore me to shreds."

Dizzy with relief, I laugh too. "Guess this will be added to our thread."

"What, us dancing?"

"Mmm hmm."

She pulls back a little and lays her soft hand on my cheek. "Dalton, why do you still want me?"

Panic speeds my pulse and parches my mouth. I'm no damn good at this part. Mooning over her is easy. Putting my feelings into spoken words, though—that's about as easy as composing a sonnet. In Swahili. "I, uh—"

Brow rumpled, she peers at me as if trying to solve a tricky puzzle. "I mean, you're sweet and tall and good-looking and funny. You could get another woman like that." She snaps her fingers. "You deserve better than a someone who's not planning her escape."

I trace her jawline with my forefinger. "I guess I still have hope you'll stay. When I lose hope, I'll be gone."

Honest, unadorned truth. That's all I can give her—and all she's asking for, it seems.

She nods and settles into my embrace again. As we step in time to the music, she rests her chin on my shoulder. Warmth blooms in my chest. She's still here. She didn't bolt. *Say something!*

"I really like your portraits."

The moment the words escape my lips, I feel the weight of my mistake—and Laurel's fingernails digging into my skin as she pushes me away, her voice raspy-tight. "Where?"

"The gallery over there."

"Shit. Shitshitshit." Grimacing, she snarls her fingers in her hair. "Agatha didn't tell me. Why didn't she tell me?"

Way to ruin the perfect moment, genius. I try a soothing tone. "She did a beautiful job. The artist really captured your spirit."

"But I wasn't prepared," she wails. "All these people will see me naked. It feels so, so...creepy."

Well, what did she think would happen when she posed nude for a popular artist? But I can't tell her that, so I just stand there, cursing my big, stupid mouth.

Her dapper friend steps up holding a paper boat of fried cheese curds, her cane beneath his arm. He shoots me a suspicious glance. "Laur-bear, what's wrong?"

"Oh, D. I'm so embarrassed." She throws her arms around the guy and whispers a flurry of words into his ear. His eyebrows shoot up. So do the corners of his mouth, but he quickly pastes on a concerned pout. "You want to get out of here?"

She nods.

The guy shrugs an apology before leading her away through the crowd. Like an afterthought, she turns to mouth, "Sorry" before disappearing.

Not as sorry as I am.

Laurel

Broadway swarms with art lovers—and just plain lovers, holding hands, smooching, gazing into each other's moony eyes.

"Ow. Stupid ankle." I collapse onto a bench. "I should go back."

Davonte sits beside me. "Nope. You'll only make it worse. Wait 'til you're thinking straight before you text him."

"But I keep embarrassing him," I wail. "School's about to start, and his students will give him all kinds of grief about dating a nude model."

"And yet, he was holding you like someone who doesn't give a shit about all that, like a man in love." Davonte pats my clenched hand. "Ain't enough of that to go around. You shouldn't waste it."

I don't respond, but the buzzing in my guts echoes the truth of his words. Stupid guts.

"Come on." I heave myself to my feet. "I need a drink."

We pass another gallery, its window full of sculptures. Davonte nudges me. "Look, there's your poster again."

I point to a display of ceramic bowls decorated with delicate vines, tiny faces peeping out between the leaves. "Maxie's friend makes these."

"In we go." He sails through the door and disappears into the crowd. I find him chatting up a man with a scruff-covered double chin. "C'mere Laurel. Meet Robert, owner of this fine gallery."

"Pleased to meet you." He grasps my hand, but his gaze stays riveted to Davonte. "Your charming friend tells me you're working on a photo display?"

"Um, yeah. For Run for the Arts."

Davonte pokes my ribs. "Rainbow something?"

I nod. "Right. Rainbow Arts Center. September fifteenth."

The owner gives me a genuine smile, as if he were talking to a real artist. "I'll check it out. We don't feature enough photography. I'd like to acquire some to round out our collection. In the meantime, would you sign this for me? I'm betting it'll be worth something."

He carefully peels the poster from the window and hands me a pen.

Holy shit, my first autograph! Giddiness tickles down my spine as I compose a swooping cursive L.

When I finish, Davonte bumps my shoulder. "Told ya."

"Hey, it's the poster girl." A pair of women closes in. One raises her phone. "When will you run with Dalton again?"

"Or are you running with this guy now?" her friend asks.

Davonte rolls his eyes and cranks up his campy tone. "Girl, I am not ruining my pedicure by running. I have much better ways of working up a sweat." He winds his arm through mine. "Laurel is my friend, not my girlfriend."

"Glad to hear it." All ginger beard and wide grin, Elmer saunters up to join us. "I've got enough competition as it is." He plants a wet smooch on my cheek. "Thanks for coming to see my work, Laurel."

I push him away. "Cut it out, Elmer. I'm with Dalton." The words fly from my lips before I can think, and the phone-wielding onlookers record every word.

"Y'all need to mind your business," Davonte huffs. He grabs my arm and nearly yanks me off my feet as he marches toward the door.

Behind us, Elmer protests, "Hey, just kidding." But the phones are already tucked away, the damage done.

Chapter Thirty-Six

♥

Dalton

Sleep is a lost cause. Sweaty and restless, I kick off the sheets, switch on my bedside lamp, and pick up my phone again.

Our hashtag is on fire tonight. Since midnight, three more photos of Laurel and me dancing in Kesey Square have been posted. I especially love this one—Laurel gazing into my eyes, her arms around my shoulders as if she were really mine. This photo must've been snapped right before she bolted.

Freakin' bizarre how her poster has focused the town's attention on an ordinary guy like me. I've even earned an abbreviated hashtag.

Aww. #ERM and his artist sweetie.

#ERM too cute. Wedding bells?

Collapsing onto the pillows, I sink into the memory—the cool caress of her hair against my neck, the warmth of her body pressed to mine. It's been six days since she melted around me, gasped my name, gifted me the most powerful climax of my life, then stormed out.

Well, that's not exactly fair, nor exactly true. More like she slunk out, reluctantly. Our amazing chemistry blew my mind and fried my judgment. She never really rejected me, just asked me to slow down. I've mentally replayed that morning a hundred times, and I'm pretty sure I never said, "I love you," but I must've said the word. Because I love being inside her, love feeling her wrapped around me, love the way she excites me and relaxes me and inspires me to hope for something better than a lonely life in a sad apartment.

Like picking at an itchy scab, I scroll through the Instagram thread. Here's Laurel, arm in arm with her too-handsome friend. *Her gay friend*, I remind myself. Small comfort, since she fled into that guy's embrace.

The next photo sets my pulse pounding: smarmy Elmer, his red beard pressed to Laurel's cheek.

#ERM, your woman's on the prowl.

Pushy bastard. I've never resorted to jealous violence, but right now, my fist itches to smash that fuzzy face.

I scroll some more.

@MamaDuck80: Some people gotta stir up drama. In the comment thread, she's posted a video clip of Laurel pushing Elmer away. The sound quality is poor, but after the third listen, I hear Laurel say, "I'm with Dalton."

I bolt upright, my pulse hammering at my temples, and push Replay.

"I'm with Dalton."

"Damn right she is." I spring out of bed and pull on my shorts and T-shirt. Then it hits me: it's three in the morning. What am I gonna do, throw pebbles at her window?

I shed my clothes, pad to the bathroom, and splash cold water on my face. "You've got it bad, my friend," I tell my dripping reflection.

Sleep deprivation, lust, and late-night madness stir a vision: Laurel's lips gliding over my bare shoulder and up my neck to nibble my earlobe. My dick throbs to life, reaching for the woman who isn't here.

Erection bobbing, I stride to the bedroom, pick up my phone, and text her:

> **Can't sleep. Miss you so much it hurts. Help me, Laurel. Tell me I have a chance. Or tell me to leave you alone. Not knowing is killing me.**

My finger's poised over the Send button. Creepy? No, just honest, and when we first met, she stressed how much she values honesty.

I hit Send, then sink onto the damp pillows. *"I'm with Dalton."* Just a ploy to keep a pushy guy at bay? To keep the social media horde off her case? Or did that ginger jackass startle her into blurting her true feelings? Once again, my memory serves up the delicious, torturous image of dancing in Kesey Square, her hips swaying to the saxophone's wail, pressing against me...

For the second time tonight, my hand slides down to grasp my erection. Pulling slowly, I imagine sliding into her wet, willing flesh. Only one night together, one incredible morning, and her memory haunts my senses. I stroke lazily, my need building. The room around me dissolves. Laurel crouches above me, clutching my shoulders, her long thighs straddling my hips as she rides me, those sweet soft breasts bobbing while she impales herself on my shaft again and again. I groan. *Laurel, Laurel...*

My phone pings. My breath stops.

I snatch it from the nightstand and tap the screen.

> **Can't sleep either. I miss you. This is crazy.**

'Crazy' perfectly describes how I feel, wide awake in the wee hours, dick in one hand and phone in the other.

I release my aching shaft and gulp a deep breath before replying.

> **Did you mean it?**

> **???**

"I'm with Dalton."

For an eternity, three dots pulse on the screen in rhythm with my hammering heart.

Yeah. I meant it.

An unfamiliar ring tone blares. Video chat! I tap the screen.

Her beautiful face appears, right here in the palm of my hand—her gray eyes luminous, her gleaming hair spread over the pillow, her shoulders bare.

There is a God.

She flashes the sweet, lazy smile she gave me after we first made love. "Hey."

"Hey." I run my thumb over her image. "There you are." I chuckle. "I want to kiss you, but that would look pretty weird."

Her laughter tinkles like wind chimes. "Yeah, I guess." She glances away and wrinkles her nose. "Maxie's snoring."

"How's she doing?"

"Okay. She and I had a long talk tonight."

"With Davonte?"

She rolls her eyes. "No, he's, uh, busy. Met a guy. They've really hit it off, it seems."

"It happens sometimes. A surprise gift, you know?"

She nods. The tip of her tongue slicks over her lower lip. My dick leaps.

"So, what did you and Maxie talk about?"

"Art, love, the meaning of life." Her lashes flutter. "And nude modeling. Turns out she's done a ton of it. She talked me down from the ledge." Yawning, she rolls her shoulders against the pillow, giving me a view of the tops of her breasts.

My breath catches.

"Listen, Dalton. I owe you a huge apology. We were having a beautiful moment, and I freaked out. I'm sorry."

"Understandable, I guess. I'm damn self-conscious about seeing my fully dressed picture around town. Can't imagine what it feels like for you."

Her mouth quirks to one side. "Well, nobody held a gun to my head."

"I wish I could afford to buy all those paintings. They're amazing. Really beautiful. Like you."

Her lips part, and her lids lower. "Aww, Dalton." Her grip on her phone must've loosened, because her breast slides into view, her pale pink nipple smooth and relaxed. My mouth waters.

"Laurel, are you..." I gesture to my own bare chest.

Her eyes widen. "Sorry, guess I should've put something on. It's warm in here." But her smile holds a playful edge. She's not sorry at all.

I let out a groan. "Naked, but too far away to touch. That's cruel, Laurel."

"It's a shame, isn't it?" Her free hand trails over her collar bone. "I'd invite you over, but Maxie..." She raises her phone, giving me a wider angle. "And it's just a lumpy single bed, as you can see."

What I can see is her naked torso, from her delicate throat down to the curve of her waist.

I gulp. "Show me more."

"I will if you will," she purrs.

Once again, my free hand slides down to grasp my throbbing cock.

Her whoosh of breath vibrates the phone's speaker. "Show me." On the screen, her long, slender fingers circle her breast, spiraling in on her nipple. It tightens beneath her touch.

"God, I want to put my mouth there," I moan.

"Guess where I want to put my mouth?" Her voice takes on a husky note. "Show me, Dalton."

Lust overrides embarrassment. I tilt the phone and fist my shaft once, twice. My balls snug up against my body, heavy and hot.

She hums deep in her throat. "So big. So beautiful. God, I want you."

"Show me," I whisper.

She does, amen and hallelujah. Her phone lens angles down to focus on her slender fingers, parting the puffy lips of her pussy to reveal the rosy inner flesh, slick with arousal. Groaning, I speed my strokes.

"Dalton, Dalton..." Her finger circles her clit, faster and faster, then slides deep inside. "Yes, like that."

I match her stroke for stroke, squeezing and pumping until a bright bolt of pleasure jolts me from toes to skull and I gasp her name. She drops her phone, crying aloud as climax grips her.

Sharp knocking. Damn, she must really be slamming her headboard into the wall.

"Laurel, honey? You okay?"

"Shit," she hisses. Rumpled sheets fill the screen. She croaks in a fake-sleepy voice, "I'm fine, Max. Just a bad dream."

Eyes wide, I smother a laugh with my pillow. My first-ever video-chat sex, and we woke Maxie.

Laurel's flushed face appears on the screen, hair beautifully mussed, eyes crinkled in mirth. "Oh God, how embarrassing."

"How delicious."

Her lids lower. "Yeah. It was. So..."

This is an opportunity. Grab it. "When can I see you?"

"I'm working all day tomorrow."

"Can I stop by?"

Her smile warms every dark corner of my heart. "Please do."

I caress the screen. "Good night, lovely Laurel."

"Good night, handsome Dalton. Sweet dreams." She clicks off.

I mop up, settle back, and sigh.

Tomorrow. Another chance to hold her, to inhale her scent, to fill my arms and mind and heart with this amazing woman. Another chance to slip through her prickly defenses, to convince her to give us a chance. Slowly, carefully, I'll show her how brightly she sparkles right here.

But how? Plotting behind the scenes only pisses her off. No matter how hot our connection is, sex alone isn't enough to hold her.

Chapter Thirty-Seven

♥

Laurel

"Laurel, can you—" With a strangled gurgle, Clara bolts to the restroom and slams the door.

Poor Clara. I swallow a wave of sympathetic nausea and shelve the last of the new picture books. The doorbell jingles.

"Be right with you." I hoist myself out of the beanbag seat.

"Here, let me help." A broad hand grips my waist from behind, steadying me. Dalton's rumbly voice sends my pulse into a manic tempo. I suck in a breath, lick my lips, and turn.

"Good afternoon, beautiful." There it is, that bashful smile I've been craving all day. I want to hug him tight, feel his strong, steady heartbeat against my chest. But a dozen customers fill the shop, so groping is out of the question.

"Good to see you." I lean close enough to whisper, "In person, I mean." Bold words, but my face flushes hot enough to melt chocolate. Just hours ago, the sight of his long fingers gripping his cock sent me spiraling over the edge.

Judging by his hot-pink cheeks, he's awash with the same heady mixture of embarrassment and arousal. He presses a chaste kiss to my lips and murmurs in my ear, "Give me a tour of the back room?"

My flush deepens. "I'd love to, but, um..."

All at once, the red door opens, the doorway bell tinkles, and a trio of chatting women stroll in from the café holding romance paperbacks.

He sighs. "Where's Clara?"

I tip my head toward the restroom, inflate my cheeks, and clutch my stomach.

"Ah. Margot?"

"Mailing a package."

"And Harry's still in Australia. Well then." He slides behind the counter and flexes his interlaced fingers, popping his knuckles like a string of firecrackers.

"Dalton, you don't have to."

He grins and passes me the scanner gun.

A few minutes later, Clara emerges from the restroom, pale and perspiring. "Hey, Dalton. Helping Laurel?"

"Any excuse to steal a few minutes of her time."

"Well, I'm done recycling my breakfast. Laurel, why don't you show him those new books in the red room?" Her smile twinkles with mischief.

I swear, these two are in cahoots, but since I have the boss's blessing, I grab the key. "Right this way, sir."

When the lacquered door closes behind us, Dalton clasps his hands behind his back and strolls around the room's edge, avoiding my gaze. "So, how's your ankle?"

"Not too bad." Why's he being so cool? I thought, after last night...

He trails his fingers over the book spines. "And your friend?"

"Davonte had to go back home."

He pulls out a volume of lingerie shots and flips through the pages. "And Maxie?"

"One of Elmer's friends is staying with her today. They're making something out of pipe cleaners." *Are you gonna kiss me, or just make small talk?*

Holding the book, he ambles to my side and bumps my shoulder with his. "You know, you'd look really good in this." He points to the page—a blonde model on a four-poster bed, wearing only strategically placed lace and a satisfied smile.

"Looks scratchy."

"You wouldn't be in it long enough to notice." He sets the volume on the love seat and slides behind me, so close his breath heats my skin. He skates his fingertips over my jaw, then lifts my hair from my nape. "Last night..."

"Mmm." I arch my neck, inviting his kiss. Dumb idea, making out at work, but his nearness has all my nerve endings dancing.

He breathes my name like a magical incantation. His lips brush my throat. His fingertips skim to my waist, a feathery dance that makes me shiver. I hold my breath.

Dalton's voice rumbles in my ear. "Does this mean..."

I pivot and press him against the door. As long as I avoid his gaze, I'll be okay. Winding my arms around his neck, I drink his mouth like wine.

But he pulls back, grasping my shoulders. "Babe, I have to know."

The question kept me up all night, even after our video tryst, when post-orgasmic lethargy melted me into the mattress. Yes or no? Stay or go?

"Listen to your heart," Davonte said.

"You aren't just playing with him, are you?" Maxie asked.

"Yes, love is worth it," Mom assured me.

My heart and the rest of my horny body vote a hard yes. Life could be so good with a steady, loving partner like Dalton at my side. But my stubborn mind and my fragile ego still cling to long-cherished visions of my career, now receding from my grasp like some nightmare scene from a Hitchcock movie. Despite my lousy track record, I have confidence in my gallery work. All I need is the right opportunity. But to bank on success as an artist? That's terrifying.

In a trembling voice, I choke out the words. "Yes, Dalton. I'm here. With you." Not quite a promise, but the best I can do.

"Really?" His gaze probes past my semantic defenses.

"Davonte's not happy in San Francisco. He may leave soon." That doesn't mean I might not bolt for some other big city, but my escape route is no longer clear.

He releases me and quirks his lips to the side. "That's not exactly what I was hoping to hear."

"Oh?" My stomach sinks.

His gaze slides to the floor. "Actually, I was hoping for something along the lines of 'I can't leave you, Dalton. I'm falling in love with you.' You know, romantic movie stuff." He massages his temples. "I should stop watching those. Makes real life seem so disappointing."

Like metal filings to a magnet, his nearness tugs the truth out of me. I stroke his cheek, smooth skin and wiry but soft golden whiskers.

"Look, Dalton. I can't just blurt out 'I love you.' It's too soon. We don't know each other that well. And that's what love's about, right? Really knowing someone to the core and embracing all of it." I rest my chin on his shoulder because it's easier to talk from my heart when I don't have to meet his piercing gaze.

"But what we have is powerful. And I want to know you. Really know you. You're open and real and..."

"Good enough." He grips my jaw in both hands and kisses me, long and hard and deep. "For now."

His tongue plunders my mouth while his hands roam over my back, slide down to my hips, and snug me tight against him. When his rigid cock presses into my belly, bright sparks of arousal dance over my skin, gathering to burn at my core.

This is wrong. I'm at work. But I'm powerless to resist. I reach for his belt.

His hand slides under my skirt and tugs my sopping panties aside. I gasp when his fingers stroke my slick center. His lips leave mine long enough to whisper, "Take these off."

My pulse pounding like a kettle drum, I lock the door and slither my panties to the floor. With his fingertips, he teases my tingling clit while digging in his pocket with his free hand. He relaxes his hold long enough to sheath his erection, then presses me to the red door, sandwiching me between the cool lacquer and his hot, muscled body. He grasps my injured leg and wraps it around his hips.

This is crazy, reckless, wild, but there's no denying my body's urgent need for his touch.

He cups my breast through my thin top, and a sharp flash of pleasure zings down my spine. The fat, blunt crown of his cock nudges my opening. "Let me in, Laurel."

I tip my hips forward, reaching for him.

With a groan, he slides home, filling me completely, then slowly withdraws—exquisite agony. He shoves into me again, jarring my bones. My bare ass thumps the door as he alternates rough, fast invasions with slow, delicious retreats, spiraling me higher and higher. I clutch his back, his muscles bunching beneath my fingers.

I clamp my jaw to restrain a scream, burying my moans in the crook of his neck.

"That's it," he murmurs. "Let me in, Laurel. I won't hurt you. Never."

My world narrows to the incredible pleasure of his body touching mine everywhere. I whimper his name as a devastating climax rips through me. Dalton follows, shuddering inside me.

No laughter this time. Our ferocious joining leaves me shaken and dizzy. Still buried deep, he strokes my hair from my damp face and rests his forehead on mine. We stay like this for a long moment, sharing one breath, until he finally speaks.

"I'm in love with you, Laurel. It's crazy how fast I fell, but I'm a thousand percent sure. You're the one for me. And I know you're not there yet, but I'm willing to wait."

My heart jolts. "Dalton, I—"

He touches his sex-scented finger to my lips. "Don't answer. Just hold on to it. See how it feels." Grasping the base of his cock, he slides out of me, and my whole body protests at the loss.

God, this man! No one has ever filled my chest with glittering butterflies like he does, and if I had a tiny fraction of the courage he gives me credit for, I'd hold him tight and never let go.

Chuckling, he knots the condom. "Should've thought this through. No trash can in here."

I pull a tissue from my pocket. "Here, I'll—"

Let's get tested. Like, tomorrow. I want to feel you inside me, bare and slick and...

I bite back that scary thought and draw a deep breath. "So, ready for our walk of shame?"

He must have missed the quiver in my voice, because he flashes a wide smile. "Laurel, I will never be ashamed of anything I do with you." He plants one last lingering kiss on my mouth. "You are the archangel of sex. Everything you do is beautiful and holy." He huffs a laugh. "If anything, they should greet us with applause."

Fortunately, no one is waiting outside the red door. I pop my tissue-wrapped contraband into a trash can as we make our way to the front. He kisses my cheek and whispers, "Call me tonight?"

"Count on it."

The doorway bell sings him out, a tinkling brass giggle. With a deep breath, I turn back and find Clara and Margot busily engaged in bullshit tasks behind the counter.

Busted. Might as well own it. Despite my gimpy gait, I put a little extra sway in my step.

Clara sets down the rag she's polishing the already-immaculate countertop with. "So, everything all right with you two?"

Mastering my grin is a lost cause. "Yeah. Everything's swell."

Clara chuckles. "The red room does have its charms."

Margot glances up from her pile of sales fliers. "Damn, am I the only one who hasn't done it in the red room?"

"Just be careful." Clara strokes her belly. "I think this little one was conceived back there."

Holy shit! Good thing I'm on birth control. That room's got magical powers.

Chapter Thirty-Eight

♥

Laurel

Three hours later, I shelve the last book on the cart and limp back to the counter. A steady stream of customers kept us busy all afternoon. No time to obsess over Dalton's declaration of love, still echoing in my brain like cannon fire.

A dad and his teenage daughter are waiting for my help.

"Books on photography? Yes, we have some good ones. Follow me." Over the past few days, I've perused this aisle well.

My phone vibrates in my pocket, but the customer keeps up a barrage of questions. Where did I get my inspiration for the poster? "Just a lucky shot, I guess." *Just Dalton. He looked so pretty in the golden sunlight.*

What kind of camera do I use? "A basic Nikon." *Though for the best photo, the one of Dalton running by the river like some sun-burnished demigod, I used my phone.*

Which graphics program do I use? "Oh, this and that." *Whatever I can borrow from Margot or Lorenzo.*

What am I working on now? "Portraits of runners." *And I'd better snap more ASAP if I'm gonna be ready for the race day exhibit!*

As I ring up their purchase, my phone buzzes twice more. I pull it from my pocket while the next customers lay their books on the counter. It's Maxie's number.

Panic flutters in my throat. "Clara, could you come here for a sec?"

Nick emerges from behind the screen. "I'll get it." While he dazzles the customers with his high-wattage smile, I call home.

A stranger answers, her voice tense and tight. "Hello? Is this Laurel?"

"Yeah, who's this?"

"Oh God, you need to come home. Like now!"

In the background, a door slams, and a male voice calls, "Maxie? What's wrong?"

My heart skids to a stop, then breaks into a sprint. "I'm on my way."

I grip Nick's arm. "It's Maxie."

Concern flashes in his dark eyes. "Go."

Ten minutes and twenty-three stop signs later, I dash up Maxie's stairs, ignoring the pain in my ankle. Elmer and a tall young woman huddle over the couch, where Maxie lies, pale and still, her purple lids closed.

"Oh God, is she—?"

The woman clutches her short dreadlocks. "I didn't see the sign on the fridge. She didn't tell me." She chokes out a sob. "We had pepperoni pizza for lunch."

Damn it, Maxie! I kneel at her side and take her cold, clammy hand.

Her lids flutter up. "Susan?"

"It's me, Laurel."

More bleary blinking. "Did I fall asleep?"

"God, Max, what were you thinking? Your legs are all swollen."

"Feels funny." She coughs, an alarming rattle from deep in her chest.

Wide-eyed, Elmer grips my arm. "She needs to go to the hospital."

Between wheezing breaths and bone-rattling coughs, Maxie shakes her head.

"Elmer's right. Let's go."

Hours later, the doctor folds her hands atop Maxie's file, open on her desk. "Congestive heart failure can lead to impaired cognition. But Maxie's a sharp cookie. I doubt she forgot pepperoni pizza is full of sodium."

Dad snorts. "She's ninety, for God's sake. I'm surprised she can remember her own name."

I wheel on him. "Shut up, Dad. If that's what you think, you don't know her."

He gapes at me, eyes bulging, but in this fraught moment, I truly don't give a crap about keeping the peace. Mom may be able to tune out his bullshit, but I am *done.*

"Dave, really." Mom lays her hand on his forearm. He subsides into his chair, arms crossed, but keeps his frosty glare fixed on me.

Elmer squirms in his seat, clearly uncomfortable with our family warfare. "Hey, let's all take it easy. We're here to help Maxie, right?"

Dad shoots eyeball daggers at Elmer. "Who the hell is this guy? I thought you were with that beanpole."

Through tight jaws, I growl, "I am with Dalton. Elmer is Maxie's friend, and he drove us to the hospital. You should be thanking him, not snarking at him."

Elmer rises, palms up in a placating gesture. "Look, this is a family matter. I'm gonna get on home."

I follow him into the hallway. Once we're out of hearing range, Elmer pinches the bridge of his nose. "Man, Laurel, your dad's a piece of work."

Still vibrating with fury, I retract my fangs. "Yeah, he is. I'm sorry."

"Poor Maxie." He sniffs hard and swipes his eyes with the back of his tattooed hand. Like a stinging slap, it strikes me how much Elmer is hurting. Focused on fending off his flirtation, I haven't spared a thought to his feelings for Maxie.

He honks into a paint-stained bandana. "Sorry. It's just—she's been like a grandma to me, you know? A wise old guru. I'm gonna miss her."

I hug him tightly. "You've been such a good friend to her. You and all her artist family. Thank you. I really appreciate it. We all do. Even my asshole dad."

"Hey now, don't call him that." He pats my cheek. "Bad karma." He blows out a shuddering breath. "You've got my number. Let me know what happens, okay?"

He makes his way toward the hospital entrance, his shoulders hunched as if carrying a heavy weight. Feeling just as weighed down, I return to the doctor's office.

Clara's voice rings firm through the phone. "Don't give it another thought, Laurel. We'll work around you somehow. Let me know when you can come back."

Wobbly with emotion, I thank her, end the call and collapse onto the waiting room loveseat and drop my head onto Dalton's shoulder.

He clasps my hand. "I told you she'd understand."

He's been a champ today, rushing over from the high school to prop me up and deflect Dad's verbal sniping while I dealt with insurance forms and getting official permission to make Maxie's medical decisions. Maxie was adamant about having me replace Mom as her medical power of attorney, and her hippie dippy lawyer friend had the paperwork drawn up and notarized within a few hours.

"You're making a mistake, Maxie," Dad grumbles as he gathers his belongings and Mom's for the ride home to Cotter's Grove. "Laurel's too young and flighty for such a serious responsibility."

"Shut up, Dave," Maxie says with a wide, sassy grin, her eyes clear and sharp now that the meds have normalized her blood pressure. "This is a matter for the Schmidt women to decide."

Hoo boy, look at the way he bristles at the use of Mom's family name!

Ignoring Dad's red-faced glare, Mom pecks Maxie's cheek, then clasps my shoulders. "I think you're eminently qualified to carry out Maxie's wishes. You two have always had a special bond."

Dad snorts and grumbles, "When the going gets tough, Laurel gets going—in the opposite direction."

Never dropping her serene smile, Mom smacks his arm. "Shut up, Dave."

A nurse pokes his head into the hospital room Maxie's sharing with an old guy who's currently breaking the world record for loud snoring. "Visiting hours are over, folks. Time for Ms. Maxie to get some rest."

"Baloney," Maxie counters. "Turn on HGTV, doll. I want to watch those hunky twins fix a house."

I give Maxie a goodnight smooch, then lean a little on Dalton's arm as we make our way to the exit.

"So, how much longer will she stay?" he asks.

"At least two days. I've lost track of how many tests the doc wants to run. Let's see..." I pull out my phone and open the calendar, too discombobulated to remember what day it is. "Tomorrow's Friday. I'm meeting with the manager of Willamette Grove at ten thirty. Hopefully, we can bump up Maxie's move-in date and nail down a meal plan that'll meet the doctor's specifications."

Dalton quirks his lips to the side. "You think Maxie will cooperate?"

"If she wants to stay alive, she really doesn't have a choice." I sink onto a bench in the entrance lobby. Dalton sits beside me and takes my hand, lacing his fingers through mine.

"God, Dalton, Maxie knows better!" Tears prickle my eyes and thicken my throat. "Do you think she was trying to—" I can't say it.

With his free hand, he rubs soothing circles on my back. "Death by pizza?"

Despite today's near disaster, I can't help giggling.

"Nah. Most likely, it was a moment of forgetfulness."

"With a dash of wishful thinking." I bump his shoulder with mine. "I can't imagine what she's going through, loss after loss after loss. All her life, she's been brilliantly in charge, and now she's taking orders left and right. That she can smile at all is a miracle."

"It's a testament to her strength." He squeezes my shoulder. "Must be a family trait."

"Pfft. I feel like a wrung-out dishrag."

"Come on. Let's get you home, fed, and tucked in bed."

When I make a wry face, he adds, "Not with me, love. As much as I want you, tonight's not the night for that kind of fun." He pulls me to my feet, slings his arm around my shoulders, and steers us toward the parking lot. "Listen, I'll understand if it's too much, but..."

"Are you kidding? After everything you've done for me, I owe you massively. What's up?"

His sheepish grin is so adorable. "A bunch of us teachers are having a Labor Day party at my place, by the pool. It starts around noon. I hope you can come, even if it's just for a little while. I'd like you to meet my friends."

I smooch his cheek. "I can't be sure, what with the whole Maxie situation, but I'll try."

Leaning against my VW, Dalton kisses me sweet and slow, then nips at my lower lip, and damn if I don't feel a zing of arousal despite my exhaustion.

I wiggle my hips against his and give him a weary grin. "You know, you're the only man who could make me think dirty thoughts after the day I've had today."

He waggles his pale eyebrows. "There's more where that came from." He drops a kiss on the tip of my nose. "Monday. By the pool. And call me if you need anything. I mean it, Laurel. Anything."

Damn, Dalton, I think as I climb into my Beetle, *you just keep racking up points in the Stay column.* Those bright city lights I've craved since forever are starting to dim in comparison with his brilliant smile.

Chapter Thirty-Nine

♥

Dalton

"When's your girlfriend coming, Dalton?" Rhonda Torres, my art teacher neighbor, squirts mustard onto her hotdog, splattering her Hawaiian shirt. "I want to talk to her about the exhibit."

I scan the crowded courtyard. Still no sign of her. "Laurel's tied up with family stuff this weekend. I don't know if she can make it."

As soon as she heard I was dating the recently famous poster artist, Rhonda set her sights on recruiting Laurel for the Rainbow Arts Center, where they're desperate for artsy volunteers. But with Maxie's illness and the ensuing family drama, more pressure is the last thing Laurel needs.

If she does show up, I hope she's ready to meet the mob. Thanks to the balmy weather, most of the staff turned out for this year's back-to-school party. While their kids bob and squeal in the pool, the P.E. teachers preside over the grill, flipping hot dogs, brats, and charred lumps that might be chicken. On the lawn, the science department crows as they trounce the English crew at cornhole.

Grinning, I scoop up a chipful of guac. Rhonda is right. We don't always agree on staff meeting agendas or homecoming week plans, but this band of goofballs has my back. I'd hoped to share this cozy feeling with Laurel, maybe show her off a little. But it's past three, and still no sign of her.

"Unka Dah-un." Aliyah waves from the pool, where she perches on her dad's shoulders. "I'm swimming." Giggling, she scoops a handful of water onto Marcus' head.

"Hey, bring me a beer?" Marcus rolls his eyes. "I'm on lifeguard duty."

I snag two cold bottles from the cooler and hand one to my friend, then sit on the pool's rim and dunk my feet in the cool water. "Well, this is it. Another summer gone."

"Blue hair." Aliyah points toward the courtyard gate.

She came. I clamber to my feet and hurry to welcome her. In a colorful sarong, a tank top, and flip-flops, she looks as cool and tasty as a mojito. *Please, God, let her be wearing a bikini under there.*

With only a slight hitch in her gait, she makes her way to the pool, beaming a smile that warms my cockles—and other places. She tugs my tacky Hawaiian shirt. "Nice outfit."

"Back to School Luau. Rebecca's idea. We're supposed to look tropical." I run my fingertips over the twist of fabric at her hip. "You nailed it."

She bats her pale lashes. "This old thing? Actually, it's Maxie's tablecloth." She glances around. "Can I kiss you in front of your friends?"

"Please do."

What a kiss. Even tastier than a mojito, and more potent.

The pitter-patter of wet little feet breaks through my love-sick, horny haze. Aliyah tugs on Laurel's skirt. "Hi."

She waves at the little squirt. "Well, hello. I remember you."

"I 'member you." Aliyah plants her chubby fists on her hips. "Come swim with me. Daddy has to go pee. You can't pee in the pool."

"That's true." She strips off her top and unwinds her sarong revealing—*thank God and all the angels in heaven*—a bikini, bright blue and very small. My heart hammers in my throat as she pulls the elastic band from her ponytail and shakes out her silky hair. "Too hard to get it out if it's wet." And there she stands in all her glory, long and lean and nearly naked.

"Oops, almost forgot." When she stoops to remove her ankle brace, her bikini bottom slides down, revealing a shadow of the cleft between her firm, round ass cheeks. I gulp to keep from choking on my tongue.

"Ready?" Clamping her arm over her breasts, she jumps in. Water splashes my shins, startling me from my stupid staring.

"Coming, Dalton?" She discreetly checks her bikini top. "God, this feels marvelous."

"Come on, slowpoke." Aliyah tugs my hand, then jumps into Laurel's waiting arms.

I shed my shirt and jump in after them.

After ten minutes of Marco Polo, Destiny appears at the pool's edge. "Come on, little one. Let's get some food."

Aliyah splashes up the steps. "Time for cake!"

Relieved of our charge, we lounge on the pool steps, Laurel's head on my shoulder. Nothing ever felt better. Well, nothing we can do in public.

"Man, I needed this."

"How's it going with Maxie?"

"About as well as can be expected, according to her nurse. Thought they'd discharge her today, but she got dizzy in the shower, so we're back to square one." She stretches her mile-long legs. "It feels good to take that brace off."

"Feels good to have you here." I slide my arm around her hips. Even underwater, her flesh radiates heat. I can't resist tracing her curves.

But when I tease my finger inside the band of her bikini bottom, she squirms away. "Lots of little eyes on us."

I snuggle closer. "Let's go upstairs."

"I thought you wanted me to meet your friends."

"There they are." I wave toward the food tables. "Friends, Laurel. Laurel, friends. Let's go upstairs." I know I'm being a jerk, but damn it, she's so near, so wet, so bare.

"There you are." Rhonda appears at the pool's edge, holding two plastic cups. Her frizzy hair floats on the breeze as she grins down at us—well, at Laurel.

I stifle a groan. Rhonda has lousy timing, but maybe she can fire Laurel up about artistic stuff going on in Eugene.

She plops down at the pool's edge and holds out a cup. "Laurel, right? This is for you. Rebecca's pirate punch."

"Um, thanks." She sniffs it and wrinkles her nose. "What's in it?"

"Better not to ask." She extends her hand. "Rhonda Torres. I teach art at Dalton's school. You gonna help us with the race day exhibit at the Rainbow Center?"

"I'm pretty busy with family stuff." Laurel sips and grimaces. "Wow. We used to make this in college."

Rhonda guffaws. "Trash can punch, right? What did you study?"

"Humanities. Art history, mostly. I wanted to be a gallery manager or a museum curator."

My brain pings. Wanted? As in, she doesn't want it anymore?

Rhonda gulps her killer punch. "Lots of art galleries in Eugene. And the art museum on campus."

I brace myself for those hateful words: San Francisco. Leaving after Christmas. But Laurel just sighs. "I'm working in a bookstore for now. I came to Eugene to help my great-aunt. She's ninety, and her health's not good."

Rhonda's hand covers Laurel's. "We're at that age, right? Lost my abuelo last year. Dalton knows what I'm talking about." She elbows me. "How's your mom, by the way?"

"She has her good days and bad days. You two want another drink? Some food?"

Laurel flashes a weary smile. "I am kinda hungry. And maybe a beer? This punch is dangerous."

"I'll make you a plate." I trot across the patio toward the food tables. A backward glance shows the two women perched on the pool's edge, heads almost touching. Excellent. If anyone can sell Eugene, Oregon to an artist, it's Rhonda.

Laurel

Dalton's friend nudges my arm. "He really likes you. It's good to see him happy."

I can't help grinning. "Yeah, I like him too." *A lot. Probably too much.*

She huffs her fluffy hair out of her eyes. "That thing with his ex-wife, what a mess. You met her yet?"

"Oh, yeah. Real piece of work."

Rhonda laughs. "Some people just have messed-up priorities. So. Your great-aunt?"

A heavy weight shifts in my chest. "Yeah, Maxie. She's an artist."

"Wait, Maxie Schmidt?"

My eyebrows shoot up. "You know her?"

"Everyone knows Maxie. She's good people. Does a lot for artists around here." Her grin slips. "She's sick?"

"Heart trouble. Won't stick to her diet."

"Well, diets suck. And old folks can be stubborn. My abuelo, he wouldn't eat right either. Doctor told him to stay away from spicy food. He just laughed."

"Did he, did his diet..." *Shut up, Laurel. None of your business.*

"No, a stroke." She trails her fingertips in the water. "He was a sculptor. The only one in my family who supported me. Told me I had the soul of an artist. Losing him was damn hard."

I mull for a moment. Kind of a rude question, but I have to know. "So, why did you become a teacher? If you wanted to be an artist, I mean."

Rhonda shoots me a puzzled look. "I am an artist. I do art all the time. After the kids leave, the classroom's all mine. The light's really good, and no one bitches if I crank up the music." She chugs the rest of her drink. "Regular paycheck, benefits too. Full-time artists don't get that."

"But doesn't it bug you, always putting other people's work ahead of your own?"

Rhonda straightens. Her dark eyes narrow.

"Sorry, I didn't mean to offend you."

"No, it's a fair question. At first, I struggled with that. You know how it is when you're young and idealistic—you think there's only one path to the promised land, right?" She wiggles her toes in the water. "But helping kids discover their talent gives my own work juice. It's a real joy to watch their passion blossom and know I had a hand in it. Dalton could tell you about that."

"He does that too?" Dalton has so many fine qualities, but so far, I haven't seen that creative spark in him. He's more a paint-by-numbers guy.

"Totally," she assures me. "Turns those odd duck loner kids into focused runners. Real creative in his classes, too. Last year, his students dressed up like people from ancient history and made presentations to the whole tenth grade. Very entertaining."

My smile slides into a suspicious smirk. "Rhonda, be real with me. Did Dalton ask you to talk to me about teaching and the Rainbow Center?"

"Hell no," she snort-laughs. "Dalton's been really closed-mouthed about you. Probably trying to protect you from all this social media mess. He doesn't get what you're going through because he's not an artist." Eyes bright, she grips my arm. "It's like you've got all this creativity in you, pushing to get out, and it feels so good to watch it take shape. Then you've got this finished work that wants to be out in the world. But letting it go is terrifying, right? Because you're hanging a piece of your soul on the gallery wall. And someone's gonna hate it."

Recognition flutters in my belly. *Especially if what's hanging on the gallery wall is your nude portrait.*

Rhonda's gaze flicks up at the sound of footsteps. "Hey, Dalton. Took you long enough."

He sets down two paper plates piled high with food. "I got a little of everything." He pulls a beer from his pocket and twists off the cap. "Help yourself, Rhonda."

She pats her belly. "Man, I'm already stuffed. Well, maybe one crab Rangoon."

Huh. Dalton saw us talking and gave us space. Smart guy.

I stab a meatball with my plastic fork. Garlicky heaven. I smooch his cheek, then turn back to his friend. So, tell me about this Rainbow Arts Center."

Dalton returns

Twenty minutes later, Rhonda pushes to her feet. "It was great meeting you, Laurel, but I've bent your ear long enough."

"And eaten half our food." I give her a smile of gratitude.

"Hey, you know what they say about starving artists, right?" She leaves us alone on the pool's edge.

Laurel nabs the last mini egg roll. "I like her."

"Yeah, me too. She's a generous soul. Good artist, too. You should come to the school and see her stuff. She paints these big city scenes full of tiny people. Lots of color and motion. I don't know the right words to describe it but—"

"I'd like to. I want to see your classroom too."

"My room? Why?"

"Just curious. I'll bet it tells me a lot about you." Her fingertips glide down my arm, leaving a tingly trail. "Rhonda says you're a very creative teacher." She sighs. "But I have no idea what this next week will bring."

"And you don't need me adding to your plate."

"Unless it's more of those meatballs. Sooo much garlic." She fans her mouth. "No vampires will bother us tonight."

Hope flares in my chest. "Us? Tonight?"

She wrinkles her nose. "Sorry, I have an early meeting with the Willamette Grove dietician. And since *someone* promised I'll be showing photos at Run for the Arts, I've got a lot of photo-editing to do. I'd better get going."

"Yeah, about that—I'm really sorry I put more work on your shoulders. Or your plate?"

She shrugs. "Done is done. At least I'm learning some new skills." Her voice sounds tight, or maybe just tired.

I help her up. "Thanks for coming. Sorry you didn't get to meet the others."

"That's cool. I'll meet them later."

Later means she'd be back. She's interested in my friends, my work. An excellent sign. "I'll walk you to your car."

She winds herself back into her sarong—damned if I can see how it stays up—then refastens her ankle brace. "Almost done with this pain in the ass."

"Can we try a run next weekend?"

"I hope so." Another sigh.

Guilt twangs in my gut. "You're under a lot of pressure now. Do you want me to ease off?"

"No, Dalton. Hearing your voice helps more than you know." She kisses my cheek and starts for the exit.

Not yet. Intercepting her, I grab her damp hair and press her lush mouth to mine in a lingering kiss.

I love the way she leans her chin onto my shoulder. Laurel's the only woman I've ever dated who was tall enough to reach. The way our bodies fit together is remarkable. But there's so much more to it than that. She just fits—in my life, in my bed, in my heart.

Hand in hand, we make our way through the dwindling crowd. At her car, I pull her in for one last hug. Her pliant body molds against me, reducing my bones to jelly, and the words just slip out, as natural and unstoppable as rain. "I love you, Laurel."

Lids half-lowered, lips parted, she seems on the verge of answering. Her fingertips trail down my chest. Her wistful smile holds so much unspoken emotion—but she slides behind the wheel of her VW and drives away.

She's not ready yet.

Soon, she will be. She feels it too, and she'll admit it, once Maxie's well.

Sudden dread stiffens my spine. But what if Maxie doesn't get well? What if she dies? Will Laurel just cut and run?

Chapter Forty

♥

Laurel

"Sorry I'm late!" I call as I sail through the door of Book Nirvana, my messenger bag flapping at my hip.

I was up at dawn for a hurried yoga routine since I still can't run on this damn sore ankle, followed by a meeting with Willamette Grove's dietician, a woman so rigid Maxie's sure to rebel—then a quick trip to Arnie's café for coffee and pastries to go, and three hours in Lorenzo's studio. That photo editing software may be a piece of cake for an experienced artist like him, but it's taking longer than I'd anticipated to master it, and Lorenzo's been too busy with a big wedding shoot to help me much.

I've got two photos complete, but I'll need at least twelve for the Rainbow Center's art show on race day, only...I check my phone calendar as I struggle into my Book Nirvana apron. Less than two weeks away. Yikes!

"How's Maxie doing?" Clara asks as she unties her apron.

"Better, thanks. They're releasing her this afternoon. Elmer's picking her up."

"Who?"

"One of her many artist friends." God knows what I'd do without them. There's no way I could hold down this job and do photography without that roster of visiting artists who keep Maxie company and make sure she doesn't deviate from the low-sodium meals I've prepared. Even with their help, I'm stretched to the breaking point.

"Well, I'm off." Clara rubs her barely rounded tummy. "I'm meeting Nick at the hospital to take a peek at this little one." She grabs her purse from under the counter. "Margot's in class. She'll be in around four. The shop shouldn't be too busy until then." She hurries out the door.

As soon as she's out of sight, I check my phone to see if Davonte has answered my text.

> **In a meeting. Call later?**

We've been playing telephone tag all morning. After Dalton's "I love you" last night, I crave my bestie's soothing voice, his gentle wisdom—or at least his snarky humor.

Because I almost said it back. The urge to echo Dalton's confession was there, fizzing in my gut as if I'd drunk too much beer, but I couldn't let the words slip past my lips. And what the hell does it mean that I'm thinking of my feelings for Dalton in terms of a belch?

I'm a mess.

I care for him so much, but with Maxie and the art stuff and decisions to be made left, right, and center, I can't spare the mental bandwidth for a State of the Relationship talk. Dalton deserves an answer, but I just can't give it to him now.

Especially considering how terrified I am by the avalanche of change those three little words could launch.

Despite Clara's prediction, a late-afternoon rush keeps me pinned behind the counter. A few minutes past three, a man's voice blares from the children's section. "Hey now, I said one book. I know youse ain't deaf."

My head jerks up. My stomach twists. *That voice. No way.*

A short, stocky man with glossy black curls barrels around the corner and hefts a toddler into his arms. The cherub points a stubby finger at me. "Blue hair!"

The man turns.

My heart stops.

Carlo.

My one great love slowly sets the child down. She toddles off to join her siblings, a sturdy boy of seven or eight, and a pony-tailed girl of maybe five, all with the same thick black hair as their father—and their mother, a short buxom woman with plump lips and sharp eyes. Leaving the kids to ransack the bookshelves, she murmurs into his ear. He nods, his gaze never leaving mine.

"Come on, kids." She claps her hands. "We'll come back for books later."

"But Maaa! I want—"

"—not fair!"

"Kitty!" The littlest one waves a shiny board book.

Carlo's voice sharpens. "Simmer down. You're gonna give your mama a headache. Go next door and get a cookie. I'll be right there."

Their mother levels a stern glance at her husband. "Ten minutes." She shoots me a glare.

When they're gone, he whistles, a low tone of escaping steam. Then he flashes that dazzling, cocky grin that first made my heart pound. He *was* my first, not in my bed, but in my heart. No one else ever came close.

Until now?

My first day at the U of O, I couldn't find my Intro to Mythology class. The professor was already lecturing when I slid into the back row, right behind a short, muscular guy. He turned, checked me out from top to toe, and his glossy black eyebrows flicked up in a cheeky greeting.

"What's up, Viking Girl?" He tugged my blond braid. That's all it took.

What a pair we made, the little Italian stallion with his square-jawed movie-star face and his big booming laugh. And me, the pale Nordic runner who towered over him. When his jock buddies teased, he'd waggle his eyebrows and say, "She's worth the climb."

He's heavier now, with a slight dad belly pooching over his belt. No doubt, his Italian-American wife stuffs him like a manicotti every night—before he stuffs her with his...

I shuffle papers on the counter while he ambles toward me. Where's a customer when you need one? The shop falls eerily quiet. Carlo folds his hands on the glass countertop, hands that once held me, soothed me, stroked me to ecstasy. His left hand bears a plain gold band.

"Viking girl." His voice is husky, as if something's blocking his throat. "I thought you were up in Portland."

"I was. My, ah—"

Behind those thick lashes, his dark-chocolate eyes hold an echo of tenderness so poignant I have to look away.

"Aunt Maxie. She needs my help."

"Feisty ol' Maxie. She must be—"

"Ninety. She's moving into an old folks' home."

"Aw, jeez. That's tough." He glances over his shoulder before covering my hand with his. So warm, so easy. "Bookstore, huh? Thought you'd be running an art gallery."

"Yeah, well, I hit some potholes. Kinda ran off the road."

He squeezes my hand. "You'll get back on track. Of all the people I knew in college, you had the clearest vision of your future. Had it all mapped out."

A sob rises in my throat, but I gulp it back down. "How about you, Carlo? Did you stay on course?"

He chuckles, and his face relaxes into a fond grin. Once upon a time, that dreamy smile belonged to me. Seeing it again slices my guts like a cleaver.

"Yeah, pretty much. I teach history now. Coach soccer, too. We're up here for a summer league tournament. Carlo Junior's team made the playoffs. Proud of him."

"He's a looker. Like his pops."

"Laurel, I—" He raises his hands, palms up, then lets them fall onto the counter.

"Hey." I sniffle. "It is what it is. Life goes on. Insert your favorite platitude." My voice hitches. "I hope you're happy."

"I am." His eyes shine glassy-bright. "But I'm sorry I hurt you. Really, really sorry, Viking Girl." He tugs the blue tip of my ponytail. "It woulda never worked out between us, you know. You're shooting for the stars. Me, I'm happy being a dad in the suburbs." His voice wobbles. "You deserve someone special, Laurel."

He squeezes my hands again, then spins away, striding fast toward the café. Gone.

I shatter. A sharp-edged sob tears my throat, stealing my breath.

The doorway bell tinkles.

"I'll be just a moment," I croak as I flee behind the wooden screen and collapse onto Clara's desk.

He's a history teacher, like Dalton. And happy in the suburbs, like Dalton. Of all the guys I've ever dated, I was happiest with Carlo, the least ambitious, the most authentic. Reflected in his eyes, I saw the woman I wanted to be. Fascinating. Surprising. Sparkly.

I'm pretty sure Dalton sees me that way too. And I'm doing my damnedest to convince him we don't fit together.

Why?

Chapter Forty-One

♥

Laurel

Maxie's artist friends are absolute gems. All week, they've been keeping her entertained. Sometimes they even join us for a salt-free dinner, and if that's not proof of love, I don't know what is.

Tonight's dinner guest is Olivia, a muralist whose mercilessly blunt talk makes us both laugh. She nudges Maxie's dinner plate. "Yeah, Max, this plain chicken and steamed veg sucks, but being alive doesn't suck, right? You were a huge help at my studio today, and I'll want your opinion once I finish the next layer." She points with her fork. "So eat your sucky broccoli and stick around for a while."

After dinner, I clear away the dishes while Olivia and Maxie stay in the dining room for a foul-mouthed round of Go Fish. When my phone rings with an incoming video call, I duck into my room, leaving the door open a crack in case Maxie calls.

Davonte's gorgeous face fills my phone screen, and I can tell by his wide-eyed, tight-lipped grin, he's got juicy news.

"Evening, doll face! Got a minute to meet my friend?"

Well, at least one of us has good news tonight. This could be good news for me too because if Davonte's met someone special, that'll be an incentive for him to stay in San Francisco, a possibility that eases some of the pressure in my chest.

Ugh. Dad's right. When the going gets tough, I look for the exit. Not knowing how long Maxie will need me is so damn stressful, and my go-with-the-flow skills are sadly underdeveloped.

Davonte props his phone up and steps back to throw his arm around a bald guy with tan skin, bushy black eyebrows, and a twinkling smile. New boyfriend waves at the camera.

"Delighted to meet you, Laurel. I'm Narek." He glances at Davonte, who nudges him.

"So, I, uh." He nibbles his lip. "I'm doing a scary thing. My uncle runs an art gallery in Sausalito, and he wants to retire. You see, he—"

Davonte rolls his eyes and elbows his friend.

"Yeah, okay. Long story short, I'm buying him out and remaking the place into a showcase for innovative contemporary art, and I'm looking for staff. You see, I've got this vision..."

Narek's dark eyes sparkle with passion as he describes the gallery I've always wanted: Avant-garde, surprising, inclusive, and with a killer view of the San Francisco Bay. And there's a vegetarian café next door! As he talks, I imagine the sea breeze blowing through my hair as I stride along the waterfront on my way to work. Already, I feel an ease, a kinship with this avid art geek. He gets it—the thrill of finding the perfect piece to open art-lovers' eyes to new perceptions.

And there's not a damn thing I can do about it.

Bitterness floods my mouth and stings my eyes. For an opportunity like this to show up when I'm mired in helping Maxie, it's just too cruel.

Narek stops blathering to catch his breath. "Davonte says you'd be the perfect assistant gallerist and, well..." He gives Davonte a side hug and an adorable grin. "I'm inclined to trust him. So, what do you say, Laurel? Are you interested?"

My bestie's eyes gleam. *Fuck me sideways with a brick*! He's laying my dream in my lap, and I can't accept it.

I breathe in one last lungful of hope, then let it go.

"There's nothing I would love more, guys, but at the moment, I'm stuck in Eugene, Oregon. My great-aunt is sick, and she needs 24-hour care."

Huddled on my bed, I feel my heart shriveling in my chest. Out in the dining room, a whoop and a burst of laughter rings out, followed by a closing door. If Olivia's leaving, I'd better wind this up.

Davonte's brows scrunch together. "But Maxie's moving into assisted living, right? Then you'll be free to move on."

"Maybe. I don't know." I scrub a hand down my face. "I'll have to wait and see how it works out." Like, will she stick to her diet? Will her artist friends continue to check on her once she leaves this funky cottage that's been their gathering place? Will she learn to be happy there, or will she wither away, her spirit squashed by the oppressive beige-ness of Willamette Grove?

Narek's smile twists a little. He and Davonte exchange a loaded glance.

"Listen," Narek says, "I'm still a couple months from opening, possibly longer, depending on financing and city hall crap. Let's talk again next month."

Davonte grabs the phone and gives me an intense, bug-eyed stare. "You think hard about this, Laurel Tree. Here's your chance to grab your dream. Time to shit or get off the pot."

Narek pokes his face into view. "Hey, family stuff is complicated. I get it. Just don't say no yet, okay?"

I nod. "Right. I'm not saying no yet."

"Love you, doll face." Davonte ends the call.

A deep voice behind me spins me around, startling me into dropping my phone.

"You're leaving?"

Dalton

Laurel clutches her shirt over her heart and gawks at me, guilt etched all over her ashen face.

Meanwhile, my heartbeat's slowing, lub dub, lub...dub, lub......dub. A clammy chill pebbles my skin.

After several seconds of opening and closing her mouth like a goldfish, she chokes out, "I didn't say that."

"But you didn't tell him no." I scrub a hand over my face. "This is what you've always wanted. There's no way I can compete with your dream job."

When Maxie welcomed me in and shooed me toward Laurel's room, I envisioned a few precious moments of privacy, some stolen kisses, a chance to drink her in at the end of an exhausting school day.

I didn't expect to be gutted.

But I can't stand between Laurel and her bright, shining plan. Even if she doesn't care about me enough to stay, I care...so damn much. And that's what love is, right? Wanting the best for your person. Wanting to see them happy.

Laurel can never be happy here with me.

"Dalton." She vaults off the narrow bed and grips my arm like she's drowning. "I haven't decided anything, except to stay here as long as Maxie needs me."

"Which probably won't be much longer." I pry her fingers from my wrist. "And I guess my feelings for you don't factor into your decision."

"Dammit, I didn't say that either," she growls through clenched teeth. "Can't you understand how hard it is, getting the perfect job offer in the midst of all of this?" She flaps her free hand, taking in the house, the street, the town. "It's like fate's laughing in my face."

"Honestly, no. I don't understand." I back toward the door. "I wish I could be more sympathetic, but you're breaking my heart, Laurel."

My voice cracks on her name. There's no air in this narrow room. My stomach flip-flops as I stumble backward, then bolt toward the front door.

"Ichabod?" Maxie calls behind me, and that's probably the last time I'll hear her voice.

Or Laurel's. Because I just can't face her again.

Too shattered to drive safely, I abandon my car at the curb and break into a run, my feet pounding the asphalt, my eyes blinded by tears, my lungs burning. Sprinting into the darkness, I try in vain to outrun the pain.

Chapter Forty-Two

♥

Laurel

You don't change your life plan just for good sex.

I've been repeating this mantra all morning—to my bleary-eyed reflection as I try to disguise the damage with concealer—and end up looking pasty on top of puffy.

On my drive to work, I grumble it to Eugene, Oregon at large. Why is everyone so freakin' irritating in traffic today?

I chant it mentally every time the urge to text Dalton strikes—about twenty-seven-million times. But Dalton's at work, and Clara's not paying me to brood and snivel. And considering she's the best boss ever, I need to get my pathetic act together.

But is it just good sex? After fights and misunderstandings, a force more profound than lust keeps tugging us back together. Until last night.

Why didn't Maxie warn me? All it would've taken is a shouted, "Hello, Dalton," and I could've spared him the shock of walking in on my not-really-a-job-interview. She's usually loud enough to hear from any room in the house, but last night she had to tone it down?

Hell, with the way Maxie's bouncing back from her latest medical episode, I may be in Eugene for a loooong time. And I'm glad, really I am. Maxie means the world to me.

So would that job in Sausalito, but some things aren't meant to be.

And Dalton thinks our romance is one of those things.

Shit, shit, shit. How can I undo this mess?

I ring up a customer's purchase: a stack of steamy romance books, thank you very much, then grab the feather duster and attack the front display table, knocking over the vase of daisies on top. Crap on crackers, I can't let this foul mood ruin Clara's inventory.

You don't change your life plan just for good sex.

Life plan? Other than clinging to my so-called plan like a scratchy rope that shreds my palms, since coming to Eugene, I haven't taken one damn step toward finding a big-city gallery job. I could've sent out résumés, made calls to Davonte's artsy friends, even looked for a gallery job here. But I haven't done any of that. Instead, I've been taking pictures. And making artist friends. And now, Eugene is starting to feel like home.

And Dad is right: my track record is pathetic. What I've called "a fresh start" after each firing, each break-up—that looks an awful lot like running away.

I duck behind the science books and pull my phone from my pocket, turning it over and over in my hand. Running off to San Francisco won't fix this—nor Portland, nor New York. Not even Paris could fix this. The answer is right here.

For once in my life, I'm running toward something.

I tap the screen to life.

Dalton, I'm sorry.

There's a helluva lot more I need to say, but before I can continue, Clara strides into the shop, her brows smashed together, her lips compressed in a straight line.

Crap, she's Dalton's good friend. Did he spend last night crying on her shoulder?

She grips the edge of the counter. "Hey, Laurel, I have a huge favor to ask."

I blink in surprise. She's not going to chew me out?

"This morning, my OB doc scolded me for stressing over the wedding. Says it's not good for the baby. But there are so many details, and Harry doesn't come back till Friday. I know you're busy with your great-aunt and your photos, but do you think you could help with the decorations and flowers?" When I gape at her, she adds, "I'll pay for your time, of course."

"Um, sure." I clear the wobble from my throat. "I mean, I'd be glad to help."

She beams. "Great. This Sunday, can you believe it?"

Through gritted teeth, I listen politely while Clara gushes about wedding plans. When I can't take a second more without screaming, I hook a thumb over my shoulder. "I need to get those new anime books unpacked."

I hide out in a rear corner of the shop, slashing away with a box cutter. *This sucks worse than the worst suckage ever.* Stab, slash. *Break up with Dalton, then go to a wedding.* Rip, tear. *His ex-girlfriend's wedding.* I yank out a staple, scratching my finger and drawing blood. *Everyone's gonna be all, "Oh, love is so wonderful."* I sniff hard and blink back tears. I will not cry at work, damn it!

The doorway bell jangles, and Clara calls, "Laurel, someone to see you."

I scramble to my feet. Dalton?

But the guy at the counter has too much hair, and it's flaming red.

"Hey, Laurel." Elmer grins over the huge bouquet he's holding. "A bunch of us are taking Maxie to her new place to unpack her stuff. Join us after work?"

Standing beside the screen, Clara raises an eyebrow.

Shit. She's gonna think he's my new love interest.

I paste on an over-bright grin. "Sure. Always glad to meet Maxie's friends. She'll love those flowers. I'll come over as soon as I get off work."

Elmer winks. "Good deal. See ya."

Clara doesn't ask, but I can't restrain my babbling. "That's Elmer. Maxie's friend. He's like a—a grandson to her. You know, an art buddy." I back away, pointing over my shoulder. "I'll just go clean up."

The hope that Dalton might still want me has dwindled to a microscopic splinter, but it's still hope, and I can't let Elmer's flirtation spoil it.

When I arrive at Willamette Grove, the party is in full swing. Music blares from a speaker on the breakfast bar while a half-dozen twenty-somethings hang pictures and open boxes. Seated on her favorite high-back armchair, Maxie directs the action. "Put that one above the couch, doll, next to the big nude."

I smooch Maxie's cheek. "Wow, you've got quite a fan club here."

"Aren't they great? Artists are generous people." She waves to a young woman in a crop top and baggy harem pants. "The lamp goes in that corner. Thanks, Chantal."

Despite her recent health worries, Maxie's grip on my hand is warm and strong. "Where would we be without our friends propping us up, eh?"

That's especially true for Maxie. Even with the seventy-year difference in age, my great-aunt and these bohemian artists are kindred spirits. "You've collected a great artist family, Max. I hope I can do as well."

Maxie shoots me a meaningful look. "What are you talking about? These are your people too. Look at you." She tugs on my chunky glass beads. "You fit right in."

"Yeah, maybe." Maxie's comment hits uncomfortably close to home. Dressing up for my art gallery jobs was a challenge. It's not easy to strike the right note: posh but approachable, modern but not too avant-garde, while the artists whose work we displayed just wore whatever funky outfit expressed their mood.

After the packing mess is put away, the workers help themselves to raw veggies and fruit, low-sodium hummus, and—

"Is that Jell-O salad?" I ask.

Maxie grins. "With marshmallows. Why not? It's not salty. Let's live a little."

I fill my plate and sit cross-legged on the floor between two women discussing their next exhibit.

"Scoot over, Kayla." Elmer flashes a flirtatious smile to the girl on my left. Blushing, she complies.

He sits beside me and leans so close his fuzzy ginger beard tickles my shoulder. "Maxie tells me you had some relationship drama yesterday."

Dammit, Maxie.

I swallow what now feels like a mouthful of mud instead of hummus. "I, uh, don't really want to talk about that."

"Okay, cool." He nudges me. "If he's a good guy, he'll be back. If not, he's an idiot. Anyway, if you need a shoulder to cry on, I'm here. I care about Maxie too. And about you." His cocky façade slips a little, revealing a sweet, genuine smile.

I sigh around a mouthful of Jello. If I'd taken a different path... Elmer is undeniably cute, and there's something sexy about his easy confidence. If I'd met him first, who knows what might've happened?

But I met Dalton first. And he's going to be so damn hard to forget.

The artists clear out after dinner. I stuff the paper plates and other trash into a sack and haul it to the dumpster. "Ready to go home, Maxie?" I ask when I return.

She looks around the now-colorful room. "You know, today made me feel a helluva lot better about this place. As long as I have my stuff and my friends, I'm home."

I've got to admit, the oppressive beige-ness of the tiny apartment has been obscured by Maxie's eclectic artwork and tchotchkes.

"Yeah, you'll be fine here," I reassure her, hoping that's true. "I'll come visit every day. Have you given any more thought to what you're doing with your house?"

She gives her head a sharp shake. "Still talking to the lawyer. You should come with me next time."

"Okay..."

Maxie drums her fingers on the side table. "Well? Have you talked to him yet?"

With a groan, I drop into a chair. "No. He won't answer my texts." Except for one terse line:

> I can't deal with this now. I'll see you at the wedding.

Right, it's the first week of school. If I'm struggling to keep my mind on work, imagine what Dalton's going through. I don't blame him for needing space.

Maxie tsks. "You know where he lives. Go see him."

"He doesn't want to talk now."

She crosses her arms and huffs. "Sounds like he's pouting. You don't need a pouter. You should call Elmer."

But I don't want Elmer. I want Dalton.

"So, you gonna tell me what happened to send your sweetheart out the door looking like the world was ending?"

My sigh empties me down to my toes. "Davonte called. His friend's opening an art gallery near San Francisco. He offered me a job. Dalton walked in on the call."

A series of silent reactions flits over Maxie's face: surprise, sorrow, maybe shock? Then she relaxes into a gentle smile and lays her hand on my knee. "You should take it."

"Maxie, no. I promised to stick around as long as you need me."

She shakes her head. "Hold on, I never asked you for that. Just until Christmas. And sweetheart, if your dream job is ready before then, I'll be okay. I have my new place, my friends." She squeezes my knee. "And I won't hold a promising young artist hostage to my needs—especially one I love as much as you."

"But Maxie—"

She waves away my protest with a flick of her knuckly fingers. "I won't hear of it." Her voice quivers. "But I'll miss you, kiddo. Now." She pushes up from her chair. "Let's go. Busy day tomorrow."

"I thought moving day was Friday. I asked Clara for the day off."

"That's right. The electrician's not done in here. But I've got things to do before I move."

"I work from noon to closing. I can help in the morning with whatever."

Maxie's grin sparkles with mischief. "I've got it handled. Chantal will give me a ride." She hooks her arm through mine as we head for the door. "You just figure out how to get Ichabod back."

Chapter Forty-Three

♥

"It's beautiful, Laurel. You have such an eye for color." Clara surveys the flower and tulle extravaganza in her backyard, then squeezes me in a tight hug. "Gotta finish getting dressed. Come have a glass of champagne with us." She dashes back into the house she shares with Nick.

Exhausted, I slump onto the deck railing. I arrived at six a.m. and, with the two undergrads Nick hired to help, festooned the wooden arbor with blue and white delphiniums, blue hydrangeas, and white roses, the color scheme a tribute to Nick's Greek heritage. To each aisle seat, we attached poufs of white tulle, anchored with pale blue ribbons and sprays of flowers. A basket of white rose petals stands ready for Nick's little niece to scatter on the aisle runner.

Framing the makeshift altar, more flowers spill from the stone urns Elmer borrowed from Willamette Grove. During the past week, I've carefully deflected his "friendly" hugs and flirtatious comments. I could use a shoulder to cry on, but I can't risk word getting back to Dalton that I've moved on even if, after four days of silence, holding onto hope feels stupidly futile. I give the yard a last once-over and snap a few photos with my phone. Maybe I can use this on my résumé. Does flower arranging count as art?

It's noon already. Guests will start arriving any minute now. Countdown to Dalton. Will he even talk to me? Nerves jittering, I fiddle with one of the lace butterflies I attached to the back porch supports.

"Really fine job, Laurel." Harry claps my shoulder. Clara's assistant and close friend returned from his Australian trip two days ago, his adorable girlfriend Evie on his arm. Both in their mid- seventies, they radiate good health and happiness, with their deep tans, strong, wiry bodies, and thick white hair—and their annoying habit of smooching in the corners when they think no one's looking. Watching two people so giddily in love turns my stomach. It's bad enough with Nick and Clara nibbling each other all the time.

Worst of all, Harry is Dalton's cousin once removed, or something like that. I can see the family resemblance in their deep-set blue eyes. Harry's probing questions make it clear Dalton hasn't been frank about our breakup. Clara seems to know, though, because her gentle teasing has dried up. Too kind to poke a fresh wound, most likely.

The doorbell rings. When no one moves, I hustle to answer it, then relax into my first heartfelt smile of the day. Arm in arm, Margot and Maxie stand on the porch in vintage floral sundresses and lacy cardigans—Margot's outfit snug and sexy, Maxie's baggy and oversized. Both are wearing heaps of colorful beaded necklaces, fingerless lace gloves, and each has a feathered fascinator pinned to her hair.

Leaning on her jeweled cane, Maxie pivots. "Whataya think?"

"Very glamorous, Max." I peck her rouged cheek.

Margot grins. "We hit three vintage stores before we found all our ingredients."

"Come in. Mimosas are in the kitchen."

"Mmm. Bubbly. Come on, kiddo." Maxie leans on Margot's arm as they make their way back. It's a huge relief to see her so spry and sharp again, after that pepperoni close call.

Nick's gorgeous Greek goddess sister trots down the stairs. "It's Laurel, right? You any good with hair pins?"

The master bedroom is a riot of color and scents. Satin dresses, silk flowers, and bathrobes litter the bed and chairs. Seated at an old-fashioned vanity table, Clara frowns into the mirror while Nick's statuesque mother fusses with her gleaming curls. "Sorry, dear, it's no use. I can't get it to stick."

"What are you trying to do?" I ask.

Clara lifts a fluff of lace, feathers, and satin roses. "This is supposed to hold my hair back, but we can't figure out the pins."

"Do you have a hair clip?"

Clara hands me a tray full of them.

"Gimme a minute." Taking the ornament and clips, I trot downstairs to my bin of craft supplies.

"There she is," Harry's hearty voice booms. The clips clatter to the floor.

He's here. Dressed in a sleek navy-blue suit, Dalton leans on the stone mantel, his back to the staircase. At Harry's comment, he turns. Emotion flashes across his face, too fast to read, replaced by cool indifference.

I stoop to collect the hair clips with trembling fingers, then dash into the kitchen to fetch a glue gun and some florist's wire. *Just run back to the bedroom. Don't look at him.*

But my feet refuse to budge.

"Well, go on." Harry shoves Dalton through the kitchen doorway.

"Okay, okay. Jeesh." He stuffs his hands in his pockets and ambles toward me.

Heart thundering, I freeze.

"Hey, Laurel." Gaze lowered, he mumbles at his shiny shoes. "You, uh, you look really pretty."

I spin to the sink, fill a glass with water, and gulp, dribbling down the front of my pale-blue lace sheath. Closing my eyes, I draw a deep breath, then face him.

"Dalton." I try for a smile, but my mouth cramps. "You look pretty too."

When his lips quirk up, I dare to move closer.

He steps back. "I think it's better if we don't go there. Not today."

A hot ball of emotion surges up my throat, pushing the words out. "Damn it, Dalton, please let me explain. I—"

He raises both palms. "We'll both just get upset. I don't want to spoil the wedding by fighting with you."

I cross my arms, protecting my center. "Right. It's their day." A tear rolls down my cheek.

His tone softens. "Oh, God. Please don't cry."

"Everybody cries at weddings. Why shouldn't I?" Snuffling, I gather my supplies. "I have to go help Clara."

He clasps my bare shoulder. For a moment, I let his hand rest there, remembering how much I love his touch. Then I pull away. "You're right, Dalton. This isn't the time."

An hour later, wobbly from three glasses of pre-wedding bubbly, I settle into my seat beside Maxie. Dalton sits across the aisle, murmuring to Harry. When his blue, blue gaze flicks up and meets mine, I wrench my focus to the back porch and watch for Clara's arrival.

The string quartet strikes up the first notes of a vaguely familiar song. I search my sketchy memory of classical music. Not Mozart, not Vivaldi—it's Elvis. *I Can't Help Falling in Love with You.* The sweetness of their choice stabs me like a stiletto.

On Harry's arm, Clara glides down the stairs, my last-minute improvisation anchoring her cascade of auburn curls. Stunning in her ivory lace gown, she glows with new love and new life.

The hairs at my nape prickle. Once again, I catch Dalton watching me, not the bride.

"We'll just get upset. I don't want to spoil the wedding."

Oh God, he's going to end it. The ache in my chest glows hot enough to melt my ribs.

Guests sniffle into tissues while Nick speaks his vows in a trembling voice. Then Clara blows my heart right out of my body with a quote from Maya Angelou, "Love recognizes no barriers. It jumps hurdles, leaps fences, penetrates walls to arrive at its destination full of hope."

Don't look at him. You won't survive this if you look at him. I grind my teeth and keep my gaze glued on the bride and groom. After their long, searing kiss ends on a giggle, they clasp hands and trot up the aisle to cheers and applause.

"Just lovely." Maxie sniffles. "You and Ichabod should have a garden wedding too. Plenty of room in the backyard, you know."

I wince. Has she forgotten? Lately, it's hard to tell what's a memory slip and what's teasing.

Feeling a hundred pounds heavier, I push to my feet and follow the other guests back to the house. While we assemble inside for photos and a champagne toast, the catering crew shifts chairs, sets up tables, and lays out a dance floor of wooden tiles, transforming the backyard into a flowery reception hall.

Clara beckons. "Over here, Laurel. I want a picture with my Book Nirvana crew."

I join Clara, Margot, Arnie, and Harry in front of the stone fireplace. Holding books from Nick's shelves, we mug for the photographer. When I glance up from my volume of erotic temple carvings, I spy Dalton watching from the doorway. The moment I catch his eye, he melts into the crowd.

Thank God Clara and Nick are keeping things casual. If there was a seating chart, I'd probably find myself beside Dalton for dinner, and that would be even worse than this stilted silence.

As the guests took their seats again, I survey the smiling, laughing faces. Couples, couples everywhere. A fucking love fest. My better angel scolds me for nursing bitterness on such a happy day, but I can't help it. It hurts so much!

Maxie waves gaily from a table full of gorgeous Greeks. "Over here, Laurel."

Good old Maxie. Never married, no kids, she spent her younger years bouncing from one lover to the next, never letting a breakup knock her off course. She just went her own solitary way.

No, that's not true. Maxie's not alone. She has tons of friends.

Ah, but is that enough? Maybe for Maxie, but for me? Because that's where I'm headed. For years, I've idolized Maxie's independent lifestyle. Now, I'm no longer sure.

After a dinner of lemony chicken and garlicky pork souvlakia, oceans of tzatziki, seasoned rice, and a feta-and-olive-laced salad, plus a low-sodium plate for Maxie, the toasts begin. Clara raises her glass of sparkling cider and thanks her friends and family for their help with the wedding. "Especially you, Laurel. Thank you for giving us such a beautiful setting to start our new life together."

Flushed with self-consciousness and a surprise burst of pride, I duck my head.

Next, Nick thanks his friend Leo for convincing him not to give up when Clara sent him back home to Berkeley. "I won't go into sordid details, but let's just say she had some pretty good reasons not to trust me." He kisses Clara's hand. "We are truly blessed, my beautiful bride and me. We both found something we thought we'd never find again." He raises his glass. "Here's to love."

My glass seems to weigh a ton, but I lift it to toast the happy couple, then chug its contents and slam it onto the table.

"Easy now." One of Nick's cousins chuckles. "That business about breaking dishes at Greek weddings, it's just in the movies, you know."

After the plates are cleared away, another Greek cousin summons the bride and groom to the dance floor for the Kalamatiano.

Nick beams. "This is proof my wife is a good sport."

His sister shouts, "Marrying you proves she's a good sport."

Twangy bouzouki music rings out. Hand in hand, Clara and Nick circle the dance floor in a rocking grapevine step. As they pick up speed, Nick grabs his mother's hand, who grabs her daughter's hand, who grabs a cousin's hand, and so on. A handsome Greek uncle pulls me to my feet. Fueled by too much wine and the group's high spirits, I dance more or less in rhythm with the lively music. Further down the line, I hear a familiar cackle. Holding Dalton's hand, Maxie trots along, her face aglow.

When the line breaks apart to loud applause, I head back toward our table.

"Not so fast, kiddo." Maxie tugs on my arm. "You owe Ichabod a dance."

No, I can't. I spin away from him, but my sandals slip on the slick dance floor.

Dalton grasps my arm. "Easy there, lightweight."

Grinning smugly, Maxie totters back to her seat.

All around us, couples sway to Sinatra. Dalton raises a sardonic eyebrow and sets his hand on my waist.

I step back. "You don't have to."

"I know. I want to." The wall of tension between us cracks, just a little. His hand closes around mine. I gulp a deep breath, and away we glide.

Hand in hand, his breath warm on my cheek, it's almost like we've never been apart. Almost. I press closer, but he shifts back, keeping a cushion of air between us. Heated air, alive with crackling electricity, but still a separation. This is only a temporary truce.

I huff a bitter laugh. "How did Maxie persuade you?"

His lashes lower. "She reminded me I'd promised her some shelves for her new apartment, then shoved me in your direction."

"Hey, you don't have to do that either."

He shrugs. "A promise is a promise."

Here it is, the opening I hope for. *Deep breath. Now or never.*

"I want you to know I'm keeping my promises. To Maxie, to Clara, to the Rainbow Center."

"You're helping them?"

"With the art show next week. Rhonda was right. It's a cool program."

"And it didn't cost you any of your sparkle."

I grimace. "Not going to let me forget that, are you?"

"Nope."

The song is nearing its end.

"Okay, so—I just wanted to tell you." I blink away the tears threatening to shatter my composure. "And to say how sorry I am. I never expected that call from California. It knocked me off balance, Dalton. But that doesn't mean I don't care about you."

Please kiss me now. Please say you still want me. Because I want you so badly, it's tearing me up. My watery gaze says all of that, but my lips still, waiting for a sign.

Couples drift back to the tables. Dalton releases me, his arms hanging limply at his sides. "I can't just snap my fingers and forget what I heard. We need to talk this out, Laurel. You and me, alone." His lips curve into the crooked smile I've missed so damn much. "And tomorrow's a school day, so—" He steps back. "I'm going to take off. See you around."

There it is—a tiny sliver of hope, shining diamond-bright. With my fists clenched over my stuttering heart, I watch him congratulate the bride and groom and take his leave.

"See you around," I whisper.

Chapter Forty-Four

♥

Dalton

"Look in the mirror, dude." Marcus sets his empty beer bottle on the low table between us. "You can't criticize her for running away when you're doing the same damn thing."

I cross my arms and slump back in the uncomfortable Adirondack chair. "I'm not running anywhere. I'm right here."

"Haven't called her yet, have you?"

"No," I mutter, barely audible. It's been two days since the wedding. I know she's waiting for my call, but every time I pick up the phone, a messy sludge of emotion clogs my throat—hurt and dread and God knows what. There's a lot more at stake than good sex. Amazing sex. Phenomenal.

Marcus fishes his phone from his pocket and taps the screen. "She's not running away now. See?"

"Fuckin' Instagram," I grumble. I've avoided social media ever since that awful night I walked in on Laurel's job interview—a surprise, she said, but I can't shake the feeling I was just her Plan B until a better offer came through.

And now one has.

Marcus thrusts his phone screen under my nose.

Art exhibit and sale this Saturday, Sept. 15. Support arts programs for Eugene's youth. #RunfortheArts. #RainbowArtsCenter

In paint-spotted jeans and a grubby T-shirt, Laurel perches on a ladder, talking to teens clustered below. Behind her, a rainbow mural stretches across the building's entrance.

"Well, I'll be damned," I mutter. "She hates working with kids."

"Apparently not. Rhonda says she's been out there every afternoon." He stuffs a handful of cashews into his mouth and talks around them. "You gonna call her?"

"And say what?"

"Man, you are dense. You got this beautiful woman bending over backward to make things right, and you're gonna keep her waiting while you make up your mind? You're taking a stupid chance, my friend. Someone's gonna snatch her up."

Destiny joins us on the deck, bearing more beers and a bowl of pretzels. No doubt, Marcus already told her everything. He always does.

She sits, slips her sandals off, and props her feet on her husband's lap. "You fixed him yet?"

"Nope." Marcus hoists his bottle, his Adam's apple bobbing as he swallows. "He's hopeless." He sets down the beer and massages his wife's feet.

She purrs, "Love you, baby," then points at me. "Let me ask you this, Dalton. Did the woman say she doesn't want you?"

"No."

"Did she insult you?"

"No."

"Refuse to talk to you?"

"No."

She takes a handful of pretzels. "So, what you're telling me is, in a moment of high pressure, she choked. And now you're cutting off a good thing because of one mistake?"

I slouch lower in my seat and glower into the distance.

A pretzel pings off my head. "Stupid man."

I pop to my feet and throw my hands wide. "Well, what am I supposed to do? Chase after her like some guy in a chick flick? Real life doesn't work that way."

Marcus and Destiny exchange sappy grins. She slides onto his lap and plants a long, juicy smooch on his mouth, ignoring my indignant snorts.

Finally, Destiny comes up for air and more pretzels. "Lemme tell you a story. On our second date, this guy—" She pokes Marcus's chest— "got the time wrong for our reservation and left me sitting in the lobby of a super-fancy restaurant for an hour. No text, no call."

Marcus pats her hip. "I was extra late because I stopped to buy her a corsage."

She laughs. "Who does that anymore?"

"Hey." He affects a wounded pout. "I was trying to be romantic. Anyway, when I got there, she was gone. Hostess told me she was mega-pissed."

"I was."

"Wouldn't answer my calls for a week."

Laughing, she hugs him, smashing his face into her boobs. "But he kept calling. He wore me down. Left flowers on my doorstep, sent chocolates to my office, even bought me one of those huge-ass teddy bears." She sighs. "Just like in a chick flick."

"And you took him back."

"Obviously." She wiggles her bottom on Marcus' lap. "Look at what I would've missed if I'd been stubborn."

I grumble, "Cute story, but—"

With ninja-like speed, her hand shoots out and yanks my shirt. "Dalton, think about what you're going to miss if you're stubborn." She releases me. "Give the girl a chance."

Marcus nuzzles her neck. "Now say goodnight, Dalster. Me and my lady have some personal business to attend to."

"G'night, guys." I leave them canoodling on the deck. At least someone's getting laid tonight.

That dance... I groan as I climb into my car. Laurel's blue lace dress hugging her slim curves, her sweet, soft body so close, inviting my touch, her storm cloud gaze probing mine, searching for forgiveness, for hope. Yeah, she hurt me, but my friends are right. She's a special lady: gorgeous, talented, funny, athletic, and astonishingly honest. And in her own way, damn brave. It takes courage to set aside your plans when life sends you on a detour. Despite her self-doubt, she's making her way as an artist in Eugene, for Maxie's sake. And maybe, just a tiny bit, for my sake too?

Crickets thrum in the cool twilight. The hollow plunk, plunk, plunk of a basketball echoes in the cul-de-sac. I close my eyes, breathe in a lungful of courage, and pull my phone from my pocket.

> **Hey Laurel, can I come by?**

No answer. Well, what did I expect? A beautiful woman like her is probably out with friends. Maybe with that fuzzy ginger guy. Regret scrapes my stomach like sharp gravel.

My phone screen lights up.

> **Maxie's place. I've got pizza. Bring beer.**

My smile blooms slowly.

> **You sure?**

> **Better hurry. I'm hungry.**

> **Be there in 15.**

Heart hammering, I add one more line:

> **I've missed you.**

Three dots, three dots, three dots. Finally,

I push aside my paper plate and hide a burp behind my napkin.

Beside me on the front steps, Laurel chuckles. "Nice one. So, you ready to start this?"

"Yeah." I pat my stuffed belly. "The grease helps."

"And the beer." She drains her bottle of IPA. "Before we get started, let's set some ground rules."

"Okaaay..." I swallow the last of my beer.

"No sex tonight."

My burst of laughter sprays beer from my nose. "Damn, I forgot how direct you are."

"What's the point of dressing the truth in lace and pearls? We know we're good at sex. The question is, are we any good at the rest of it?" She folds her tense, white-knuckled hands in her lap. "You get the first question."

She's waiting for the obvious: *Why do you run away?* But I dig deeper toward the question that matters most. "Why is art so important to you? Help me understand."

"Wow. Playing hardball, aren't you?" She unclenches her hands and sucks in a deep breath. "Art is so powerful, you know? It takes those feelings that are so hard to pin down and splashes them across a canvas. Or shapes them into a sculpture." Her voice firms, her eyes sharpen, her hands wave like an orchestra conductor's. "You look at good art and, even though you can't quite form words around it, you *feel* it. Big soaring emotions: pain, and yearning, and hope, and awe, and—"

"And love?"

Her gaze drops to her lap. "Yeah, and love."

See? You said the word. And you didn't die. I take her hand as gently as I'd hold a wounded bird. "So why not here?"

"Sorry?"

"Why can't you do the work you love here? Eugene's an artistic town."

Her voice wavers. "It's hard to break in if you don't know anyone. In SF, Davonte has lots of friends..."

"Maxie has lots of friends."

She huffs a strand of hair from her forehead. "You're making this hard on me."

"That's my goal, to make it hard for you to leave."

"Why? Because we have good sex?"

I wait until her skittish gaze meets mine. "Because you're so damn bright, Laurel. I don't mean smart, though you're that too. Your spirit just shines. When you talk about art, when you push your body on a run, when you're in my arms, you're just—brilliant. And none of it is fake. None of it's for show." I cup her face in my hands, emotion scraping my throat raw. "You can make amazing art right here. Don't go, Laurel."

She twists from my embrace. "I'm afraid I don't have what it takes."

I nudge her arm. "Is this the part where I remind you how your poster went viral?"

Her snarl is so damn sexy. "If that poster's good, it's because when I took the picture, I was feeling so much for you."

Hope tickles deep in my gut. "What else do you feel so much for?"

"Huh?"

"What do you want to take pictures of?"

She gazes into the darkness, her brow furrowed. "People, I guess. Their faces. Their stories. Regrets and loves and dreams fulfilled and unfulfilled."

I nod. "At the risk of repeating myself, there are plenty of interesting people in Eugene."

"Yeah." Chuckling, she takes my hand and weaves her fingers through mine. "I'm sitting next to the best of them. On the porch he fixed." She leans onto my shoulder, her hair cool and silky against my cheek. "Do you forgive me for running away?"

"I'm here, aren't I?"

She averts her gaze but presses her leg against mine. "You're a good guy, Dalton."

My pulse revs, but I breathe through it. There's too much at stake to let myself be distracted by desire. "You're a good woman, Laurel. And a good artist. What's it going to take for you to believe that?"

Her gaze slides to somewhere far away. "I'm glad you have faith in me, but I can't help comparing myself to the artists I see in galleries."

"Are you at least willing to try?"

Her hand hovers over my knee, then settles, her grip warm and firm. "I guess I've already started trying. And you've helped." She pushes herself upright. "And now I'm gonna say good night, before I cry or kiss you or otherwise mess this up. We've both got stuff to think about." She tugs me to my feet. "Good night, Dalton. See you at the art show on Saturday?"

"Before the race, yeah."

Her shy, hopeful grin could melt an iceberg. "I hope you'll like it. The kids have put a lot of work into it."

So have you. But I leave that unsaid. Rubbing it in won't help my case.

"G'night, Laurel." Not kissing her is like resisting gravity, but I leave her on Maxie's porch with her thoughts. Laurel's porch, now. I've done all I can do. The decision is hers.

Chapter Forty-Five

♥

Laurel

"Cheeeeeese." Vamping for the camera, two dozen kids cluster beneath their new mural at the Rainbow Arts Center. Their goofy antics are a welcome distraction from my jittery nerves. Fifteen minutes to showtime. I've poured more heart into this exhibit than in any previous gallery job, and I'm damn proud of what we've accomplished: the kid artists, the Rainbow Center staff, and me, the one in charge of shaping it all into a cohesive presentation.

Bouncy freshman Mia Lopez tugs on my T-shirt. "Where's Miss Maxie? She said she'd be here."

"She'll come by later. Elmer's bringing her."

"The ceramics teacher?"

I nod.

"I like him. He's funny."

Yeah. And persistent. Every time I turn around, there he is—toting lumber, building display stands, even hooking up old laptops to ancient TVs to display performance projects. The kids love him, but his constant presence and flirty glances add pressure I don't need right now.

Shading my eyes, I peer into the parking lot. Runners mill around the starting line, but no shiny shaved head towers above them.

He'll be here. Relax.

I barely slept last night, knowing I'd see Dalton this morning. Will he like the exhibit? Not calling him over the past few days has been as tough as resisting fresh-from-the-oven brownies and wiggly puppies and—well, sex with Dalton. Again and again I picked up my phone, then set it down because a sex-sated brain would dull the edge I need to sort my next steps.

The Rainbow Center's director claps her hands. "Okay, kiddos, to your battle stations." Mia and her mom man the front door, ready to hand out programs. I'm heading inside for a final check when a shrill voice spins me around.

"Coach Garvey!" Mia squeals and dashes across the patio, nearly knocking into him. "You came."

"I said I would, didn't I?"

His nearness steals my breath. He's dressed for the race in, well, not much, and his long, muscled limbs gleam in the sunlight. When our eyes meet, he flashes a lopsided grin that weakens my knees.

Holding my gaze, he ambles closer. The morning sun glints off his shiny dome, his thick lashes, and the golden scruff on his jaw. Do I dare to hug him in front of all these kids and parents? Dalton bites his lip, gives me a lingering up and down glance—but instead of taking me into his arms, he crouches at my feet.

"You sure you're ready to run on this ankle?"

"The nurse at Maxie's place is a runner too. She says I'm good to go."

Pinching his lips together, he rises again and takes my hands. Is he trying as hard as I am not to grin like a goofball? "So, have you—"

Mia jitterbugs closer, her patience clearly exhausted. "Come see our art show, Coach."

"Okay, okay. Show me some art, Lopez." Before releasing me, he whispers, "After the race."

The squirrelly young artist tows her favorite teacher toward the new mural framing the Rainbow Center's entrance. "See where I hid you in the picture?"

He peers closely, massaging his upper lip. "No, sorry."

Mia points to a bald figure peeping out from behind the rainbow. His T-shirt reads #EugeneRunningMan.

Dalton throws back his head and laughs. "Good one."

Inside, I follow Mia and Dalton past ceramic sea creatures, dinosaurs, and superheroes, past a glass case of original comic books, past battered mannequins painted in rainbow swirls and draped with handmade jewelry, past old tablecloths tacked onto wooden frames, backgrounds for paintings and drawings.

"See my octopus?" Mia points.

He nods. "I like his smile."

"Miss Laurel helped a lot. She's good at mixing colors."

My cheeks heat. "Naw, that was all you, Miss Mia."

Next, Mia leads us to the professional artists' displays. Between Maxie's connections and Elmer's, we've wrangled thirty donations. "Here's Miss Laurel's pictures. That's my brother, running up a tree."

I hold my breath as Dalton leans in for a closer look. He furrows his brow, grunts, and sidesteps to peer at the next image.

"See, we're all running on the river here. Like Jesus." She slaps her hand over her grin. "Don't let my mom hear that."

He finally straightens and blows out a long breath. "Laurel, how did you—"

"Rhonda told me your team runs in the park on Fridays, so I snapped some pictures last week. Lorenzo helped me edit them."

"Lorenzo?"

"My photography teacher." I point to his display. "He's a real sweetheart."

He surveys Lorenzo's photos, then grips my arms, his face solemn. "Laurel, your work is just as good."

I manage a nonchalant shrug, but inside, his praise lights me up like fireworks. "No way. He's won all kinds of awards. You know how much his pictures sell for?" I point to a price card with lots of zeros.

Dalton shakes his head slowly. "Look, I knew you had talent, but this is really—wow." He pulls me tight against his chest.

For a moment, I forget we're surrounded by kids, many of them Dalton's students. All I know is I'm back in his arms, and it feels damn good.

"Hey, look, it's that running guy from Instagram," someone calls.

"Aww, how sweet."

He stiffens, but he doesn't let go. His lips at my ear, he murmurs, "Wanna go run?"

I nuzzle the delicious spot where his neck meets his shoulder. "I'd rather go make out in the broom closet."

"That'd start a whole new hashtag." His laughter rumbles against my cheek. "Who'd a thought a beanpole like me would have to worry about paparazzi?"

I let my fingertips trail down his back. "Make that two beanpoles."

His voice softens. "Laurel, you're no beanpole. You're beautiful." He presses a tender kiss to my forehead. "Now, let's go win this race."

Running this far without training first was a deeply stupid idea, but I push my leaden legs toward the finish line, knowing Dalton is waiting for me on the other side. The cheering grows louder as I round the final corner.

"Here she comes, the artist who gave us Hashtag Eugene Running Man, number 1027, Laaauuurelll Jepsennnn." Too winded to laugh at the announcer's corny theatrics, I dig deep for my last iota of strength and power my exhausted body across the finish line.

The bubbly KVAL reporter trots toward me, but Dalton reaches me first. With a loud whoop, he lifts me off my feet and spins me around. "You did it." He covers my sticky face with kisses. We're both disgusting—smelly and sweat-drenched and beet-red—but I'd happily stay in his arms all day.

"How's your ankle?" He angles his broad shoulders to block the microphone the reporter's trying to jab between us.

"Not too bad. What's my time, did you see?"

"Fifty-six something. Pretty damn good, considering."

I lace my fingers behind his slick, sunscreen-smeared head. "I'll do better next time, Coach."

The fuzzy microphone cover tickles my cheek. "Laurel, Dalton, how do you feel about—"

A beefy arm shoves the reporter back. "Leave her alone." Elmer scowls, his face flushed and blotchy above his fiery beard. "Laurel, I've gotta talk to you."

Dalton rounds on him, fists clenched. "Just a goddamn—"

Elmer doesn't flinch. "You too, man." Grabbing each of us by the arm, he propels us away from the news crew.

My already-racing heart picks up speed. "What's wrong? Where's Maxie?"

Elmer presses his fists over his eyes and shakes his head. His muscular shoulders shudder.

The crowd and noise fade as if I've plunged deep into icy, stinging water. I raise my hands, pushing back against the awful news. Dalton's arms close around me, his solid presence my only anchor.

"Babe, I'm so sorry," he murmurs.

"How can that be?" I sob into his chest. "She was fine last night. She ate a huge dinner. She—"

Pain pulses through me. I should have noticed. I should have been with her. I've been so damn busy with the art show. Did she know it was the end? Was she scared? Did she call for me?

Such a big, bright spirit, wise and generous and wonderfully weird. My mentor, my guiding light.

Maxie's gone.

Chapter Forty-Six

♥

My hands dangle between my knees as I sit on Maxie's front porch, watching the last swallows swoop low over the cooling asphalt. Soon they'll move on, chasing the summer southward. Something in me still yearns to go with them.

Hard to believe Maxie's been gone only four days. I'm exhausted to the marrow of my bones, and oddly grateful for the numbness that comes with shock—because if I felt the full force of grief right now, I wouldn't be able to handle all the tasks her death set into motion.

Dalton nursed me through the worst of it, letting me cocoon in his arms during all those wrenching phone calls when I informed Maxie's loved ones of her passing. He took time off from work to hold my hand at the funeral home. Despite his distrust of Elmer, the two of them coordinated with Maxie's artist family for the memorial service we'll hold on Saturday. Dalton brought me tea, soft music, books I stared at without comprehending a word, food I barely tasted. He massaged my sore body, patiently ignoring his obvious arousal. No demands, no pressure, just steady warmth.

And now the time has come to, as Davonte put it, shit or get off the pot. Moving on with life is so damn hard, but it's what Maxie would want me to do. Enough dithering. Enough stalling. It's go time.

I shield my eyes from the headlights' glare as Dalton pulls into the driveway and climbs out of his dented station wagon. He must've come straight from team practice, because he's still wearing his track suit. Smiling that crooked smile I love, he lowers himself beside me on the front stairs, sets down a sack of takeout food, and wraps his arms around me, pulling me tight against his chest.

"Sorry, didn't stop to shower."

I shelter in his arms, soaking up his warmth. "I like your smell."

"You're a weird woman, Laurel." He kisses the top of my head, then unwraps his monster sandwich and takes a huge bite. When I leave mine untouched, he nudges me. "Gotta eat, babe."

The scent of the pastrami calls a rumble from my belly, which feels somehow disconnected from the rest of me.

Dalton wipes his mouth with a paper napkin. "So, how'd it go with the lawyer?"

"Not what I expected." That's putting it ultra-mildly. I'm still reeling from the news.

Concern flickers in his eyes. "Is your family selling the house?"

"We can't." I unwrap my sandwich and fiddle with a shred of lettuce. "*I* can't."

Ever patient, he raises his eyebrows and waits.

"Maxie left me the house, but with strings attached. If I stay for two years, it's mine to keep or sell or whatever."

"And if you don't?"

"It goes to a foundation that supports arts education." I nibble my bread. "She's still pulling the strings, even after she's gone."

The corners of his mouth inch upward. "I learned the hard way how much you hate that."

I bump his shoulder with mine. "I still don't like the way you went about it, but I have you and Clara to thank for my new side gig as a window dresser."

"Visual merchandiser," he corrects me with a chuckle. "So, what's your next move?" The quaver in his voice contradicts his outward calm. He's afraid I'm going to run away again.

I take his hand and thread my fingers through his. "You know, I thought this would be the hard part, the final capitulation. But letting go of that stale, stubborn plan of mine doesn't hurt at all."

He raises an eyebrow, still doubtful.

"Well, maybe it hurts a little, but things have changed. I'm actually starting to see myself as an artist, thanks to Maxie, and Agatha, and Lorenzo, and Maxie's artist friends."

The hope glowing in his eyes could light the whole town.

"The social media attention for my poster helped too, and the five new requests I have from downtown merchants to redo their window displays." I squeeze his hand. "It's still terrifying, but if Maxie could face the end of her long, colorful life with so much courage, I can be brave too. Especially with you by my side. And being an artist is what I've wanted since I was little, long before I gave up and switched the plan to owning an art gallery. So..." I fill my lungs with cool night air. "I'm staying right here."

Dalton grips my shoulder. "You mean it, Laurel? Because if you change your mind again, I'll probably explode." He spreads his fingers wide—kaboom.

God, this man! After all I've put him through, he's still here, still hopeful when I've given him every reason not to be. Time to put his doubts to rest.

I swivel on the step so our knees are touching and sink into his twilight-blue gaze. "You believed in me, and you helped me believe in myself. I won't change my mind, Dalton. I'm in love with you."

He tenderly cups my jaw and brushes his thumbs over my cheekbones. "Really?"

"Really really." And if we don't get naked soon, I'm going to combust from sheer happiness, relief, and pent-up desire. I flash him a naughty grin and tug him to his feet. "Now, come inside. Let's talk about renovations. If we're gonna live here, this old house will need some TLC."

"We?" His slow-blooming smile is a thing of beauty.

"Well, there's no pool, but it's bigger than your apartment. I figured, why not take advantage of the opportunity?" I clasp the back of his neck and hover my lips an inch from his. "It's what Maxie would want."

He flattens his palm on the small of my back, pressing our bodies together. "What happened to taking it slow?"

"You can't fight fate." I stroke the golden scruff on his jaw. "Well, you can, but it's exhausting. I'm done fighting this, Dalton. This is my home, and you're the one I want to share it with."

His whoosh of breath tickles my cheek. Then he mashes his mouth to mine and kisses me until I'm dizzy and panting, desperate to know his body again. His molten kiss melts all my doubts. Dalton is my friend, my perfect match, my forever lover. And I am the luckiest woman in Eugene, Oregon, in the state, the West Coast, the whole wide, wonderful world.

I break the kiss and back toward the stairs, tugging him after me. Sandwiches forgotten, we stumble through the front door. He kicks it shut and rains hungry kisses over my face and throat.

"God, I've missed you." He breathes into my hair. "I've missed us."

With one hand, he clutches my ass and pulls me tight against his erection while his other hand tugs my shirt free from my jeans.

As I pull his shirt up, our arms tangle overhead in a snarl of half-discarded clothing, and we dissolve into laughter.

I extricate myself and smooch the tip of his nose. "How about you take off yours, and I'll take off mine?"

"Good plan." He bends to pull off his warm-up pants without first removing his shoes. Off- balance, he topples onto the couch.

Giggling like a horny lunatic, I peel off my own clothes, then help him free his hobbled ankles. "C'mere, gorgeous man." I beckon him into the hallway. "Let's get you cleaned up."

"Yes, ma'am." Rigid cock bobbing, he follows, pausing by the guest room when he spots the new queen-size bed.

"An early birthday gift from my parents." I wiggle my hips. "Just in time."

"Amen." Drinking me in with his hooded gaze, he skims his hands up my sides to cup my breasts. My eyes close on a moan of pleasure. It's been too long since I've felt Dalton's touch. We've got a lot of making up to do.

I reach for his jutting shaft, but he slips from my grasp and flashes a wicked grin. "Shower first. Wash my back?"

Fitting two tall people beneath Maxie's too-low shower head isn't easy, but feeling his soap-slippery skin beneath my fingers is worth the effort. Water cascades over his muscular chest, plastering the blond hairs to his skin.

"Let me." I take the soap from his hand and stroke it reverently over his skin. His head drops back on a sigh. Bubbles slide down his belly, following the golden happy trail to his cock.

But as tempted as I am to lather him there, I first want to enjoy the rest of him—every last inch.

"Turn around." I soap his back, then glide over the enticing curve of his ass.

"Look." I point to our steam-blurred reflection in the bathroom mirror. While he watches, I work up a lather between my palms and stroke slippery bubbles over his hard length. He groans and thrusts into my fist, his shaft sliding like greased steel. I press my breasts to his back, teasing him with my hardened nipples.

"Your turn," he growls and grabs the soap to slide it between my legs. I'm already slick with desire, but the soap transforms his probing fingers into something miraculous—gliding, thrusting, exploring, until...

I squirm away. "The soap stings."

Devilish fire sparkles in his eyes. "Let's rinse you off." Unhooking the shower head, he adjusts the spray to a pulsing massage and aims the stream between my thighs while his nimble fingers spread me open. The water dances over my clit, a blissful sensation that's almost too intense to bear.

"God, Dalton, I'm going to—" My words dissolve into a whimper.

"Not yet." He turns me to the wall. By now the mirror is completely fogged, the bathroom floor soaked, but I'm too far gone to care. My whole world narrows to his touch, his rumbling voice, his hot breath on my wet skin. Hands starfished on the tiles, I spread my legs as far as the tub allows. He clutches my hip with one hand while the other aims the spray, making me buck and squeal.

I grope behind me until my fingers close on his iron-hard length. "Now, please. I need you inside me."

"Condom?" he rasps.

That's right, we've never had the awkward STI talk. "I've been tested, and I use birth control."

"Thank God. Me too. I mean..." With a guttural grunt, he bucks his hips forward.

I arch my back and seat his plush crown at my entrance. He slides home.

Sweet Jesus.

The water is going cold, but bright pleasure scalds me. Dalton's broad, thick shaft plunders deep, hard, blindingly good. My voice rises in a crescendo of animal cries as he slams into me.

"Help me," he murmurs, pushing the shower head into my hand. I angle the now-cold spray onto my clit, and the powerful sensation of icy water against molten heat pushes me over the edge. Spinning through fire and ice, I shatter.

He hunches over my convulsing body and sinks his teeth into my shoulder. His groans echo off the tiles as his cock throbs inside me—a storm of sensations that forges us together. No matter what delights the future holds, I'll never forget this moment.

Later, we lie on my new bed, my head cradled on his chest, our limbs entangled. His voice rumbles beneath my cheek. "This is perfect." He chuckles and strokes my back. "Sorry, babe. Not very poetic. You wore me out."

I nestle into his warmth. "I don't need poetry. Just you." I trace figure eights around his golden-furred pecs. "No more running away."

He captures my fingers and presses them to his lips. "Just running side by side."

"Nope." I nibble his flat nipple. "I'll be running behind you so I can watch your yummy ass."

"No fair. I love the way your butt jiggles when you run." He squeezes a big handful.

I poke his ribs. "Are you trying to start something, mister?"

We both glance down at the protrusion tenting the sheets.

Dalton's earthy laugh fills my chest with glowing happiness, not to mention the giddy tingle between my legs. I flash a wicked grin before sliding down beneath the covers. "Excuse me for a moment while I go say hi to a friend."

His breath catches when my fingers close on his shaft. I stroke slowly, then lick him from root to tip. He smells of herbal soap and sex.

He squirms on the mattress. "Did I mention I'm in love with you?"

I swirl my tongue around his plump purple crown. "You did." I nibble his plush balls. "I love you too," I add, and fill my mouth with his

rigid flesh.

"Luckiest guy in the universe," he groans.

Chapter Forty-Seven

♥

Laurel

The day of Maxie's memorial service dawns cool and clear, the autumn leaves shimmering bright against the cerulean sky.

Funny how, since I've finally admitted I'm an artist, details like this jump out at me—glorious colors, vivid shapes, subtle movement. It's like I've given myself permission to really notice the beauty all around me.

And I owe that to Maxie.

"It's perfect, Laurel. Just what Maxie would've wanted." Standing beside me in the backyard, Elmer gazes misty-eyed at the bejeweled urn resting on a satin-draped pedestal. It took Margot and me many weepy hours to cover the plain stone vessel with swirling patterns of rhinestones and beads from Maxie's trove of art supplies. The rose bushes flanking the urn flutter with photos of Maxie tied on with colorful ribbons. Maxie's colorful scarves wave like banners from the trees. Everywhere you look, there's glitter, shine, mementoes of Maxie's bright, sparkly life.

I wipe a tear as I survey the scene. Helped by Maxie's friends, Dalton and I pulled weeds, mowed the scraggly grass, set up folding chairs, and picked up food from Maxie's favorite restaurants. Elmer brought beer. Nick and Clara sent a spray of bright-yellow lilies and hot-pink roses. Margot brought a sound system. And now, reggae tunes float on the crisp autumn air as Maxie's friends stream into the yard.

Dalton steps to my side and laces his fingers through mine. "Maxie would love this. You've truly captured her spirit."

I sigh. "I hope I can hang onto some of her shine."

He gathers me into his arms, warm and strong and gentle. "You will, love. Your shine is different from Maxie's, but it's just as bright."

How could I ever want to run away from this man? After just one week of dreaming in his arms and waking up to his crooked smile, my former doubts seem ridiculous.

I rest my chin on his shoulder—then stiffen when Dad strides around the corner, face scrunched as if smelling something rotten. Mom follows, along with Willow, her husband Frank, and their new baby, Hazel.

Mom hugs me tightly while Dalton introduces himself to Willow and Frank.

Dad grumbles, "Don't see why we couldn't have the service in a church, like a normal family."

I meet his critical gaze with steel in my own. "This is exactly what Maxie wanted. She left detailed instructions." I link my arm with Dalton's, and we walk to our seats in the front row.

The other seats fill quickly, with still more guests standing on the back porch and on the lawn. It seems in the few months I've been here, I barely scratched the surface of Maxie's enormous circle of friends.

I hope, when it's my turn to go, I'll gather even half as many loving companions for my final send-off. Maxie has touched so many lives.

The officiant, a silver-bearded guy with a round belly and a beatific smile, takes his position behind the borrowed podium. His purple clerical robe flutters in the breeze.

"Friends, we gather today to celebrate a life well-lived. We are here to honor a rare and precious spirit, Miss Maxine Delores Schmidt."

A murmur of ascent arises from the congregation.

"I had the honor of living next door to Maxie these past twenty years, and never have I known a kinder, more generous, more creative and playful person. She touched many lives during her too-short time here on earth. Yes, I know our friend was ninety, but to those who loved her, ninety wasn't nearly long enough."

"Amen," someone calls from the back row. I turn to see Agatha dabbing her eyes with her fringed scarf. Beside her, Lorenzo waggles his fingers at me.

"Friends, please join me in a prayer, an invocation, whatever you want to call it, for the transition of Maxie's soul to the spirit realm, where I'm sure she'll light the place up with her art, her laughter, and her love."

I bow my head.

"Maxie, as we continue our journey in this life, we promise never to forget you. We will honor your memory by living our lives as brightly and truly as you did. We promise to keep alive the spark of joy and pleasure you had in life, and to share it freely with those we meet along the way. Until we meet again, dear lady. We love you."

"Amen," I mutter as a tear drops onto my lap.

Dalton silently hands me a tissue. I lean on his shoulder as I dab my streaming eyes.

The next-door reverend gives me a smile of encouragement. "Today's eulogy will be delivered by Maxie's grandniece, Miss Laurel Jepsen."

All the preparations for Maxie's memorial service left me very little time and energy to collect my thoughts, so I have the barest outline to guide my tribute.

With quaking fingers, I unfold my notes on the podium, then face the crowd. Their warmth and love steady my voice. "I guess we all have our favorite Maxie stories, and I hope you'll share them today. I'll keep mine short." I meet Dalton's gaze. He nods.

"Twice, I came to Maxie with a broken heart. Back then, I had some pretty messed-up ideas. I thought the applause of strangers was what I needed to be happy. But Maxie gifted me with her wisdom." I sniffle hard before continuing. "She taught me to find art and beauty all around me. She taught me that true sparkle comes from within, and once I find my inner light, no one can ever dim it. She helped me stop running away from failure and start running toward new opportunities, new friendships, new love. For that, I can never thank her enough. But I'm going to try."

I flip the page. "Many of you already received invitations Maxie sent for her Christmas party on December fifteenth. She had a reputation for hosting epic parties, and she put a lot of time, thought, and love into this year's event. She wouldn't want us to miss it, so I hope you're still free on that date because you're all invited to the first annual Maxine Schmidt Festival of the Arts. Bring your best work to display or sell."

This next bit brings a smile to my lips. "Another thing I've learned since coming back to Eugene is the power of social media, so help us spread the word: Hashtag Art for Maxie. It's gonna go viral."

Maxie's final gift to her artist friends was a rented exhibition hall with ample parking, support staff, catering, and even a band, all arranged and paid for before her death. I'm guessing she knew it would be her final fabulous bash. I've already contacted that bubbly KVAL reporter, who promised to give the event lots of publicity.

After the speeches are given, the stories shared, the tissue boxes emptied, the food eaten, and the beer kegs drained, a few friends remain to fold up the chairs and clear away the debris.

Dalton's long arms slide around my waist from behind. "Happy, babe?"

I cuddle against his chest. "I am. Feels weird to say at a funeral, but I think Maxie would be pleased."

"Of course she would." He kisses my temple, a gesture of comfort I've come to love.

"You know what would feel good right now?" he asks, a note of mischief in his voice.

I elbow him. "Not while guests are still here."

His low laugh rumbles beside my ear. "Not what I meant, though that always feels good." He kisses my neck. "Amazing." He peppers kisses along my jawline. "Phenomenal. But how about a run along the river? There's nothing better to shake off a sad mood. We've still got a few hours of light, and Elmer volunteered to handle the rest of this."

At the food table, Elmer and Margot are covering the leftovers with foil. Margot holds a strawberry to Elmer's lips. He gobbles it, then seizes her hand and kisses the inside of her wrist.

Well, well! "Good idea. Looks like someone could use a little privacy."

Leaving the lovebirds in the backyard, we change clothes, lace on our running shoes, and head for the riverside trail—cooler now than our first summer runs, but just as beautiful. Golden leaves litter the pavement, and the evening sun sparkles on the glassy green water. Side by side, we fall into an easy, comfortable pace, our breathing in sync, our feet slapping a rhythm that goes on and on and on...

Thanks for reading Dalton and Laurel's story! Want to spend a little more time in Book Nirvana? For my newsletter subscribers, I've compiled some juicy, spicy deleted scenes from Edition One of ***Runaway Love Story*** that didn't make it into Edition Two. To claim your copy, visit sadirastone.com and find the Subscriber Bonuses page.

Don't miss Margot's funny, steamy, complicated love story ***Love, Art, and Other Obstacles: Book Nirvana 3*** coming April, 2025.

Read on for more books by Sadira Stone. But first...

Reviews are the lifeblood of hard-working authors like me, so if you enjoyed ***Runaway Love Story***, I'd be so thrilled and grateful if you'd leave a review. Even a line or two about what you enjoyed helps so much! Just find the book's retail page on your favorite online bookseller's site and find "Leave/Write a Customer Review" – usually located near the stars or book title. Thank you from the bottom of my heart! Extra virtual smooches for reviews on Goodreads and Bookbub.

Books by Sadira Stone

♥

Next in the **Book Nirvana** series: *Love, Art, and Other Obstacles*, coming April 2025.

I can't help craving my rival.

Margot

Who needs family? On the cusp of launching my graphic arts career, I'm all about freedom—no fences, no limits, and no more bigoted family weighing me down. Between college, work at Book Nirvana, and a high-stakes art competition, I barely have time for my part-time girlfriend, much less a flirtation with my competitor, even if his cocky, ginger-bearded hotness makes me question my "no strings" rule.

Elmer

Family is everything, and I've found my family of the heart in the Eugene, Oregon art scene. But something is missing ...until Margot, my rival for an art grant we both desperately need. That prickly little sprite lights me up body and soul, but she fears I'm out to clip her wings. I'm not made to share my heart with more than one, and falling for Margot could wreck me.

Come to Book Nirvana for a red-hot love triangle that forces two young artists to redefine success, family, and freedom.

Love, Art, and Other Obstacles was previously published and has been revised and updated with new chapters.

And did you miss *Through the Red Door*: Book Nirvana One?

Two good men vie to heal a widow'sheart—but it only holds room for one.

Clara

Unless I find a lifeline, my bookstore will close its doors forever. My best shot at saving Book Nirvana is my late husband's collection of rare, racy books, but I'm not ready to open that red door and face the flood of memories. And I'm not ready to open my heart again, even if the two new men in my life tempt me to try.

Nick

I came to Book Nirvana in search of antique bawdy books and fell hard for lovely, lonely Clara. As a widower, I understand her skittishness, but the spark between us is undeniable. My academic connections could rebuild her clientele, but if she discovers my secret scandal, her fragile trust will shatter.

Dalton

I'm over the moon for beautiful, bookish Clara, but how can a teacher like me compete with a suave professor like Nick? Clara and I have so much in common, and our sweet friendship could bloom into something deeper if it weren't for my rival's grip on the vulnerable widow. I don't trust him, and neither should she.

Come to Book Nirvana for chosen family, laughter and tears, sizzling passion, and a love triangle for the ages.

Through theRed Door was previously published and has been revised and updated with new chapters.

Bangers Tavern Romance Series

Come to Bangers Tavern for super-steamy rom-coms featuring chosen family, diverse characters, creative cocktails, and the best tater tots in Tacoma. Four full-length novels and one novella each deliver a satisfying HEA and an unforgettable holiday bash in the neighborhood bar that feels like home. One night in Bangers, and you'll want to return again and again!

Trappers Cove Romance Series

Welcome to Trappers Cove, a quirky Washington State beach town nestled among the pines. Here you'll find steamy, small-town, grownup romance, laughter and tears, heart-warming chosen family, Madame Zora's Psychic Emporium, and all the best beachy fun!

For bookish news, reader exclusives, and romance freebies, visit sadirastone.com and **<u>subscribe to Sadira's reader newsletter.</u>**

About the author

Award-winning contemporary romance author Sadira Stone spins steamy, smoochy tales set in the U.S. Pacific Northwest. Her stories highlight found family, friendship, and the sizzling chemistry that pulls unlikely partners together. When she emerges from her writing cave in LasVegas, Nevada (which she seldom does), she can be found shaking her hips in dance class, blowing bubbles with her granddaughter, playing her guitar (not very well, but improving!), exploring the Western U.S. with her charming husband, cooking up a storm, and gobbling all the romance books. For a guaranteed HEA (and no cliffhangers!) visit Sadira at sadirastone.com.